ON A DAY LIKE TODAY

A Selection of Recent Titles by Nicola Thorne

THE PEOPLE OF THIS PARISH SERIES

THE PEOPLE OF THIS PARISH (Book I)
THE RECTOR'S DAUGHTER (Book II)
IN THIS QUIET EARTH (Book III) *
PAST LOVE (Book IV)*
A TIME OF HOPE (Book V)*
IN TIME OF WAR (Book VI)*

THE BROKEN BOUGH SERIES

THE BROKEN BOUGH *
THE BLACKBIRD'S SONG *
THE WATER'S EDGE *
OH HAPPY DAY *

COPPITTS GREEN *
A FAMILY AFFAIR *
HAUNTED LANDSCAPE *
THE HOUSE BY THE SEA *
THE LITTLE FLOWERS *
REPOSSESSION *
RETURN TO WUTHERING HEIGHTS *
RULES OF ENGAGEMENT *

* available from Severn House

ON A DAY LIKE TODAY

Nicola Thorne

This first world edition published 2008
in Great Britain and the USA by
SEVERN HOUSE PUBLISHERS LTD of
9–15 High Street, Sutton, Surrey, England, SM1 1DF.

British Library Cataloguing in Publication Data

Thorne, Nicola
  On a day like today
  1. Mothers and daughters - Fiction 2. Traffic accident
  victims - Fiction 3. Psychological fiction
  I. Title
  823.9'14[F]

ISBN-13: 978-0-7278-6659-2   (cased)
ISBN-13: 978-1-84751-076-1   (trade paper)

Except where actual historic
described for the storyline of
publication are fictitious and
is purely coincidental.

All Severn House titles are prin

Typeset by Palimpsest Book
Grangemouth, Stirlingshire, Scotland.
Printed and bound in Great Britain by
MPG Books Ltd., Bodmin, Cornwall.

Author's Note

A few years ago I was the victim of a serious motor accident, an event which had a profound effect on me, my family and my career. Daily we are surrounded by media reports of disasters and accidents that change peoples lives, but it is true that until it happens to oneself you don't really know what it is like. It not only changes your view of the world but how people feel about you. As a novelist it was something I felt I wanted to write about and the result is this, my first novel for five years.

But I must emphasize that this is not an autobiography. I am not Eleanor and, except for the accident itself and subsequent hospitalization, the events and people in the story are fiction. That said there are many people I should like to thank for their help, concern and messages following my accident. It would be invidious to single anyone out, nor is there the space, but they know who they are.

However, I feel an exception must be made in the case of my son Stefan and his wife Rebecca for their love and support, particularly in the immediate aftermath of the accident, and Ruth Wrixton whose kindness, good humour, ceaseless energy and practical common sense contributed greatly to my recovery and still do. Lastly, although she can't yet read, I know my eccentric cat Pinky would be justifiably aggrieved to be left out from an acknowledgement because of the vital part she played in my convalescence simply by being there. She and Melody might well recognize each other. In fact this is the one character in the novel I can say with truth is based on real life.

One

It began as a day like any other.

Eleanor leaned back from her desk and gazed out of the window. It was a fine September day, the sky blue and inviting. A day for a walk to the sea? Since her move there had been so little time for leisure. The countryside around her was beautiful; the sea a mile away via a tranquil road restricted to traffic, through woodland and undulating fields rich with grazing sheep and cattle. On a day like today, now that she was settled in and the few outstanding jobs left over from her career as a magazine editor had been completed, it seemed a good time to begin to take advantage of her new life.

Six months earlier she had completed a move from London, forsaking a career that had become a burden, a large house that had become too large once the children and the husband had left. But beginning again was all very well in theory, but more difficult to accomplish in reality. Finding the place to which to move had been the easiest part, the coast of West Dorset. They had always thought they would retire there, one day, very far away, a long way off. Together. But the time had arrived sooner than she expected when her husband Dick announced he wanted to marry his girlfriend, Karen, because she wanted a baby. To Eleanor it was a shock, but also it seemed a way of release from a marriage which, in retrospect, had settled into a dull routine. The shock was that she and Dick had always been good friends and as such she hoped, and thought, they would remain once the knot that had bound them together was finally untied. But now there was little communication. Dick had settled into a new life that, inevitably, excluded her.

Breaking away; cutting ties. In one's late fifties, it was a good time to begin again because to leave it any longer would be too late. The new house was pretty, not thatched, big enough if the family wanted to visit, compact and, more importantly, only a short distance from the sea. That was the easy part. It had taken much longer to complete the purchase and make all the final arrangements than she had expected. Also, without Dick it had been just that bit more difficult. Anticipating, or perhaps hoping to accelerate events, Karen was already pregnant and there had been a quick divorce. But now it was all done and she had no regrets. None at all.

Eleanor put aside the article she had been working on. She had not abandoned her career completely, intending to freelance whenever an attractive opportunity arose. Her magazine had promised to give her work and she had many other contacts after a lifetime in Fleet Street, or what had been Fleet Street. It had not been her intention to become a pillar of the Women's Institute, but to enjoy her new life in a variety of ways.

Eleanor ran down the stairs and went into the small cloakroom off the hall to find her walking shoes. She was edging them on when the telephone distracted her. She thought she would ignore it, then, maybe . . .

Just as the answering machine kicked in she lifted the receiver.

'Eleanor? Hello, this is Jean Walker. I wondered if you'd like a spot of lunch?'

'Well . . .' Eleanor gazed out at the blue, blue sky. 'I was just about to go for a walk, actually.'

'Well, we can still have a walk. Maybe lunch at a pub?'

Eleanor was tempted. She quite liked Jean and she didn't know many people, what with all the packing and moving around and trips to London and back. It was a business settling into her new home and, besides, she was slow to join things and neither a frequenter of pubs nor a regular churchgoer.

'Good idea,' she said. 'Where shall we meet?'

'The George in West Bay. Say, half an hour?'

It was one thing leaving London and the past behind her, Eleanor thought, resetting the answer machine, but no man was an island. You couldn't live completely alone. She went upstairs, changed, slapped on fresh lipstick – she had good skin and wore little make-up – ran a comb through her hair, got her keys from the dining-room table and went round for the car. She backed out of the garage, put on her sunglasses, turned on the radio and drove up the hill.

Coming down from the brow of the hill with no cars in front of her but a line on the other side going in the opposite direction, she saw a car suddenly emerge from the line of traffic and head towards her.

'I don't believe this,' she gasped.

Darkness.

'What is your name?' she heard a voice asking.

'Eleanor.' Her response was very clear but she could see nothing.

'Can you call my husband? Dick Ashton at Ashton Associates, South Audley Street, London.'

Aware of people but still seeing nothing and with no feeling of fear, though she knew something terrible had happened, she asked, 'Am I dying?'

'You're not dying,' said a strong male voice.

And then there were the helicopter blades going round, and then into a scanner with a woman looking kindly down at her.

She didn't like flying and was afraid of enclosed spaces, which was probably why later she could recall those, just little snippets of life; lightness in the dark.

'Have you had a tetanus injection in the last ten years?' a voice said.

'No.'

Brief interludes of consciousness; unaware of the passage of time; still no feeling of fear. In retrospect that was the most curious part because, despite an appearance of strength, she had always been a rather nervous, fearful person.

She was aware that Dick was standing by the bed gazing down at her. He sank into a chair at the side of the bed and put a hand over hers.

'I couldn't think of anyone else to call,' Eleanor murmured apologetically. 'I'm sorry.'

Dick said something, which she couldn't hear.

'You'll have to speak louder,' she said.

A look of concern on his face, he put his mouth to her ear. 'I said, don't be silly. It's perfectly all right.' The pressure of his hand tightened. 'Alex is on her way.'

'But isn't she in India?'

'She's left. Caught the first plane out.'

'It must be bad,' Eleanor murmured. 'Hugo won't be pleased.'

'You had a very bad accident.'

Eleanor gazed at the ceiling, then her eyes wandered around the ward making her aware for the first time of where she was.

'How long have I been here?'

'Since yesterday afternoon. About 24 hours.'

'Anyway, I'm so glad you're here. It was good of you to come.'

Eleanor tried to squeeze his hand but found it impossible. She seemed to have no strength and no feeling. She looked closely at Dick.

'I can see two of you,' she said almost in amusement.

'It will pass,' Dick said. 'The thing is –' he edged his chair even closer aware of her hearing difficulty – 'I can't stay. Karen had a baby yesterday. She wants to come home.'

'Oh, I'm so glad for you, Dick.'

'A boy,' Dick continued.

'Is she OK? And the baby?'

'They are both fine.'

She had no real emotion on hearing the news about Dick's new child, almost thirty years younger than James, their son. It seemed ridiculous to be a father again at sixty. She wondered how he would cope, as he had never been much use when his own children were tiny.

'James wants to fly over.'

'There is no need. Nothing he can do.'

'I think he'd like to see you.'

She looked steadily into his eyes. 'Dick, tell me honestly. Am I dying?'

'No,' Dick said just as authoritatively as the unknown man had by the roadside, 'but you are very ill. It was a very serious crash.' Dick paused. 'The man who went into you had a heart attack. He's dead.'

'As a result of the crash or before?'

'They think before. He was quite old.'

'They probably think I'm quite old.'

A nurse approached the bed and looked critically at her. 'You mustn't exert yourself, Mrs Ashton,' she said checking the drip feeding into Eleanor's arm.

'I must go, anyway,' Dick said, getting to his feet. He addressed the nurse. 'My daughter is on her way back from India; she should be here tomorrow morning.'

He stooped and lightly planted a kiss on Eleanor's brow, accompanied by a brief squeeze of her hand. Then he and the nurse left the bed together and stood for quite a time by the door of the ward talking, glancing occasionally over at her. They were talking about her. She was very ill.

Eleanor closed her eyes. A pain was starting in her ribs, spreading across her abdomen, up to her head and then down again, through her body to her legs.

As she saw Dick disappear a deep feeling of sadness overwhelmed her.

She wished now that she and Dick had never divorced. Part of him still belonged to her, but it was a very small part. Gradually, foolishly, perhaps, she had ignored what was going on confident that the affair would pass. She had known about Karen for some time and although, with hindsight, it defied logic she had been quite prepared to put up with the situation, until the pregnancy. She guessed that Karen had intended it that way. Karen was nearly forty and the time clock was ticking away.

Dick seemed to have created a space and now that he had gone she felt very alone. But she was also overcome with weariness and as the pain grew more intense she called out for the nurse who came running.

Eleanor looked up at her, speechless.

The nurse said something to her that she, again, couldn't hear. Leaning over her she repeated it. 'Is the pain very bad?'

Eleanor nodded.

'The doctor will give you something,' she said and suddenly there was a lot of activity by her bedside, a tube was inserted into her back and the relief was instant and overwhelming, and Eleanor fell back on the bed.

When she opened her eyes again she saw her daughter sitting by her side. She didn't know how long Alex had been there, but it was comforting to see her and she reached for her hand, whispering, 'I'm deaf and there is something wrong with my eyes.'

'I know, Mum. I had a long talk with the doctors.' Alex tightly clasped her mother's hand, her face close to her ear. 'They say it won't last –' Alex tried to sound reassuring – 'at least they don't think so. You've been very badly injured, Mum.'

Eleanor nodded to indicate she understood, murmuring, 'It was very good of you to come. Was Hugo very cross?'

'Of course not; he understood. It was the least I could do.'

Eleanor felt disloyal wishing that it had been James. She and Alex found it so hard to communicate. It seemed as though Alex could read her thoughts because she leaned back and looked critically at her mother.

'I said you should never have gone to the country to live.' She leaned closer again. Even then Eleanor could hardly hear what she said and Alex had to repeat herself.

'You can have an accident anywhere,' Eleanor replied weakly, the pain beginning again to spread across her body. She gripped Alex's hand.

'Could you call the nurse, darling?' she grimaced. 'Quickly.'

Alex opened the door of the house and looked around. It was a very strange, eerie feeling knowing that her mother had left only two days before. Her things were still lying around as though she had just discarded them; a coat flung across one of the dining room chairs, a washed cup and saucer left to dry on the draining board. Suddenly there was a plaintive miaow and she looked up the stairs to see her mother's precious cat, Melody, standing at the top; precious to Mother, but not to the rest of the family whom she kept at an imperious distance. She was a very beautiful cat, small and delicate with soft fur that was more pink than ginger, interspersed with white. Eleanor had rescued her, and to her Melody felt she owed her fidelity and undying loyalty. Everyone else, she ignored, despised or ran away from.

'Melody,' Alex gasped, but the cat stayed where she was looking reproachfully down at her. Alex wondered how long it was since she had been fed and immediately went into the cloakroom where Melody's food and litter tray were kept. The tray looked clean and there was still food in her bowl, water by the side. Also, there was a small stack of letters on the dining-room table. Someone had been in. Alex walked slowly up the stairs, her hand outstretched in a placatory, almost imploring gesture towards the cat, but she backed away and disappeared under the bed in Eleanor's room. There was a deep dent in the middle of the duvet, where Melody had obviously been sleeping. Again, there were a few things tossed around as though Eleanor had just left the house in a hurry; a lipstick on the dressing table without its top, a tissue tossed hurriedly aside, a shoe in the middle of the rug next to the bed. It was so like her mother, Alex thought, never leaving quite enough time to do all the things she had to do. Suddenly overwhelmed with sadness, mixed with guilt, she wandered to the window and stood looking down into the lane.

Always in a hurry, elegant, smartly turned out as behoved the editor of the English edition of an international women's magazine, Eleanor was a slim, tall, good-looking woman, with short, slightly wavy, dark hair, stylishly cut, a good complexion and looked years younger than she was. She was a presence, heads turned in her direction when she came into a room, yet she was friendly, approachable, imperturbable, used to dealing with crises in a calm, efficient way. However, though undoubtedly caring and loving, in her domestic setting Mother had presented a different picture to her daughter. Alex had always found her remote, a little distant so that their relationship was uneasy and, craving affection from someone she instinctively adored, she had often felt sidelined. Younger brother James was his mother's favourite, and Alex rather wished James had been the one to come. She knew Eleanor would have preferred it, but he was held up in New York, his wife expecting their third child. Everyone was producing, unlike her. She had still not got used to the idea that Dad was a father again, not sure really that she approved.

Alex glanced at her watch. She would telephone James later on.

Just then the doorbell rang; she heard the door open and a voice called out tentatively, 'Hello?'

Alex went on to the landing and peered down the stairs where she saw a rather beautiful young woman of about her age gazing up at her.

'I'm Niobe,' the woman said. 'You must be Eleanor's daughter. I live just across the road.'

Alex walked down the stairs, hand held out. 'Yes, I'm Alex. How do you do?' She said, shaking Niobe's hand. 'We didn't meet before, did we? I'm afraid my visits here have been very brief. Have you been feeding the cat?'

'Yes, because your mother was often away she left a key with me.'

'That's very kind of you.'

'We read about the accident in the paper,' Niobe said with a shudder. 'It sounded awful. How is she?'

Alex shook her head. 'Not very well, I'm afraid.' She passed a hand wearily across her brow. 'Frankly, at the moment it's touch and go.' As she spoke she led the way into the sitting room and pointed to a chair, but Niobe remained standing.

'I won't stay,' she said. 'I saw the car and just wanted to be sure.' She paused. 'We were very upset about your mother. What a terrible thing to happen. She was just getting settled in.'

'Beginning to enjoy life, I know.' Suddenly overwhelmed by a feeling of complete exhaustion, verging on despair, Alex perched on the arm of a chair. 'My father rang me and I got on a plane straight away and flew back from India. I only got in during the night, hired a car and came straight down. Mum is still on the critical list; she has internal bleeding, which the doctors consider very serious. She also has fractured her skull, has broken ribs and extensive bruising. It is amazing that she is still alive. Her eyes have been affected, also her hearing. She can't see straight and you have to sit very close before she hears you.'

'Can I give you something to eat, drink?' Niobe looked at her. 'Would you like to come over for a snack?'

'Oh, no thanks.' Alex shook her head. 'I got a few things in the town before I came on here; milk and bread. At the moment sleep is more important than food. It has been an awful shock. You've been very kind. Poor Melody might have starved to death.'

'Oh, we'd never let that happen. We love animals.' Niobe turned towards the door. 'When will you be going back?'

Alex shook her head. 'Really, I have no idea. I was on assignment in India. I'm a travel writer.'

'I know, your mother told us.'

'I shall have to sort things out here. I can't leave until Mum is out of Intensive Care. My brother might come over, but his wife is on the point of delivering their third child. Dad's new wife has just had a baby.' Alex gave a wry smile. 'Everyone seems very productive.'

'We'll do all we can –' Niobe turned towards the door – 'feed the cat anyway. Anything, just ask.'

'Thank you very very much –' Alex opened the door – 'you're awfully kind.'

'And any time you want to chat or have something to eat . . .'

Alex nodded and thanked her again. Right now all she wanted was to be alone and sleep.

The door opened and Dick came into the room carrying the baby. It was so unusual that Eleanor was quite astonished. She hadn't even known he was home from work. Alex was playing in her pen, which was on the lawn in the garden and Eleanor could see her out of the kitchen window.

'He was as good as gold,' Dick said, 'loved his walk.'

'I wish you'd have taken Alex, too,' Eleanor said, 'she'd also have loved a walk.'

'Strange you didn't ask me.'

Strange of him to walk the baby, Eleanor thought, feeling angry with herself because Dick so seldom helped in the house or had anything to do with the children and now she was being critical.

*As if to justify her apprehension, Dick said, 'Well, if that's
all you can say when I try to help . . .'*

*She knew she was being peevish, but she was tired,
constantly tired and overworked. Having two children so
close together had been a terrible mistake. Get it over, she
had thought, before I'm too old. A career woman, she was
already in her late twenties, ambitious; certainly there would
be no more.*

*She looked at Dick and then at the baby who was staring
fixedly down at her.*

*'But Dick,' she cried, her tone close to panic, 'that is
not our baby. Dick . . .' She ran towards him, arms
outstretched and started to cry. 'Dick, what have you
done . . .?'*

'Stop talking to yourself,' a voice said sternly. 'There's no
one there.'

Eleanor seemed to drift back to reality. This was not the
house in Primrose Hill with its view across London, and she
knew instantly where she was and why and how long it had
been since the children were tiny.

The nurse was standing staring down at her as though
she had done something wrong. Instinctively, she disliked
this woman and knew this woman disliked her. Why? What
had she done? It was something imperceptible, indefinable.
Eleanor watched the nurse as she walked away, her trim
uniformed figure outlined in the darkened ward. She was
a very sick person and no one had any business to dislike
her. She knew her anger was clouding her judgement,
distorting it. She thought back to her dream. The sight of
Dick with the strange baby had been so clear, so vivid, but
she was in a hospital ward and she knew quite well where
and why.

The nurses were magnificent technicians, highly trained
to deal with the complex equipment necessary in an intensive ward where the narrow borderline between life and death
was a daily occurrence. You couldn't help admire them and
their expertise. Most of them were nice as well as accomplished, but not the night nurse who ignored her calls and
was brusque and perfunctory when she did answer them.

Most of the time Eleanor was in a great deal of pain; to her shame she even screamed when they tried to turn her. The oxygen mask she was expected to wear all the time was a continual irritation, and whenever she attempted to remove it it was shoved firmly back on her face. That, and the pain and continual cough that wracked her body, meant she never felt at peace except when she was asleep and, thankfully, there was a lot of that.

She knew she had been hallucinating. With the morphine it happened all the time. She had so clearly seen Dick with a strange baby at their house in Primrose Hill where they'd lived all their married life, bought for a song and sold for an enormous profit at the time of the divorce. Karen didn't want to live in the house Dick had shared with his former wife, and Eleanor hadn't wanted to live there either. It was a very nice Georgian house overlooking Primrose Hill where the children used to play and from the top of which they could see the dome of St Paul's and beyond as far as the Surrey hills on a clear day. Happy memories of Primrose Hill; happy, happy . . .

'I wish I were there,' James said, his voice over the phone sounding tired and stressed.

'I wish you were too and so does Mum, I bet.'

'Nonsense.'

'Oh, come on James!' It was, Alex knew, unnecessary to explain to him that he was their mother's pet. James annoyed her when he tried to pretend otherwise, but then James was like that, easy-going, always trying to please, wanting to be liked, ironically resembling his father more than his mother. Eleanor and Alex were temperamentally alike, which was probably why they so frequently clashed.

'How is Beverley?' Alex asked.

'Sick of being pregnant. Uncomfortable. The baby's now late; only a few days, but once she is born I will fly over and see Mum. Bev's mother is here.'

'Oh, you know the sex?'

'Yes.'

'And are you pleased?'

'Yes.'

'I bet.' There were two boys, now they would have a daughter.

'Seriously, about Mum,' James said sombrely, 'is she going to make it?'

'Just at the moment they don't know,' Alex said and to her surprise suddenly she felt like crying. 'The internal bleeding is the worrying thing. If they have to operate it could be fatal. Oh James, I do so wish you were here. I feel so inadequate.'

And she did, almost unable to cope. She felt the whole weight of their mother's illness, possibly death, on her shoulders and how would she be if she did recover? It was certain she would never be the old capable mother again, and what strain would that put on the single daughter with no encumbrances, apart from a demanding boyfriend with whom she had been in India and who, indeed, had very much objected to her leaving. Hugo was a cameraman and they often worked together on assignments, which was how they'd met two years before and Alex, like Hugo, preferred living out of a suitcase, having no ties, no encumbrances.

All that was now going to change.

'Try again Mrs Ashton,' the physiotherapist urged. 'You've got to try and spit.'

'I can't,' Eleanor gasped trying with all her might to produce the phlegm that seemed to be essential for her survival. She knew it was there, somewhere, deep in her tortured lungs because the coughing hardly stopped. The young woman, and she was very young, looked at her critically as if she were a recalcitrant child. Eleanor gazed back at the two faces peering at her like identical twins, which merged when she closed one eye again. The pain suffusing the length and breadth of her body was by now excruciating.

'I can't,' she cried again. 'I can't, I can't . . .'

The doctor who controlled pain relief was once again by her side.

'What's the matter?'

'I'm in terrible pain,' Eleanor managed to gasp.

'When did it start?'

Eleanor stared at the physiotherapist who looked over to the doctor with a helpless shrug of her shoulders.

He dismissed her with a wave of his hand and bent over Eleanor. Once again the needle was inserted in her back. Blessed relief.

She lay looking up at the ceiling of the flat on Hampstead Heath, familiar now after so many visits. The man at her side was breathing deeply and she turned to watch his face in repose, uneven features, craggy, pleasing, not strictly handsome, a man of experience, a kind, patient man. She knew it couldn't last. They both did. She didn't even know why it had started, boredom she supposed after so many years of marriage. She knew she was deeply committed to Dick, and Michael, the man by her side, felt the same about his wife. They were both just out for a little excitement, adventure, a change. In a way it went with the journalistic profession. You met so many people, were often away, too many parties, lots to drink. Often you knew it was silly and sometimes risky. People got hurt. Why do it then, one could ask in the cold light of day, but invariably one didn't. It was not her first affair and it was not his and she was sure that Dick wasn't innocent either. Everyone knew that the public relations profession was a hotbed of sexual intrigue.

Eleanor had known Mike for years. They met when she was a travel writer, as was he. That was before she reached the giddy heights of editing the magazine, but Mike had continued to travel, though now he appeared a lot on TV, a pundit on the travel scene.

Mike opened his eyes and looked straight into hers, a funny half smile on his face, almost as though he knew what she was thinking.

'Penny for your thoughts,' he said, sliding an arm around her waist, his fingers pressing into her skin.

'I was thinking I had to get back to work,' Eleanor said in a practical tone of voice looking at the watch on her wrist, once more the busy editor rather than a lover. It was nearly three. The long lunch hours that journalists invariably took provided good camouflage for illicit romances. The flat belonged to her close friend and personal assistant Marge who covered up for her at work. Marge, unmarried, unattached, thought nothing of providing a refuge, as well as

*excuses when required, for her philandering boss who she
adored, perhaps even envied. Wasn't she the woman who
had everything – looks, a husband, children, lovely home,
good job* and *a lover?*

'*I have to go to Thailand next week,*' *Mike said raising his
head and looking, too, towards the window.*

'*For how long?*' *Eleanor swung her legs over the side of
the bed glancing at him over her shoulder.*

'*A month, at least. I'm doing a feature.*'

*She wondered what Mike, with his strong sex drive, would
get up to in Thailand. Perhaps it was time, after all, that the
affair finished. One had to think about disease these days
and unfortunately one rarely did. At her age, just fifty, they
were happily free of the necessity of taking precautions,
which made sex these days all that much more fun. She gave
him a wry smile.*

'*I'll miss you,*' *she said, not entirely truthfully.*

'*And I'll miss you . . . darling,*' *he added after a pause.*

It was the last time they'd slept together, Eleanor thought
opening her eyes, which were fastened on the ceiling. She
stared at it for a long time, blinking before realizing that
she was in a hospital intensive care ward and not the attractive bedroom in Marge's flat with its lovely view across
London and the Heath. It took her several minutes to adjust
to reality. She was nearly ten years older than she was in
the dream, ill, perhaps dying, wired up to tubes and drips,
an oxygen mask over her face, a urine bag hanging by the
side of the bed. Oh, Mike, if you could see me now, she
thought. But the affair had finished years ago and Mike had
since remarried.

People were moving quietly around the ward. The woman
in the bed opposite her was obviously gravely ill as the
medical staff were always congregating round her, switching
tubes and drips. She was very elderly, but perhaps they
thought that she was elderly too; a rather cantankerous, difficult patient who disliked doing what she was told, being
treated like a child, unable fully to accept the state she was
in and the intensity of pain, the humiliation of her situation, all caused by something for which she was in no way

responsible and which had so drastically interfered with her plans for a new start in life.

After her affair with Mike there had been no others. It all seemed rather pointless, juvenile. Besides, she and Dick had always enjoyed a reasonable sex life, a few troughs but on the whole good. They liked and enjoyed each other's company, were friends in fact. Why play around just for kicks?

What would Mike think of her now even if he knew, which she supposed he didn't? But news got around. It had made the papers, so Dick had said. 'Get better soon' cards were beginning to flood in so she supposed Mike might find out; maybe there was one from him. She didn't care and she couldn't read them, didn't even feel she wanted to, didn't have the heart for anything. She was tired, drugged and it was surprising how little anything seemed to matter.

Alex sat by the side of her mother's bed watching her face in repose, wondering what she was dreaming as occasionally her mouth twitched, her eyelids flickered. She looked almost normal. It was only when she was awake that her expression gave any indication of the torments she was enduring. They had never been close, yet in this very short time, hours more than days, in fact very few days, they seemed to have begun to realize how much they needed each other; Alex a mother; Eleanor a daughter. Impulsively, Alex felt for her hand and Eleanor stirred and woke up.

'I want to talk about my death,' she said to Alex leaning towards her, trying to focus, trying to hear.

Alex felt shocked. 'Don't be silly, Mum. You're not going to die.' Alex pressed her hand reassuringly. 'I've got good news. I had a long talk with the doctors while you were asleep. The bleeding has stopped, so a major crisis has passed. There is no need for an operation. The doctors are pleased with you. Really, you are making good progress.'

'I don't feel it,' Eleanor grumbled. 'I'm having hallucinations.'

'Really?' Alex looked amused.

'Very odd. It usually happens after they give me morphine. I seem to be reliving bits of the past, down to when you and James were tiny and when,' she paused, 'I had a lover.'

'Mum!' Alex didn't know whether to appear amused or
shocked.

'His name was Mike. I was dreaming about him. It was
very vivid; the places, the situation, the things we said. Marge
used to lend us her flat on the Heath. When I opened my
eyes it was hard to believe I wasn't there.'

'Did Dad know about Mike?'

'Oh, no, your father and I were discreet about our affairs.
Oh, yes, he had them, too.'

'You had more than one?' Now Alex did begin to feel an
irrational sense of disapproval. One didn't expect parents to
have sex, let alone lovers.

'And Dad . . .?'

'Of course he did. How do you think he got to know
Karen? He was carrying on with her for years.'

'And what happened to Mike?'

'Oh, the thing just petered out.' Eleanor sounded offhand.
'Not very important, really. I thought your dad and I would
stay together forever. I never took Karen seriously, but it
wasn't to be.'

She sighed.

'I think you do regret it quite a bit, don't you, Mum?'
Alex said earnestly.

'I suppose so . . .' Eleanor leaned back aware of the
morphine beginning to wear off, the pain starting again. '. . .
especially now.' Her voice faltered. 'That's why I wanted to
discuss my death, my possible death, with you.'

'I don't want to talk about it,' Alex said robustly. 'You are
not going to die. You are going to get better and continue
life just as it was before.'

'If only . . .' Eleanor said and, as her eyes closed, Alex
watching her wondered if, in fact, it were possible that her
mother could ever lead a normal life again.

Alex slept a lot, but at odd hours, sometimes during the day,
to make up for all the times when she didn't sleep because of
the worry about her mother and other things. After a few hours
she would wake up in the middle of the night, fully alert, then
everything, all her worries and fears, would crowd in to prevent
her sleeping again, often until dawn, sometimes not even then.

This time sleep had evaded her and finally she got up just before six, let Melody out into the garden and made a cup of tea. She drank it slowly standing by the kitchen door and looked out on to the expanse of low-lying land and hills that shielded the sight of the sea from the house.

It was indeed a beautiful situation. Her mother had chosen well and she should by rights have enjoyed many years of happiness here, making new friends, entertaining old ones from London, continuing to write for the magazines. Whatever her mother said she knew the divorce had not been easy, though now that she had learnt to her astonishment about the affairs both her parents had apparently been engaging in she was not so surprised after all.

A lot of the time she had been abroad with Hugo and she preferred it that way, keeping out of it but perhaps at the same time not being of much help or support to her mother. In retrospect she felt guilty. In so many ways she'd failed Eleanor, maybe subconsciously getting her own back for that real or imagined lack of affection in the early years.

Alex finished her tea and called Melody who slunk in reluctantly, sulkily and looked apathetically at her bowl. She and Alex had achieved a kind of *modus vivendi*, but Melody spent most of the day on her mother's bed and Alex felt some pity for the cat and wished she could explain to her what had happened. As Melody stared peevishly at her bowl, then accusingly at Alex, implying that the food on offer wasn't much good, Alex bent to stroke her, feeling a sudden affinity with the cat, but Melody skipped away out of reach and scurried up the stairs to resume her lonely vigil on the empty bed.

Alex put on a coat and went out by the side of the house locking the kitchen door and slipping the key into her pocket. It was a glorious morning, but a chilly one and as she passed the farm where Niobe lived she saw a muscular, good-looking man loading thatch on to the back of a truck. Thinking it must be Niobe's partner she waved. He looked at her a little surprised, not knowing who she was and then he raised his hand and smiled at her before resuming his task.

Alex felt guilty that she had made no attempt to contact

Niobe since that first meeting and decided she would call in on the way back. She thought her man looked rather nice.

She loved that walk to the sea down the narrow road flanked by high hedges and thought it no wonder that it was a favourite of her mother's. The ground sloped gently, fields on one side, woodland on the other, the soft colours of autumn now beginning to proliferate and very soon she came in sight of the sea, a triangle of blue nestling between the surrounding hills. She quickened her pace and the roofs of the small hamlet, just a cluster of cottages scattered on the hillside dominated by a pub came in sight. The pub, The Smugglers' Arms, had been there for almost two centuries from the time when the hidden cove was a favourite haunt of smugglers, notorious in the area.

The sea, as if caressed by the early morning sunlight, was as still and calm as if it were a pane of glass reflecting the deep blue of the sky. Several gulls flew noisily overhead, swooping low as they came to the sea in the hope of an early morning catch. Hands deep in her pockets, Alex perched on a wall by the side of the pub overlooking the water. It was so early that no one was yet about and it seemed as though she had the entire world to herself. Across the bay she could see Lyme Regis hazily outlined and, far away to the left, Portland Bill. To one side of her a man appeared walking purposefully along the beach, an outboard motor clasped in his arms. He stopped by the hull of an upturned boat and slung the motor inside, then began to push it out towards the sea. She watched him idly as he jumped aboard, fixed the motor onto the stern and then rowed out into the sea until it was deep enough for him to start the motor. He shipped his oars, fired the motor and sped away towards the horizon doubtless in search of lobster pots he had put out the previous day.

Alex stretched her legs and then stumbled across the rocks to the beach and walked to the water's edge, her eyes following the progress of the boat until it disappeared from sight.

She strode along by the side of the water and then turned and retraced her steps towards the pub where there were now signs of activity. A young man who she had seen behind the bar, in jeans and a white T-shirt with the pub logo on the front, was rolling an empty barrel down the slope towards the others that stood at the side of the road awaiting retrieval by the brewer's dray. He stood upright as she approached.

'How is your mother?' he asked, a look of concern on his face.

'Progressing, thanks.' Alex stopped. 'How nice of you to be concerned.'

'Everyone is concerned,' the young man replied. 'The pictures of the accident were in the papers. It looked horrific. It was a miracle that she wasn't killed. She hadn't been here very long, had she?'

Alex shook her head. She had only visited the pub once with her mother before the accident and was surprised he remembered her.

'Did Mum come here much?'

'Not much,' the young man said. 'She sometimes took a walk, usually in the early evening, then occasionally she would pop in for a drink or stay for a meal.'

'She liked it here.' Alex gazed towards the sea. 'I really wonder if she will ever be able to make this walk again.'

'Her injuries are that bad?'

'She has a lot of internal injuries, broken ribs, that sort of thing. Thankfully, the internal bleeding has stopped; that really might have finished her off, but she also sustained a fracture of the skull, which has left her deaf and with double vision. She can't see well enough to read and can hear very little of what you say. For one used to communicate, she feels terribly cut off.'

'That's awful,' the young man said with a shake of his head.

'I don't know your name, I'm afraid,' Alex said apologetically. 'I'm Alex.'

'George.' The young man held out his hand. 'My dad is the licensee.' He looked at the empty barrels still lying outside the open door. 'I'd better get on. Please give your mother our best wishes.'

'Oh, I will and as soon as she is well enough I'll bring her down to see you.'

'Let's hope she can make it herself.' George however didn't sound too convinced as with a wave of his hand he turned towards the pub again.

How nice people were, Alex thought resuming her walk up the hill. That was the thing about the country, everyone knew, everyone cared, or at least was concerned. In London it would not even have made the local papers unless it had happened to someone very famous.

She came to the top of the hill and paused by the farm where the man had been loading his truck of which there was now no sign. It was half past seven. Niobe would be getting the children off to school, she supposed; best call back another time. Then she saw her come around the side of the house, a basket of washing under her arm, and walk towards the clothes line. She saw Alex, put her basket down and waved a cheery greeting.

'Hello,' she cried gaily, coming towards her.

'Morning,' Alex replied, 'and a lovely one, too. I just went down to the beach for a walk.'

'Your mother loved the beach.'

Alex noted with a jerk the past tense.

'I know. I saw George at the pub just now and he told me. I'm going to take her there as soon as possible when she comes out of hospital.'

'Any idea when that will be?'

Alex shook her head. 'She is still in Intensive Care and I don't think it will be very long before she goes to a general ward. Her condition has stabilized, thank God, but it will be a long time before she is able to be discharged.'

'How long are you staying?'

'That depends.'

'Come in for a coffee or tea, whatever.' Niobe beckoned towards the house. 'Have you had breakfast?'

'But aren't the children . . .?' Alex gazed questioningly towards the house.

'Oh, Francis takes them to school. They left a few minutes ago.'

'How old are they?'

'Freddie is eleven, Sam – Samantha, that is – ten.'

'And you? Have you any?' Niobe looked at her as they walked towards the house.

'No children, but I do have a bloke, Hugo. He's in India and pretty fed up that I've had to abandon, at least for the time being, the assignment we were working on. I can't leave Mum at the moment.'

'Of course not.'

Niobe led the way into a large, pleasant farmhouse kitchen with check-curtained windows, lots of flowers prettily and artistically arranged in various containers – jugs, jam jars, pots of all kinds. At one end was an Aga on which a kettle was simmering. The floor was flagstoned and a large deal table in the middle had on it the remnants of breakfast: packets of various cereals, mugs, a milk bottle, used dishes and plates.

'Can I get you some toast?'

Alex shook her head. 'But a cup of coffee would be lovely. And you had time to do the washing, too!'

'Oh, we're early risers. Have to be. There are animals to feed. We have a smallholding you know: chickens, geese, a few pigs and some sheep. Francis is a thatcher and has to be at work early.'

Alex sat on a chair and looked round appreciatively. 'It is very nice, spacious. How long have you lived here?'

'Getting on for ten years.' Niobe gestured towards the window indicating one of the outbuildings opposite. 'That's my studio. I'm an artist.'

'Really?' Alex rose and stared out of the window. 'What a lovely place to paint. You must show me your work.'

'I will, one day.' Niobe sounded guarded and sat a mug of coffee on the table in front of Alex.

Alex started to say something, then hesitated. 'Do you . . .?' she trailed off.

'Do I sell? Is that what you're trying to say?' Niobe gave a brittle laugh. 'Not very much. It's very hard to make headway here. That's why I miss London.'

'Oh, you came from London? I didn't realize.'

'You thought I was a local?' Niobe appeared mildly offended by the suggestion, leaning heavily on the word local. 'No thank *you*.'

'Don't you *like* the locals?'

'Some of them are all right,' Niobe sniffed.

'But your husband . . .' Alex trailed off not wanting to appear to pry.

'Francis is local born and bred. He's all right. Incidentally, he's not my husband. We never tied the knot. People don't these days, do they?'

'No and I haven't either,' Alex paused. 'But if I had children I might. I don't know. I never gave it much thought.'

'Well, we might some day.' Niobe took up a pack of cigarettes as if she wished to change the subject and offered one to Alex who shook her head.

'I gave it up, fortunately.'

'I should, too.' Niobe stuck the cigarette in her mouth and lit it. 'Socially, it's becoming very unacceptable. Francis smokes like a chimney, when he can, not when he's thatching of course.' She gave a hoarse laugh.

Alex, deciding that Niobe was a more complex person than she had seemed at first, with perhaps a complicated domestic life, watched her with renewed interest as she moved gracefully across the kitchen floor and perched on a chair by the table, legs crossed. She was a striking looking woman, unusually tall, maybe five feet nine or ten with rather untidy, shoulder length jet black hair. She had large brown eyes under plucked eyebrows and a full, sensuous mouth. Her firm, dimpled chin made her seem strong and determined, not a person to trifle with. She wore jeans and a loose tunic fastened at the neck with thongs, and had sandals on bare feet. Several large ornate rings adorned her fingers and strings of beads round her neck fell to her waist. Alex saw that Niobe's large knowing eyes were fixed on her.

'I don't *look* a country girl, do I?'

'Well . . .' Alex considered the question. 'I don't really think there is such a thing as "a country girl" is there? I mean . . . well, women are pretty much universal these days aren't they?'

'I wouldn't have said you were from these parts,' Niobe said, 'nor your mother. I always admired her style. She looked elegant in anything. She did . . . does,' Niobe corrected herself.

Alex smiled sadly. 'I haven't a clue how she'll be when she leaves hospital or, for that matter, what will become of her. I can't stay here forever.'

'I'll do all I can,' Niobe said. 'You can count on me.'

When Eleanor woke it was dark, just a light over the desk where the night nurse sat making notes. It was very warm, but a stiff breeze blew across Eleanor's back making her uncomfortable. The nurse, the one she didn't like, came over to her and briskly consulted a chart hanging from the bottom of her bed. This she then unhooked and tucked under her arm in a businesslike manner.

'Could you turn down whatever is making that breeze?' Eleanor said. 'I'm cold.'

'It's a *very* warm night, Mrs Ashton.'

'I don't care. I'm cold. Please turn it down.'

The nurse didn't reply and with the chart still under her arm returned to her desk to resume her scribbling. The breeze remained unabated and Eleanor called out to the nurse who ignored her. Eleanor felt she actually hated the bloody woman who left her feeling hopeless, helpless, agitated and inadequate.

After a while, the nurse got up and with a sheaf of papers now in her hand came over to Eleanor.

'We're moving you, Mrs Ashton.' There was a note of triumph in her voice.

'Now?' Eleanor protested, 'but it's nearly midnight.'

'Now. We need the bed,' the night nurse said tersely. She then began to clear Eleanor's locker and put her things on a trolley.

A porter appeared by the side of her bed and, unlocking the brakes, moved it towards the door. The nurse followed and putting the papers on Eleanor's chest walked behind her along corridors, down in a lift, along more corridors. Idly Eleanor grasped one of the papers and made to look at it when it was snatched from her hand by the nurse who restored it to the sheaf on her chest.

The bed stopped outside a ward where another white-coated nurse stood awaiting her. 'Goodbye, Mrs Ashton,' the night nurse said with her customary lack of warmth.

As she turned, Eleanor said with a sincerity she did not feel, 'Goodbye and thank you for looking after me.'

She raised her eyes to see two identical heads bending over her.

'You poor thing,' the white-coated nurse said in a voice full of compassion and at that moment it came home to Eleanor, finally, how awful and abject her situation really was.

Two

Eleanor sat by the side of the bed gazing at the clock high up in the corner of the ward. The minutes seemed to pass by so slowly that each one was more like an hour, the whole day an eternity.

She had been in this ward for several days but she had lost track of time so she could not exactly say how many. Alex had gone back to London and it seemed as though her lifeline had gone with her. She would be back soon, she had said.

Eleanor was in a ward for trauma victims, but they were mainly geriatric patients, people either with Alzheimer's, or verging on it, who had fallen and broken a limb. They would lie in bed calling out wildly, often in desperation, pathetically, occasionally weeping, but mostly groaning, feeling, as she did, lonely and lost. Yet, although she did not identify with them the fact that their plight was similar made her want to reach out to them, even help them, but she couldn't.

In the bed next to her was a quiet young woman who had had a stroke and kept on trying to get out of bed as if, like Eleanor, she was desperate to get away. She repeatedly called out for help, strange strangulated noises that were sometimes answered and sometimes ignored whereupon she would attempt to get out of bed herself and would inevitably collapse on the floor dragging the bedclothes with her. Sometimes before then there would be a chorus from those patients watching her: 'Nurse, nurse, Sandy is trying to get out of bed,' in which Eleanor occasionally joined not wanting to see the young woman do herself any harm. Sandy was usually reprimanded, treated like a naughty child and bundled back into bed. Some of the nurses tried more than others to be compassionate and understanding of this poor woman who was a mother herself, and had been reduced by some terrible misfortune almost to an imbecilic state. In a way, their impatience as well as her frustration was understandable and Sandy should clearly have been elsewhere. Occasionally, she attempted to engage Eleanor in conversation and Eleanor was ashamed of herself for her reluctance and her inability to do more to help.

But Eleanor could do little to help her or anyone else. She was one of them: helpless, pathetic, all dignity gone. How was it possible that she, always a busy and active woman, independent, a doer rather than a receiver, had landed up in a situation like this?

Brain injury, Alex had told her. They probably thought she was mad or, if not now, soon would be. Turning her head Eleanor saw a nurse peering at her through the window next to her bed linking the ward with the duty desk, as if trying to get her attention. Eleanor stared back without acknowledging her.

She was angry and her anger was channelled against everyone including herself. Anger was almost a permanent state, bubbling below the surface, welling up inside her. She hated the ward and she wanted to be out, but she could scarcely make the chair by the side of her bed unaided and once she was in it she longed to be back in bed again.

At first, when they had come round in the morning selling papers she had bought *The Times*, but it was useless. Reading was so difficult that she had ceased trying. She had to skew her neck at such an angle that the words disappeared off the page and after a while she abandoned it.

Eating normal food at first had been almost impossible. She had choked on every morsel and only managed to swallow it urged on by a sympathetic, male orderly who put his arms round her shoulders in a valiant attempt to encourage her.

She could not walk, but had to be ferried to the lavatory in a wheelchair and be washed and, ignominiously, even have her bottom wiped.

She was aware that she was still being stared at through the window, someone trying to get her attention. Still feeling angry, she glanced impatiently sideways and a hand enthusiastically waved in greeting, a smiling familiar face gazing back at her.

'Marge!'

Joy immediately replaced anger. She wanted to wave, to reach out and hug her but she scarcely managed a weak flip of her hand. Marge slowly entered the ward, a large bunch of flowers clasped to her bosom.

'Oh, *Marge!*' Eleanor gasped as her friend stooped to kiss her. 'How wonderful to see you.' She felt tears prick behind her eyes and Marge's face seemed to crumble.

The two old friends embraced clinging to each other for what seemed an age before letting go.

'Don't say it,' Eleanor murmured. 'I look a mess, don't I? I daren't look in the mirror.' She pointed to her ear. 'I'm deaf, too, so you will have to shout.'

'Oh, you poor, poor darling.' Marge laid her flowers down and perched on the edge of the bed. 'The main thing is that you are *alive*. We all thought you were dying when we got Alex's email.'

'Oh, Alex emailed, did she?'

'Everyone in the office was deeply upset. They are all coming to see you, even Candy.'

'Candy!' Eleanor said, impressed. 'What an honour!'

Candy Huber, who had once been her deputy, was her successor. In between, as she was an American national, she had worked in head office in New York and had risen high in the hierarchy of the newspaper corporation that owned the magazine. She now controlled Europe, too, so Candy was a very important person, indeed.

'I wonder she has the time.'

'Oh, she is very fond of you. She owes you a lot.'

'She certainly does.' Eleanor had promoted Candy in the face of considerable opposition from people who thought she was not sufficiently experienced as she had been quite a junior sub, but Eleanor had seen her potential.

'Did you get my card?'

Eleanor shrugged. 'I'm afraid I've hardly looked at them or taken them in.' She indicated the white patch that covered one eye. 'Alex went through a few, but frankly I found it difficult to take much interest when I was in Intensive Care.

'Can't you see?' Marge was concerned.

'I can see, but not with both eyes at the same time, that's why this one is covered, as you can see. The other one . . .'

Marge nodded sympathetically. The other eye looked at her nose in a fixed squint so that Eleanor had to turn her head sideways to look at her.

'Horrible, isn't it?' she said. 'It has a name: diplopia. They say it might improve. Give it time. They say that about everything.'

'They didn't know if you would want to see me. That's why the nurse was trying to get your attention. I was standing just behind her.'

'Of *course* I want to see you, Marge. It was awfully good of you to have come such a long way.'

'I'd go to the end of the earth to see you, Eleanor. I have missed you. We all have. Candy is not quite the same.'

'She could be prickly, to put it mildly.' Eleanor gave a wry smile.

'She is also trying to get me to retire.'

'But you're miles away from retirement.'

'Not for Candy. I'm not quite "with it" enough for her. Anyway, I'm staying until pushed.'

'You could run that magazine yourself,' Eleanor said angrily, but still she knew what Marge meant. Pushy young women like herself were what Candy would be after. The other older, more experienced, but less fashionable women could be put out to grass. Eleanor was rather sorry now that she had done so much to advance her, but she had been good and her fairly rapid promotion was deserved. Under her the magazine had modernized, been revamped, prospered and revenue had increased.

'You could stay at my house for the night if you want.'

Marge shook her head. 'Thanks, no. When you are better, I'd love to, but right now I have to get back. I came by train and have a return ticket, besides, Candy expects me. I don't want to get the sack! By the way, who is looking after Melody? You still have her, don't you?'

'Oh, I do. A neighbour, a nice woman called Niobe. Look,' Eleanor paused, 'I've suddenly thought of something.' Her pallor was replaced by a flush of excitement. 'I wonder if

Candy would like a sort of diary from me, you know, of my recovery. And I shall recover.' Eleanor said firmly as if to reassure herself. 'It will give me something to do, keep my hand in.'

Marge nodded. 'I think it's a wonderful idea. You were so popular. I'm sure Candy will jump at it. As soon as you feel like having more visitors she will be down, I'm sure, and you can discuss it with her. Also, let me know who else you want to see. Believe me, you have a lot of friends there who miss you and are all very, very concerned.' She paused as the nurse appeared beside them, pushing a wheelchair, smiling apologetically.

'I'm sorry to disturb you, Eleanor, but the doctors in ENT want to see you to try and get some of the blood out of your ears. It should help you to hear a lot better.'

'Oh, but . . .' Eleanor glanced in dismay at Marge. 'My friend has only just come all the way from London.'

'I'll be here when you get back,' Marge promised. 'Don't keep them waiting.'

The room was completely white, small, brightly lit, devoid of furniture except for the surgical couch on which she lay. Two doctors were leaning over her and were delicately probing her ears with an instrument that sounded a little like a dentist's drill and which performed, they had told her 'microscopic suction'. Finally, one of the doctors stood back with an apparent air of satisfaction, the palm of his hand extended towards her. 'This was what was causing all the trouble,' he said cheerfully. 'Your hearing should improve a lot now.' Eleanor found herself staring at a solid, thick string of dried blood about an inch long that resembled a fat worm. It was a hideous sight and a spasm of nausea shot through her as, momentarily, the room seemed to spin.

The two doctors conversed for a moment and then left the room without further explanation. Eleanor remained on the couch staring up at the ceiling and to her surprise instead of elation at the thought of regaining her hearing she felt completely paralysed with fear, claustrophobic in this small room, terrified of being left alone.

In a stricken voice she called out, 'Please don't leave me

alone.' But her plea was not answered and she repeated it. She felt marooned, isolated on this couch, unable to move, overwhelmed by the irrational terror claustrophobia inevitably brings. She was practically on the verge of hysteria when the nurse who had brought her re-entered the room cheerfully pushing the wheelchair and paused, gazing with concern at Eleanor's stricken face as, gently, she helped her from the couch and into the chair. Eleanor found she was shaking.

'What's the matter?' the nurse enquired.

'I was terrified of being alone. I don't know why.'

The nurse patted her shoulder. 'It's all over now,' she said comfortingly.

'It was horrible. That tiny room made me feel claustrophobic, all by myself.'

She sat back and tried to relax, aware now of sounds to which she had hitherto been deaf.

'You will feel much better now,' the nurse said as they re-entered the ward. Eleanor was looking eagerly across to her bed expecting to see Marge sitting there, but there was no sign of her and the staff nurse came over to her as she was helped back into bed.

'I'm afraid your friend had to go. She said she'd miss her train.'

'Oh.'

Dejection once again.

Eleanor settled back in her bed and closed her eyes aware of a deep sense of loss.

Marjorie Grafton was aged fifty-five, rather a large woman who had worked for the magazine since her teens. In fact, she was one of the oldest employees in the organization. She had worked her way up from a temp in the typing pool to personal assistant to the editor. She had by now served three and one of them and her undoubted favourite was Eleanor Ashton, who had a humanity, a concern for others, which the other two conspicuously lacked, a not uncommon phenomenon in the cut and thrust world of journalism.

Marge was by now an institution, capable, dependable, expert at her job. Candy Huber was in her early forties, elegant, chic, not particularly good-looking, but managed to be by employing every skill in the book from hairdressers to beauticians to *haute couture* clothes, most bought in Paris and Milan. To encourage the dream of youth she liked to surround herself with nubile young women who wore lots of make-up, dressed fashionably, smoked, drank and probably took drugs, though this would have been neither admitted nor tolerated if it ever became known.

Marjorie, though popular, was not of this ilk. She lived alone at the top of Hampstead Heath in a handsome flat, which had belonged to her parents who had unwittingly bequeathed a small fortune to their daughter, thus guaranteeing her future, when they bought it not long after the war.

Candy, whilst aware of Marge's good qualities, felt that her image didn't fit in with the ones she wanted to project of the office. She would have liked to have pensioned her off, and one day quite soon now she probably would and replace her with someone much younger, smarter and prettier and not nearly as capable, knowledgeable or faithful.

Candy's office was on the fifth floor of a glass building with a view of St Paul's Cathedral and the Thames on one side and Tower Bridge and city skyscrapers on the other. Her office was partitioned from the rest of the open-plan office by more glass so that she could see everyone and everyone could see her.

Marge's desk was immediately outside the office and she was able to control who had access to her boss and who didn't. She fielded all her telephone calls and dealt with all her appointments, correspondence and business emails. Those of a personal nature Candy liked to send herself from a computer on her desk.

Marge had started work in the days long before computers. She had trained as a stenographer and had excellent shorthand and typing skills. She had a pleasant middle-class accent and her own unique brand of personal charm.

Marge now sat in front of Candy's desk with a sheaf of papers before her, going through the business of the day. It was eight thirty in the morning and the office was still almost empty, but Candy liked to start the day early before her hectic round of meetings and engagements began, which inevitably included a lunch in some fashionable eating place. Marge was always there before her. She had dealt with e-mails that had come in overnight and was ready to start as soon as Candy, and possibly the day's post, arrived.

Today was a particularly busy one because of Marge's day off the previous day. There was a stack of mail to see to, schedules to draw up, invitations to accept or decline. Candy seemed to have forgotten Marge had been to see Eleanor the previous day, and she wasn't mentioned until just before the end as Marge was standing up.

'I saw Eleanor yesterday.'

'Of *course* you did!' Candy exclaimed, momentarily abashed. 'How forgetful of me. How *was* she?' Candy always spoke with emphasis on certain words.

'I was quite shocked when I saw her,' Marge said sombrely. 'I hardly recognized her. She looks terrible. She has a fractured skull, which has left her with a pronounced squint. This gives her double vision so she can't read.'

Candy shook her head. 'Really *awful*,' she murmured. 'I don't even like to think about it. That that could happen to someone like Eleanor…' She paused shuddering.

'She is also very deaf at the moment. Of course things might improve. They were about to remove the dried blood from her ears soon after I arrived. Unfortunately she was gone such a long time I couldn't stay, so I don't know what happened.'

'Poor, poor Eleanor,' Candy said. 'I am so sorry to hear this. She was always so smart, so well turned out; someone I admired, even envied. She taught me a lot about life as well as journalism.'

'I am sure she would like you to visit her, maybe when she gets out of hospital? I told her you might.'

'Mmm.' Candy's eyes gazed fixedly at her desk, her shoulders hunched in an expressive gesture. 'I don't think I could possibly do that. I'm afraid anything to do with eyes makes me quite queasy. You know, it makes one so, well, *vulnerable*. I think you were terribly brave, Marge.' Candy straightened up decisively. 'Tell you what, I'll send her a *huge* bunch of flowers. Can you arrange that for me like a darling?'

'We already sent her one,' Marge said frigidly.

'Then send her another, larger –' Candy looked up – 'and don't say anything about my not coming, but I just couldn't do it.'

'It may improve,' Marge said. 'They are not sure of the outcome. She will probably have to have surgery.'

Candy's hand shot out in a forbidding gesture. 'Please, please don't go on, Marge. I don't want you to think I'm horrible, but I have heard *quite* enough about poor Eleanor. Now, is that all for the moment?' She reached for the telephone.

Marge paused nervously in the act of making for the door. 'The thing is, Candy, she suggested she might write a diary . . . you know, for the magazine.'

'A diary!' Candy exclaimed, replacing the receiver. 'What sort of diary?'

'About her progress; her recovery. She is determined to get better. You know she was editor for so long, so many people knew her. She was so popular. She thought it would do her good to keep her hand in.'

'Hmm . . .' Candy tapped her desk thoughtfully again. 'I'm not so *sure* about that. You know, however much we love her, and we all do, she is past history. She's also getting on. She must be well into her fifties by now.'

Marjorie felt herself colouring furiously. 'What has age to do with it?'

'Everything,' Candy said. 'The readership of this magazine is getting younger and younger. People forget very quickly and pretty soon no one will know or care who Eleanor Ashton was. Besides, people don't want to know about squints and deafness. Put squints and deafness with *age* and you've had it. It is so uncool! You want something heroic, particularly if they're young: masses of broken limbs, arms in slings, all that is acceptable, even cancer, as long as it is curable of course. Why, she might die on us and what then? We will lose readers in droves if we start printing that sort of thing. Illustrated with photos, no doubt.' Candy shook her head in obvious distaste. 'No, *please!*' She gazed earnestly at Marge. 'No, I think we must definitely shelve that idea, Marge.' She looked at her squarely. 'Just don't bring it up again if you see her. Be as tactful as you can. I do think she is brave,

I really do, and we don't want to hurt the poor woman's feelings.'

'Lean on my arm,' the physiotherapist said, encouragingly gripping Eleanor firmly round the waist. 'You can do it.'

Eleanor gritted her teeth but she felt she had no strength in her legs; they seemed to buckle at the knees. She put her arm firmly round the waist of the physio and leaning heavily against her walked falteringly into the middle of the ward. She was watched with some interest by the patients who, she imagined, tended not to like her because she was so uncommunicative. Some of them chatted to one another all day long, or called out in ringing tones, making you wonder why they were in hospital if they were so well. Eleanor remembered that when the children were born the maternity ward had been a very jolly affair. In those days one stayed in hospital for days rather than hours, but not now, not here. But having a baby was quite a different matter to being the victim of a road accident. She wanted quiet, but the ward rang with sound all day long and visiting hours were endless with bored young children using the highly polished floor as a running track.

It had been a warm, sunny September morning but Eleanor could recall so little of it except that the beams of the sun had been reflected in the polished wooden floors of the hospital. She had not once glanced outside the window and had no wish to do so now as, teeth firmly clenched, she tried to concentrate on her steps, longing for the day when she could propel herself unaided and thus be able to go home.

Slowly, they came to the end of the ward and Eleanor glanced briefly at the window, but still not out into the sunshine and the sunlit streets beyond with normal, fortunate people – how fortunate they most certainly didn't realize – going briskly about their business, shopping, working, eating, entertaining. Engaged in everyday things that people took for granted were impossible for her now and she wondered if they ever would be.

Reaching the end of the ward, slowly they retraced their steps still hanging on to each other but Eleanor, exhausted when they reached her bed, flopped thankfully down on it.

'That was good,' the physio said briskly ticking her name off a list in her hand. 'You are making good progress, Eleanor. You'll soon be skipping about. Sooner than you think.'

'If only,' Eleanor said, knowing how very far from the truth that was.

'I want to go home,' Eleanor said to the consultant who was making one of his rare visits. In fact, he was someone she hardly knew, a man she had scarcely seen and almost certainly would not have recognized had she not been told who he was. One night in Intensive Care she had watched a man standing at the foot of her bed, dressed in a dinner jacket, his back to her, studying her records. She remembered wishing he would turn and speak to her, whoever he was, but his task done he had left without looking at her. However, he had apparently been the doctor in charge of her case and as such she had a lot to thank him for. He had decided not to operate on her to stop the internal bleeding and had probably saved her life.

'You really are not ready, Mrs Ashton. A long period of convalescence is called for. You had a very serious accident.'

'I want to see my cat, be in my own home,' Eleanor insisted.

'You must not be alone, not for the time being.'

'I shan't,' Eleanor persisted mulishly. 'I shall have my daughter.'

'Well . . .' The important man glanced at his watch. 'I shall have to have a word with the neurologist.'

'Why?'

'Because you had a serious brain injury. It will take you a very long time to recover.' And with an abrupt nod of his head in the manner of a schoolmaster dismissing a naughty pupil he walked with the nurse who had been standing docilely next to him, out of the ward.

Three

'You don't know how much it means to me, bringing you back like this,' Alex said, glancing sideways at her mother. 'A day that at one time we never thought we'd see.'

Eleanor nodded, but she was preoccupied. 'Are you sure Melody is all right?' She leaned forward, peering nervously through the windscreen as the road seemed to merge and converge with the surrounding hedges and fields.

'Of course she is all right, Mum.' Alex had already tried to reassure her mother on this point. She wondered if she was in fact leaving hospital too soon as the surgeon had suggested when he reluctantly signed the papers allowing her release.

Eleanor could not believe that a nervous cat like Melody could have spent five long weeks virtually alone except for Niobe or Alex who had fed her. She suspected that they'd been concealing the fact from her that Melody had disappeared.

Finally, they arrived. Eleanor looked with some emotion at the house she had left so gaily on that warm September day five weeks before. Alex studied her and then swiftly bent across to kiss her, an uncharacteristic gesture that Eleanor in her emotional state found almost overwhelming. Her daughter was the least demonstrative of people and gestures like this were rare. Between them there had always been a distance.

She waited while Alex got out of the car and, retrieving her sticks from the boot, opened the passenger door and helped her mother out.

'Go carefully, now,' she said, half jokingly. 'No rush.'

'Don't worry, I shall be very careful,' Eleanor replied.

Eleanor grasped the stick and painfully, with difficulty and with the help of Alex's guiding hand, extricated herself from the car. Carefully, Alex unlocked the front door and Eleanor, once inside, stood for a long time looking round.

'Melody,' she called gently and waited, but no Melody appeared and she called again, this time more loudly. Nothing. She turned a stricken face to Alex who was bringing in her bag and some shopping.

'Now, don't panic, Mum,' Alex cautioned. 'She *is* here. She was here this morning and I assure you she is here now. She's hiding. She's cross with you.'

Eleanor, unconvinced, turned into the sitting room and gazed through the French windows into the garden. It looked sad and untended. The grass badly needed cutting, dead heads hung sadly from the roses.

'Cup of tea, Mum?' Alex suggested from the doorway. 'I'll take your things upstairs first.'

Eleanor shook her head. 'I'd love a cup, but I think I'll go upstairs and have a little rest.'

'I'll bring the tea up.'

Alex looked on as her mother slowly, leaning heavily on her sticks, made her way to the foot of the stairs, paused and then taking a deep breath began to mount them very slowly, one at a time. She would pause on each stair to get her breath before heaving herself onto the next. When finally she got to the top she paused to get her breath back.

'The last time I was on these stairs I ran down,' Eleanor said, looking back at her daughter, noting the concern on her face. 'Down the stairs and out of the house . . .' She seemed on the point of tears

'It *will* get better. I promise it will,' Alex called. But as Eleanor continued slowly into her bedroom she felt on the verge of tears herself.

Eleanor flopped thankfully on the bed and looked round a room that was so restful and welcoming, so normal after the hospital ward.

'Melody . . .' she called again but still no sign of that capricious pet.

Eleanor's eyes closed as she lay back on the bed, her bed, her home. Now that she was here she would recover, she knew that, but there had been times in the hospital when she felt she would never leave it.

She opened her eyes as Alex appeared with a tray, which she put by the side of the bed, then began to pour the tea.

'I'll slip into my gown,' Eleanor said, 'in a moment. I'm just luxuriating being in my own bed.'

'Take your time,' Alex handed her her cup. 'Still no sign of that pussy cat?'

'She *is* here, isn't she?'

'She certainly is. I heard her bell as we came through the door. Look, Mum, are you able to come down for supper or would you like me to bring it up here?'

'No, I want to come down,' Eleanor said firmly, sipping her tea. 'I am determined to make an effort. I feel I've been an invalid for far too long.'

Alex perched on the side of the bed and put her hand over one of her mother's. 'Mum, it will take a very long time. The staff nurse said you must be very patient with yourself, give yourself time to recover slowly. You must accept the fact that your recovery *will* be very slow. After all, you nearly died.' She got up. 'I'll go and see what I've got in the fridge. It will be pretty basic. Steak and chips?'

Eleanor nodded. 'Sounds good to me.' She wasn't hungry but she didn't want to tell Alex that, didn't want to diminish in any way the gratitude she felt to her daughter for all she was doing. She felt it was like a new beginning, a fresh start between the two of them, busy distant people for so long. Alex hadn't even been around when the divorce was going on and she'd moved from London to the country. Yet James had taken leave and made the journey from America.

Alex reached for her mother's gown and threw it on the bed.

'I'll change when I get up,' Eleanor said. 'Just at this moment I'm loving the rest and my beautiful cup of tea.'

'Call if you need me.'

Eleanor finished her tea and lay back shutting her eyes once again and thinking back on the momentous events of the day when she finally got her much wanted release. Then Alex had arrived just after lunch, by which time she was dressed and had everything packed up.

The farewells were sincere, but not tearful. Eleanor had hated the hospital, knew she had not been a good patient and had made herself unpopular. She was sure they would be glad to be rid of her. The moment Alex appeared the nurse put her in her wheelchair and she was taken to the hospital entrance where Alex had left the car. The drive home was scary, the extent of her double vision all too apparent; bad enough inside, but terrible when she was out in the open.

At that moment there was a familiar plop on the bed, a feline grunt and a soft furry body rubbed itself alongside her.

Eleanor opened her eyes and saw Melody staring at her with an expression that seemed to suggest she had never gone away.

'Melody,' she said tenderly, her hand curling round that soft body, pressing it to her side. Her eyes filled with tears while Melody settled down to a deep throated purr, now that normality was restored and things were once again as they should be, mistress and cat reunited at last.

It was one thing to say you must make an effort, another to put it into practice. Once she was in her gown and had made her way downstairs again, Eleanor was visited by that sense of helplessness, of exhaustion, which was to be a feature of her life for many weeks to come.

She sat toying with her food, anxious not to disappoint Alex who had gone to so much trouble. She had made a nice starter of smoked salmon, which Eleanor would normally have enjoyed, followed by fillet steak, chips and salad. There was a freshly opened bottle of Shiraz.

'I have so little appetite,' Eleanor said apologetically placing her knife and fork together on the plate. 'I'm so sorry, darling.'

'Do try to eat something,' Alex pleaded. 'You have lost so much weight. You need to get your strength back.'

'In time,' Eleanor said, 'and thank you so much for taking so much trouble.' Alex was not the most domesticated of creatures and so it had been an effort. 'I can't tell you how much I appreciate it,' Eleanor continued, 'and also all that you have done for me. I don't know where I would be without you.'

Now Alex leaned back from the table and a slight flush stole over her face. 'Mum, there is something I have to tell you. It's not very nice and I know you will be upset, but . . .'

'Good heavens.' Eleanor looked at her in alarm. 'What on earth is it? Don't say you are ill . . .' She pressed her hands fearfully to her face.

'No, no, it's nothing like that,' Alex smiled reassuringly. 'It is just that, Mum, I have to go back to India.'

'Oh, no, when?'

'Tomorrow, I'm afraid.'

'*Tomorrow*!' Eleanor experienced a sharp feeling of panic.

'Don't worry,' Alex said. 'You are not being deserted. I have made arrangements for someone to come in and look after you. I have known for some time, but I was sure you would prefer to be here rather than in hospital or a convalescent home.'

'Of course . . .'

'An agency was recommended and they will supply someone to look after you during the day and someone to sleep here at night. You will have twenty-four-hour care.'

She stopped as she saw her mother's crestfallen face.

'Oh, I know it is not the same as having me and I will be back as soon as I can, that's a promise.'

'It's Hugo, isn't it?'

'Partly Hugo,' Alex confessed. 'He more or less delivered an ultimatum, but if I don't go back we shall lose our commission. He has done all the photography he can by himself and I can't give up the job, Mum. It is my career.'

'Of course . . .' Eleanor sat back. She must be brave, not whinge or moan. It was not in her nature and Alex, so like her in temperament, wouldn't expect it, but strangers in the house, people she didn't *know*. It would in fact be rather like being in hospital again.

'It will be terribly expensive,' she faltered.

'I know, but ultimately your compensation will take care of that. I have also consulted our solicitors who are on the case. They say it is cut and dried as it was clearly not your fault.'

'Couldn't Niobe . . . ?' Eleanor began.

'I did ask Niobe to recommend an agency and she said these people are supposed to be very good.' Alex paused. 'I think that if she thought it was something she could do she would have said. I didn't like to presume too much.'

'Of course,' Eleanor said. 'I quite understand.'

'And she is there, willing to help. But she has a partner and kids, animals to look after. She is a very busy woman.'

'Oh, I know.'

'She said any time, just ask. I will stay until the woman arrives tomorrow, but I am booked on a night plane from Heathrow. It was a very hard decision, not taken lightly, I assure you. Anyway,' she smiled and playfully tapped her mother's arm as she said, 'you know we'd fight if we saw too much of each other.'

That was it, Eleanor thought gazing into the night unable to sleep despite a sleeping pill, her arm tightly encircling Melody who was still purring. She and Alex would always disagree about something; loved each other but couldn't live together, the usual story.

But oh, why now, at this moment, when she was so weak, so feeble, so unlike her old self, when she so desperately needed someone she loved, a familiar face, did she have to go?

Eleanor sat in the chair where her carer left her each morning so that she could look out of the window and watch the birds in the garden where winter was setting in. Beside her was a table on which was an array of things she might need: water, medication, tapes for her talking book – what a godsend that was and, above all, the telephone.

Alex had been gone a week and the routine of her new life had settled down into a dreary monotone of repetition, things done at the same time every day. The caring had not quite gone the way she had expected. The woman who slept in at night was the same but she scarcely ever saw her. She would arrive at ten by which time Eleanor was in bed, and leave at seven placing a cup of tea and toast on Eleanor's bedside table. Her name was Marion and she was very pleasant. So far Eleanor had never had to summon her during the night and she didn't suppose she ever would, but it was nice to have someone there. She did not dread loneliness so much as being alone, especially during the night because her poor sight and hearing made her feel very vulnerable. She was never able to go to sleep until she knew that Marion had come and had popped her head round the door and bade Eleanor goodnight.

Melody took exception to all these intruders and disappeared into various hiding places when they arrived. At night, after Marion had gone to bed, she emerged from under Eleanor's bed and spent the night happily sleeping by her mother's side.

The garden looked very autumnal and so much needed doing to it. Eleanor wanted a gardener and various people to help in a way she never had before. She also found she was yearning for companionship, also something new to her; someone to talk to, someone to see. She spent a lot of time thinking about the accident almost with a sense of disbelief that it had ever happened, that her life could have undergone such a radical change in such a short time.

Whereas Marion kept regular hours it was not the same with the carer who came daily and it was not always the same person. Sometimes they would come early and sometimes late according to who it was. In a country area they had long distances to cover and this had to be allowed for, but it was still very inconvenient. The carer got her up and helped her into the shower. Eleanor longed for a bath, but it was impossible for her to get in and out of one. In the hospital it had taken two nurses to help her when she bathed.

The carer helped her to dress and then left her downstairs with her coffee and all the little bits and pieces that were a part of invalidism. As soon as the front door had shut Eleanor felt a pang knowing that some hours would pass before the woman came who gave her lunch and took her upstairs for her afternoon sleep.

When she complained to Alex, who telephoned every day, about the dreariness of her routine she was reminded quite sharply that she was very lucky to be alive and she supposed she was, and grateful too. James also rang every day worried because his wife and new baby were both very weak and he didn't want to leave them yet and get over to see her. Eleanor put on a specially cheerful voice for James assuring him that she was doing well, was well looked after and he must not worry about her but concentrate on his family.

Alone. She felt very alone, isolated, cut off.

Eleanor sat back in her chair, her hands resting in her lap, her eyes on the birds who kept visiting the bird feeders hanging from the trees in the garden. A brightly coloured bullfinch was busy pecking at the seeds while two blue tits waited patiently on either side for their turn. The bright red of the bullfinch was a glorious splash of colour against the dark green background of the trees. As a city person Eleanor had been very ignorant about the countryside, and one of the joys in coming to Dorset had been the discovery of birds and the routine that governed their lives. There was a time-lessness about the business of breeding and feeding, the little quarrels they had, the mating rituals, the skirmishes that reflected, after all, so much of human life.

Unexpectedly Eleanor was visited at that moment by a sharp sense of euphoria that slowly swept over her like a wave creeping gently up on the seashore. It was a feeling she had not experienced for a very long time, maybe ever, quite in this way. With it came the realization that life after all still had so much to offer: the unending progression of the seasons, the beauty of nature, the continuity of human existence regardless of wars, natural disasters or the number of people injured in road accidents. Devastating wars left huge areas of the earth barren, only for nature to reassert itself time and time again. Into her mind's eye came that vivid, familiar picture of the petrified landscapes of France devastated by the First World War, acres of skeletal trees and rain-soaked, pitted craters to be replaced in time by fertile woods and fields, acres of corn interspersed with bright red poppies waving in the sun.

She realized that she was indeed fortunate to be alive here in this place, well looked after, gazing out into the tran-quillity of her garden, observing the plant and bird life with Melody sleeping on the sofa beside her: that little cat, once a stray unwanted and unloved, who was such a companion and who had waited for her for five long weeks.

For several moments Eleanor luxuriated in her newfound

feeling of hope and gratitude, the sheer joy at being alive, and vowed to remember this moment whenever pain and depression and that sense of hopelessness she so often had got the better of her again.

Company, of course, was a good tonic. She thought of Jean Walker, one of the few people she had met since her move, a bright intelligent woman who had taken early retirement as a school teacher in a large inner city comprehensive. It was Jean who had telephoned her on that fateful day. But for Jean she probably would not have had her accident, been safely on the seashore before the man who was nearly to kill her came over the horizon. She knew there had been a card from her but no word from her since.

She consulted her address book on the table by her side and took up the phone. It rang for a while before it was answered.

'Hello?'

'Jean?'

'Yes, Jean Walker speaking.'

'Jean, it's Eleanor.'

Pregnant pause.

'Eleanor Ashton,' she repeated.

'Oh, Eleanor, yes of course! How wonderful to hear your voice!'

'Thank you very much for your card, Jean.'

'Oh, that's nothing.' Pause again, Jean was struggling. Then: 'How long have you been home?'

'Just over a week, ten days, I don't know; I lose count of time.'

Another long pause. This was turning into a very difficult conversation, the tone of which took Eleanor by surprise.

Eventually Jean said in a subdued voice, 'Eleanor, I am so sorry not to have come to the hospital to see you . . .' Her voice trailed off.

Eleanor picked up the conversation quickly. 'Oh, that's perfectly all right. Don't worry about that.'

'I had a bad dose of flu, took me an age to get over it.'

'Don't worry, really. I was very deaf anyway and the eyesight is not too good even now.'

'Oh, I am sorry. Eleanor, I feel so awful, you know, thinking the accident was partly my fault.'

'But that is nonsense . . . I never gave that a thought.' Not quite true but she certainly didn't blame her.

'Didn't you really? That is very generous of you. I couldn't help thinking that if I hadn't called to invite you to lunch that day it would never have happened. You said you were going for a walk . . .' Jean's voice faltered again. She sounded almost on the verge of tears.

Eleanor hastened to reassure her. 'Jean, *please* don't distress yourself. It is absolutely nothing to do with you, nothing at all. It was one of those things. They happen. Some people say they are meant.'

'If that's how you feel.' Jean sounded dubious. 'But I thought you *must* somehow reproach me.'

'Of course I don't, not at all. It never occurred to me. Now, why don't you come and see me? I'd love that.'

'Oh, I will.'

'When? This afternoon? Tomorrow? You say.'

Another long pause.

'Can I give you a ring? I have rather a lot on at the moment and my sister hasn't been well. Say in a week or two?'

'Of course.' Eleanor experienced a sharp feeling of disappointment. 'I'll leave you to get in touch and please don't for a moment think that I blame you in any way. I really, truly don't.'

'I won't, Eleanor,' Jean said with relief in her voice, 'and *thank* you.'

It seemed then that she abruptly replaced the receiver and the phone went dead. Somehow, Eleanor thought, sitting back and not feeling so tranquil now, it had all seemed so false.

The dreams that night were some of the worst she'd had. Not of the crash but of chaos, disorder, moving house, leaving home, being alone, loss and desolation. She kept on waking up and not knowing where she was until she felt Melody slumbering by her side and pressed the cat to her for comfort. She would have a drink of water and then grabbing her sticks by the side of the bed make her way ponderously to the loo, return to bed and lie there for ages until finally she drifted off to sleep and the dreams would start all over again.

Eleanor woke with a start.

Melody was no longer by her side, her duvet was half off
the bed and bright sunlight was apparent through the curtained
window. Some noise she was sure had awoken her and she
looked in front of her realizing that her view was blocked
by the bulky form of Janice, one of her day time carers, her
face glaring down at her.

'Come on, Eleanor,' Janice boomed seizing the duvet and
removing it completely from the bed, 'time you got up. It's
nearly ten. We're short-staffed, which is why I am late.'

Eleanor, feeling almost naked without the protection of
her duvet, stared back at her.

'Who do you think you're talking to?' she demanded.

'I'm talking to *you*, Eleanor. No use lying there feeling
sorry for yourself. That's not the way to get better.'

Eleanor snatched the duvet from her and covered herself
with it again. She didn't like Janice, she never had. She felt
she was more suited to be a jailer at a prison for particularly difficult women than an assistant employed by an
expensive agency supposedly caring for sick or elderly
people. She dreaded the days when Janice was on duty, and
there seemed to be more of them lately because they nearly
always had some kind of confrontation. It was like being
in hospital again, being told what to do, ordered about by
people half your age who treated you like some kind of
imbecile, geriatric at the very least. One or two carers she
liked very much and responded well to them, but Janice was
not among them. It was obvious too that her feelings about
Eleanor were reciprocal.

'I had a very bad night,' she said wearily. 'I kept on waking
up.'

Janice looked at the untouched cup of tea by the side of
her bed that Marion must have left at about seven. She
seemed to relent a little and smoothed the duvet across
Eleanor.

'I'll bring you another cup of tea to wake you up,' she
said in a gentler tone of voice and disappeared through the
door. Seconds later Melody crawled from under the bed and
arranged herself alongside Eleanor sympathetically.

'We don't like her, do we?' Eleanor murmured. 'She's
horrible.' Melody looked up as if in agreement but moments

later was back under the bed again as Janice entered carrying a fresh cup of tea.

'That cat doesn't like me,' she said peevishly looking at the disappearing tail, putting the cup on the bedside table.

'She's a very nervous cat,' Eleanor said wanting to add that Janice might well be right, but thinking better of it.

'I haven't got very long.' Janice began to go busily around the room moving this and that. 'I've already tidied up in the kitchen.'

Eleanor finished her tea and swung her legs over the bed sitting there for some time staring at her feet. 'My toenails could do with cutting,' she said.

'We don't cut toenails. We are not allowed to.'

'Oh, why not?' Eleanor looked curiously at her.

'It's the rule. I think it's because of Aids. You know . . . if there's any bleeding.'

Eleanor, who was easing herself out of her nightie, looked at Janice in astonishment. 'I haven't got Aids! What an outrageous suggestion!'

'I'm not suggesting you have,' Janice said silkily, 'but *we* don't know that, do we? We have to be very careful, it's the rule.' She then assisted Eleanor into her en suite, stood her under the shower and closed the curtains.

Eleanor turned on the taps and stood relishing the water running over her, trying to refresh herself and banish the horrible dreams of the night. She was not yet able to have a bath, which she longed for, because in addition to not cutting toenails the carers were not allowed to do any lifting.

'Ready,' she called at last turning off the shower, but there was no reply. Usually, the carer stood just outside the door holding a bath towel ready.

'Janice,' she called more loudly gingerly edging to the side of the shower. Still no answer, so, hanging on to the side of the cubicle, she peered round the corner as Janice came into the bedroom casually swinging the towel.

'Sorry,' she said offhandedly, 'I was in the kitchen.'

'I thought you were meant to be there in case I fell,' Eleanor said.

'Well, you didn't, did you?' Janice gave her a malicious smile and, holding out the towel, wrapped it with exaggerated tenderness around Eleanor's body as if in fact she would have preferred to have smothered her.

After Janice left, Eleanor sat in her chair looking out onto the bleak landscape. Winter was setting in and the ground had a sad, barren look, the falling leaves carpeting the lawn. Even the birds looked cold. After her encounter with Janice she felt acutely and abjectly miserable. Beside her was a cup of cold coffee that Janice had practically thrown at her in her anxiety to be gone. Eleanor simmered with indignation, but was at a loss as to what to do about it. She simply didn't feel strong enough to cope with outright war.

Suddenly there was a tap on the window and turning she saw Niobe looking through the front window with a big smile on her face.

Oh, what a welcome sight, Eleanor thought, raising her hand in greeting. Heaving herself up she hobbled over to the door to let her in.

'How *lovely* to see you,' she said stepping aside. Niobe, normally a constant visitor, had not been seen for a few days.

Niobe had a basket in her hand and held it out. 'Brought you a few things: some new-laid eggs, a cake I made and some ham – one of our pigs,' she said with a regretful sniff. 'I hate doing it, but that is what they are for.'

'Exactly,' Eleanor said sympathetically, 'I know how you feel.' She indicated the sitting room. 'Do come in. I was just feeling sorry for myself.'

'Sorry I haven't been for a few days. Sam was off school with a cold.' She held out her basket. 'I'll just pop these in the kitchen.'

'Make yourself a cup of coffee.'

'Would you like one?'

'Yes, please. I had the awful Janice woman this morning. She practically threw it at me. It tasted horrible. I don't think the kettle even boiled.'

'Now you just go back and sit down,' Niobe said solicitously. 'Leave everything to me. Would you like something to eat? Toast?' Eleanor shook her head and returning to her chair sat down thankfully.

'You know,' she said as Niobe entered the room with two cups on a tray together with large slices of what was obviously her home-made cake. 'I don't know what to do. That woman Janice drives me mad. She seems to think there is nothing wrong with me. That it's simply a question of pulling myself together.'

'What rubbish.' Niobe took a seat opposite Eleanor and gazed at her sympathetically.

'She even suggested I might have Aids.'

Niobe gaped at her, nearly choking on the piece of cake she had just put into her mouth.

'She *what*?'

'I said that my toenails needed cutting. She said they were not allowed to do that in case there was any bleeding as I might have Aids. I said I hadn't and she said but they didn't *know* that, did they!'

'I would report her to the agency.'

'I don't like to lose her her job, besides if they have these rules there is not much I can object to. I don't like her manner and that is another thing. I don't think she has a very happy personal life so she takes it out on other people. She's always muttering darkly about her boyfriend.'

'I still feel you should get someone else,' Niobe said.

'Yes, but who? That is the question.'

'I'll ask Francis's mother. She knows everyone. She may think of something. Look . . .' Niobe rummaged in her basket. 'I bought you a paper.'

Eleanor put out her hand to take it. 'That is sweet of you, but you know I can't read at all easily. I have to rely on my talking books. I see the news and so on on the TV. It is so difficult looking at everything sideways.'

'Any improvement in the eyes?'

'No, I see my surgeon again in a few weeks' time.'

Eleanor had had painful Botox injections in both eyes with a view to relaxing the muscles that had been affected by the injury to her brain, forcing her to squint and have double vision. She looked wryly at Niobe.

'I feel a fright. I look a mess don't I?'

'Not really, probably not as much as you think. I did find it disconcerting at first but now I am used to it. I think you are wonderful the way you cope.'

'What else can I do? I have no alternative except to go

under and I don't want that. I want to get better.' Eleanor leaned forward clasping her hands in her lap. 'That's enough about me. Now, tell me what you've been up to, Niobe. How is Sam?'

'Better. Back at school.' Niobe grimaced. 'Trouble is there is so much work in the house and on the farm that I can never find the time to do what I really want to do.'

'And what is that?'

Niobe tossed back her hair, a characteristic gesture of hers and looked towards the window as if seeking inspiration for a way to express what she wanted to say.

'You know I am an artist, a painter. I trained at the Slade. I knew it was difficult making a living through art alone so I also did a course in graphics, ceramic design, and for some time I worked in a studio not far from here. That was how I met Francis; he was thatching the cottage belonging to the couple who ran the studio. It was a case of instant attraction.

'Francis was very different from the men I'd known in London who were mainly from the artistic community. He was straightforward, sincere, robust, a man of the soil with his small farm holding, his independence. Still is,' she added after a pause, 'that's partly the trouble.' She tossed back her hair again and looked despairingly at Eleanor. 'After a while it is not enough. He has no artistic interests at all and at the end of the day all he wants is to have a few beers after work at the pub, come home to a meal waiting for him, watch telly for a while and go to bed. I am so exhausted at the end of the day that I flop into bed at about the same time too . . . and that's our life. The whole point is that, although I love Francis – and he is such a nice bloke you could not love him – I find him very boring, and then I think I'm going to spend the rest of my life like this and I am only thirty-five.'

Again she looked at Eleanor as if imploring her for help.

Eleanor knew it was not an uncommon problem that affected so many marriages. It had affected hers and Dick's. Although they did share a number of interests and enjoyed life together, it was a condition that somehow seemed endemic to the married state, which was when you diversified into other things, most often affairs. There was a lot she could have learned from what happened to them and she wondered how much of this she could impart to Niobe, or how much was relevant coming from a much older woman.

'You know relationships are tricky things. Once passion is spent there is sometimes a gap. The problem is you come from very different backgrounds. I suppose you were born in London?'

'No, I was born in Birmingham where my father was and still is a businessman, very active in local politics, cultural pursuits of all kinds. He and my mother do a lot of charity work as well.'

'And what did they think when you settled down with Francis?'

'They just hoped I wouldn't marry him and that it would blow over. When the children came along, of course, it was a very different matter. I think they've washed their hands of the whole business.'

'But do they see you, come to visit? Do you visit them?'

'Very rarely now. I usually go alone with the children because one of us has to look after the animals and Francis, if the truth be told, likes to stay where he is. Given the chance he would never move from here and rarely does.'

'No foreign holidays, that sort of thing?'

'Oh, no!' Niobe looked astonished at the very idea. 'He hates "abroad" and of course I love Italy, France, any place where there is plenty of art. Not that I've ever been, but I'd like the chance.'

'Couldn't you leave the children with your parents and go alone or with a friend?'

'I don't think Francis would like that either.'

'It seems to me,' Eleanor said, 'that you should set up time to talk or maybe . . . have you thought of a marriage counsellor? Some people say they are very useful. We did an article on it in the magazine I used to edit. It was very interesting.'

'Are you joking?' Niobe said standing up. 'That's the last thing we need. I don't want to be rude, but frankly I think they're a complete waste of time. Look –' she glanced at her watch – 'I must go and pick up Sam. She is only at school for half the day until she is quite better. And I'll ask Francis's mother about a help for you.'

Eleanor gazed rather sadly out of the window as Niobe made her way briskly down the path to the gate, wondering if she had upset her. When it came to it people didn't really want to be deflected from their opinions, their view of themselves and others. Attitudes became entrenched.

But how she envied her her energy, as well as her youth. Perhaps she envied that most of all. Or did she? Did she want all Niobe's anxieties and uncertainties? But for her accident she felt she had developed a plan for the rest of her life that would, hopefully, have led to a serene and contented old age.

How easy it was to plan. How different the reality. Now she had to confront a future that seemed every bit as uncertain and fraught with difficulties as Niobe's.

Four

Roger Mallett had known Eleanor most of his adult life. He had joined his father's firm, Mallet & Mallet of Lincoln's Inn, after he graduated and succeeded him on his retirement. Now, his son Christopher was poised one day to succeed him. Roger also had a daughter in the firm.

Mallets, as it was simply known, was one of those old established firms with a loyal and occasionally distinguished clientele. Eleanor's family had used Mallets, and Roger's father had acted for her until his retirement when Roger, who was only a few years younger than Eleanor, had taken over and looked after her affairs. He had handled her divorce, the sale of the old house and the purchase of the new one.

Even Dick had greatly respected the firm, which had eased the passage of the divorce for both parties. It was Dick who had told Roger of Eleanor's accident and asked him to act for her.

Eleanor was very fond of Roger and his arrival had brightened her day even though he could not hide his sense of shock when he had first seen her.

'I am much better than I was,' she said trying to sound reassuring.

'I can imagine.' Roger shook his head. 'A terrible thing but, from a legal point of view, an open and shut case.'

'Thank heaven for that.'

'It still won't be simple,' Roger said shaking his head again mournfully, 'these things never are.'

Eleanor leaned towards him. 'Roger, I want to take a look at my will.'

'But you only made it a couple of years ago, when the divorce was finalized.'

'I know. I just want to take a fresh look at it.' She leaned

back, hands folded in her lap. 'This accident has made me
focus on a lot of things. We don't know how long we have
got, do we?'

'Not really,' Roger agreed.

'I don't think I want to make many changes, but I worry
about Alex. I divided my estate between her and James, but
really Alex is the one who will need the money. James has
his own business and I believe does very well.'

'He has three children.'

'Yes, well, no need to hurry, just something we must talk
about one day.'

Eleanor looked up as the door opened and a pleasant
looking woman came into the room.

'Oh, there you are, Cathy,' Eleanor said with a smile.

'Sorry I'm late,' the woman said. 'I got held up by traffic.'

'That's perfectly OK. Let me introduce you to Roger
Mallet, our family solicitor. Roger, this is Cathy who is
helping to look after me. Cathy is the mother of Francis who
lives opposite. She has very kindly agreed to help out and,
more importantly, to sleep here at night. I am like a child
again and don't like being alone in the house at night.'

Roger stood up and held out his hand. 'How do you do?'

Cathy shook his hand and muttered something unintelli-
gible. 'Is your guest staying for lunch, Eleanor?' she asked.

'I hope so. Roger?'

'I hoped I might take you out.'

'I think Cathy has something prepared.'

'Chicken casserole,' Cathy said helpfully.

'Well . . .' Roger gestured helplessly. 'What can I say?'

'He seems a nice man, that solicitor,' Cathy said as she cleared
the table after seeing Roger to the door.

'He is. I have known him a long time. It was a big help
when I had my divorce. My husband liked him too, so that
helped even more.'

'So you remain friendly with your husband?' Cathy asked
curiously.

'Well, not so much friendly, but shall we say civilized?'
Eleanor hesitated, reluctant to release details about her
personal life, so soon anyway, to someone she scarcely knew.

'That's about it,' she said with an air of finality looking at her watch, aware suddenly of what a strain Roger's visit had been.

'I expect you miss him now.' Cathy seemed reluctant to let the matter drop so easily.

'Not really. He has remarried and his wife has recently had a baby. He has a whole new family and obviously that excludes me.'

Cathy looked at the clock. 'You look awfully tired. Time for your snooze. The meeting with your solicitor has tired you out.'

Before her afternoon nap Eleanor would always listen to her talking book before she drifted off to sleep, often waking with the headphones still on, the narrative long having finished. Sometimes it was just a short nap, sometimes much longer. This afternoon after Roger had left and Cathy had helped her up the stairs to bed she only drifted off for a few seconds, her mind too active to sleep. She removed the headphones and lay for a long time thinking, luxuriating in the warmth of the bed, the feeling of being at home, safe, of being alive.

As usual, Melody slumbered by her side, head on her paws, whiskers twitching occasionally, tail flicking as if in pursuit of some small furry animal through the delicious undergrowth by the stream at the bottom of the garden. In fact it was a long time since Melody, as if aware of her years, like Eleanor, had undertaken such vigorous activity. Eleanor's arm tightened round Melody's soft body and the cat stretched her limbs, blinked at Eleanor and closed her eyes again. It seemed ridiculous to depend so much on a cat for company, Eleanor thought. She had been catapulted into solitude by her decision to retire, the divorce, the sale of the house where she had lived all her married life. The move had, indeed, marked a new beginning. It was sensible and logical. There seemed so much to look forward to. Now no longer self-sufficient she seemed so much more dependent on the world about her, on other people. It was as though she had completely lost direction.

Cathy was a find. She had come into her life just in time. She had arrived unannounced a few days before saying that

Niobe had asked her if she knew of someone to help Eleanor and had volunteered herself. A widow, she lived alone and occupied her time with various tasks paid and unpaid, and with helping to look after her grandchildren. She was of medium height with short mouse-coloured hair, which she tried rather unsuccessfully to lighten, brown knowing eyes and a comforting and ready smile. She had the rather worn air of someone who had lived, had seen it all. She was brisk, practical, yet kind. She seemed to have endless time to help Eleanor who was so slow in her movements, so awkward in getting about, yet there was something detached about Cathy as though you did not entirely absorb her attention, inhabit her being and never would. When she was not with you you felt that she would not spend her time thinking about you – in fact in all probability would not think about you at all, but would turn to the job in hand. Eleanor, in fact to Cathy was the job in hand, and when she was with her she gave her all her attention. One could not ask for more. Cathy's husband had been in his family's building business and had been killed in an accident when he was thirty, leaving her with her only son, Francis.

A feeling of drowsiness once again overcame Eleanor and she turned on her pillow preparing to take another nap when she heard the sound of a car drawing up outside and, seconds after that, noises in the hall. She half sat up on the bed listening and Melody took a swift dive off the duvet and disappeared underneath the bed, a sure sign of a visitor.

Then there was silence and thinking that maybe it was a casual caller, or that Francis had come to have a word with his mother, she lay back again and closed her eyes. Dimly aware, because of her faulty hearing, of steps in the room she opened her eyes and saw the face of her beloved son, James, gazing down at her. For a moment she didn't believe it and wondered if she had somehow taken a turn for the worse and was once again hallucinating.

'Mum . . .' The familiar voice said softly as if fearful of disturbing her.

Slowly Eleanor propped herself on her arms, again blinking. 'Is it really you, James?'

He sat down on the bed beside her and, leaning towards

her, took her hand between his. She saw that his eyes brimmed with tears and her own suddenly welled over and she made no attempt to stop them coursing down her cheeks.

'Oh, James,' she said and opening her arms she drew him towards her and hugged him.

Later, after a celebratory dinner prepared for them by an excited and, one sensed rather approving, Cathy, they sat closely together in the sitting room, hands clasped.

The arrival of James had been a tonic and Eleanor had felt as though some renewal of life had surged through her.

'I can't believe you're here, really here.' She squeezed his hand tightly.

'I feel so guilty, Mum, that I couldn't come sooner, but Bev had a bad time with the baby. I couldn't leave her.'

'Is she all right now?' Eleanor sounded anxious. The seriousness of the situation had been withheld from her. James's expression was not that of a happy new father.

'Physically, she is OK, but it took its toll. She has a touch of the baby blues, but the doctor doesn't think it is especially serious. However, baby is fine. You'd love her.'

'I wish I could see her.' Eleanor had always gone over to the States when the other children were born.

'You will, Mum. If necessary, we'll come over and see you, but not for a while. You can imagine what a ghastly time it was for me worrying about Bev and the fact that you had this terrible accident and I couldn't be with you. The news at first was so bad I really thought I might never see you again and I dreaded the sound of the telephone, thinking it might be bad news from England. For nights I hardly slept. I would have come sooner but with Bev a little depressed it was impossible. It is also the reason I can't stay long.'

'Oh, I hoped . . .' Eleanor's voice trailed off.

'I know, Mum. I have a return ticket for the day after tomorrow.'

'We must make the best of it, then,' Eleanor said stoically, determined not to whinge. 'We mustn't lose a moment of the time we have together.'

It seemed quite wrong to admit, even to oneself, that one preferred one child to another, but James had always been special. He was two years younger than Alex and had been a sickly baby, in and out of hospital with a variety of complaints all of which, thankfully, disappeared as he got older. Now he was a tall, studious looking man of twenty-eight with thick brown hair, a spectacle wearer who might easily have been mistaken for an academic. His career after university had been steady, almost mercurial, and he had gone to America to a senior position in an Anglo-American bank.

They drove slowly along the coast road in James's hired car, Eleanor well wrapped up against the cold.

'It is a lovely spot,' James breathed deeply. 'Sometimes I regret the move to New York, but we're buying a place in the Hamptons, just for the weekend and holidays.' He glanced at his mother. 'Bev likes it there. Her parents have a place nearby.'

'You must be doing well,' Eleanor said and smiled at him contentedly, relishing every moment of his company, relaxed for the first time in many weeks.

'Not bad,' James acknowledged. 'Mum, I hope you'll come over soon and visit.'

'Not for a long time, I'm afraid.' Eleanor nervously raised a hand to her face. 'I have to get my sight sorted out. Frankly, I've hardly the strength of a cat.'

'I'll come over for you.'

'Eventually,' she said, knowing in her heart that it would not be for months, maybe years.

A mist had descended over the sea. It was a damp, chilly day and there were few people at the pub. As Eleanor was ushered through the door into the cosy bar where a fire burned in the grate, the man behind the counter looked at her with incredulity and then, abandoning the task in hand, went round to greet her.

'Eleanor,' he exclaimed. 'George told me you were out of hospital. How are you?'

She proffered cold cheeks to be kissed and clung on tightly to Martin, the proprietor's, hand.

'All the better for seeing my son,' she said. 'This is James. He has come all the way from America to see me, just for two days.'

Martin and James shook hands while Eleanor took a seat next to the window from which she could look out onto the familiar stretch of sea, a view she might never have seen again. Unexpectedly jolted by the thought she looked away, realizing that she was hungry, and carefully studied the menu scribbled on a board over the fireplace. James came over with a beer in one hand and a glass of white wine in the other, which he offered to his mother.

'These are on the house,' he said. 'Martin insists.' Both raised their glasses to Martin who had resumed his place, polishing glasses behind the bar.

'Fish pie is very good,' he said. 'Joan made it this morning.'

'Then we'll have fish pie –' Eleanor looked at James – 'or would you prefer a steak?'

James shook his head. 'Fish pie sounds good.'

'Joan is a marvellous cook.' Eleanor sipped her wine carefully trying hard to conceal the fact that she was almost overwhelmed by emotion. 'It is *really* good to be back.'

James was gazing thoughtfully into his glass. 'Mum, be honest. How long can you stay in these parts? Cut off, no car, few friends as you haven't lived here long.'

'Oh, I'll be OK. I'll make friends. I have Cathy and Niobe and . . .' She thought hard. 'There is a very nice woman called Jean Walker. She is a freelance journalist. Mind you, I haven't seen her since my accident. She appears to be very busy. You know, people do keep away from you. I think they feel you might impose, be a burden. The neighbours keep themselves to themselves. I suppose one can understand it. Here is this stranger in their midst who suddenly might become dependent on them.'

'You wouldn't be tempted to come and live with us?'

'In the States?' Momentarily, Eleanor looked horrified. 'Oh, no! Definitely not. I was never keen on America. Besides, Bev would probably have a fit at the very idea.'

'She wouldn't. She likes you. She even suggested it. She thought you might be lonely and cut off.'

'No,' Eleanor said firmly. 'It is completely out of the question, but thank you for asking.'

Realizing she might have hurt his feelings, she reached up and lightly stroked his face. 'You are a dear, dear boy, and I am terribly grateful to you and Beverley even for thinking about it, but I am going to be absolutely fine.'

After the fish pie, which was indeed excellent, and a long talk with Joan who had emerged from the kitchen, they strolled along the pebbled beach, Eleanor clinging on to James's arm because the stones made walking difficult. The mist that hung over the sea had descended even further, obscuring everything down to a few yards.

'I wish you could see it. It is so beautiful,' Eleanor said making a despairing gesture. 'You will come again James, won't you?'

'Of course.'

'Maybe bring Bev and the children?'

'Some day, Mum, yes.'

But she could tell by his tone of voice that it was as unlikely to happen soon as her going to America.

'It is awful to have my children so far away,' she burst out. 'I don't want to sound dependent but my one hope might be that Alex will come back.'

'Well, she's got to come back some day, hasn't she? I mean, they are only on an assignment. India is not permanent.'

'And I'm wondering how permanent Hugo is. They have a lot of rows. Frequent clashes.'

'Artistic,' James said briefly.

'I think it's more than that. Very different people.'

Finally back in London, but not yet having seen her mother, Alex was in her flat looking through the stills of the Indian project. She experienced, not for the first time, a feeling of desperation. Masses of pictures littered the floor, difficult to know which to choose for submission to the weekly colour supplement which had commissioned the project. These trips abroad were very costly and didn't always cover expenses, so they had to distribute material as widely as they could, think of an original angle, careful to retain the copyright. Hugo was out at the moment trying to flog the extensive footage he'd taken for a documentary, but this was proving hard to sell. It was a very competitive business and even though they were both experienced and had good track records times could be hard.

She crouched on the floor, chin in her hands pouring over the photos until she was disturbed by the sound of the key in the door and Hugo came in. She could tell by the expression on his face, his silence, that the news wasn't good.

'No luck?' She rose to pour him a drink but, ignoring her question, he had already beaten her to the sideboard. He poured a substantial measure of whisky into a glass and drank it unadulterated, straight down, not offering her one. Then, still standing, he refilled his glass.

'I've had a bad day, too,' she said straightening up. 'We have so many shots I just don't know which one to choose and haven't even begun the text.' She also poured whisky into a glass, added soda and took it to the sofa on which Hugo had sprawled.

Hugo Sandeman was the stereotype of the professional cameraman, a legend in his craft. He had travelled all over the world, sometimes in dangerous places, including the first Gulf war. He was tall and lean, not conventionally good looking, with a receding hairline and a strong forceful jaw, hard, determined-looking blue eyes. He had charisma, which made him very attractive to women. He was forty and he and Alex had been together for several years during which they had spent very little time in her somewhat impersonal flat in Camden Town. The wandering lifestyle suited Alex. She liked anonymous foreign hotels, seedy bars where journalists congregated and difficult assignments. She and Hugo had met on an assignment in the States and he had jettisoned his current girlfriend for her. Somewhere he had a divorced wife and two children whom he scarcely ever saw and to whom he never referred, as if they didn't exist.

Eleanor had met him only once, he had been so often away, and she was very circumspect in her remarks about him. Alex knew she didn't really like him and Hugo, indifferent to her, or anyone's, opinion of him, had not set out to charm. Alex found him irresistibly sexy and was obsessed by him despite, or perhaps because of, her suspicion that he was no good for her and would never want to settle down. Despite her own journalistic background and free lifestyle, Eleanor was quite conventional, at least when

it came to the welfare of her children. Alex was very interested and not a little shocked to find that her mother had
had a lover.

'Tell me what happened,' Alex cajoled putting a hand
lightly on Hugo's knee.

'Justin says there is too much of this sort of thing about;
too much poverty. We see it all the time and the public is
sick of it.'

'Too much poverty!' Alex exploded. 'They should see it
as we do.'

'Oh, I know what he means. I don't like it, but I do know
what he means.' Hugo got up and went over again to the
drinks trolley.

'Hugo, don't hit the bottle every time something goes
wrong . . .' Alex began irritably and regretted it as soon as
the words were out of her mouth.

'Please don't tell me what to do, Alex,' Hugo said coldly.
'I'm quite able to look after myself and I can hold my drink.'

'For now,' Alex retorted, 'but you are drinking more. I've
noticed it a lot lately.'

'It is absolutely nothing to do with you.'

'But it is,' she insisted.

Hugo finished the fresh drink, banged the glass down on
the table and went into the bedroom. A short time later he
emerged in jeans, T-shirt and a leather jacket and, gathering
his keys off the hall table, opened the front door, banging it
hard after him.

Hugo did not return that night or the following day or
night, and early in the morning the next day Alex threw some
things into an overnight bag, hired a car and drove down to
her mother. It was a bright beautiful December day with a
slight frost still dusting the fields as she drove through
Wiltshire and Hampshire and into Dorset, glad to be out of
the city, away from the stress and pain of the relationship
with Hugo.

When she arrived at her mother's house there was a car
at the gate and a man was helping her mother, who still used
two sticks, alight with some difficulty. As she looked at her
daughter Eleanor's expression changed from initial delight
to one of concern.

'Darling,' she said as Alex stooped to kiss her, 'is everything all right?'

'Everything is fine.' Alex looked at the man who was taking some carrier bags from the back of the car.

'Darling, this is Francis, Niobe's husband. Francis, my daughter, Alex.'

'Hi,' Alex said as Francis looked helplessly at her indicating his full hands. 'Sorry, I can't shake hands.' His quiet, gruff voice had a strong Dorset accent.

'I saw you briefly from the road once. You won't remember,' Alex said and Francis, nodding, turned his back on her and walked up the path towards the door.

'Man of few words,' Eleanor said *sotto voce* as Alex took her arm, 'but very nice. Niobe has a bad cold so, not wanting me to catch it, he took me to the doctor for my check-up and then to do a bit of shopping.

'What did the doctor say?'

'What she always says. "It will take time."' Eleanor sighed. 'But what brings you here? You usually ring.'

'Impulse. Just wanted to see you, Mum, how you were getting on.'

Eleanor looked at her suspiciously.

'Is that all?'

'Why not?'

'You look strained.'

'Oh, Mum, it's quite a long drive down,' Alex said with increasing irritation, as Francis emerged from the front door. 'You worry too much about everything.'

'Thank you so much, Francis,' Eleanor said gratefully. 'I can't tell you how I appreciate all you and Niobe do for me, to say nothing of your wonderful mother.'

'That's perfectly all right, Mrs Ashton,' Francis said, 'any time.'

He nodded at her, glanced briefly at Alex and got into his car.

'Where is Cathy?'

'She had something else on. She doesn't work for me full time, you know, just when I need her. Normally she would drive me, but not today.'

They made their way into the sitting room and Eleanor,

casting her sticks aside, dropped gratefully onto the sofa and stretched her legs. 'I am extremely lucky in the people who work for me.'

'Anyone else help you out? That Jean you talked about?'

'Well, I have not actually seen her. Frankly, I have stopped telephoning. If she doesn't want to come I can't make her, or anyone else for that matter. Marge vaguely keeps in touch. Candy told her she was coming to see me, but as yet no sign.' Eleanor looked up at her daughter who was warming her backside on one of the radiators. 'Let's face it, I don't know many people here and I can't expect friends to come from London. They all have busy lives. Besides, I'm OK. I have my talking books and plenty to think about and I have Melody, the most constant companion of all.'

'It's not much of a life, Mum, compared to what you were used to.'

'But I was beginning again, wasn't I? Starting a new life in the country. I had scarcely got things organized before this happened. I'm lucky to be alive and I have to remind myself of that constantly.' Eleanor got slowly to her feet and grabbed one of her sticks to get her balance. 'Now look, Cathy will have left something in the kitchen so why don't we have lunch? How long can you stay? Have you brought a bag? Left it in the car?'

Alex shook her head, overwhelmed by a feeling of bleakness that verged on despair, unable now to hide her crestfallen expression from her mother.

'Alex, there *is* something wrong, isn't there?' Anxiously Eleanor seized her arm and looked into her eyes, which were now brimming with tears.

'It's Hugo, isn't it, darling?' Eleanor led Alex to the sofa and sat down beside her as she began scrubbing her eyes to try and rid them of this unwanted display of feminine weakness.

It was always Hugo. Eleanor didn't know him well, had scarcely met him, but she knew he wasn't good for Alex. Like any mother she wanted happiness for her daughter and Hugo, with his failed marriage and propensity for deserting women – as he had done to go off with Alex – had seemed to her a disaster from the very beginning.

'We had a row. Work is difficult. It wasn't much of a row but he walked out and hasn't come back.'

'Then where is he?'

'I haven't a clue.'

'Has he done this before?'

'Not disappeared for two nights. He will walk out and come back. Took nothing with him.'

'Have you tried to contact him?'

'I've left a message, several, on his mobile but he doesn't respond. I mean, I'm not *worried* about him or anything. He's perfectly able to look after himself. It's just . . .' Alex rubbed her eyes again. 'It's just such a horrid thing to do, especially when we've both been under a lot of strain.'

'To which I have contributed. You left India to come to me.'

'I had to, you're my mother. You couldn't help it, Mum, be reasonable. I don't blame you at all; I blame him and my ridiculous inability to rid myself of him.'

'That's love,' Eleanor said sadly gently brushing Alex's hair away from her eyes.

'It's not love, it's stupid,' Alex said straightening up, angry with herself for making such an exhibition. Here she was, a seasoned traveller, an intrepid investigator, making an idiot of herself in front of her mother who really had got something to complain about yet hardly ever did, even when her husband left her for a younger woman – always a humiliation as though you had nothing more to offer – or when she had this dreadful accident that nearly killed her.

'Sorry, Mum,' she said, blowing her nose. 'Let's have lunch.'

Later that afternoon, Eleanor stood by the window in her bedroom watching Alex walk round the garden. It was a crisp, clear day, unseasonably warm and one could almost imagine spring was in the air. Occasionally she stopped either to gaze out at the view or to study some plant or shrub that interested her. Although Eleanor was upset by Alex's distress she felt closer to her daughter than she had been at almost any time in the past. Alex had seldom confided in her mother, particularly about her affairs. Eleanor realized that at the age of thirty she knew really very little about Alex's past, or what went on either in her heart or mind.

Alex had told her over lunch that she was afraid that Hugo was, if not an alcoholic, then close to becoming one. She had noticed it a lot in India where it was difficult to get drink, but somehow Hugo had always managed, however remote their location. She was afraid now that he had gone off on some bender, and although he was supposed to be able to look after himself she was afraid that he would do himself harm.

'I imagine him lying in a gutter somewhere,' Alex had said with a shudder, 'and I am absolutely powerless to do anything about it.'

Eleanor had pointed out as gently as she could that it was most unlikely that Hugo would find himself in such a situation. After all, he had plenty of friends and it was more likely that he had holed up with one of these. She didn't like to speculate whether it could be a man or a woman. At that point Alex had got up to clear the dishes and helped her mother up the stairs for her afternoon nap, but Eleanor was too restless to sleep. It seemed very ironic that it had taken a major accident to help her get closer to her daughter, but in her heart she was glad it had.

A car drew up at the gate and Francis got out, once again laden with carrier bags. Alex went over to open the gate and took the bags from him and for some time they stood there chatting, their heads bent close together emphasizing the differences in their colouring. They were similar in height but Francis was dark, almost swarthy with black hair and a tanned weather-beaten face. Alex, with her father's colouring, was a natural blonde with attractive highlights and very fair skin, deep blue eyes that sometimes, in certain lights, appeared almost violet. She was really an exceedingly attractive woman, slim but voluptuous at the same time, and in her mother's opinion deserved a good man who would make her happy. She and Francis looked well together. Not that it mattered, Eleanor told herself sternly, as they were both very attached to other people.

At that moment, Francis looked up and seeing her at the window waved. Alex also turned and held the carrier bags up for her to see.

'Lots of fresh goodies,' she called out as Eleanor opened the window and shouted her thanks to Francis who, with another word to Alex, got back into the car and drove off. When Eleanor got downstairs Alex had put the contents of the carriers on the kitchen table: Brussel sprouts, cabbage, potatoes and tomatoes.

'Where does he get all these?' she asked.

'From a market garden nearby. He does it once a week. I pay, of course.'

'Lovely,' Alex said sniffing the cabbage. 'He really is a very nice bloke. He quite opened up.'

'Oh, in what way?'

'Nothing earth shattering,' Alex said with a smile, 'about the weather mostly. He asked me where I lived and I told him we'd just come back from India. He seemed amazed and said he had never been further than Birmingham. Isn't that strange?'

'I know,' Eleanor laughed. 'Niobe told me he hates going away, even to see her parents who live in Birmingham.'

'Then how did they meet? She told me she came from London.'

'How do you know that?' Eleanor began putting the vegetables away in the larder.

'Well, when you were in hospital I went down to the sea one day and on the way back saw Niobe. She invited me in and we had a chat. She told me she was an artist and was very offended that I thought she was local.'

'Really?' Eleanor grimaced. 'Well, she is certainly very different from Francis. An attraction of opposites, I guess. She told me she was doing a course locally and met Francis who was working nearby. She always strikes me as not a very happy woman, but I might be wrong. I hope I am.' She looked across at Alex who had her back to her and was once more gazing out of the window.

'Do you know, Mum, I think I'd be happy in the country. I really am very tired of wandering all over the world, living out of a suitcase and being messed about by Hugo.' She turned towards her mother who had finished putting the vegetables away and had sat down heavily at the table.

'Every blinking little effort makes me so tired,' she said

crossly and then, looking at her daughter, 'well, why don't
you try it? You know I'd love to have you, for a while anyway.
You can look around, rent something if you want to be independent as I expect you do, knowing you.'

'No, it's out of the question –' Alex shook her head – 'for
now. Thanks, Mum, but I have a lot of things to sort out
first, besides, I don't think I'm *quite* ready to make the break
from Hugo.'

'The problem with your mother's eyes,' Mr Ferguson the
consultant eye surgeon said to Alex patiently, as if explaining
an elementary matter to a somewhat dim child, 'is that the
nerves affecting the movement of the eyes were damaged in
the accident, leaving her with double vision. One eye is more
affected than the other. It is possible to correct this by an
operation on one of the muscles controlling eye movement.
There are three to each eye,' he continued in the same patient
tone of voice. 'I want to try and centralize her vision so that
she is not looking sideways all the time which, of course,
has a bad effect on her neck.'

While all this was taking place Eleanor remained silent,
feeling as though she was either invisible or considered incapable of understanding something that seriously affected
her own health.

Resentful though she might feel, for the moment anyway,
she did admire his competence and expertise and was grateful
to him for the trouble he was taking to explain it all to Alex.

Her sight problems were horrible. To have any direct vision
at all she had one of her eyes occluded by a white patch.
Coupled with the use of sticks, she knew this gave her the
appearance of an invalid. This she hated because inside she
was still the active, vigorous woman she had been before
the accident, driving back and forth to London in a day if
necessary. She found her infirmities very hard to take,
however brave a face one put on it.

She was glad Alex had come with her, not only for the
companionship, but also because she felt it somehow involved
her in her predicament.

'So, when will the operation be?' she heard Alex asking,
again as if she were not present.

'When it suits your mother, as everything is being taken care of by the other side's insurers.'

'Will it be painful?' Eleanor found her voice at last.

'You might have a bit of discomfort afterwards, some redness, but you could leave hospital the same day if you wished, or an overnight stay.'

'And will it be permanent?'

Mr Ferguson glanced at his watch and as he got to his feet looked patiently down at her. 'That, I can't say.'

'I feel he knows what he is doing,' Alex said later as they were driving back from the appointment.

'He is supposed to be one of the best for this condition,' Eleanor said doubtfully.

'How do you feel about it, Mum?'

'I just want to be better,' Eleanor said. 'I want to be able to see properly again. He says I will always have a certain degree of double vision because he is moving the muscle. I will have to put up with that.'

'You are great, Mum.' Alex leaned towards her. 'I can't tell you how much I admire you. You never moan, never whinge.'

'I don't see the point,' Eleanor said practically, 'if I did, I would.'

Alex drove on in silence concentrating on the road. This was just the sort of remark her mother would make. In fact, people thought she was so capable she would deal with anything. She knew her father had thought that, which was maybe why he went for a woman more for her vulnerability than her youth. It had been painful to see the effect of the accident on her mother. The eye defect was very obvious, and she knew how much a woman as smart and as proud as her mother would hate it. As yet she had hardly ventured out and never unaccompanied, and in a way it made Alex feel important. Maybe for too long she had been in Eleanor's shadow.

Eleanor, a successful, powerful woman was someone you had to stand up to. Now, they were more equal.

'What are you doing about Christmas?' Eleanor asked.

'Hadn't thought about it.'

'It is less than three weeks away. Had you and Hugo any plans?'

Alex snorted. 'Plans! Hardly!'

'I don't want you to think you have to come, but if you do you are very welcome, you know that, with or without Hugo.'

'I do.' Alex touched her mother's hand as they turned into the road and stopped outside the house. Then, spontaneously she leaned across and kissed her cheek, an untypical gesture that momentarily brought tears to Eleanor's eyes which she hastily brushed away before Alex could see them.

Again that afternoon Eleanor found it hard to sleep, rest yes, but not sleep, thinking about her visit to Mr Ferguson, the forthcoming eye operation but, above all, the subtle, yet gratifying way in which Alex had changed towards her: softer, gentler, more concerned. It seemed to her that for the first time in many years mother and daughter had begun to understand each other, and it was because she needed Alex rather than that Alex needed her. Maybe all her life she had been too strong, too self-contained, not revealing enough of her needs to other people.

She was aware of a phone ringing downstairs but knew that it was Alex's mobile, and gradually she drifted off to sleep until Alex shook her gently and told her that supper was ready.

'Good heavens! Is it that late? I didn't think I would sleep, but I must have.'

She threw back the duvet and Alex helped her up.

'I'll be OK, down in a minute,' Eleanor said and went into the bathroom to tidy herself and change into a housecoat.

When she got downstairs the table was laid and an enticing smell wafted from the kitchen. She seated herself as Alex emerged carrying two plates, one of which she put in front of her mother.

'I didn't know you were such a good cook.'

'You have to thank Hugo for that. He can't cook at all. By the way –' she uncorked a bottle of wine and poured some into her mother's glass – 'Hugo rang.'

'Oh, I guessed who it was. I heard your mobile just before I dropped off.'

'Full of apologies.'

'Of course.' Eleanor couldn't keep the sarcasm from her voice.

'Don't be like that, Mum. He said he had gone to see his children; two girls, you know. They miss their dad.'

'Quite understandable,' Eleanor said in measured tones.

Alex had prepared delicious Dover sole and sauté potatoes, but Eleanor suddenly discovered she had no appetite. She put the glass of wine to her lips and gazed over the rim at Alex whose face had gone slightly pink. 'He could have told you, of course.'

'Well,' Alex said defensively, 'you know how it is. We both were to blame. I can't pretend I'm easy. Anyway –' she looked brightly over at her mother – 'he said he'd love to come down for Christmas, so that's nice, isn't it? You don't mind us both, do you, Mum?'

'What about his girls?'

'I didn't ask him. I guess they will be spending it with their mother, they usually do. I think she goes abroad, Bermuda or somewhere like that. She likes the sun.'

Five

Eleanor was not religious in the sense that she had no strong belief in a personal deity who directly intervened in the life of human beings, but she had never eschewed religious experience altogether, or denied that there might be a spiritual dimension to life that had never affected her. Even when she was seriously ill after her accident she had never resorted to prayer. When she was close to death she had never had any sensation of an afterlife. Consequently, on Christmas Eve she sat in the candlelit parish church listening to the prayers, occasionally taking part in the hymn singing, aware somehow that she was there to give thanks, that she was after all alive and glad to be alive. Despite still suffering from the effects of her injuries, she was nevertheless able to get about, her faculties were as far as she knew intact and her pleasure in life and what it had to offer was, if anything, enhanced.

On one side of her was her daughter, on the other, Hugo who had not taken part in the service at all but remained either standing, kneeling, but always silent, absorbed in one did not quite know what.

She was tired. It had been a long day, Alex and Hugo not arriving until nightfall. Cathy had made a casserole for supper and after that there had been some discussion about whether to go to the midnight service or not. Alex had been the only one who had really wanted to go. Eleanor thought she should go and Hugo professed his indifference but offered to accompany them if it pleased them.

'We aren't in any danger,' Eleanor had said more sharply than she intended. 'The church is only up the road. We are quite capable of getting there and back on our own.'

'Oh, Mum,' Alex said impatiently, 'don't be so churlish.'

'I am not being churlish,' Eleanor had insisted, colouring, rather regretting her asperity; but there was something that always irritated her about Hugo, as though he did what he did because he felt he should not because he wanted to. 'If Hugo doesn't want to come there is no need for him to make an effort for our sakes.'

'Seriously, I'd like to come,' Hugo said with his detached smile. 'It will be a new experience for me.'

'Never been to church before?' Alex looked at him teasingly but he ignored her.

The church had been packed and after the service was over it took some time to get to the porch where the vicar stood shaking hands.

'So nice to see you are able to get about, Mrs Ashton.'

'Thank you.' The vicar had visited her quite soon after she had got home. 'This is my daughter, Alex. Hugo Sandeman.'

They shook hands and moved down the path towards the gate where a small group engaged in conversation broke away to let them pass.

'Why, *Niobe*,' Eleanor exclaimed with pleasure as she stepped forward. 'I didn't see you in church.'

'We were late,' Niobe said with a shrug, 'as usual. Had to stand at the back. Beautiful wasn't it?'

'Lovely,' Eleanor agreed. 'You know Alex, don't you? Her friend, Hugo.'

As Niobe was shaking hands Francis appeared behind her and was also introduced.

'Mum's babysitting,' Niobe said, 'we must hurry back.'

'Come and have a drink tomorrow?' Eleanor said abruptly. 'Before lunch? We don't eat until evening.'

'Oh . . .' Niobe looked at Francis. 'Well, we usually have lunch.'

'How about later on? Bring the children.'

'Well . . .' Niobe still looked doubtful. 'That would be nice. Thanks, Eleanor.' Niobe tucked her arm through Francis's and waved as they separated at the gate.

'I don't think they really wanted to come,' Alex said as they walked down the hill.

'Oh, I think so. They could have said, no.'

'You put them on the spot, Mum.'

'Why must you always be so critical, Alex?'

'I'm not being critical; I'm just saying what I think. Don't you agree, Hugo?'

'I'm not getting into this,' Hugo said opening the gate to the house and standing back to let the women through. 'You ladies can sort it out between you. I'm ready for bed.'

To bed, but not to sleep. Hugo and Alex lay for some time in silence after putting out the light. It was a strange uneasy silence, not warm and intimate, not conducive to lovemaking.

Hugo said quietly, 'Has your mother always been cantankerous and bad tempered?'

Alex sat up in bed and gazed indignantly at his recumbent figure. 'I do object to that. She is not cantankerous and bad tempered. She has had a very bad accident.'

'Well, she has always been a bit like that with me. I remember when I first met her I thought she was a very tough cookie.'

That had been about two years ago. Alex could recall it quite well and how nervous she was about introducing the two rather strong personalities to each other.

'Mum was going through a difficult time. The divorce, selling the home where she'd lived all her life, making plans for a fresh start.'

'You're always making excuses for her. It was obvious from the start she didn't like me. "Not suitable for her daughter", she thought, "older and divorced, a loose canon". I could see it in her face.'

'Well, you didn't try very hard to get on with her. I didn't notice you making much of an effort.'

'Why should I?'

'Because she was my *mother*,' Alex said with emphasis. 'Look, I don't know why you came down, and why bring this all up now, for God's sake?' Alex withdrew even further to the far side of the bed.

As if in self defence, Hugo pulled what he could of the duvet up to his chin in a gesture of self-protection. 'I wanted to please you. I did behave rather badly going off, and I wanted to make up for it. I even went to church tonight, didn't I? What more proof could you want of my devotion?'

Tentatively he reached across for Alex, but she remained unresponsive.

'Mum didn't believe it was to see your daughters,' she said peevishly knowing that he was trying to be nice mainly because he wanted sex.

'Oh, she *would* say that, wouldn't she?' Hugo exploded. 'Anything to cause trouble.'

'I didn't really believe it either, if you want to know.'

'What did you think? That I was holed up with another woman?' Hugo didn't hide the sarcasm from his voice.

'Perhaps, or even a bloke, you know, a friend. Drinking, as you have been accustomed to of late, assuaging your misery, or trying to. I'm not insinuating anything else, like an affair.'

'Oh, well that *is* something,' Hugo said teasingly changing his tone of voice. 'Look –' he reached for her again pulling her roughly towards him – 'don't let's mess about.'

Lying still in her bed, one hand resting on Melody's back, unable to sleep, worried by the tension introduced to the house ever since the appearance of Hugo and Alex, regretting her own lack of warmth towards her daughter's boyfriend, Eleanor was suddenly startled by the noise from the bedroom opposite. It was a sort of stifled scream that made her sit up sharply in bed. For a moment she wondered if Hugo could possibly be hurting, even attacking Alex. Easing herself groggily out of bed she grabbed her stick and tottering across to her door leant her ear against it.

For a while there was silence and she opened the door a crack and looked out into the dark hall.

Then there were murmurs, endearments, the sound of the bed beginning a rhythmic creaking noise and, smiling to herself, reassured, she gently pulled the door to and hobbled back to bed drawing Melody to her as she settled down. After all this time she had forgotten the way most lovers' quarrels ended.

'Love is a funny business,' she observed to the purring cat. 'Somehow I'm not sorry all that sort of thing is behind me.'

Niobe stood awkwardly at the door, Francis behind her as though he wanted to hide.

'Come in, come in,' Eleanor said backing away from the open door, which admitted an icy blast. 'Where are the children?'

'Well, Sam has a bit of a cold. We didn't want you to catch it so Mum is staying with them. We can't be very long.'

Eleanor led the couple into the sitting room where Alex and Hugo stood waiting to greet them, drinks already in their hands. On the table was an ice bucket with an open bottle of champagne and tall glasses beside it.

'Cathy and the children can't come,' Eleanor said as she introduced them, 'isn't that a pity?'

'Sam has a cold,' Niobe explained. 'We don't want to give it to your mum.'

'How thoughtful of you.' Alex smiled across at Francis who was still sheltering behind Niobe. He looked as though he had been well scrubbed and had somehow been poured into an ill fitting suit which had the shiny look of one that was perhaps cheap and also a little worn. Niobe on the other hand looked quite ravishing, dressed in the modern style in a knee-length black dress over faded blue jeans, with a pretty gold silk scarf slung round her shoulders She wore little make-up except green eye shadow which enhanced her limpid brown eyes, and blusher. Her full, sensuous lips were naturally red with a mere touch of lipstick.

Gazing at their guests, who had obviously taken a lot of trouble over their appearance, Alex had the feeling that the invitation had not been a good idea. She and Hugo were very informally dressed in jeans and shirts, though she had care-lessly strung a row of ethnic beads round her neck which dangled between her breasts. At ease with themselves they presented a contrast to the two guests.

'Hugo, can you dispense the champers?' she said with forced jollity holding up her own glass. 'I'm afraid we've started. We thought something to celebrate was Mum's recovery.'

'And thanks a lot to you and your family,' Eleanor said warmly addressing Niobe. 'You have all been marvellous. I don't know what I'd have done without you.'

'It's terribly bad luck that Mum had the accident so soon after moving here,' Alex said taking a glass from Hugo and handing it to Francis. 'She hadn't the time to make new friends. Francis, you looked harassed. Fill yourself up with champagne.'

Francis gurgled and reddened putting the glass hastily to his lips and gulping down the contents. Alex smiled encouragingly at him, and crossing to the sofa patted it inviting him to sit beside her which he did rather clumsily looking awkwardly across at Niobe, as if reluctant to be too far away from his anchor.

'I must go and baste the turkey,' Eleanor said. 'Excuse me a moment.'

'Mum, I'll do it.' Alex made to get up but her mother gestured at her.

'No, you stay and entertain the guests. I have a few other things to do; besides I want you to get to know one another better.'

Hugo handed Niobe her glass and leaned against the wall by the drinks table.

'That leaves us,' he said. 'I'm afraid you won't find me very entertaining.'

Niobe leaned beside him. 'On the contrary, I think you seem *very* entertaining. Eleanor says you are a well-known journalist.'

'Cameraman, actually.' Hugo pointed to Alex now deep in conversation with Francis who appeared to have opened up to her and was chatting quite animatedly back. 'Well, photo journalist. Alex is the real journalist.'

'I envy you what you do,' Niobe said and took a deep gulp of her drink. 'I would simply love to travel. I feel absolutely stuck and cut-off here.'

'Really?' Hugo looked surprised and reaching for the bottle refilled her glass. 'You do surprise me. Are you not a local girl, then?'

'Not at all. I was born in Birmingham, but studied in London at St Martins for three years. I came down here to do ceramics and that's how I met Francis.' She glanced across at him, almost resentfully. 'I never in the least bit intended to spend the rest of my life here.' She paused for a moment. 'He seems to be getting on very well with Alex, she's drawing him out. He doesn't say much, usually.'

'That's where her journalistic skills come in. She's used to interviewing difficult people. But to get back to you, don't you have a farm, children? All that must keep you very busy.'

'Oh, it does,' Niobe said, finishing her drink whereupon Hugo refilled her glass again. She looked at it rather doubtfully as though she felt she should have refused. 'I am busy, but not fulfilled, if you know what that means.' Observing the expression on Hugo's face she added with a note of bitterness, 'I don't for the moment suppose you do. You must lead a very fulfilled life with the work you do.'

'Well, most of it is very mundane. It might sound glamorous, but it isn't. Some of it is quite dangerous.'

'Have you been in any wars?'

'Oh, yes, Lebanon, the first Gulf war; I was nearly captured by the Iraqis. In fact, I might go again if there is yet another war there and it looks as though there will be.'

Before she could reply, Hugo looked up to see Alex gazing quizzically at him. 'You two seem very absorbed,' she said.

'Oh, we are,' Hugo replied. 'Did you know Niobe was an artist?'

'Yes, I did.' She looked behind her. 'I'm afraid Francis thinks it's time to go. I'm trying to persuade him to stay a bit longer.'

'But you've only just come.'

'That's what I said. Francis,' she called, 'Hugo says you've only just come.'

Francis had stood up; hands in his pockets and the stubborn expression on his face spoke volumes.

'What, not going already?' Eleanor exclaimed entering the room clasping a new bottle of champagne. 'I haven't even had a drink with you yet.'

Niobe carefully put down her untouched glass on the table. 'Francis is quite right. We told Mum we wouldn't be long. It was just to say, hello.' She smiled at Eleanor. 'We'll see you soon again anyway.'

'I'll see you out,' Alex said turning to her mother. 'Mum, you stay here and have a drink.'

'Oh, well . . .' Eleanor slumped into a chair, faint beads of perspiration on her brow. 'I am sorry I was away so long. I didn't realize you'd be going so soon.' She held up her hand to Niobe who bent and kissed her cheek. 'Happy Christmas,' she said.

As Alex came back into the room, Hugo opened the new bottle of champagne.

'What a strange couple,' he murmured handing Eleanor a glass, shaking his head, 'very odd.'

'They're not really odd,' Eleanor said defensively. 'Francis is a bit shy, awkward in company. He is a very nice person, very helpful to me.' She struggled out of her chair. 'I'll just go and look at the turkey.'

By the time they sat down to Christmas dinner it was nearly nine o'clock and Eleanor was in fact very tired. Despite Alex's promises she had had to do most of the preparations for the dinner herself. Her faulty eyesight slowed her down and putting things in the oven and taking them out was tricky. She frequently burned herself. It had been a mistake to invite people to drinks beforehand. She kept on forgetting that she was not the woman she used to be, that she was slow and awkward. But in fact she'd had little choice, neither Alex nor Hugo had appeared before midday when they decided they wanted to have a walk to the beach and a snack at the pub to save her getting lunch, which Eleanor thought rather rich. Not a word was said about helping her, but then she had always been so capable and Alex could not rid herself of the feeling that somehow she still was.

Whether she liked it or not, most of the preparations had been left to her, so not only did she prepare most of the food, but also she had made an effort with the table: a splendid table decoration in the middle, red candlesticks burning in silver holders, the best china, Meissen – it had been a wedding present – and crystal glasses, a cracker by each plate. In the dim light everything gleamed and Alex exclaimed as they went into the dining room, 'Mum, it all looks lovely. You've gone to so much trouble.'

A melange of smoked fish was already prettily arranged on plates and the dumb waiter stood by the side with the turkey on top.

'You've worked awfully hard, Mum,' Alex said sitting down and unfolding her napkin. 'You should have called me. I feel quite awful.'

'I wanted you to enjoy the party.' Eleanor looked up. 'Hugo, dear, would you pour the wine?'

As Hugo started to remove the cork, Eleanor continued as she cut into her smoked salmon, 'Anyway, I think now it was a bit of a mistake to ask them.'

'Why?' Alex put down her knife and fork.

'Well, it was a silly time for them, with young children. I should have thought it out more, maybe arranged a proper party, inviting neighbours, the vicar, maybe tomorrow or the day after. I thought tonight was a bit awkward, a little strained, and most of the time I wasn't even there. It must have seemed rude of me. Obviously they both had dressed up, made a bit of an effort and yet they stayed only about half an hour.'

'That's because Hugo was flirting with Niobe,' Alex said. 'I think Francis got fed up with it.'

'I *beg* your pardon?' Hugo, looking furious, stopped in the act of pouring wine.

'You know you were. It was quite obvious and a bit silly if you ask me.' She stuck out a hand, half covering the top of her glass. 'Only an inch for me, I already feel a bit drunk. I've had lashes of champagne.'

'So I noticed.' Hugo poured about an inch in her glass and then rather obviously filled his to the brim.

'And how much did *you* have?' Alex retorted. 'Did you notice that?'

'Oh, shut up!' Hugo said, sitting down. 'This is all silly. I was not flirting with Niobe. She doesn't interest me at all. If anything, I thought you were making eyes at that clodhopper Francis, trying to overwhelm him with your cosmopolitan charm.'

'What an absolutely ridiculous thing to say.' Alex slammed down her knife and fork and pushed back her chair. 'And nasty, too. Francis may be quiet, may be a countryman, but he is not a clodhopper. In fact, if you ask me he has got a lot more charm and intelligence than you. I've had quite enough.'

Eleanor watched helplessly as her daughter got up, threw down her napkin and flounced out of the room.

'I said she'd had too much to drink,' Hugo said triumphantly. 'Eleanor, would you like me to carve the turkey?'

*   *   *

It was nearly midnight as Eleanor and Hugo sat on either side of the fire gazing at the embers. Dinner had been finished and everything cleared away without the reappearance of Alex, but Hugo and Eleanor had gone through the charade of eating and pretending to enjoy themselves. It was, after all, Christmas. Now Eleanor felt past tiredness and could hardly contemplate the thought of climbing the stairs to bed. Hugo had his hands wrapped round a rather full glass of brandy and as he had finished the champagne and almost a bottle of Burgundy, Eleanor wondered if Alex's fears about his drinking mightn't after all have some foundation.

Yet he didn't in any sense appear drunk. He had helped clear away, load the dishwasher, his speech remained completely clear and his mind apparently lucid. He was, after all, a seasoned journalist and they were used to this kind of thing.

'I do love her, you know,' Hugo said suddenly speaking into the fire, 'but I don't really think we have anything in common.'

'I would have thought you had a lot in common,' Eleanor found herself saying. 'I mean, you are both journalists, you like that kind of life.'

'Mmm.' Hugo nodded as if contemplating the matter carefully, which was when he did appear a bit under the influence, the way drunks seem to weigh every word. Then he looked lugubriously over at Eleanor. 'I'm talking about values.'

'Values!' Eleanor exclaimed in surprise.

'You see, I don't have any. Now you have values and she has got them from you.'

'I think we all have values,' Eleanor said, then, after a moment's pause, 'of some sort.'

'Yes, but conventional values, you know what I mean. You see I don't want to get married again or have any more children. I have been a very bad husband and father. Disastrous. It doesn't suit my lifestyle and I think that's what's bugging Alex. She has values and they are conventional, like yours, if you don't mind my saying?'

'In what sense?'

'Marriage and a family, that sort of thing.'

'Yes, but you once had a marriage and a family.'

'But that is all over. Alex has not been given the chance, if that's what she wants.'

'Have you asked her?'

'No.'

'Then why don't you?'

'I don't want to lose her, I suppose. It will bring things to a head. If I tell her all this then I think she will just go away.' He looked at Eleanor. 'Well, won't she?'

'I don't really know. I don't know what she wants.'

'You've never discussed it with her?'

'No, not really. Alex keeps her inmost thoughts to herself.'

'Oh, she does from you, too?'

'We are not terribly close as mother and daughter, though I think the accident has made us closer. I adore her, of course, and I think this has made her realize that maybe she values me more than she thought.'

'Oh, I'm sure she does. She idolizes you.'

'Isn't that a bit strong?'

'Not really. You should have seen how upset she was when she heard you'd been badly hurt in a car accident. She couldn't wait to get on the plane. Now I don't think she wants to leave you for long and, frankly, I haven't told her this but in a way I'd rather she didn't. You see, I'm thinking of going to Iraq.'

'Oh,' Eleanor exclaimed in alarm, 'isn't that terribly dangerous?'

'It's very dangerous, but I know I can take care of myself and that is where the opportunities are and frankly the money – the Americans might be interested. Or if I can manage to be embedded with the British troops in Basra I'd go like a shot.'

'When did you decide this?' Eleanor asked quietly, realizing suddenly that she was wideawake.

'I haven't decided anything. Oh, it's been in my mind for quite some time, but don't worry I don't want Alex to go with me or even contemplate it. Yes, it is dangerous but I know the Middle East. I covered the first Gulf War. I thought they should have gone on to Baghdad and finished it off. We would not have had all this trouble if they had done that.

The Allies have completely mishandled the situation. They made no plans for what to do after the fighting was finished. Now we have all this sectarian conflict and we could be there for years.' He looked at her anxiously. 'Please, Eleanor, not a word to Alex. Anyway –' Hugo got to his feet and tottered slightly – 'I think I *have* had too much to drink.' And suddenly he bent down and kissed her on the cheek, then looked into her startled face. 'You know, you're not so bad after all.'

'Why, thank you,' Eleanor said and felt herself blush, grateful for the half light so that Hugo couldn't see it.

Now that Christmas was over and Hugo and Alex had left, Eleanor felt bleakness descend on her. It had not been an altogether successful visit, but nor had it been a complete disaster. She had even grown quite fond of Hugo and instead of being annoyed had been strangely touched when he told her she wasn't as bad as he'd thought. With Hugo, what you saw was what you got. He was nothing if not direct and in a world full of insincere people, or people who one thought were friends but who were not, this was an advantage.

They left the day after Boxing Day, Hugo because he had some unspecified business, but Iraq had never again been mentioned and Eleanor wondered when he would feel he should tell Alex. Her one dread, of course, was that she would insist on going with him. She paid more attention than usual to the news, particularly about the situation in the Middle East.

It was a very frightening, uncertain world, Eleanor thought as she gazed out of the window at her wintry garden. The only cheering aspect was the bird table and the hanging bird feeders packed with nuts and wild birdseed, which were extremely busy with finches and tits while blackbirds and the odd strutting pigeon hopped hopefully about underneath. A mist hung over the distant hill crowned with fir trees, an aspect that sometimes made it look like Switzerland. Disturbed by a noise in the hall, Eleanor turned to see Cathy framed in the doorway clutching the inevitable array of carrier bags.

'Hello, I didn't expect you,' she said, relief apparent in her voice at the sight of a friendly face.

'Well,' Cathy said taking off her coat and disappearing for a moment to hang it in the hall, 'I wanted company.' Re-entering the room she plopped herself down in a chair opposite Eleanor.

Eleanor laughed. '*You* wanted company! You're just being kind.'

'Also, I thought there are a few jobs I can do. Frankly,' she said joining her hands in her lap, 'I did think you might be lonely now that Alex has gone.'

'How very sweet of you, Cathy,' Eleanor said warmly. 'Yes, I am a bit down. Sometimes I feel so useless and at holiday time one remembers past ones, especially Christmas, I suppose.'

'I'll get coffee –' Cathy got briskly to her feet – 'and I've bought you a few things.'

'As usual,' Eleanor said looking at her fondly as she left the room.

There was something on Cathy's mind, Eleanor could tell as she sat down again, her cup carefully balanced on her lap. Cathy was normally one of those buxom, unfailingly cheerful women, but today her manner was different, unusually subdued.

'What's up?' Eleanor enquired, stirring her coffee. 'I can tell you're not yourself.'

Cathy sighed. 'Well, I don't want to burden you with our problems, you have enough of your own, but Niobe and Francis had a terrible row the other night. Things haven't been the same since and he wants me to have the children for a while. He says he and Niobe aren't speaking and the atmosphere is bad for the kids.'

'Oh, dear.' Eleanor, concerned for Cathy, was also thinking of herself. If Cathy looked after her grandchildren there would be no time for her. 'Is it as bad as that? Somehow I always had the impression that on the whole, allowing for the odd row, they were a happy, well-suited, couple.'

'That's what they like people to think, or Francis does. The fact is Niobe is a discontented woman. She always has been, considering herself better than Francis and now it has come out. She picks on him a lot, you know, niggly little things. I think I notice it when I'm there more than my son, who thinks the world of Niobe and can see no wrong in her. Well, when they came back from your place Christmas night they had a terrible row and Niobe walked out of the house. He went after her, of course. It was dark, very late, and he just stopped her driving away in her car. He almost dragged her back and there was another terrible scene. The children woke up and it was awful. I stayed the night to try and calm things down.'

'What were they rowing about?' Eleanor said though she felt she already knew.

'Francis said that Niobe was flirting with your daughter's boyfriend,' Cathy blurted out. 'I hate to say it, but that's what started the row. It was very unlike Francis. He is normally so mild, very quiet, doesn't say much. I think he'd had a bit too much to drink.'

'There was quite a lot of champagne.' Eleanor glanced down at her knees. 'Maybe he wasn't used to it.'

'Well, he said some very nasty things to her and she said nasty things back, like that Hugo was a gentleman and Francis wasn't, that sort of thing. Finally he called her a slut and at that stage she ran out and I told him to go after her in case she hurt herself.'

'I am so sorry.' Eleanor hardly knew what to say. 'But if it is any comfort the atmosphere here was not peaceful. The atmosphere was tense. I have come to the conclusion that Alex and Hugo are an ill-suited couple too, but Alex is obsessed with Hugo. She knows something is wrong but can't do anything about it, doesn't want to, in fact. I am so afraid that if he goes to Iraq as he said he wants to, she will go with him. But please keep this to yourself.'

Cathy, whose mind lingered on her own woes rather than Eleanor's went on murmuring almost to herself. 'I've always been so worried about those two, you know. They are very different. Not getting married even after two children, I can't understand it.' Cathy shook her head wearily and turned her eyes once again to Eleanor.

'Who didn't want to get married?' Eleanor asked, 'or was it mutual agreement?'

'I think it was Niobe's choice,' Cathy sniffed, dabbing at

her eyes with her handkerchief to keep the tears at bay. 'Francis was always very keen to get married and that's what made me think from the very beginning that she was restless. *Why* doesn't she want to get married, I asked myself? But then the children came along and they seemed happy enough. Niobe looks after the house and the farm and she does it well, but her real love is her painting. Money has always been tight and Francis works all the hours God sends.' She blew her nose hard. 'Francis is a good lad and he deserves better.' Cathy's expression turned from tearfulness to anger. 'Niobe is so restless. She always has been and lately it has got worse. It doesn't seem to bother Francis. It's almost like he doesn't notice it, but I do. I think Hugo seemed very glamorous to her compared to Francis and I suppose he is. Did *you* think they were flirting?'

'I was hardly here,' Eleanor confessed. 'I thought with four young people together, let them talk and get to know one another. I was busy in the kitchen and as you know how slow I am it all takes time, but I was very surprised when they said they were going and it was Francis who wanted to go. Niobe was reluctant, so maybe she was enjoying herself with Hugo. You know, someone different. That also was what my two were arguing about, each accusing the other of flirting! Maybe it got out of hand, or seemed to in a charged atmosphere. But Alex and Hugo were bickering all the time they were here about something or other, silly little things. Frankly, I was quite glad to see the back of them.'

Eleanor rose to her feet, stretching. 'Now look, why don't we forget this silly business and go to the pub for lunch? I'll treat and you drive.'

Silly business it might be, but it was not really all that easy to forget. For one thing, Niobe, who usually popped in every day or so, stayed away and Eleanor wondered if she felt guilty about what had happened.

At the beginning of January the notice of her eye operation came through from the hospital and, using this as an excuse, she went across the road and tapped on the door of the farmhouse waiting for some time before it opened. Niobe stood there wiping her hands on a cloth and looking rather flustered.

'I'm sorry, Niobe, did I disturb you?' Eleanor asked apologetically. 'You look busy.'

'Not at all,' Niobe said stepping back. 'Do come in, Eleanor. I've felt guilty about you. It is a long time since I paid you a visit, but I have been very busy.' Her expression suddenly became animated. 'There's a chance I might get an exhibition in Blandford, sharing it with others, you know.' She thrust towards Eleanor hands stained with paint as she led her into the pleasant kitchen with its wood-burning stove and held out a chair for her.

'Children gone back to school?' Eleanor asked, sitting down.

'Yes, thank heavens, though . . .' Niobe paused and shot Eleanor a guilty look. 'Well, I suppose you know from Cathy that she had them for a few days, Francis being very irrational and silly about . . .' She stopped again.

Eleanor nodded. 'Cathy did mention something.' Her voice trailed off as Niobe continued agitatedly.

'Francis was absolutely ridiculous.' She stared indignantly at Eleanor. 'He accused *me* of flirting with your daughter's boyfriend. As if I would dream of such a thing. I can't think what got into him and I was very cross. I was enjoying myself that evening. It is very rarely that I meet intelligent people like Alex and . . . I've even forgotten his name.'

'Hugo,' Eleanor said, though she doubted the truth of this claim.

'I spend all my time with Francis's friends – builders, farmers or thatchers and their wives or girlfriends. I'm not saying there is anything wrong with them, don't misunderstand me. I am not a snob, but I have little in common with them and occasionally, just occasionally, I like to meet people who know something of the world, who have been somewhere. Francis has never been further than Birmingham,' Niobe said derisively, hands placed firmly on her hips. 'Do you know he has never been abroad, never been to London, never even *wants* to go? He wants his own little furrow, if you like, and to stay there living happily ever after. Well, no thank you, not me.' Her voice rose as she spoke leaving

Eleanor with the impression of what a very discontented and frustrated woman she actually was. As if reading her thoughts, Niobe flung her hands in the air in a wild gesture. 'Sometimes, I think of leaving Francis, I really do.'

'Oh no, you *can't* do that,' Eleanor cried, shocked.

'Why can't I?' Niobe demanded, hands once again pressed to her hips.

'Because of the children. You can't leave them.'

'Oh, I wouldn't leave the children, at least I don't think so,' she added doubtfully. 'I mean, I would always want to see them, but Francis is very good with them and they adore Cathy.'

Eleanor found herself wishing that she were not hearing this. To see Niobe with new eyes as a rather footloose, uncaring mother was painful for her.

'I'm very sorry to hear all this,' she said.

'Oh, don't worry, it will never happen,' Niobe cried with an abrupt change of mood once again and Eleanor realized what a very volatile woman she was. 'Forget I said anything. Only dreaming.'

'Look,' Eleanor said, 'to a rather practical matter and the reason I am actually here. I have to have an eye op next week and I wondered if you would take me to the hospital and collect me the next day? I'd be so grateful. Alex can't come and Cathy has something else to do.'

'Oh, I'd do anything for you, Eleanor, you know that,' Niobe said. 'Of course I'll come with you. When?'

Six

Eleanor lay dressed on her hospital bed ready to be collected. There was a white patch over her eye but otherwise she felt quite well and relieved now that it was all over. Mr Ferguson was pleased with the operation but said it would be a few weeks, possibly months, until the full results could be assessed.

She was in no pain and was pleasantly somnolent after her sleeping pill the night before, routinely administered in hospitals. She had always hated hospitals, even visiting people in them, had tried to avoid seeing doctors unless it was strictly necessary, so that being subjected, as she was now to frequent medical inspection was a kind of added torture to her general situation.

The door opened slowly and Niobe put her head round the door.

'OK?' she asked, smiling at Eleanor as she closed the door and approached the bed, then her smile vanished. 'Oh, dear.'

'Oh, dear, what?'

'You look awful.'

'I just had an operation.'

'I mean that patch over your eye.'

'Oh, that is only temporary until I get home.' Eleanor touched it tentatively with a finger. 'I still have one good eye to see out of. All ready?'

'All ready.' Niobe stepped back and prepared to help her off the bed.

'I have to sign something in reception. I have all my bits and pieces –' Eleanor pointed to her overnight bag – 'drops, eye shield, the lot.'

'You're a plucky person,' Niobe said taking her arm.

'Have to be,' Eleanor said with a shrug, 'no choice.'

When the formalities were signed, they stepped out into the wintry sunshine towards the car, parked nearby.

'OK?' Niobe asked as they settled in.

'OK,' Eleanor replied and sat back to enjoy the drive home. She had only had the use of one eye for so long now that the patch made no difference. One can, after all, see as well out of one eye as two. She glanced at Niobe who was concentrating on the road, leaning forward, hands tightly clasping the wheel of the car. She thought that Niobe resembled an animal about to spring or, maybe, one that was caged yearning to be free. There was in fact a similarity between them in that they were both trapped by circumstances, one by her health the other by the constraints of a family life that it was now apparent she did not altogether enjoy.

Suddenly Niobe turned to her with an air of suppressed excitement.

'I may have a chance to exhibit in London,' she said.

'London!' Eleanor exclaimed. 'I thought you said Blandford?'

'There is an art show in Battersea. You have to pay and it is quite a lot, but it would give me a chance, wouldn't it?'

A chance to be free, Eleanor thought.

'I've only just heard about it,' Niobe went on. 'I have all this stuff I was going to exhibit in Blandford, but *London* . . . The thing is . . .' They were approaching a lay-by and, swerving dangerously, she turned off the road and parked. 'The thing is, Eleanor, and I hate to ask you this, but I do need money to enter the exhibition and we are very strapped for cash. Trouble is, I really don't know your circumstances . . .'

'How much?' Eleanor asked, swallowing.

'Five hundred? Something like that,' Niobe sounded vague.

'Something like that?' Eleanor repeated slowly. 'You don't know exactly how much? Could it be a thousand?'

'Mmm, maybe; not more,' Niobe said trying to sound reassuring. 'I really do *hate* to ask, but it is such a chance.'

'I'll do it if I can,' Eleanor said. 'My finances aren't marvellous, but I think I can help you, and if I can, I will.'

'Oh, Eleanor!' Niobe reached across and hugged her. 'Oh, you are a darling. It will only be a loan, you know. I can pay you back.'

'Of course,' Eleanor said and smiled reassuringly, 'when you sell all those pictures. And there is always my compensation.'

'Of course, as you are retired you can't claim loss of earnings.' Christopher Mallet sat back and looked across the table at Eleanor who experienced a feeling of indignation at the very mention of the word. She never thought of herself as 'retired'. 'That greatly reduces the amount you can expect in compensation.'

Christopher smiled at Cathy who hovered by the table in the dining room where the excellent lunch she had prepared had been served.

'I don't think I could eat another thing,' the solicitor observed, wiping his mouth on his napkin. 'That was excellent. How fortunate you are, Mrs Ashton, to have such an excellent cook.'

'Don't I know it.' Eleanor prepared to rise. 'Shall we finish this discussion over coffee?' Much as she valued Cathy, she didn't want her to know all her business, especially the financial side and she slowly made her way into the sitting room followed by Christopher.

'I've been awfully fortunate in my help.' Eleanor sat down and pointed to the chair opposite her. 'Cathy is wonderful and her son lives opposite with his partner, Niobe, who is also a very good friend. Without them, I don't know what I should do. But, Christopher, what you say worries me a good deal. I am not a wealthy woman and have had enormous expenditure since my accident. Moreover, I don't consider myself "retired" as you put it. I intended to continue a career as a freelance journalist. I'm appalled to learn that my extensive injuries and suffering, the fact that I was nearly killed, apparently count for nothing.'

Eleanor paused as Cathy came in with a coffee tray and, as she seemed inclined to linger, smiled her thanks and with a wave of her hand said she would pour.

'I'll be off then, Eleanor, if that's all right?' Cathy said. 'Everything is stacked in the dishwasher and there are some cold cuts and salad in the fridge for you tonight, but I'll be back at bedtime to put in your drops.'

'Angel,' Eleanor murmured as Christopher shook hands with Cathy and saw her to the door.

'She comes at seven in the morning to put in my eye drops and then again last thing at night. I tell you, after I came out of hospital I looked like a creature from a horror movie.'

'You're not nearly as bad as I expected,' Christopher said comfortingly. 'Dad said you were in very bad shape.'

'I've recovered a lot. It may be that in future even my sight will improve.'

'Can you read?'

'Yes, but not easily. I can glance at the newspaper, but for entertainment I rely on talking books. Now, about the claim.'

Christopher took out some papers from a briefcase he had left by the side of his chair and cleared his throat. 'The defendant's insurers have admitted liability. There is no doubt that the man who caused the accident, Mr Jones, was responsible. He overtook a vehicle when there was not room to pass and consequently crossed the centre of the road where he collided with you. Numerous witnesses, fortunately, testified that this was the case. However, as he is dead he cannot be personally prosecuted but we will try and prove that he should not have been driving. He had a very serious heart condition and had not long been out of hospital. It is not clear if he had taken his medication and we will never know, but it is a very complex issue and could take years for the insurance companies to battle it out. In fact –' he looked gravely at Eleanor – 'there is no doubt that it will take a long time. Have you sufficient funds to last?'

'How long?' Eleanor swallowed.

'Two to three years, maybe more. I can of course apply for interim payments, but you have to have a number of medical examinations to determine the extent of your injuries and their permanence or otherwise. I hate to say it but the worse you are the better.'

'I want to recover,' Eleanor said firmly, 'as much as I can.'

'I'm sure you do, but also you don't want to live in poverty for the rest of your life, do you? We want to get you enough money to enjoy a reasonable standard of living. But it will take time and you must have patience.'

Patience: it was easy to say but hard to achieve. Eleanor,

her hand resting on Melody, lay waiting for Cathy to come and do her drops. She felt very depressed by Christopher's visit and had thought of very little else since he'd left.

She had sat for a long time watching dusk settle over the garden, not even bothering to switch on a light; toyed with the food Cathy had left in the fridge and had gone upstairs to bed even earlier than usual. There was no doubt that she felt depressed. She had been warned about the possible onset of depression; had resolved never to give in to it. After all, was she not a strong woman used to being in control?

Melody suddenly raised her head preparing to leap off the bed, a sure sign that there was a visitor, and Eleanor looked at the clock and then ahead expecting to see Cathy's comfortable figure framed in the doorway.

'Niobe,' she exclaimed in surprise. 'I didn't expect you.' She patted the side of her bed. 'Lovely to see you anyway.'

'I've come to do your drops,' Niobe said perching by Eleanor's side. 'Cathy had a meeting with the mothers' union and I think after that they went to the pub. Anyway, I just wanted to have a word.'

'Nothing wrong, I hope?' Eleanor looked at her anxiously. 'Children all right? Francis?'

'Everything is fine.' Niobe got up and, picking up the tube by the side of the bed, took off the top and leaned over Eleanor. 'Let me get the hang of this. I used to do it with Sam when she had conjunctivitis. I'm sure I'm not as good at this as Cathy. Open wide; don't want to poke out your eye!'

Eleanor, suppressing a giggle, did as she was told and the procedure was soon accomplished. She blinked her eyes and then dabbed at them with a tissue.

'You're very good,' she said. 'I can, of course, do it myself. I am spoiled. Now, what did you want?' She patted the bed beside her again.

'It's about that money.' Niobe perched beside her. 'You remember I asked?'

'Yes, of course.'

'Well, I wondered if I could have it now. I don't mean this minute but in the next few days.'

'I didn't think you wanted it so soon.'

'Neither did I, but they want a deposit and, yes, it is a thousand pounds. They would like half. They are doing me a favour fitting me in. I should have applied well before Christmas.' She looked anxiously at the woman lying on the bed looking so helpless and felt, somehow, that she was taking advantage of her. 'I did hate to ask and Cathy said your solicitor was here today and you seemed rather worried. Really, Eleanor, I am sure I can try elsewhere if . . .' She paused again. 'You see, I don't want my parents to know. Like Francis, they feel I'm wasting my time. They have no faith in me. They'd be furious at the cost.'

'The solicitor was nothing about money, well, only indirectly. It was about the claim against Mr Jones, or rather his insurers. It will just take a lot of time but, yes, I have some money and of course I can let you have it. Five hundred now, you say?' To her surprise and discomfiture Niobe started to cry, head in hands, whimpering like a small child.

'Oh *please*.' Eleanor put a comforting hand on her back. 'It is nothing to weep about. It is a big chance for you and I am seriously and sincerely very glad to help.'

'It's not just that.' Niobe groped for a tissue from the box beside Eleanor's bed and blew her nose vigorously. 'It's the whole business. I will have to tell Francis.'

'You haven't told him yet!' Eleanor was astonished.

'No, I mean, now that they want the money and the die is cast I shall have to tell him.'

'Of course you will. I don't want to be censorious but you should really have discussed that beforehand.'

'I know he'll be cross. He doesn't take my painting seriously. Never has. Thinks I'm fooling about. It will cause all sorts of trouble. Supposing he says no?' Niobe's expression was anguished.

'Well then, I would talk to him as soon as you can and it's not just about the money as far as I am concerned. Don't think that, because you can have it at any time. It is there for you. But it is getting it straight with Francis and Cathy. I don't suppose she knows either?' Niobe shook her head.

'She'll have to help look after the children,' Eleanor went on as there was no answer.

'I wondered if you'd talk to her,' Niobe began snivelling

again. 'Make out how important it is for me, you know. I'd be so grateful.'

And looking at the weeping woman beside her Eleanor experienced a sense of foreboding, knowing not only that she had no choice but also that she was getting into much deeper waters than she would have wished.

Eleanor was very fond of Cathy, appreciating her robust common sense, her no-nonsense approach to life. She felt the affection was mutual. The two women usually had coffee together. It was a break for Cathy who arrived at eight to take Eleanor her breakfast and then help her shower and dress. It was still too difficult to bathe. Eleanor had problems getting in and out of a bath so a luxurious soak, which she loved, was out of the question for the time being.

Still, she was much more agile than she had been, she reflected. She could get down the stairs by herself and potter about instead of just sitting in a chair all day staring into the garden, although that had its own pleasure, as birds foraged for food in the weeks of winter and the bird table was emptied almost as soon as it had been filled.

'I wish spring would hurry up and come,' Eleanor said taking her coffee from Cathy who plopped down in the chair next to her. 'It is such a dismal time of year, it can't come soon enough for me.' She gazed across at Cathy who, although not a woman of moods, had seemed to her to be rather downcast that morning. Eleanor wondered if, after all, Niobe had said something to Francis overnight. Cathy was usually very chatty but this morning, less so. 'You OK?' she asked.

'I'm all right,' Cathy replied robustly. 'It's Francis I'm worried about.'

Eleanor felt her pulse quicken as she waited for her to proceed.

'His business is not going well; his little thatching business, you know. There are a lot of competitors and Francis is a one-man band. The trouble is if he goes in with someone else he earns less money.'

Eleanor's heart sank. Obviously it was not a good time to introduce another subject. She rather wished she had left Niobe to do her own dirty work, and a feeling of irritation overtook her to be replaced almost immediately by guilt because of everything Niobe did for her; her loyalty and willingness to help. She took a deep breath.

'Cathy, this may not be quite the right moment but Niobe has asked me to do her a favour.'

Cathy replaced her cup on the table and looked questioningly at her. 'Don't tell me she wants to leave Francis,' Cathy began.

'Oh no, nothing like that, but she has an opportunity to exhibit some of her work in London and it will of course mean leaving home for a while. I think she was a bit nervous about telling you as she hadn't yet told Francis.'

'Oh!' With an audible sigh of relief Cathy leaned back in her chair, a grim smile contorting her features. 'Oh, is that all? She is always coming up with daft ideas like that and we never take any notice.'

'Well this time I think you should. She is serious. I thought as you seemed in a funny mood she might already have told Francis.'

'Why didn't she tell me herself?' Cathy demanded. 'Too scared, is she?'

'Nervous, I'd say,' Eleanor said gently.

'Well, there is no need for her to be nervous because it will never happen,' Cathy said firmly preparing to rise from her chair as though she had put an end to the matter.

Eleanor leaned forward with a motion of her hand to indicate that Cathy should stay where she was. 'Look, Cathy, now that we've started let's discuss this a bit further. I do think Niobe is serious, you see she has asked me to lend her the money she needs to enter the exhibition, and I have agreed.'

'You what?' Cathy sat back again, her expression one of incredulity. 'You agreed to help her in a hare-brained scheme like this? This is why she never goes to any of these things because she can't afford to. Now you help her and she can. It is absolutely nothing to do with you. *Really*, Eleanor.' This time Cathy was visibly simmering with anger and jumped up from her seat. 'Is this the way you say thank you for all, we, and I mean Francis and I, have done for you?'

Eleanor put up a hand. 'Please, Cathy, please don't take it like this. Let's discuss it rationally.'

'There is nothing to discuss as far as I am concerned,' Cathy said wrathfully, 'and I thought you were my friend.'

'I am your friend and always will be, but I am Niobe's friend, too, and she asked me at a vulnerable moment, I admit, a moment when she was driving me home from the eye hospital.'

'Oh, did she? Had it all worked out I bet?'

'I don't think it was like that at all, but had it happened at another time I might have asked a few more questions, the effect on the family and so on. She told me she had an opportunity to exhibit in London and asked if I could help her financially. It does not involve a very large sum and I felt I couldn't refuse.' Eleanor looked appealingly at Cathy. 'Well, could I?'

'She took advantage of you, scheming bitch!'

Eleanor looked shocked. 'Oh, that is a very unfair thing to say. Niobe is not a scheming bitch. She is a very nice young woman and I am very fond of her.'

'Well, I can tell you that she is not a "nice young woman" if you want to know. She has made my son's life a misery with her fancy ways, her art! She has always refused to marry him despite the fact they have two children. Never wanted to be tied down, she said. I always warned Francis she was a bird of passage. He works all the hours God sends to keep them alive and this is what he gets. Why can't she do something useful instead of all this art business?'

'Like what?'

'Well, work properly; like me, like him. She could do a job of some description while the children are at school.'

'There are the animals,' Eleanor said weakly. 'She looks after the farm.'

'What farm?' Cathy retorted. 'The little stock they have presents no problem. They only need to be fed twice a day. Instead it is always her "art". She is a lazy little bugger and sometimes I think Francis would be much better off without her . . .' Cathy paused. 'The trouble is the poor sap loves her and I think, if you ask me, she doesn't love him and never has!' Finally Cathy rose from her chair and looked purposefully towards the door.

'Oh, Cathy, please try and understand.' Eleanor made one last desperate plea.

'I don't understand *anything*, Eleanor, least of all why you, struggling with your own problems, which God knows are bad enough, should want to get involved in something that is absolutely none of your business.'

And taking up both empty cups Cathy hurried out of the room.

Hugo and Alex sat in front of the television absorbed in the latest news bulletin about Iraq. It was a situation which seemed to be getting worse every day despite the promises made by the occupying powers, the hopes of the world.

With an exclamation of irritation Hugo suddenly leaned forward and switched off the TV, then went to the drinks table and poured generous measures of Scotch into two glasses, one of which he handed to Alex. There was a spring in his step and a gleam in his eyes that Alex recognized and knew well. This was a man who was at his happiest when in action and if danger were added to that, so much the better.

'You know that is a place I'd really like to be,' Hugo said flopping down beside Alex again.

'You're joking, aren't you?' Alex shot him a sideways glance.

'No, I'm serious. There is a lot of material to be got out there that hasn't been covered already, I'm sure. How the people are reacting and so on. Lots of new angles.'

'And be bumped off or disappear.' Alex suppressed a shudder. 'Don't even think about it.'

Hugo put an arm on her shoulder and drew her close. 'I'm perfectly serious. I've even put out a few feelers. There's a lot of interest from an American TV company. Can't say which one at the moment.'

'Then I don't see why I can't go with you.' Alex rashly drained her glass and held it out for a refill, feeling slightly heady already. 'I thought we were a team.'

Hugo slowly refilled it, added a large dollop of soda and handed her back the glass. 'Not so quickly this time,' he said perching on the futon next to her and putting his arm round her shoulders again.

'We are, only this time you are not going with me, at least not to start. I'd be much better on my own until I can suss out the lie of the land. I would feel too responsible for you, and your mother would hate me.' He paused and drank deeply from his glass. 'More than she does already.'

'Oh, don't let's start that again,' Alex said irritably moving away from him.

'Really darling, there would be no place for you. This is a war of extremes. It's a jungle out there. I have been very busy in the last few weeks chatting up my contacts. I'm in with an extremely good chance of a commission, but on my own not with you, for the moment anyway.'

Alex gazed at him in astonishment. 'How can you have done all this without me?'

'Because I knew how you'd react and, believe me, darling, I don't want you there, but if the situation improves and the chance arises I promise you I'll find a place for you if I can.'

'Nothing can stop *me* going to Iraq as a private individual if I wish,' Alex said stubbornly.

'Oh, yes they can. I can. It is much too dangerous and I doubt, anyway, you could get there, even now. There are too many obstacles, transport to start with. No one can guarantee you a safe passage from the airport to Baghdad without an escort. You can't just arrive and call a taxi!'

Alex leaned back against his arm, gazing abjectly in front of her at the bare flat with its stripped pine floors, sparsely furnished with a few items from Ikea, which gave it a transitory air of impermanence, of people who were passing through. It was above a shop in Camden Town close to the main street but near the park. The street was full of shops and cafes, pubs, a bookshop, a dry cleaner, a launderette, a dentist, solicitors, estate agents and a doctor's surgery: people of all nationalities, ages and colours. It was a vibrant, cosmopolitan atmosphere in which they both felt at home, although Alex liked the country more than Hugo. It had a bedroom, a sitting/dining room and a small kitchen and overlooked a children's playground on one side and the street on the other. Alex had bought it with money given to her by her father in a moment of guilt after he left Eleanor and knew the family home would be sold.

'Say something,' Hugo said pressing her shoulders again.

'What can I say?' she turned to him wearily. 'I feel our

life at the moment is so unfulfilled. It seems to have no purpose.'

'It *has* a purpose. We love each other, need each other.'

'Do we?'

His expression changed to one of astonishment. 'Of course. Don't you think so?'

'I think you have a funny way of showing it, Hugo, planning to go to a place like Iraq without me, without even *consulting* me.' Alex brushed his hand away and rising wearily from the futon stretched herself and went across to the window overlooking the street. People were passing, going about their business. They all seemed to have a purpose, which at the moment was more than she had. They had shared so many adventures she couldn't understand how he could contemplate one without her, didn't even seem to want her.

She was aware that Hugo had got up and, moving silently across the room, now stood behind her, his hand on her shoulders digging into them.

'I think a little break would do us good,' he whispered in her ear, nuzzling it with his lips. 'It will give us time to think and reassess where we stand.'

His words seemed to send a chill through her heart, confirming her hidden, secret fears.

'Supposing you don't come back?' She turned seeking reassurance in his eyes.

'I will come back,' he said, 'don't worry about that.'

A few days later Hugo took the long awaited call from America and, convinced this was the big chance, he threw a few basics in his bag as was his custom and was off. Alex knew it was useless to protest and let him go with the best grace she could muster. Almost immediately, unable to bear the worry about Hugo and the isolation of London in that flat, denuded of all warmth and comfort, she packed her bag and fled to her mother.

However, there she found the atmosphere far from peaceful with a little domestic war all of its own in place. A rift had occurred between her mother and Cathy who blamed her for encouraging her son's partner to indulge in lofty ideas about exhibiting her work in London. Eleanor had not backed down and, as a consequence, Niobe spent almost all her time in her studio furiously painting.

'Cathy said it was nothing to do with me,' Eleanor concluded after explaining the situation to Alex soon after her unexpected arrival. 'She was right.' She looked anxiously at her daughter. 'But what could I do? What would you have done in the circumstances?'

'When did all this happen?' Alex asked, perplexed.

'Soon after I came out of hospital. She asked me on the way home.'

'But that was weeks ago!'

'And it hasn't got any better. Cathy comes in as usual, does her work and goes. We no longer sit and gossip over our morning coffee. I think she would like to quit completely but basically she is too decent a person to leave me in the lurch.'

'Have you tried to discuss it with her?'

'She says she doesn't want to talk about it. People are like that, aren't they? I always want to get things sorted if I can, but some people don't.'

'Like Hugo,' Alex said. 'He would rather brush everything under the carpet, or under the sheets,' she said as an afterthought. 'He thinks everything can be settled by sex.'

'And can't it?' Eleanor enquired gently.

'No, it can't. Most definitely, it can't.'

It was good to be home, Alex thought as she unpacked the few things she had brought in a rucksack. Home? She paused in her unpacking and gazed thoughtfully out of the window. Did she think of it as home? Outside it was a cold, wintry day and fleetingly her thoughts flew to the hot sands of Iraq where Hugo might soon be assessing the worsening situation. Occasionally, she had a brief call from him on his mobile, never more than a few words and no information about progress in America.

She looked round the pretty room, tastefully but not fussily furnished. After all, hadn't her mother been the editor of a stylish women's magazine? It had a comfortable armchair, an attractive duvet cover with matching curtains, a desk in case she wanted to work, a small dressing table with a stool and a television with a DVD player. It was specifically furnished with her in mind, no doubt of that. It was her room.

Home?

Yes, it was. It was much more homely than the Camden Town flat and much quieter, too, almost ethereally quiet. Alex had always thought of herself as a city girl, a wanderer, restless and insecure. The relationship with Hugo hadn't helped. He was a very dynamic, exciting man, but no home-maker with his failed marriage and yearning for adventure. Alex had decided she was like him, too. He was the man of her dreams and they were ideally suited. She had never before considered her mother's house as home, and she thought it was odd that this was how she felt now. She perched on the bed and stroked the duvet, freshly made with a towel waiting for her, flowers on the dressing table, doubtless hastily arranged when she had phoned her mother that she was coming.

Had Cathy done it all? Presumably, as her mother was still able to do very little.

Now her mother needed her even more with this storm in a teacup about Niobe and her artistic ambitions. Yet, to the people concerned, it was all too real, just as real as the situation in Iraq, only perhaps on a drastically smaller scale.

She put her last few things into drawers, ran a comb through her hair and went downstairs to where Eleanor was still sitting where she had left her in a chair by the fire, looking thoughtful, rather sad as though she had a lot on her mind.

'Mum, should I go and have a word with Niobe?' Alex asked impulsively.

Eleanor looked up in surprise. 'What about?'

'About all this. How it is upsetting you and your rela-tionship with Cathy which, after all, is a very important one.'

'Oh, no, please don't,' Eleanor cried, 'I think it would only cause more trouble.'

Alex gazed at her mother, saw the injured, slightly un-focused eyes, the thin almost emaciated body, deeply etched lines on her face that had not been there the previous summer and was filled with a surge of love that made her kneel down on the floor beside her and take her hand.

'Mum, I do love you,' she said with emotion.

Eleanor looked even more surprised. 'Well, this is a lovely thing to say darling, but why now?'

'Because I do and I think I have been remiss as a daughter. You need me, not Cathy. You need me to look after you, to take care of you, at least until you're better.'

'But, Alex, what about your work?'

'I haven't any. I have no projects on at all at the moment. I am simply an appendix to Hugo Sandeman and that is the honest truth. My man is going to a dangerous place without me and I'm waiting for him to return. I am just like women over the centuries, incomplete without a man. Until then, if you want me, if you can put up with me, you can have me.'

'I can't afford to offend Cathy, Alex. I mean, as you say, you are not going to be here forever.' She smiled at her gently, sadly. 'As you say, once your man comes home you'll be gone and I wouldn't wish it any other way. Let's just hope it all ends soon.'

'No, I don't want to offend Cathy either, but I would quite like to talk to Niobe, as a friend. Just chat, you know. See what she has in mind; plans for the future. I'm interested, frankly, in the set-up. Can't blame me, can you?'

'Not really.' Eleanor pressed her hand. 'But do be careful.'

Alex got up from the floor and stretched.

'I shall go for a walk before it gets dark and just pop in to see her on the way back. Make it look casual. I'll go and have a look at the sea; breath in some good salt air.'

Alex stood on the doorstep of Niobe's house and looked up. The last time she had been here was when her mother was still in hospital. It was also the first time she and Niobe had met. She remembered the impression Niobe had made on her; an unusual, beautiful woman with a domestic life perhaps even more complex than hers because of the children. You couldn't just walk away where children were concerned. She also recalled the rather flirtatious Niobe on Christmas night, which had occasioned a row between Hugo and herself, though Hugo had said she was flirting with Francis, which was absurd.

The front door now was shut and the place seemed deserted. It was five o'clock and already the days were getting longer.

She knocked again and was about to leave, thinking she was rather foolish to be here anyway – asking for trouble in a sense, no, courting it – when she remembered that Niobe on that previous occasion had shown her a studio at the back of the house. She retraced her steps, went round the side of the house and surveyed the number of outbuildings, most of which appeared to be in bad repair and empty. A few hens wandered disconsolately about in the yard, pecking apathetically and looked at her as an interesting diversion. As a farm the place had an air of neglect. Obviously, it had been rundown: not enough time spent on it, perhaps not enough money, or interest, certainly on Niobe's part.

Suddenly, a door to one of the outbuildings opened and Niobe appeared at the doorway cleaning a brush on a cloth. When eventually she looked up and saw Alex her expression was hard to divine as slowly she came towards her.

'Hello,' she said her manner not altogether friendly, 'how long have you been here?'

'Just arrived,' Alex replied. 'I knocked first at the house and was about to go when I remembered your studio.' Then she added, rather breathlessly, 'And also that you promised one day to show me your paintings.' She didn't know what mysterious, unconscious impulse had put this little lie into her head to explain her presence. 'I'm sure it's not at all convenient, you're obviously extremely busy. It is just that I had my walk to the sea and was passing.'

'Come in and see.' Niobe's tone was anything but welcoming as she stood back pointing towards the interior of the studio. 'It's a mess but then it always is.' She looked at Alex curiously. 'Was there anything in particular you wanted?'

Niobe was very shrewd, a hard person to deceive, Alex thought ruefully, silently, as she walked slowly along by the walls on which some of Niobe's work was displayed.

There were a few rather striking colourful abstracts – Niobe obviously liked strong primary colours – and some simple watercolours of rural scenes. As Alex had anticipated her work was not outstanding. Hers was not an undiscovered talent; she was a gifted amateur.

'I studied at St Martin's School of Art,' Niobe said defensively as if she could read Alex's mind, 'I'm not completely untrained.'

'So I see,' Alex said, examining intently one of the abstracts. 'I think you have a gift, just as I thought,' she added diplomatically turning to Niobe with a smile. 'Mum said you are to exhibit in London.'

'Yes, in Battersea. It's very soon now. I'll have to start packing up my stuff.'

Alex looked round. 'All this?'

'Well, a lot of it.'

'How will you get it up?'

'Francis has a van and he'll run me up. At least, I hope he will. He doesn't know it yet. He is being so bolshie about the whole business. Doesn't approve. If not, I'll hire a van and drive myself.'

Niobe looked at her defiantly and Alex suddenly felt a surge of admiration, mixed with pity, for this rather tough but sad woman who clearly felt nobody understood her.

'I'd help if I could.' Her voice tailed off. 'Trouble is Mum needs me right now because I expect Cathy is looking after the children.'

'I'll be all right. Don't worry.' Niobe began visibly to relax and her expression softened. 'It was *very* kind of Eleanor to lend me the money. I expect she told you. Without her the whole thing would have been impossible. A thousand pounds. I will pay it back, I promise.'

'Oh, don't worry about that. Mum is glad to help.' Alex looked at her thoughtfully. 'Where are you staying?'

'Oh, on the Embankment, I suppose. I hadn't thought about it. That's the last thing for me to worry about.'

'Oh, you can't *sleep* on the Embankment,' Alex looked horrified. 'Look, I have a flat in Camden Town, which is empty at the moment. Hugo is in the States looking for a commission and you are very welcome to use it.'

Niobe sat down abruptly on the nearest chair and gazed across at Alex. 'Oh, but I couldn't.'

'Oh, but you could. It's a way for me to help and I'd like to. It's quite comfortable and pretty central. *Please*, I'd like you to accept.'

'Well, if you're *sure*.'

Rather to Alex's surprise and embarrassment, Niobe jumped up from her chair and, throwing her arms around her shoulders, hugged her tightly.

Alex, aware that Niobe had begun to sob, reluctantly tightened her arms around her. 'Hey, no need for tears.'

'But you don't know what it means to me to have people so kind.' Finally, Niobe stood back, vigorously wiping her eyes. 'I never get it from my own family. No one understands me, least of all Cathy who thinks her son is too good for me. In her opinion I'm an idler and a waste of space. I think the honest truth is that she'd like me to go and not come back, and then Francis could find a good woman who he could marry and who would look after him.'

'I'm sure that's not true,' Alex said, but in her heart she wondered if it were.

Relating the scene to her mother over supper that evening Alex found it all a bit unreal. Eleanor had listened in silence until Alex finished, then she leaned back in her chair and put her elbows on the table.

'You know, sometimes I think we have got a bit too emotionally involved with that family. It is so hard to be objective. I rather wish I hadn't lent her the money, or given it rather, because I am sure I'll never get it back.'

'Oh, Mum . . .' Alex looked at her mother in dismay. 'Why do you think that?'

'Because where would she get it from? She hasn't got any and if, as you say, her painting isn't up to much she won't make a fortune there.'

'Well, it's all right. The watercolours are quite sweet, but I think there is much better abstract art around for those who know about that kind of thing. Why didn't she borrow the money from her family? I had the impression her dad was quite well off, a business man in Birmingham.'

'Oh, I can understand that,' Eleanor said. 'Too much pride. She says she doesn't want them to know. I don't think they really approve of the relationship either; think she could have done better. That's probably why she wouldn't marry Francis. Anyway she doesn't seem all that close to them. No, I don't mind her having the money. They have been good to me and your father once said you should only lend as much as you can afford and not expect to get it back. I can't really afford as much as a thousand, but she has it and that's the lot. But now she's staying in your flat. That's quite another matter.'

'Well, there's no harm in that. It's only for a few days.'

'Supposing she likes it there?'

Alex looked at her in astonishment. 'What do you mean?'

'She's restless. She's unhappy. Who knows what could happen?'

'Well, she can't stay there for long. Hugo could come back at any time and I can't stay here forever, either. I shall have to make that clear – a few days only and that is it.'

Seven

Niobe stood by the window watching the people pass in the street below. Night was falling and the lights were coming on in the shops and in the windows above them. The one-way street was full of traffic, stationary because of the traffic lights at the junction with Camden High Street.

She turned and looked back into the room which, though sparsely furnished, was to her a place of awe and wonder. A London flat!

She had never lived in London despite having told people she had trained at the Slade or St Martin's School of Art. Both were lies, but Niobe was not so much a liar as a fantasist who sometimes came to believe all the stories she told because she so badly wanted them to be true. She had had one or two day trips to London, once to the Royal Academy Summer Exhibition and once to the National Gallery. She had done a brief course in art at a school in Birmingham and she had done ceramics in Dorchester, which was where she had met Francis. Bits of her past were true and sometimes she forgot which bits she had told to whom.

Niobe was a woman who felt deeply unfulfilled, whose potential was unrealized and as she got older she felt life was passing her by, was going all too quickly and soon she would be old and all her chances would have gone. This was why she had seized so avidly the opportunity when she read about the Battersea Exhibition to go to London. In order to qualify she had even had to invent a gallery that exhibited her work and called herself Dorset Arts, so that the abstracts were by her and the watercolours by someone else, also exhibited by a mythical gallery based in Bridport. As someone used to making up stories Niobe had no difficulty with this at all and, indeed, enjoyed it. The part she had not enjoyed was asking Eleanor for money, but she had because she believed fervently that the cause was just.

And now she was here in London, in a real flat, living the dream, a dream realized at last even for a few days. Life could never possibly be the same again.

The freedom of the flat! She couldn't believe it and here for how long? Five days, six maybe? Perhaps she could extend it a bit, though Alex had been pretty adamant about a time limit. Maybe she was nervous Niobe would meet her boyfriend? She wouldn't have minded. She had liked him, found him vital and attractive. He was about as opposite to Francis as it was possible to be. But the boyfriend was abroad, so there was no chance of that happening.

They had left well before dawn in the morning, the van packed with her paintings. Francis had helped her hang them in the small space she'd rented in Battersea, and then he'd gone with alacrity as though London terrified him, as it probably had. They had spoken very little on the way up. She knew he resented her going. The chasm between them seemed to have grown, be widening all the time.

The fair was intimidating. It was so large, stretched along by the side of Battersea Gardens within sight of the Thames. Everyone seemed to know one another and there was a lot of chat, frenzied greetings, effusive kisses and corks popping, which made Niobe feel isolated and, for the first time, a few doubts about what she'd done had entered her head. Unlike other artists she seemed to have very little to show, and when she compared them to some of the work on the walls she was almost tempted to take them all down again and go home.

Officially the fair started the following day and, rejoicing in this unaccustomed freedom she had walked part of the way back to the flat, across Battersea Bridge, along the Embankment, past the Houses of Parliament and Westminster Abbey, which she gawped at in awe. Then, feeling hopelessly lost as well as tired, she had got a taxi the rest of the way and resolved not to take one again because it cost a fortune.

Her hand had trembled as she put the key into the door of Alex's flat and now she was here, alone in London. A dream fulfilled at last.

The kitchen was small and the fridge was empty except for a carton of milk, which was practically solid, a jar of pickled gherkins and a half pound of rancid butter. In the bread bin was some very stale bread, green and covered with mildew.

Well, Alex had been gone a few days and she supposed Hugo had, too.

Niobe realized she was very hungry, but she didn't feel like cooking so, putting on her coat, she descended the stairs from the flat which was over a cafe and wandered up the road looking for a takeaway or store where she could buy milk and a sandwich.

The street was very busy and crowds were pressing home-wards, people leaping on buses, cars hooting. It was exciting – it was London – and, on impulse, Niobe retraced her steps and went into the cafe under the flat, which was already filling up with early diners. It wasn't a threatening place. It was an egg and chip sort of cafe, so that's what she ordered with bread and butter and a cup of tea. She would actually have liked a drink but the cafe was unlicensed.

She liked it. Above all, it was cheap, impersonal and she decided she would come here a lot, well, in the time she had left.

'Do you know anywhere I can buy milk?' she addressed the man behind the till as she paid on her way out.

'If you go up the road towards the park there is a deli-catessen. It is just off the main road, the first turning to the left past a row of houses. It's Greek but it sells everything. But if you only want milk I can let you have some.'

She pointed at the ceiling. 'I'm staying in the flat upstairs.'

'Oh, Alex's place?'

'Yes, I'm a friend.'

The man held out a hand. 'Oh, I know Alex very well, and Hugo. You know Hugo?'

'I've met him,' Niobe said, taking his hand. 'I'm Niobe.'

'Unusual name. I'm Tony. How is her mother? She had that bad accident.'

'She's much better.'

'Come from those parts, do you?'

Niobe nodded. 'Dorset. I'm a neighbour of Eleanor, her mother.'

'Ah.'

Tony gave her her change, shook his head when she proffered a tip. 'No, you keep it. I'm the boss.'

'Oh, sorry.'

'No need to be sorry.' Tony pointed towards the road. 'That way, first left, you can't miss it.'

'Thank you very much,' Niobe said. 'I'll see you again.'

'I hope so.' With a smile Tony turned to the customer behind her.

The man behind the counter in the delicatessen was Greek and greeted her as if she were an old friend. She even told him it was her first visit, real visit, to London and about the exhibition. He said he hoped he'd see her again and she assured him he would.

On her way back, clutching her provisions of bread, butter, honey and milk she experienced a feeling of elation, of sheer euphoria of an intensity that she could not recall having felt for years. This was London, shops open until all hours, a buzz about the place, restaurants full of people. It was nearly nine o'clock and even the bookshop was open with people browsing by the shelves. In Dorset everything was shut down just after five, the streets almost deserted. It was strange and it was different, yet when she got back to the flat it was almost like coming home. Alex had told her where fresh bedclothes were, and within half an hour of her return, Niobe was in bed and fast asleep.

It was surprising after all how nice people at the art fair were; how helpful to a novice, but on that first day, though lots of people meandered past her booth and a few came into it and looked around, she didn't sell anything. One man appeared to loiter in front of one of her watercolours for so long that she even asked if he knew the place, but this seemed to scare him and without even glancing at it any more he left.

She was told by the woman exhibiting in the next booth to her that this was the kind of thing that happened and you got used to it.

'Been painting long?' she asked Niobe, looking at her

curiously, cigarette in one hand, mug of tea, or maybe it was wine, in another.

Niobe thought she'd better not give her the spiel about the Slade or St Martin's in case the woman was an ex student and said, 'On and off for years. This is my first exhibition.'

Her friend who had introduced herself as Dilys, nodded.

'Well, this is a good place to start. Never came across your gallery before.' She squinted at the sign which was very small.

Niobe thought silence was the best policy and said nothing.

'Cheers,' Dilys said and having just espied someone entering her booth left with a wave.

Except for one or two calls to the loo and to get a sandwich and a drink, Niobe spent all day in her booth waiting hopefully for a buyer.

In the afternoon quite a few people came and several of the other exhibitors wandered round and made encouraging noises, but the more she saw the more she knew she was not in the league of the professional artist, which most of them seemed to be. Everyone was kind to her, perhaps out of pity, but some were patronizing and peered sceptically at the sign that timidly proclaimed the gallery: Dorset Arts.

At the end of the day she was less euphoric than she had been and knew without any doubt that she would not be coming here again. She had paid a lot of money to enter and at this rate she would not be able to pay Eleanor back a penny.

On the grounds of economy she decided not even to eat at the cafe, although she was starving, but bought some more provisions at the Greek shop as well as a bottle of wine. However as she passed the cafe beneath the flat she was astonished to see a light on in the sitting-room window above and, with some trepidation, went upstairs. The door was unlocked and as she entered she was greeted with a loud noise from the TV and the powerful smell of cigarette smoke.

There was a bag in the hall and photographic equipment and, her heart sinking, she went into the sitting room to find Hugo sitting in front of the television, glass in one hand, cigarette in the other, oblivious so far to her presence.

She stood for some moments in the doorway, uncertain

what to do when Hugo looked up, saw her and, his face registering intense surprise, got slowly to his feet. She was sure he didn't know who she was, searching his mind for a name. Slowly she entered and put her purchases down on the table.

'Niobe?' he said hesitantly. 'It *is* Niobe, isn't it?'

'It is,' she said. 'Didn't Alex tell you I was staying here?'

'Ah, Alex . . .' His voice trailed off as he stubbed out his cigarette. 'I'm afraid she doesn't know I'm here. I just landed from the States and I'm stopping over on my way to Berlin.'

He rose and came towards her. 'Have a drink?' His manner subtly changed from surprise to affability.

'Well, thanks, I will.'

'Whisky OK?'

Niobe screwed up her nose. 'I'd prefer wine.' She pointed to the bottle she'd brought. 'I've had a hard day.'

'Me too –' he reached for the corkscrew and expertly drew the cork – 'that's why I didn't tell Alex. I'll give her a call from the airport. I was going straight to Berlin, but I had to stop over and see the FO. It seems that at last I'm on my way to Iraq. I guessed that if Alex knew she'd rush up and try and stop me. I would have thought that by now she would have realized it was futile, but that's Alex.' He pulled a face.

'I understand why she wouldn't want you to go.' Niobe accepted the glass from him and as the futon was the only place to sit besides the solitary chair, collapsed on it. Hugo refilled his glass with whisky and sat beside her.

'So,' he said looking at her. 'Have you left your husband?'

'No, not at all. I'm exhibiting at the art fair in Battersea. Why should I leave my . . . well, Francis?'

'Oh, isn't he your husband?' Hugo looked at her with interest.

'We are not married, but we have been together for a long time and we have two children.' She gave him a withering look.

Hugo looked chastened. 'Sorry. I'm not married either and Alex and I have also been together for a long time. Tell me about your art fair.'

So she told him and when she'd finished she got up and put her empty glass on the table.

'I suppose I'd better find somewhere else to stay.'

Hugo looked surprised. 'What's wrong with here?'

'Well, it's hardly the thing is it? Only one bedroom. What will Alex say?'

'Alex will not know and I wouldn't dream of taking your bed from you, or sharing it, if that's what you think I have in mind.'

Niobe coloured and looked away.

'I'm sorry,' Hugo said quickly. 'I didn't mean that. It was a crass thing to say. I can sleep on the futon which, after all, is what it is for and I shall probably be out before you've even opened your eyes and, hopefully, be on my way to Berlin by the afternoon. Now look, why don't we go out and have some food? You must be starving. I am and I believe there's nothing substantial here to eat.'

'I bought some ham,' Niobe said lamely, 'and there are eggs and . . .' She pointed to the half empty bottle of wine.

'There is a very nice Greek restaurant five minutes away,' Hugo said. 'Why don't we eat there?'

'Do you like Greek food?' Hugo looked at Niobe across the table after the waiter had handed each of them a menu.

'I don't really know,' she replied. 'I have never had it before. Why don't you order for me?'

'Let's have the meze in that case.' Hugo closed the menu and instructed the waiter. 'In that way we get a bit of every-thing. And a bottle of Othello,' he added, still addressing the waiter. 'I prefer it to retsina,' he said to Niobe and, extracting a crumpled packet of cigarettes from his breast pocket, offered it to her.

'I'm trying to give up,' she said taking one from him and leaning forward as he lit it.

'I couldn't live without cigarettes.' Hugo inhaled deeply.

'Francis says we should both give up. It's so bad for the children.'

'Tell me about Francis,' Hugo said encouragingly.

Niobe felt herself instinctively withdraw. 'What about him?'

'Everything, you know. I thought he seemed a nice guy.'

'He is a nice guy.' Niobe studied the table. 'Too nice for me.'

'Oh, I can't believe that.'

'He is, really. He is good and kind.' She paused.

'But . . .' Hugo smiled encouragingly as she looked across at him.

'Well, I don't know. I just can't see myself spending the rest of my life with him, that's all. He's not interested in my painting, thinks it is affected. Of course we both adore the children and, well . . .' She sighed deeply. 'I don't suppose we will ever part, not at least until the children are older.' Her tone of voice changed, became sharper as though to indicate that was all she would say on the subject. 'And Alex?'

The waiter put a tempting array of dishes in front of them and another approached from behind him and began to pour from a bottle of red wine.

'I hope you don't mind red?' Hugo said to Niobe. 'I should have asked.'

'Oh, no, I like it.' She held out the glass towards him. 'Cheers.'

'Cheers,' Hugo said and, observing Niobe looking at the dishes in some bewilderment, took a piece of warm pitta bread from the basket and used it as a scoop as he attacked one of the plates.

'Seriously, you've never had Greek food? Not even when you lived in London?'

'I never lived in London.'

'Oh, I thought you did. I thought Alex said . . .'

Niobe shook her head and said nothing, following Hugo's example and scooping the humous from the central dish. 'This is really tasty,' she said. 'I'm so glad we came.'

Hugo sat back, lit a fresh cigarette from the stub in his mouth and studied her quizzically. 'You're not answering my questions are you?'

'And you're not answering mine,' Niobe replied.

'So, shall we leave all personal questions out of the conversation?' Hugo suggested humorously, 'and talk about the war.'

'I'm afraid I don't know anything about that either. You're going to find me very boring.'

'On the contrary, I find you quite intriguing. Mystery woman.'

Niobe ignored his slightly flirtatious remark.

'Why do you want to be where there's fighting?'

'Well, I am a photo journalist and if that's where the action is, that's where I want to be and I must admit that, yes, I do find it exciting. There is something about danger that is very intoxicating. I can't quite explain it but I feel drawn to it. I am having trouble with this situation, however, because all the papers and news stations are sending their own people and I am essentially freelance. But I think I have an assignment from an American TV station, nothing signed, can't pin the bastards down, but they're interested. I am going to have to make my own way as best I can, but I do have a contact with the British forces in Berlin and I think he can swing it for me.'

'Tell me where you've been,' Niobe said and, as course followed course, she found herself absorbed by the account of his adventures, which had started with the war between Iran and Iraq when he was only twenty.

'Then I went to cover the civil war in Lebanon, but it got too dangerous,' Hugo said.

By now they were on their second bottle of wine and were near the end of the feast with a variety of roast meats, kebabs, chops and meat balls.

'That was the time they were taking hostages, so I got out. My next was the first Gulf War war and I was with the troops when they decided to stop just before they got to Baghdad. What a mistake that was.' He looked up as the waiter hovered.

'I couldn't eat another thing.' Niobe patted her stomach. 'Full to burst.' She felt much more relaxed now. Relaxed and happy, very happy with this strange, attractive man opposite her.

'Just coffee,' Hugo said and nodded to the waiter, 'black, dark, Turkish.'

'White for me,' Niobe said, 'or I shan't sleep.'

'After that there were no more wars. I had a number of assignments, one of which was the American election in 2004 and that's where I met Alex and —' he stared at his watch — 'the rest is history.'

After they'd finished their coffees, he summoned the waiter.

'I think we should make tracks or neither of us will be

able to get up in the morning. Tell me, do you hope to sell a lot of pictures?'

Niobe shrugged. 'I have to, you see . . .' She paused but by now the wine had helped release her inhibitions. 'I owe Eleanor Ashton a lot of money. She lent me a thousand pounds, or else I would not have been able to exhibit. If I didn't take it then I felt I never would. It weighs on me how much I owe her and sometimes I wish I'd never asked her, but it was my great chance.' She looked at him eyes shining and there was something at once childish and pathetic about her, at odds with her veneer of sophistication. 'If I can't repay her I will be forever beholden to her, and I'd hate that.'

More than ever Hugo warmed towards her, and gave a low whistle as he helped her on with her coat.

'Oh, dear. Sounds bad.'

'Well, it's bad if I don't sell any pictures. So far I haven't sold any.'

'Not one?' Hugo stared at her in surprise.

'Not one,' Niobe replied and Hugo whistled again.

'That sounds really serious,' he said, but Niobe didn't answer.

They stood outside on the pavement, Niobe shivering from cold, or excitement, she wasn't sure which. She couldn't remember when she'd had a more heady or exciting evening, well, since Christmas when she had last met Hugo.

As if he could read her thoughts he gently brushed her arm with his hand.

'I really have enjoyed this evening,' he said, 'though I don't feel I know as much about you as I should. Maybe another time?'

'Maybe,' she said aware of a deep sense of regret that she didn't know when that would be. When they reached the door of the flat they saw Tony standing outside the cafe smoking a cigarette.

'Hey, Hugo!' he called out in surprise and held out his hand. 'I didn't know you were back.'

'Just briefly,' Hugo said and indicated his companion. 'Do you know Niobe? She's a friend of Alex's.'

'Sure, she ate here last night.'

Tony smiled at Niobe.

'It was Greek tonight,' Hugo said.

'Maybe breakfast?' Tony suggested.

'Maybe, but we both have to make an early start.'

They said goodnight and climbed to the top of the stairs switching on the lights as they went. Niobe took off her coat and turned to Hugo who was locking the door.

'Are you sure about the futon?'

'Of course I'm sure. It's too late to go anywhere now. I wouldn't turn you out. It would have to be me and frankly I ain't going nowhere.' He gave a big yawn.

'I'm only a bit sorry Tony saw us,' Niobe murmured feeling embarrassed.

'Oh, I don't care about Tony,' Hugo said robustly. 'Besides we've nothing to hide, have we?'

'Nothing at all, only I don't think it would be a good thing to tell Alex, or Francis, maybe. He is very jealous.' She looked appealingly up at Hugo. 'We don't want people to get the wrong idea, do we?'

The morning was a little busier than the one before and Niobe did sell one of her small watercolours for fifty pounds. She felt elated because it was the first painting she had ever sold, but fifty pounds would not inflict much of a dent in the money she owed Eleanor. Most people just came, looked around and shuffled out again, hoping she wouldn't see them. In such a small space it was hard not to.

She had not slept well, tossing and turning, too aware of the man in the next room. When she did finally get to sleep it was almost dawn and when she woke up he had gone. The futon had become a couch once again and the room was conspicuously tidy. A still warm mug on the kitchen sink indicated that he had not been gone long. She felt a pang. She knew it was irrational, but she would have liked to say goodbye, wished him well. She thought all morning about Hugo and what a difference knowing someone like him could have made to her life. For an intelligent, sophisticated, cosmopolitan man, one who had travelled all over the world, a war correspondent, he had been extremely nice to her, not patronizing in the least, seeming even to care.

Was it possible that he did care? He had paid her a lot of

attention at the Christmas party. There had been a hint of intimacy between them that she couldn't quite explain, enough to have made Francis very jealous. How furious he would be if he'd known about last night. She didn't think Alex would have been too amused, either.

She smiled to herself as she stood at the entrance to her booth, surveying the scene around her with an air of detachment and then suddenly she saw him, as though a dream had come true, looking around, peering first into one booth then another. She waved frantically in case he missed her and, seeing her, he quickened his step almost bumping into her as they came to a stop. For a moment they just looked into each other's eyes, their faces almost touching.

'I had to come and see your pictures,' he said prosaically stepping back and glancing at his watch in the manner of one who was pressed for time. 'I haven't very long. I've got a car waiting.'

'I don't know what to say,' Niobe said leading him in. 'It's *very* kind of you.'

She saw him looking quickly round. 'I'll have that one,' he said pointing to a large abstract gouache on the wall.

'Are you *sure*?' Niobe looked confused. 'Don't be silly. You don't have to.'

'I want it and I'm certain,' he said smiling and produced a cheque book from his breast pocket. 'How much is it?'

'Well, I wanted £300,' she said, 'but you can have it for . . .'

But he was already writing swiftly in his cheque book, tore out the cheque and handed it to her. Staring at it she saw it was made out for £1000.

'I can't *possibly* take this,' Niobe said, almost breathless with astonishment, trying to thrust it back to him.

'Take it,' he said with that disconcerting expression on his face as he looked into her eyes and his hand closed over hers holding the cheque. 'I want you to have it to repay Eleanor.'

'But *why*?'

'I just do, because I sense how worried you are about it. Look, I never particularly liked Eleanor because she doesn't particularly like me. I'm sorry about her accident and all that but to my mind she's an old bitch, always trying to separate me and Alex, and I'd hate to see you suffer on her account.'

Niobe tried to free her hand, but he clung on to it.

'I can't possibly take it,' she said. 'I can't *possibly*. I may sell enough paintings, anyway. I sold one this morning. Besides you don't want it. What will you do with it?'

'Hang it for me on the wall of the flat. I do want it and I do like it and, besides, I want you to pay Eleanor just in case you don't sell enough paintings, which I am sure you will. Then you'll have a bit left over. Buy something nice for the kids, Francis, anyone.'

'I will give it you back,' Niobe said firmly.

'No,' he insisted. 'It is not charity, nor a loan. It is payment for a beautiful painting. You don't charge enough. I shall enjoy looking at it when I get back. Honestly, Niobe, money means nothing to me. I have stacks of the stuff and who knows? Iraq is a very dangerous place . . .' His voice trailed off as he freed her hand, jerking back his sleeve to consult his watch again. 'Look, I must go. Take it. Enjoy it and seeing Eleanor's face when you pay her back and, by the way, I think you have great talent. I love the painting, I really do: worth every penny.' Then he gave her a quick peck on the cheek and swiftly retreated the way he had come.

She followed his progress until he was out of sight, her heart almost bursting with emotion.

Alex sat watching the rolling news on twenty-four-hour TV. She hardly missed a bulletin now that Hugo was there, some-where. He had arrived in Baghdad and he was safe, but communication was difficult and maybe he used it as an excuse to say very little except that he sounded excited, on a tremendous high. At last he was doing what he wanted to do, but she didn't know exactly what. She felt that he was keeping the truth from her, that his vagueness was delib-erate, but she had no proof. Whenever she tried to pin him down the line went dead and she was sure this was delib-erate not a fault on the mobile. But she couldn't be sure. She couldn't be sure of anything, except that a lot of nasty things were happening in Iraq: massacres, suicide bombers, atrocities inflicted not only on the occupiers but also against their own countrymen; people disappearing, bodies found in the streets, floating down rivers.

When she managed to wrench herself away from the TV screen, Alex occasionally would take a walk in the garden or down to the sea to try and free her mind momentarily of the awful sense of dread that seemed perpetually to be gnawing at her heart. One day on her way back, she passed the farm and observed clothes blowing on the line. Impulsively she went up the path and knocked on the door. Once again there was no reply so she went round the back and saw that the door of Niobe's studio was wide open. She approached quietly and stood outside hesitantly, peering in where she could see Niobe stacking canvases against the wall.

'Oh, you're back,' she called, whereupon Niobe turned with a startled almost frightened expression on her face.

'Oh, Alex,' she said nervously brushing hair out of her eyes. 'Yes, back a few days. I meant to come over, but I've been so busy.' She made an awkward gesture as though she was trying to stand in front of the wall in an attempt to hide the canvases from Alex's eyes, a futile gesture but one not lost on Alex. 'Just trying to sort everything out. Masses of washing to do, of course.'

'So I see,' Alex said amiably. 'Cathy not doing her stuff?'

'Oh, Cathy was brilliant. She had the children with her, but Francis,' Niobe said and pulled a face, 'is incapable of looking after himself. There's all my stuff to wash from London. I never had a moment to spare.' Niobe moved towards the door and, without inviting Alex in, pushed it firmly shut behind her. 'Come and have a coffee; just a quickie. I have to pick the kids up from school.'

Alex shook her head. 'No, I should get back. I am worried about Hugo and I don't want to miss any calls.' She put a hand in her pocket, 'I have my mobile but the reception is bad.'

'He arrived then?' Niobe said offhandedly.

Alex thought it was strange question. 'Oh yes he arrived in Baghdad, but I don't know what he's doing.'

'Very worrying for you,' Niobe said sympathetically, pushing open the kitchen door. 'But I'm sure he'll be OK. He seems the type to look after himself.' Then she went over to her handbag on the kitchen table and taking a cheque book from it, opened it and started writing.

'If you're going home, maybe you'd do me a favour. I have a cheque to give your mother.' Niobe finished writing, tore the cheque out of the book and held it out, her face wreathed in smiles.

Alex studied it, trying heard to conceal her surprise.

'Oh, but that's wonderful. Mum will be pleased, but, more importantly, it means you must have sold a lot.'

'Enough.' Niobe sounded cautious, but she had been rehearsing for some days how to explain that she was able to refund the loan while selling practically nothing. She had decided that the less said the better. 'I was going to come over this afternoon, but maybe you can take it for me and I'll call in later.' She glanced at the clock on the kitchen table. 'Golly, I didn't realize the time. I have to pick up the kids. How is your mum?'

'She's great. Worried about Iraq, like me.'

Niobe nodded not wanting to seem too interested, not wishing to give away the fact that she too was concerned about Hugo and what happened to him. For, after all, why should she be in Alex's eyes?

'Tell your mum how grateful I am for the loan. And, Alex, thank you *so* much for the loan of the flat as well. It was marvellous. Really kind of you.'

'Oh, I'm so glad everything went well.'

'Couldn't have been better. I'll tell you all about it. Now, I must fly.' She picked up her car keys from the kitchen table and, shepherding Alex firmly in front of her, moved towards the outside door.

Eleanor sat in her comfortable chair in the sitting room, but it was now turned to the TV rather than the window, though the sound was down. She knew how upset and worried Alex was about Hugo and she had urged her to take a walk. She tried to keep her as busy as she could but it wasn't easy. Alex seldom brooded and when she did it meant she was unhappy. Alex by nature was an extrovert rather than an introvert, which was why the active life appealed to her and why she would be attracted to a man like Hugo. However,

Alex was also impulsive and temperamental, so she did have mood swings and when she was down she was very down indeed. Her mother thought how Alex had changed in the short time they'd been together, an Alex she hardly knew: caring, concerned, thoughtful. It was the accident that had caused this change. She knew how much she loved Alex, but maybe Alex had not known how much she loved her mother.

Eleanor's hand rested gently on Melody who was snoozing on her lap, her fingers softly caressing the cat's back. She leaned back against the chair and emitted a deep sigh, part contentment, part, well, a bit worried like Alex. Events in Iraq were deeply disturbing and in common with a large part of the British population she had been against the war and the occupation of a foreign country. If she'd lived in London, or even if she'd been well enough to travel, she would have been up there demonstrating.

She thought how dramatically her accident had altered her view of life, given a completely different meaning to it. Her life span was now divided into pre- and post-accident. In no way was she the same person as before. It was rather like a rebirth, though not in a religious sense.

She had had her rest, but she was still a little drowsy and felt herself nodding off again when she heard the sound of the front door closing and was jerked awake. She looked up as Alex came into the room.

'Were you nodding off, Mum?' Alex asked gently. 'Did I wake you?'

'Not really,' Eleanor said defensively, 'just feeling relaxed.'

Melody raised her head, glanced at Alex with a slightly cross expression and settled her head firmly between her paws again as though indicating her displeasure.

'Sorry, I mustn't disturb Melody,' Alex said contritely.

'Did you have a good walk?'

'Lovely. The sea looked so inviting. Could have jumped in.'

'I wish I could walk to the sea.' Eleanor's expression was nostalgic as though for a vanished dream.

'Well, Mum you *can.*'

Eleanor shook her head. 'Impossible, it's too far.'

'Mum, we could try and if you can't make it, I promise I'll come back and get the car.'

Eleanor smiled wanly. 'We'll see.'

'I popped in to see Niobe and she gave this to me.' With a dramatic gesture Alex handed her a piece of paper.

Eleanor studied the cheque with a bemused expression. 'Well,' she said after a pause, 'I never expected to see this again. Not quite so soon, anyway.' She glanced up at her daughter. 'What a pleasant surprise. Did she sell a lot of pictures?'

'Must have.' Alex's expression was thoughtful. 'Though I must say there were an awful lot of pictures left.'

'I thought you said she wasn't much good?' Eleanor said.

'It was only my opinion. Obviously other people thought differently.'

'Well, I'm very glad for her.' Eleanor tucked the cheque into her pocket. 'And for me. I must say I had misgivings, but for once I did the right thing and this is my reward.'

Alex went over to the television and, staring at the screen, turned up the sound. There was nothing about Iraq so she switched off the TV and went and sat next to her mother.

'There's something rather odd about Niobe's behaviour,' she said shaking her head. 'I can't quite put my finger on it.' She gazed at her mother. 'She's kind of evasive. I don't quite know how to explain it, but when I went into her studio she seemed alarmed rather than pleased to see me and, although it was quite ridiculous because the area was so large, it was as though she was trying to hide from me all the pictures she had stacked at the back by standing in front of them. Then she got me out of the studio as quickly as she could. Said very little about the exhibition. Practically nothing. Didn't want to chat.'

'Maybe she felt awkward about the money.'

'Why should she if she was about to repay it? And why did she take so long? She has been back a few days apparently.'

Eleanor nodded. 'Cathy said last week. I forgot to tell you.' She indicated the TV screen as if to explain why. 'At least did she thank you for the use of the flat?'

'Oh, yes, she was very grateful, no doubt about that.'

'I think we're making a mystery out of nothing,' Eleanor said gently, easing Melody off her lap, who jumped off with an indignant squawk. 'Shall we start thinking about some supper?'

Niobe lay right on the edge of the bed, so far away from Francis that it seemed as though any minute she might fall off. She knew he was awake even though he'd been so tired when he'd got home after working late. He did work hard, but she felt no pity for him. He'd slumped on the bed and turned his back to her pretending to sleep, but she knew he wasn't because of his pattern of breathing. She felt quite out of tune with Francis, especially after meeting someone like Hugo. What a different kind of life that had offered, just a glimpse of what might have been, possibly could be if she took the plunge and moved away. Since she'd been home the atmosphere between them had been terrible. Sometimes she just wanted to pack up all her things and leave. Leave the children, too? That was the rub. That was the part she couldn't face.

With a grunt, Francis suddenly turned and lay on his back as if talking to the ceiling and what he said startled her. 'Why didn't you tell me you paid Eleanor back?'

'Why should I have? I didn't think of it, to be truthful.' In fact she wasn't being truthful at all. Then: 'How did you know?'

'Eleanor told Mum. Made me feel a fool.'

'I would have told you, sometime. It was no secret.'

'But you told me you didn't sell many pictures. Besides, I know you didn't. You brought back almost as many as you took. Surely if you had sold enough to pay her back you would have been hopping about, but you were very quiet. You would have been happy and would have told me?'

'Not necessarily.' She turned to him. 'Look, Francis, what is this all about?'

'I want to know what happened in London.'

'What do you mean, what happened in London?'

'Something happened. I can feel it.'

'Well, you're wrong. Nothing "happened" except the exhibition. I don't know what you're getting so uptight and suspicious about.'

'Then how did you get the money?'

'I tell you I earned it. One picture I sold for quite a lot. Someone paid much more for it than I expected.'

'Why?'

'I can't tell you. I mean, I don't know why. I think he liked it so much.'

'He?'

'Yes, he.'

'Who was "he"?'

'I have no idea. He went away, abroad, he said.'

Francis's tone was incredulous. 'Someone you didn't know paid more for a picture than you asked and then just went away?'

'Yes.'

'I don't believe you.'

'You can believe what you like. I don't care. You have a nasty jealous nature, Francis, and I'm sick of it.'

There was a heavy silence as though he were weighing his options.

'Anyway, you're not going again. I won't let you,' he said at last.

'What do you mean, you won't *let* me?' she asked furiously.

'I won't, that's all. And I mean it. People are beginning to talk about you, Niobe.'

'Oh, are they?'

'Yes, they are.'

'And I suppose you defend me?'

Francis was silent.

'I suppose you defend me, don't you, Francis?' she repeated more loudly.

Again there was silence.

She hauled herself up, sat on the edge of the bed and studied the floor, her head clasped between her hands. Moonlight shone through the uncurtained window and made an uneven pattern on the floor. She didn't know what time it was; past midnight, long past midnight. She was terribly tired.

'I'm going to leave you, Francis,' she heard herself saying.

'Oh, no you're not,' he said also rising and seizing her by the waist he drew her roughly back to the centre of the bed again. After a struggle she lay still, panting, looking up at his angry face glaring down at her. Momentarily she wondered if he was going to kill her. You heard that sometimes men were driven to do things you would never ever believe them capable of. Kill her or make love to her? And love in these circumstances would be rape, a kind of death against which she felt defenceless.

However, he did neither but, after a few seconds in which his whole body quivered with tension, he relaxed his grip and lay down again. Then he turned over and burying his face in the pillow began sobbing loudly.

Eight

Did the sea look particularly beautiful, or was it just because it had been such an effort to get her here? No car, just walking as Alex had wanted her to do. It had been difficult to get her going, such an amount of persuasion that Alex had almost despaired, promising to get the car if her mother faltered, and now promising to get the car if necessary to drive her back. Eleanor had assured her that it would be necessary. One way would be quite enough.

It was sunny and quite warm, the early spring sea was calm and there were quite a few people on the beach. Eleanor and Alex were sitting on the sea wall watching all the activity around them: children playing, being reprimanded by anxious parents for going too near the water and being dragged back; dogs chasing energetically after pebbles thrown in the sea or balls hurled in the air or along the shore; people putting up tents to shelter from the sea breeze. At sea, a motor boat whizzed past and even further out a shipping vessel could be seen on the horizon. There were the usual optimistic few tapping the cliff face for fossils, seldom found, and several fishermen, again optimistic, lines stretching out far into the water.

It was a happy, normal, joyful scene and Eleanor felt her heart lift once again at the thought that she had been spared to see it. Alex was largely silent as if sharing her mother's pleasure, and then almost by mutual accord they rose and began making their way slowly up to the pub and into the bar where they were greeted by Martin, who came round from behind the counter to kiss Eleanor warmly on the cheek.

'It is so good to see you again,' he said. 'You look better than when I last saw you.'

'I am, much,' Eleanor replied. 'And this is my first walk to the sea.'

'How did it go?'

'Very well. With Alex holding on to me, of course.'

'Mum said she couldn't do it,' Alex said, 'but I knew she could.'

'Just a matter of willpower.' Eleanor sank down in a seat near the window.

'Of which you have plenty. Have a drink on me,' Martin said going back behind the bar, 'both of you.'

'White wine would be lovely. Small glass,' Eleanor added.

'Same for me.' Alex removed her coat and sat down next to her mother.

It was just past noon and only a few people were in the pub, but they decided to order lunch. Martin brought their drinks, took their orders for soup and sandwiches and then indicated a man sitting in a corner who had been looking at them intently.

'There is someone over there who wants to say hello to you, Eleanor.'

'Oh?' Eleanor looked up as a man rather hesitantly rose from his seat and ambled over to them. He bent down and shook her hand. 'My name is Henry Bankhurst,' he said. 'You don't know me, but I know you.'

'Really?' Eleanor found the way he stared at her disconcerting.

'I was in the car behind you when you had your crash. I never thought I'd see you again,' Mr Bankhurst said and his eyes moistened behind his spectacles. 'It was a terrible scene. I don't know how you survived.'

Impulsively Eleanor reached for his hand and pressed it. 'It must have been,' she said gently. 'I am so sorry.'

Alex moved up so that Henry could sit next to her mother. He was of indeterminate age, fifties maybe or early sixties and dressed for walking. He'd been having a beer when they came in. She wasn't sure that this encounter was altogether a good thing, or how it might affect her mother.

'Martin says you have made a marvellous recovery,' Henry said still clasping her hand.

'I have, except my sight isn't great, nor my hearing, but the improvement continues.'

'I saw you lying in the road and then the helicopter arrived, very quickly. The paramedic saved your life.'

'So I believe,' Eleanor said and began to feel emotional, too. She remembered asking if she was dying and the firm strong voice that reassured her that she was not, probably with more hope than conviction at that time.

She and Henry remained staring at each other as if mentally reliving the scene until he shook himself and got up.

'I must get on. The weather looks as though it might break and I'm walking to West Bay.' Once again he shook Eleanor's hand. 'I do wish you continued recovery, Mrs Ashton.'

'And I hope I see you again,' Eleanor said. 'You must let me buy you a beer.'

Henry smiled, went over to where he had been sitting, finished his drink, still standing, put on his cap, took his stick and his backpack and waving to her left.

'What an odd encounter,' Alex said as the door closed behind him. 'Did it upset you, Mum?'

'It brought things back, but not really. It must have been terrible for him.'

'I thought he was quite nice. Perhaps he fancies you, Mum.' Alex glanced at her slyly.

'Don't be silly,' Eleanor said robustly. 'Who would fancy me, looking as I do?'

'Well, you never know your luck.'

As they ate Eleanor kept glancing through the window endlessly fascinated by the wonderful view of sparkling sea and undulating hills. Maybe the encounter with Henry Bankhurst had reawakened the sense she had that she was indeed fortunate to be sitting in this place with her daughter by her side.

'Do you know,' Eleanor said looking at Alex 'I really do think I could manage to walk home after all'

Eleanor lay in bed in the early hours of the morning, a time that suited her, a time that she loved, always had, but perhaps it was best in the country. It seemed that everyone and everything was still asleep except the birds: the call of the blackbird and chaffinch in spring and early summer, the year round cries of the gulls as they swooped low over the hills towards the sea. She thought maybe that it was this that had awoken her and through her window she could see them perched on the roof of Niobe's farmhouse, heads bent as they inspected the yard below for any pickings.

Beside her Melody stretched out her paws and yawned looking back over her shoulder to Eleanor whose hand rested on her back. In the old days, the pre-accident days, she and Melody used to go down the stairs in the morning – Melody scampering ahead of her – and into the garden where together they made a leisurely inspection of what slight changes may have taken place overnight. Or maybe it was just enough to breathe in the fresh morning air and see the sun breaking over the hills to the east.

But now there was no scampering down the stairs. She didn't even go down until after she was bathed and dressed. Alex brought her breakfast, usually after her bath. What a luxury it had been to be able to ease herself gently down into a bath once more instead of relying on the shower. Yes, gradually things had improved, gradually but not fast enough. She was more aware now than she had ever been of the changes that had taken place inside her body, if not her mind, and that she was not the vigorous, energetic woman she had been. Melody knew that the routine of going down the stairs into the garden was over and usually curled up again and went back to sleep, or sometimes she disappeared downstairs maybe to have her breakfast and a little inspection of the garden all on her own.

Eleanor got gingerly out of bed and crossed the floor to the en suite where she filled the kettle to make her morning tea. Even being able to do this had been a luxury, and after the brief ritual performed on the table by her bed she got back into bed again and flicked on the TV for the news. One always hoped for some breakthrough, but the downside was that even if the situation in Iraq did improve Alex might be leaving her either to join Hugo – that still seemed unlikely – or to be with him when he came home. With an acute anticipatory sense of loss Eleanor realized how much she had come to rely on her and how terribly she would miss her. She had not many things to thank her accident for, but this closeness to her daughter was undoubtedly one of them. Maybe they had been thrown together by mutual need and it would all disappear, for Eleanor at least, as though in a puff of smoke when Alex and Hugo were together again, restlessly roaming over the face of the earth in search of adventure. How Eleanor hoped Alex would settle down, but with someone like Hugo it seemed remote.

She heard the sound of the telephone, dimly, so she knew it must be Alex's mobile. It rang for some time before it was answered. Alex would have been roused from deep slumber. She always went to bed long after her mother and was a late riser in the morning. Eleanor had a sudden sense of apprehension and realized how often in her life it happened that, just as she thought things were going well, misfortune struck, like the time she was beginning to enjoy her new life in Dorset and she'd met Mr Jones head on up a hill not too far from her home.

But why should she feel apprehensive now? There was no reason. As usual her pessimism was illogical. If Hugo was calling it was good. It didn't necessarily mean that Alex was about to leave or that something terrible had happened.

At that moment her door was flung open and the object of her thoughts appeared dramatically in the doorway, still in her nightie, tangled hair almost obscuring her face.

'Mum! He's back! He's here!' She flung herself across her mother's bed and hugged her, causing Melody to leap off the bed with an indignant squawk and dive underneath.

'Sorry, Melody,' Alex said contritely. 'Mum, *Hugo* is back in London.'

'Why, that's wonderful.'

'Oh, it is and I'm going up straightaway.' She looked back and gazed at her mother. 'Mum, you don't mind, do you?'

'Of course I don't mind.' Eleanor leaned forward and drew her close. 'I'm very happy for you, sweetheart. I really am.'

'You don't know what it means to me to know that he's safe.'

'Of course I do,' Eleanor said hugging her fiercely, wondering how long it would be before she was able to do this again.

Alex left soon after breakfast, throwing a few things into her car because she didn't expect to be gone long, having no idea of Hugo's movements. There was time to telephone Cathy and tell her about the change of plan, in exchange for which she got a few non-committal grunts at the other end.

'Didn't seem too pleased,' Alex had murmured when she put down the phone.

Eleanor sighed. 'Well, there has been this sort of strangeness between us ever since the exhibition. She didn't like my lending Niobe the money.'

During the time Alex had been here Cathy had come in only once or twice a week to clean, had done her work and left. There definitely had been an atmosphere, which pained Eleanor who so much valued Cathy as a friend as well as a helpmeet.

'Well, she has paid you back, so that is all done and dusted.' Alex had finished stuffing her things in her bag. 'I'm sure she won't let you down, Mum, and if she does I bet there are plenty of other people.'

Eleanor didn't feel so confident and watched with a heavy heart through the sitting-room window as her daughter drove off. 'Do be careful,' she had cried, but Alex hadn't heard her. Car crashes, accidents of any kind, disappearances, anything could happen in the list of possible disasters that always lurked somewhere in the recesses of Eleanor's mind. She realized how much she had come to depend on her and after she'd left she mooched about the house like a hen looking for its chick. She went disconsolately into Alex's bedroom and then quickly shut the door because it was so untidy.

Well, just supposing Cathy didn't come? She suddenly felt rather lost and afraid. This was the new post-accident Eleanor and she didn't like her. She had always been the capable one, but now she seemed unable to face the prospect of being alone, of looking after herself. She thought of Niobe across the road. She had hardly seen her since the exhibition and not for the first time realized what a lot of harm had been done by lending her that money and wished she hadn't.

Eleanor wandered out into the garden and was joined by Melody who was soon interested in the discernible passage of a mole under the flower bed and gazed at it intently, occasionally sticking out a paw as though to halt it in its tracks.

The garden looked neglected. She'd have to get someone in. She had scarcely been there long enough to get anything established, though it had been quite a mature garden when she bought the house due to the enthusiasm of the previous owner. She stooped with difficulty to pick up a few weeds, still needing to use her stick to get about, even in the garden. Momentarily, she felt close to tears, immediately hating herself for it. She must not give in to self pity and she sank down on the garden bench determined to divert herself by the joy of watching the birds attack the bird feeder, queuing up on the fence for their turn and Melody's hopeless and hapless pursuit of the tunnelling mole.

She heard the door close in the house and looked back, suddenly filled with a wild and irrational hope that somehow it would be Alex having changed her mind and decided to return. Instead she saw Cathy standing in the doorway, looking uncertain as to whether to proceed or go back into the house.

Eleanor beckoned to her. 'Hi, Cathy! Come and sit down. It's not too warm but just about bearable. I was feeling a bit sorry for myself.'

Cathy came across the lawn and perched on the bench next to Eleanor, seeming ill at ease. 'Yes, I thought you might be. You'll miss Alex. Have you had coffee? Shall I get it?'

'That would be lovely,' Eleanor lightly placed a hand on her arm and looked at her intently. 'Are you OK?'

'Yes, I'm all right,' Cathy said, but somehow she didn't sound all right. Then she got up, saying, 'I'll go and get the coffee.'

'Let's have it inside,' Eleanor said rubbing her arms. 'It's really quite chilly.'

She followed Cathy into the house, shutting the garden door behind her. She hovered in the kitchen as Cathy put on the kettle and spooned coffee into the cups, still not speaking. That feeling of apprehension Eleanor had had since early morning deepened, and she went slowly across the hall into the sitting room, taking up her usual seat by the French window overlooking the garden. They had been right to come in as the sun was now obscured by clouds.

She cleared a space on the coffee table for the cups. Cathy put down the tray and sat opposite her.

'It's a long time since we've done this,' Eleanor said sipping her coffee. She paused still disconcerted by Cathy's attitude and decided to take the plunge. 'I hope you're not going to tell me you're leaving me?'

Cathy immediately registered shocked surprise. 'Oh, no, Eleanor. Why should I do that?'

'There's been an atmosphere. I know it hasn't been easy, I thought it might be something to do with my lending Niobe money and I'm often sorry I did it.'

'She would have gone anyway.' Cathy carefully put down her empty cup. 'She'd have found a way She's a crafty so and so.'

'You really are off her, aren't you, Cathy?' Eleanor, too, finished her coffee and replaced her cup.

Cathy sat back, arms folded across her breast. 'I've got to tell you this, Eleanor, and it is difficult, but I saw a cheque in Niobe's handbag for a thousand pounds. It was not signed by you, Eleanor, but by Hugo Sandeman and the date was around the time Niobe was in London.'

'Hugo?' Eleanor gasped, not quite understanding. 'Did you say, *Hugo*?'

'I said, Hugo.' Cathy nodded. 'I was not snooping and it was the last thing I expected, I assure you, but I was looking in Niobe's handbag for the keys to her house. I had the children and she'd just taken her purse and gone to the village. That was very soon after she came back from London.' She looked fixedly at Eleanor. 'I know she paid you back the money she borrowed. I wondered how and now I know. She told Francis it was for selling pictures, but he knew she'd hardly sold any.'

'Have you told Francis this?'

'I certainly have not. That poor man has been through enough misery on account of Niobe without knowing she'd been unfaithful to him.'

'Unfaithful!' Eleanor exclaimed. 'How on *earth* can you say that?'

'Well, what else can I think? She stays at your daughter's flat and comes back with a cheque for a large sum of money from your daughter's boyfriend.'

'But Hugo has been in Iraq and has only just got back. As far as I know he was thousands of miles away when Niobe was in London.'

'Ah, but was he?'

'Yes,' Eleanor looked at her defiantly. 'Of course he was.'

'Then the whole thing is very funny, isn't it?'

'Very,' Eleanor replied. 'In fact it is extraordinary.' She stared hard at Cathy. 'I suppose you're sure? I mean, there is no question of any mistake?'

'None at all,' Cathy confirmed and shook her head. 'It was a funny bank. Not one of the usual ones. Is it Cutts?' She put her head on one side.

'Coutts,' Eleanor corrected her. 'That is Hugo's bank.' Then, after a pause: 'I suppose he couldn't have sent it to her?' She realized she was clutching at straws.

'As far as I know he hardly *knew* Niobe, did he? They only met here at Christmas and that was before she had this crazy notion of an exhibition.'

'She asked me soon afterwards. Her entry was late.'

'Believe me, Eleanor,' Cathy said earnestly, 'I don't put any blame on you for all this. But the whole business has had a very unfortunate effect on my family, and I feel my son and grandchildren will suffer for it. Also, Alex has been deceived as she obviously knows nothing about all this. I feel very sorry for her indeed.'

'Well, she certainly doesn't know the cheque came from Hugo. She can't. How could she?'

Cathy shook her head. 'Don't ask me.'

'So what are we to do?' Eleanor attempted to sound practical. 'There must be some explanation.'

'I don't think there's anything we can do until the truth comes out and, believe me,' Cathy said ominously, rising and gathering up the cups, 'one day, it will.'

Alex's hands were shaking as she put the key in the door only to realize it was open and Hugo must be there. She paused for breath before climbing the stairs and then again before entering the sitting room. It was ridiculous to be so nervous. Yet she was. It seemed like a lifetime since they were last together. So much had happened and war was a momentous thing. It was as if a chasm had opened between them, which they had somehow to cross. They had never been separated for so long since they had been a couple. She opened the sitting-room door and at first didn't realize what was different until her eyes became fixated by the large painting on the opposite wall, which dominated the room. Strangely familiar. And then she saw Hugo standing in the doorway of the bedroom, drink in one hand, cigarette in the other. Familiar, darling, Hugo.

'*Darling!*' he cried and came towards her, locking his arms around her, still with his hands full.

She leaned her head on his shoulders and gazed at his face. He looked very tired, almost ashen. She raised her hand and tenderly stroked his brow.

'Was it awful?' she asked finally breaking away and taking the glass from his hand, while he put the cigarette in his mouth with the other.

'Interesting,' he replied as he leaned towards the table and stubbed out the cigarette. 'Very interesting.' He took her hand and pulled her down on to the futon beside him, then embraced her for a long time.

'I missed you so much,' she said close to tears. 'I was so afraid.'

'Piece of cake,' he said. 'I fell in with the Coalition forces and that gives you some protection. There is a heavily fortified green zone. But living outside it is tough and that's where the danger is. I got some very good footage and I've come home to try and flog it.'

'For the Americans?' Alex looked at him, hopefully. Hugo shook his head.

'In the end they didn't bite, the bastards. Weeks wasted schlepping around. But ITV might take what I've got. It could lead to a documentary and a commission.'

'So how long have you got here?'

Hugo shrugged. 'Let's talk about it later.' He rose and took her by the hand, pulling her up.

But Alex was looking at the painting and Hugo noticed the direction of her gaze.

'Not really my taste,' he said offhandedly.

'It's by Niobe,' Alex said. 'You remember her? She had an exhibition in London and stayed here for a few days. She

must have left it as a thank-you present.' She turned towards
him. 'Nice of her to think of it, but if you don't like it we
can hide it.'

Nothing more was said about the picture and they went
to bed where they alternately slept and made love until
nightfall.

'What time is it? Hugo asked drowsily squinting at the clock
by the side of the bed.

'Time to eat,' Alex turned on her back stretching luxuri-
ously. 'I'm very hungry.'

Hugo sat up and lit a cigarette. 'Would you like Greek?'
'Why not?'

There was something wonderful about walking through
the streets of Camden Town, arms entwined, to be together
again, very special. They were greeted at the Greek restaurant by Pavlos the proprietor who insisted on buying them a
drink and hovered while they ordered.

As they studied the menu, Hugo was rather uncomfortably
reminded of the last time he had been there and the vision
of the painting on the wall flashed through his mind with all
its unanswered questions. He should have removed it, but
where to put it was another matter. It was so large. He had
a sudden impulse to tell Alex all about it; clear the air, but
then decided not to. The atmosphere between them was so
close and tender he didn't want to risk disturbing it with a
silly row. He knew that Niobe would never have mentioned
it. She had been right in thinking Alex might not understand.

There was an intimacy about the restaurant that perfectly
suited their mood and Alex, for her part, had never felt closer
to Hugo or more in love.

'When will you go back?' she asked.

'I can't say at the moment. It depends on whether I can
unload my stuff. There is an awful lot to be decided and I
don't think the Coalition forces or their commanders realized the magnitude of their task. I think it is a hopeless cause.
The Coalition countries want their forces home. Too many
lives have been lost. You are not just going to have a demo-
cratic state where previously you had a brutal dictatorship.
Also the tensions between Sunni and Shia are considerable

and Saddam was able to keep this under control. But, yes, I will go back eventually.'

'And can I come with you?'

'Maybe,' he held out a hand for hers. 'But not until it is safe. Tell me, how's your mum?'

Walking back through the dark streets illuminated by the lights of the shops and the noise of busy traffic it was very London and Alex realized how much she loved it and she felt at home here. They held each other very tightly, saying little, Hugo softly humming a tune.

Again there was the thought of the night ahead, which they would spend together after so long apart, making love, enjoying all the things they shared in common.

When they reached the door of the flat Tony was standing outside his cafe smoking a cigarette. He looked pleased to see them and discarding his cigarette on the pavement extended a hand.

'Hey, you're back,' he exclaimed. 'How was Iraq?'

'Pretty busy,' Hugo said putting his key in the door.

'Come and have a drink,' Tony urged, standing back from them.

'No, really, we're very tired,' Hugo said. 'Perhaps breakfast.'

'And your friend?' His remarks were still addressed to Hugo. 'Was she happy with her exhibition?'

'I think so,' Hugo mumbled as the relaxed, happy expression on Alex's face changed to one of bewilderment.

'It was certainly a very big picture.' Tony smiled at Alex. 'Do you like it? She's your friend, too, isn't she? A very nice lady.'

'I'm not sure,' Alex said confused, and hurried up the stairs ahead of Hugo who, with a shrug at Tony, slowly followed her. It was now Tony's turn to look bewildered and he turned back into his cafe shaking his head.

Alex was standing gazing at the picture as he finished locking up and putting on the lights.

'So, she's your friend, too, is she? I don't understand this at all.' Alex turned round and looked at him. 'Do you mean that *you* and *Niobe* were here together? How and when? Or is it silly of me to ask?'

Hugo lit a cigarette and went over to the drinks table.

'Don't you think you've had enough?' Alex said.

'Please don't start this again,' he said wearily, half filling a glass with whisky. He held the bottle towards Alex but she shook her head. 'If I want to drink, I'll drink,' he said and put the glass to his mouth. 'Yes, I was here at the same time as Niobe. I had no idea she was here of course . . .'

'But *when*?' Alex distractedly ran her hands through her hair. 'That's what I just don't understand. You were in *London* and you didn't tell me?'

'I didn't tell you because it was for a very short time and I thought you'd rush up and try and stop me going. It was just a stopover and I stayed here one night on my way from New York to Berlin.'

'With Niobe.'

'No, not *with* Niobe,' Hugo said irritably. 'Well, yes, she was here, but that was all. She slept in the bed, I slept on the futon and the next morning I left early.'

'Yet Tony saw you together. Did you go out?'

'Well, yes, it seemed a civilized thing to do. I took her to the Greek. Tony saw us on the way back.'

'How very civilized,' Alex said bitterly. 'A wonder Pavlos didn't mention it tonight. You were lucky. Pity Tony caught you out.'

'Alex, don't be petty and jealous,' Hugo said crossly. 'I did not sleep with Niobe, if that's what you think. I didn't want to. It never crossed my mind. I'm sure it didn't cross hers. We're not rabbits, you know. I took her out to dinner because as I said it seemed a civilized thing to do. She was here alone. She is, after all, your family's friend. It didn't mean we had to have an affair for Christ's sake! We talked mostly about Iraq and she told me a bit about her life and that was that. There was nothing more to it than that.'

'What I really mind,' Alex said, aware she was over-reacting, 'is the secrecy. Or am I imagining it all? You never once indicated you'd stopped over in London until it was dragged out of you and that by chance. Why didn't she mention you were here? That she'd met you, you'd had dinner together? I've seen her since she came home. She never said a thing.'

'I have no idea.' Hugo shook his head wearily. 'No idea at all. I'm sure I'd have got round to telling you sooner or later, simply because there is nothing to hide. Would I have carried on if you'd gone out to dinner with a friend? No, I would not. Niobe on closer acquaintance struck me as a very strange woman, unhappy with her partner and wanting to achieve something in life. To tell you the truth I felt sorry for her. Well, we all know that feeling, don't we? But for you to do the jealous woman act is unworthy of you.'

'Niobe is a schemer,' Alex said pursing her mouth. 'Maybe I will have that drink after all.'

Eleanor thoughtfully put down the phone and sat back in her chair. Alex didn't sound happy at all, not the kind of rapture she would have expected after the reunion with Hugo. But Hugo was a difficult man and, well, Alex wasn't easy. They would always have a difficult relationship and she often wondered if Alex would ever settle down with anyone. Instinctively she seemed to have an unrelenting wanderlust too. Eleanor also wondered if Alex had found out about the cheque Hugo had given Niobe. If she had, this would explain her attitude on the phone, brief, to the point. She told her mother she did not know when Hugo was going back and would probably stay in London until he did. It was even possible she might go with him, an idea that made Eleanor's heart contract.

Several times she had been tempted to talk to Niobe, but she was not meant to know about Hugo's cheque and she didn't want to strain any further her relationship with Cathy, for to confront Niobe would be to betray a confidence.

She picked up her headphones and was about to put them on and continue with her talking book when she heard the doorbell ring. Cathy had left so she got up and went to answer it.

At first she couldn't put a name to the man's face that greeted her with a half-smile on his lips, even though it was familiar.

'Mike,' he said quietly, stepping forward and putting a very large bunch of flowers in her hand. 'Remember me?'

'Mike,' she repeated as she took the flowers, confused,

wishing she'd done her hair, put on make-up, all the silly things that might pass through the mind of a woman when confronting a former lover. 'Mike Cathcart.'

'The very same,' he said uneasily. 'May I come in?'

As Eleanor ushered him in he kissed her very gently on the cheek. It was nevertheless an intimate, familiar gesture she rather resented and she stepped away from him. Sensing her disapproval he said quickly, 'I should have telephoned, but I thought you might not want to see me, so I took the risk of being flung out.'

'Of course I wouldn't fling you out,' Eleanor said with a rather forced smile and firmly shut the door. 'What a suggestion!'

'I thought you might let me take you out to lunch.' He looked hard at her. 'That is if you're fit enough. How *are* you, Eleanor?'

'As you see me,' she said nervously touching her hair. 'Had I known you were coming I might have done something to my face, my hair.' She laughed awkwardly. The situation seemed to her bizarre; it was so many years since she'd seen Mike. 'How on earth did you know where to find me?'

'I'd heard you'd left the magazine and I got in touch with Marge and she gave me your address. You remember Marge?'

'Of course I remember Marge.' It was in Marge's flat that they'd mostly conducted their affair, which was now all of ten years ago.

He had changed, but not much. His hair was a bit grey, he had put on weight but he looked well and in control, which was more than she felt at the moment.

She took the flowers into the kitchen and he followed her.

'They're wonderful,' she said smelling them, unseasonal and must have cost a fortune. 'Are you passing or . . .'

'Well, I had business in Bristol and I thought . . . I'd heard you'd divorced and moved to the West Country, but didn't know about your accident until Marge told me. I was very shocked. She said you were nearly killed.'

'True.' Eleanor nodded and stacked the flowers into a large vase. 'I'll arrange them properly later,' she said. 'Come and sit down.'

'It's a nice house,' Mike said as he followed her into the

sitting room and took up a position by the window, hands in his pockets. Then he turned to face her. 'Look, Eleanor, I hope you don't mind my walking in on you like this. It was a bit tactless and I may have done the wrong thing, but I did genuinely want to see how you were, especially when Marge told me about your accident. After all, we did once upon a time mean quite a lot to each other.'

'A lot of things have happened in ten years, Mike,' she said smiling ruefully. 'Are you still married?'

'Just,' he said. 'You know I married again?'

'Yes, I did hear that.'

'I think if I'd known you and Dick were going to divorce things might have been different, Eleanor. I thought you two were somehow a fixture.'

'So did I.' Eleanor studied his face for a moment. 'Look, Mike, things have moved on. We have moved on. I am very pleased to see you, but I don't necessarily think we want to go over the past, do we?'

'Let's go and have lunch.' Mike looked at his watch. 'Actually, I don't have all that much time. I'm sure you know somewhere nice we can eat.'

As she quickly changed, did her hair, make-up, Eleanor wondered if she had really wanted to see Mike with all the memories of their affair it would inevitably bring back. He didn't look very different, but she certainly did. She knew she looked gaunt, she walked badly and her eyes didn't quite focus. Even if she didn't fancy her former lover, she didn't want his pity or much value his curiosity. It would have been better had Mike stayed away. He was still standing by the French windows when she returned to the sitting room looking into the garden.

'You always liked a garden,' he said turning towards her. 'My, Eleanor, you do look good. You really haven't changed much.'

'Don't be ridiculous,' she said sharply. 'I don't need to be flattered, Mike, or told untruths. I look awful, but I am alive and for that I am very grateful.'

'Just the old Eleanor,' he said smiling and took her arm in that rather intimate, proprietorial manner she resented as they went to the door. She collected her stick from the stand in the hall as she opened the front door and brandished it. 'See, I have a stick.'

'Look, I really don't care,' he said as she locked the door. 'You must think I am very superficial if all I am concerned about are appearances. It is you, Eleanor, the person I remember and that hasn't changed. Where do we go for lunch?'

'There's a nice pub down the road. It overlooks the sea.' She gazed at the sky. 'There are one or two clouds about, but . . .'

'Let's go there,' he said opening the car door for her. 'It sounds great.'

He insisted on lunch in the dining room rather than in the bar and ordered wine. He even remembered that she liked a good dry white and got the best the pub had to offer, which wasn't saying very much.

She ordered the famous fish pie and Mike ordered the same.

'It is really a lovely place,' he said looking round appreciatively. Eleanor thought he looked relaxed and quite at home. He appeared to have none of the uneasiness she felt.

'Do you ever miss London?' he asked.

'I did when I first came, but not now although had I stayed in London I would not have had my accident, an event that changed everything. If I'd stayed married to Dick we would probably still be in the same house and I might even still be working, though I doubt it given the ageist attitudes of magazine proprietors these days.'

'What happened with Dick, or don't you like to talk about it?'

'I don't mind talking about it. He went off with his secretary, the usual story. Well, didn't "go off" exactly. He'd been having an affair for some time and I guess I knew, but wanted to leave things as they were. But then she wanted a baby. In fact she became pregnant, probably deliberately, and that was that. It was all quite civilized. I wasn't bitter. I'd had affairs. We more or less lived our own lives, but it was quite pleasant. We were both busy people. Something one took for granted and then it all goes haywire. I don't think Dick really wanted to marry Karen, but he felt he had to do the right thing by her. Dick was like that. *Noblesse oblige*. He even came to see me as soon as I had my accident, felt some responsibility I suppose as both the children were abroad. The house came to me, but I decided it was too large. The children were abroad and I decided I'd make a new start in the country. Not quite in the way it happened . . .' She looked over at him. 'But you do learn a lot about yourself and other people.'

'How?'

'People do avoid you. They are embarrassed. They don't know what to say. They look at you differently. Candy, the new editor, avoided me altogether after repeated promises to come down. I'd trained her, after all. On the whole I'm rather glad she didn't. I feel my image has suffered. Marge promised to come often, but I've only seen her once. I don't blame her. I don't blame anybody. I have become extremely philosophical about life.'

Mike leaned over and put his hand over hers. Again, like the kiss on the doorstep, it was a gesture she didn't welcome. It was an attempt to recapture their old rapport and she knew without any doubt that that had gone completely.

'Tell me what you do,' she asked gently withdrawing her hand and taking a fork to the fish pie, which had been set before them.

'Well, I'm still in the boring old travel business, but instead of writing about it I arrange tours to far-off places. I work for an agency.'

'You've had plenty of experience. Were you fired?'

Mike nodded. 'I was too old at fifty. I was redundant for some time. Sheila and I had already split and I was lonely and so I married a woman called Tessa who was a divorcee with two teenage children who bitterly resented me and still do. I was very glad when this offer of a job came up through someone I knew when I was writing. It gets me away a lot. Can we smoke here?' He looked around.

'I think so. They'll soon tell you if you can't.'

Mike pushed his fish pie to one side and lit up.

'It's very good, but I'm not very hungry. I do smoke a lot and probably drink too much. Yes, the marriage isn't a great success.'

'Does Tessa work?'

'Yes, she's younger than me and has a small boutique. She does quite well, actually. But I travel a lot and keep out of her way. The children are really awful; low achievers, into drugs, I'm sure of that. They don't like me and I don't like them'

'But you had children, too, Mike.'

'A child. Matthew is now grown up, of course, and lives with a girl. He's actually doing all right. Works in a City bank in London, not just counting the cash but some sort of executive. I don't see much of him. He was quite close to his mother.'

Eleanor gazed at the table and realized she had also lost her appetite. It all sounded very depressing. In fact, the former, exciting lover she used to dash across London to see had turned into a rather sad man. She looked at him closely. Could it be the same person? Undoubtedly it was as he stared back at her through wreathes of smoke. She remembered how they used to fling off their clothes almost as soon as they got into the flat and dive into bed. Torrid stuff. She was sure, too, that Mike remembered that by the way he was looking at her now. Was he, too, wondering how it had ever happened? Here she was wounded, older, a shadow of her former self.

'Tell me about your kids,' Mike said, as though reading her mind.

Putting as good a gloss on it as she could, because she didn't want to imitate his dreary litany of failure, she said that James was in America and happy with three children and a good job and Alex was a journalist and mostly out of the country. If she'd felt any rapport at all with Mike she might have told him more about Alex, but she didn't. She just wanted him to go: a boring man, part of her life long ago. She didn't know what she ever saw in him.

After lunch they wandered along the shore for a while and then, saying she was very tired and always rested in the afternoons, she rather conveyed to him that she wanted him to go. He dropped her off at the house without coming in, promising that he would keep in touch, a promise she hoped he wouldn't keep. He didn't attempt to kiss her as she got out of the car, and she stood waving to him as he drove off.

Alex sat looking at the picture and then came to a decision. She got up, placed a chair under it and standing on it took it down. It no longer dominated the room and already she felt better. She would have liked to have put her foot through it, but already it had come between her and Hugo for long enough and if she destroyed it it might only aggravate the situation.

For it had come between them, something had. Their relationship was not the same as it had been before he went to Iraq or before he and Niobe had spent the same night in the flat. Something had changed, she wasn't quite sure what. She knew that if she persistently nagged Hugo about Niobe the situation would be worse, but there it was, like an invisible barrier. It wasn't only Niobe but the deception that irked her; not even telling her that he had stopped over in London on his way to Berlin. The euphoria, the elation of their first meeting two weeks before had gone. He was out a lot, trying to sell his footage of Iraq, but by now there was so much of it about that so far there were no takers. What had once been sensational was becoming commonplace, for all the wrong reasons. His own depression and dejection didn't make the situation any easier. He seemed to be smoking and drinking more than ever and she was in danger of turning into a perpetual nag. Maybe it was time to quit, go home? Change something?

Hugo had gone out early and it was only eleven o'clock. What was she doing mooching around all day harbouring negative thoughts? She was an independent woman with a living to earn. She should go out and find some work, not hang around waiting for Hugo to direct her life. But then he had done nothing to draw her into his latest undertaking so she could hardly start writing about it.

What to do with the picture? It was so large that the only place for it was under the bed. She felt slightly ridiculous lying on her stomach and trying to find space for it with all the other stuff they hid there, inevitable in a flat with little storage place.

She jumped up, dusted her hands and went to consult her notebook to see if she could get any inspiration from the names she had listed there of people she had worked for in the past.

She spent the next half hour making calls, finding people either out or busy and was about to make another when her mobile range. It was her mother.

'Alex.'

'Mum.'

'Alex, Melody has gone missing.'

'Oh, Mum, when?'

'She didn't come in last night. Frankly, I'm frantic with worry. It's so unlike her. Oh, Alex, I really feel I couldn't live without Melody.'

'Mum, she may just have got shut in somewhere. Have you asked about?'

'I've been round myself putting notices on all the lamp posts. Niobe has been very sweet and Cathy has been all round the block. Oh, Alex can you . . .?'

'I'm coming straight away, Mum. I need some things anyway.'

She phoned Hugo on his mobile, but he wasn't answering. She left him a message and also wrote one which she put on the table. It was with some relief that she found her way down to Dorset. At least it gave her something to do.

It was late afternoon when she arrived and she was greeted at the door by Eleanor whose expression told her that the cat was still missing. Alex kissed her and standing back to study her face tenderly stroked her brow.

'Mum, you look all in.'

'Of course, I didn't sleep.' Eleanor took her daughter's hand and led her into the sitting room. 'I know it's silly and she *is* only a cat . . . but I've had her such a long time. She has been such a comfort to me.'

'Of course, Mum.' Alex sat beside her still holding her hand. 'We'll find her.'

'I've looked everywhere, all sorts of outhouses, the various barns on Niobe's farm. It's so unlike Melody. Usually she goes round the garden and that's it. You know how timid she is.'

'Have you had your nap?'

'No time for a nap. Can't relax.'

'Then go and have one. I'll bring you a cup of tea and I'll set out on my search.'

Relieved to have someone in charge Eleanor did as she was told and had scarcely lain down when Alex appeared with the promised tea.

'Oh, you are a darling,' Eleanor said taking it from her. 'I know I fuss.'

'Don't worry, Mum, we'll find her.' Alex bent and kissed her on the cheek and impulsively Eleanor grabbed her by her shoulders, drew her down and hugged her.

'You don't know what it means to me to have you, Alex,' she said. 'I don't know what I'd have done without you.'

'Next to Melody, I'm sure I am the most important person in your life,' Alex took her mother's cup and briskly drew the duvet over her.

'How's Hugo?' Eleanor asked.

'Oh, Hugo's fine. Busy trying to sell his stuff from Iraq. I hardly see him.'

'No news about going back?'

'I suspect it might be quite soon. He needs a job, a commission. For one thing he is getting desperately short of money.'

Eleanor's eyes spontaneously filled with tears after Alex closed the door. She felt an idiot calling for her daughter, who surely had enough to do, but she had felt desperate and she knew Alex would understand in a way that others didn't. It was difficult for practical people like Cathy and Niobe to understand the symbiotic, almost unnatural relationship between her and her cat. Wondering if she would ever see her beloved pet again, through sheer exhaustion she fell asleep.

'Oh, hi,' Niobe said in that detached, rather brittle tone she seemed to reserve for Alex, 'I suppose you've come about the cat?'

'No sign of her, I suppose?'

'She could have been run over.'

Niobe still didn't ask her in. It seemed unusually offhand, even for Niobe, to keep her standing at the door. Difficult to realize this was the same woman to whom she had done an exceptional favour. Something had definitely happened in London. Niobe felt guilty. Alex was sure of that.

Leaning against the doorpost Niobe rambled on. 'I mean, if she has never gone missing before it does seem strange. I'm afraid I can't ask you in. I have to go and pick up the children. Must do some shopping first.' She turned as if to go back indoors.

Alex felt suddenly angry. As if to remind her of the debt Niobe owed her, she said, 'By the way, thanks for the picture. It was a thoughtful present, but you didn't have to'

'Oh? You like it, do you?' Niobe's tone changed.

Alex avoided a direct answer. 'It was very kind of you. Anyway, I won't keep you. Are you sure you had a good look in all your buildings for Melody?'

'Of course I did,' Niobe said brusquely and shut the door.

Alex went slowly down the path more convinced than ever that more had happened in London than either Niobe or Hugo were prepared to divulge. She didn't know why she hadn't mentioned the fact that she knew Niobe and Hugo had been in her flat together. What would have been the purpose? What would she have said and how would Niobe have responded? Things might have been said that she didn't really want to know, would rather not know.

Doing her best to stifle the jealousy, suspicion and rage in her heart, Alex walked down to the sea and sat for some time on the sea wall looking out towards Portland. It was cold, a little foggy and she felt beset by anguish and worry; worry about the cat and the effect of its loss on her mother, anguish about Hugo's and Niobe's relationship. On impulse she decided to have a drink and went into the pub. The bar was almost empty except for a solitary drinker sitting in the corner reading the paper. He looked up as she came in and his face broke into a smile.

Although the face was familiar, at first she couldn't place him.

He rose and came towards her.

'I suppose you don't remember me.'

The penny dropped. 'Of course I do. You were behind Mum's car when she had her accident. Is it Henry?'

'Bankhurst,' he smiled. 'Yes, right behind. I don't think the memory will ever leave me. How is your mother?'

'Rather distraught, I'm afraid. She has just lost her cat.'

'Oh, I'm sorry. Was it old?'

'I mean literally lost. Disappeared. She, the cat, meant a great deal to her especially since her accident. Lay on her bed all the time.'

'What sort of cat was it? Look, may I buy you a drink?'

'Lager, if I may.'

They both moved up to the bar and rang the bell and Martin appeared from the back.

'Hello, Alex,' he said greeting her. 'Nice to see you. Been away?'

'In London,' Alex said. 'Hugo came back from Iraq. Mum has lost her cat. She disappeared two days ago. You haven't seen a sad, lost-looking car?'

Martin shook his head as Henry ordered the drinks.

'What sort of cat?' Henry turned to Alex.

'She's a moggy, but a very pretty white and ginger cat. Looks younger than her age.'

'White and ginger . . .' Henry paused in the act of taking the glass from Martin and sorting through his wallet to pay for the drinks. 'Now, I did see a white and ginger cat in the field next to the car park when I was parking my car. It did look a bit lost. Sort of purposeless. A pretty little thing.'

'Oh, Henry!' Alex spontaneously clasped his arm. 'Do you think we could go and have another look?'

'Of course.' Henry took a sip from his drink and replaced it on the bar. 'I don't want to get you too excited. It was only about an hour ago, so if by any chance it is your mother's cat it might still be around.'

The trouble was that it was getting dark. Alex and Henry went round the side of the pub towards the field where Henry said he had seen the cat, Alex calling Melody's name gently so as not to frighten her. Martin followed them and began opening various doors to his outbuildings and with the help of a torch peering in, but there was no sign of the cat and after half an hour they returned disconsolately to the pub.

'I must get back,' Alex said. 'Mum will be worried. She'll

think she's lost me as well.' She turned to Henry. 'It was nice to see you again. Thanks for your help.'

'Sorry I raised false hopes,' he said contritely.

'No, you didn't at all. If it is Melody and it does sound as though it might be, it means she is somewhere around and still alive. I'll come out again tomorrow when it's daylight.'

Eleanor took the news that Henry thought he had seen Melody with guarded optimism.

'We have been here long enough for her to know where she lives,' she said doubtfully.

'I don't want you to be too optimistic, Mum. She never leaves the garden, does she?'

'No. She can if she wants to, but doesn't, not that I know anyway. Maybe someone left the gate open.'

'Perhaps she's in love. Saw a handsome male cat passing . . .'

'Perhaps.' Eleanor smiled. 'I think she's a bit too old for that, like me.'

'Oh, come on.' Alex looked at her mother. 'If Mr Right came along . . .'

They were sitting in the kitchen having a drink before supper, which Alex was cooking.

'No, seriously,' Eleanor continued. 'You remember I said I had an affair before your dad and I split up?'

'Yes. I must admit I was a bit shocked.'

'Were you? I'm sorry. Anyway, he turned up unexpectedly the other day, his name is Mike. Just showed up at the door. He'd heard from Marge about my accident.'

'And . . .?'

'And, nothing. Sorry to disappoint you. I wondered what I had ever seen in him. It happens, you know. Ten years has passed and ten years is a long time.'

'Maybe he still fancied you?'

Alex who was a reasonable cook when she chose was making an omelette, half of which she skilfully slid onto her mother's plate.

'Eat it while it is fresh,' she said and poured some more wine into her mother's glass.

'I don't think he did. Certainly not like this.'

'Mum, don't do yourself down all the time. You haven't changed as much as you think you have, you know. You're still you.'

'That's what Mike said, but I have changed a great deal, in mind as well as body.'

'I wish I could say the same about me.' Alex put her half of the omelette on her plate, helped herself to wine and sat opposite her mother.

'Oh, go on darling. You're much too young to think like that. You have the whole of your life ahead of you.' She looked anxiously at her daughter. 'There *is* something about Hugo, isn't there?'

Alex took a sip from her glass.

'Well, yes there is, frankly. We have not had a very good time in London. Of course it is a bad time for him. He has done a lot of work in Iraq, been in considerable danger, if you ask me, but being Hugo he never spelled it out. As he was not officially embedded with the troops he did a lot of fringe filming about the effect of the war on the general population; how it was affecting ordinary people and so on, but he is finding it quite hard to sell. He wants to turn it into a proper documentary and is trying to get some people interested. American interest went cold. It didn't leave an awful lot of time for us to develop our relationship which, frankly, I feel is in the doldrums. Besides, there is this Niobe thing . . .'

Eleanor looked up, startled. 'What Niobe thing?'

'Well, while Niobe was in London Hugo popped into the flat on his way from America to Berlin. He was trying to get himself embedded with the British troops and had a contact in Berlin. He said he didn't tell me because he thought I would want to come up and try and stop him and he was probably right. The thing is they both spent the night at the flat which bothered me a bit knowing how attractive Niobe is and what a bad relationship she has with Francis. Hugo is very sexy, too, of course. They would probably think nothing of it. He denies anything happened and says I am being ridiculous and suspicious, but it did put a damper on things.'

Eleanor, who had been listening keenly put down her knife and fork.

'But do you actually know . . . anything happened?'

'He wouldn't tell me if it had. I realize it might not mean very much to him, but I think it would mean a lot to Niobe and she has been very strange with me since her return. I popped in to see her today to ask if she'd seen Melody and she didn't even invite me in. She was cold and remote. Well, she would feel guilty if she'd fucked my boyfriend, wouldn't she? Whereas he wouldn't feel guilty at all, the shit. Men have a different aspect on these things.'

Alex got up and restlessly began to pace the room, her meal left half finished on the table.

'You know how they carried on at Christmas. He did flirt, whatever anyone said. They both did. And I did *not* flirt with Francis. That was absurd. Francis is a sweet guy, but I don't fancy him at all and I am positive he didn't fancy me, whereas there was something rather suitable about Niobe and Hugo. They seemed to go well together. I didn't like it at all.'

Yes there was, Eleanor thought, eyeing in her mind that scene when the two were so earnestly talking in the sitting room. She knew that Niobe would find Hugo very attractive. Most women did. Even she could see his attraction, something atavistic, not pure good looks because he was not conventionally good looking. She was also sure that his profession would excite and appeal to Niobe who was always belittling the talents of her own man, although to Eleanor the occupation of thatcher was no mean skill.

Alex, who had been standing by the kitchen window, said suddenly, 'We have a caller.' She looked at her watch. 'Wonder who it can be?'

She left the kitchen and was gone quite a long time while Eleanor heard first an exclamation and then low, excited murmurs. She was about to get up to satisfy her curiosity when Alex returned clutching a frightened-looking cat who was desperately trying to escape from her arms. Behind her, looking very pleased with himself was Henry Bankhurst.

Eleanor sat back in her chair uttering a deep sigh of relief, as tears sprang to her eyes. She felt foolish and brushed them away.

'Oh, Melody, you *naughty* little girl,' she said holding out her arms. 'Where *have* you been?'

'I found her in the car park near the pub, Mrs Ashton,' Henry said. 'It's where I took Alex. I think she was looking for a lift.'

'Oh, Melody.' Eleanor, hugging her, stroked her and gazed into green eyes that looked at her gratefully. 'You are a very *very* naughty girl. It's amazing that she let you catch her,' she said to Henry. 'She is normally very timid.'

'I think she'd had enough,' Henry said. 'She came to me quite willingly, but I didn't want to put her straight in the car in case it frightened her. I wrapped her in a rug and took her to Martin who told me where you lived. She was very subdued. I think, though, she knew she was coming home.'

After Henry was given a drink, an invitation to supper, which he refused and had been profusely thanked, Eleanor and Alex stood at the door seeing him off as he got into his car and shot up the road towards the village.

'What a very nice man he is,' Eleanor said returning to the kitchen and the half-eaten and, by now, stone cold supper. She resumed her seat and drank her wine. 'He went to an awful lot of trouble.'

'I do *really* think he fancies you, Mum.' Alex, taking a seat opposite looked at her mischievously.

'Why must you always bring sex into it?' Eleanor said irritably. 'I suppose it's because you're young.'

She got up and taking her plate to the bin scraped the contents into it. 'Pity to waste this, but it's so wonderful to have Melody back.' The cat had refused any food, quickly disappearing upstairs and was by now probably settled on Eleanor's bed nursing her grievances at being so badly treated. 'I wonder where she went? She's been gone *two* nights.'

While Alex stacked the dishwasher, Eleanor went back into the sitting room thinking about the conversation they had been having before Henry appeared. She wondered whether she should tell Alex about the cheque or if she should keep it to herself. Alex was already unhappy and suspicious, why make things any worse or her even more unhappy? On the other hand it was a mystery that was not going to go away. Might it not be better to bring it into the open?

Her mind was partially made up for her by Alex's first

words as, another glass of wine in her hand, she sat down opposite her mother.

'Sometimes I think I should have it out with Hugo. Try and clear the air.'

'Have what out?' Still playing for time, Eleanor sat opposite her.

'Our relationship. You know. Where we are going. At the moment it seems like nowhere.'

'Alex, there is something I should tell you,' Eleanor began hesitantly. Immediately, Alex's expression became one of alarm. It was, of course, the silliest way to start and Eleanor could have kicked herself. She went on hurriedly: 'I've been wondering whether to say anything and it might mean absolutely nothing. However, as it concerns Hugo and you might find out anyway, maybe it is best I tell you. Forewarned is to be forearmed.'

'Go on. He and Niobe *did* sleep together,' Alex said, her voice deadpan. 'Is that what you're trying to tell me?'

'No, I don't know anything about that. I didn't know they had met in London, not at all. I knew nothing about that, honestly, but the money that Niobe gave me to repay the loan almost certainly came from Hugo.'

'How do you know that, Mum?' Alex's tone didn't change. 'Did Niobe tell you?'

'No, Cathy did. She saw a cheque for a thousand pounds in Niobe's bag, signed by Hugo.'

'I don't believe it.' Alex's voice now sounded relieved. 'That is utter rubbish.'

'Why should she make up such a story? Besides, it was Hugo's bank, Coutts. Not many people bank there, do they?'

'Cathy *told* you it was a Coutts' cheque?'

'Yes, because I asked her. Knowing how she feels about Niobe it occurred to me that she might be trying to make mischief. Unworthy of me, but there you are. She couldn't make up a thing like that.'

'No wonder Niobe is acting strangely,' Alex said, but reflectively her voice now strangely detached. 'If she is having it off with Hugo, she must . . .'

'Oh, darling, she is not "having it off". There must be some kind of explanation,' Eleanor faltered.

'A thousand pounds is a lot for a fuck. I hope it was value for money.'

Alex got up and went over to the window staring out into the night. 'He *said* it was only one night he was in the flat, but who can believe anything?' She turned and looked despairingly at her mother. 'I really feel I don't know what to do.'

Eleanor rose and put an arm round her daughter's shoulders. 'Just sit on it for a while. Don't do anything for the time being at least. You never know, but it's something that may just sort itself out.'

'I wish you'd never told me,' Alex said despairingly. 'I just wish you had kept it all to yourself.'

Nine

A lex put her bag on the floor and stood looking round the flat. It seemed more desolate than ever, somehow too clean and tidy, empty. Hugo had gone, summoned back to Iraq by the promise of work. He'd rung her from the airport when she was halfway to London; too late to turn back. She had felt then that she'd like to take off, to anywhere; Scotland, Ireland, Wales, maybe cross over to France; anywhere to try and forget; anywhere to try and stop brooding on why Hugo had left such little time to tell her.

He'd said he'd only got the call that morning. Someone had been taken ill, or funked going back to Iraq where the situation was deteriorating, and he was a replacement in a team making a documentary. It was a chance he couldn't lose, but how could one believe Hugo anymore? That was the point. What trust could you place in someone you felt had at the worst lied to you, at the best misled you? Maybe he'd gone to get away from her and her jealousy and suspicion? She had become the species of female she had always despised: a nagging woman who didn't trust her man. How she'd pitied friends in the past who had got into this situation. How sure she'd been that it would never happen to her. Her one desire had been to confront Hugo with the fact that she knew about the cheque, longing for a simple, straightforward explanation, not the sort of thing one could talk about on the phone, and now it was too late.

The fridge was reasonably well stocked, which seemed to indicate that Hugo had genuinely suddenly been called away. There was butter; fillet steaks and salad; a packet, unopened, of smoked salmon; eggs; milk that seemed reasonably fresh; a bottle of white wine; bread in the bin and fruit in the bowl on the sideboard. It looked in fact as though Hugo had been prepared for her, looked forward to sharing a meal with her and that was the fact that made the flat seem so cold and lonely.

Alex took her bag into the bedroom and flopped on the bed, gazing at the ceiling. She felt dreadfully tired. It seemed that all this, coupled with the worry about her mother, her uncertainty about Hugo's affections, had caught up with her. It was very unusual because normally she was a very active person, full of energy. What had happened?

She was beginning to have an awful suspicion of what might have happened, but she wouldn't let herself dwell on it: couldn't. Tomorrow she would make some more phone calls and try and get herself a job. She might even explore the possibility of going out to Iraq, whether Hugo wanted it or not.

Sara Clements was both a friend and colleague, a woman who had had the sense to progress up the journalistic ladder in a sensible way, going from one job to another in orderly progression, a little more promotion, with each step carefully calculated. They had met in journalism school and, whereas Alex had gone freelance after her first few newspaper jobs, Sara was now the features editor of a broadsheet whose views carried a lot of weight, and a person of some importance. She was actually the same age as Alex and someone whom Alex admired and not a little envied. They were lunching in Soho a few days after Alex had returned to London, made endless phone calls and finally secured a date with Sara, at her invitation.

'It's been a long time,' Sara said, holding her glass up to toast Alex. 'Tell me what you've been up to. How is that gorgeous man of yours?'

A few months before the paper had run a piece by Alex with pictures by Hugo. It was the one they'd been doing on India, just before her mother had had her accident.

'He's in Iraq,' she said.

'Oh.' Sara's face darkened. 'Worried?'

'Of course I'm worried. The situation hasn't really improved, has it, despite all the euphoria about victory?'

Sara nodded. 'They say there was no plan for what to do after Saddam was overthrown; no plans to restructure Iraq.'

Alex decided to come directly to the point. After they'd given their order she leaned across the table and lowered her voice. It was a busy restaurant in Soho and invariably either or both of them might know other people lunching there, with ears always attuned for gossip.

'If I went out to Iraq would there be the possibility of a commission?'

'Are you serious?'

'Very.'

'It could be dangerous for you. A lot of people out there are paying huge sums for protection. We couldn't pay for anything like that. You'd be on your own.'

Alex's heart rose. 'I'd take the risk.'

Sara frowned. 'I'd have to consider it. I do find the idea quite attractive, but I am worried about the consequences of anything happening to you. It is *very* dangerous territory out there now. Presumably you'd be with Hugo?'

'Not necessarily. I have no idea where Hugo is right now, or who he's with or even quite why he went. I was in Dorset with my mother – you know she had a very bad accident? – and we were going to meet up in London. Suddenly he had a call to go on a job and that was the last time I heard from him. Mobiles don't seem to work so well from Iraq.'

'Even getting to Baghdad from the airport is dangerous,' Sara said. 'I would think very carefully about it if I were you, but the idea is attractive. Let me get back to you on this.'

Alex felt reinvigorated and quite euphoric after the lunch which finished shortly before three. As women watching their diets they ate sparingly, cutting down on calories and the amount of alcohol, too. Time was when a bottle of wine was preceded by a few drinks. Not any longer, although Hugo might have been an exception to this rule. There had been very little girlish chat between them. Sara wasn't into gossip. It was all serious stuff about the progress of the war, its effect on the nation and job opportunities of which there seemed precious few. Sara was guarded about her private life, which suited Alex who didn't want to say too much

about hers. Maybe it was because they were both getting
old; over thirty, a watershed. One thing she did know was
that Sara would not keep her hanging about with an offer of
work.

She bought the *Evening Standard* to search for a film to
see, but nothing interested her. Instead, she made her way
across Trafalgar Square and on to the Embankment where
she hung over the wall gazing for a long time into the water,
looking across to the Festival Hall and the South Bank and
thinking what a wonderful place London was and how much
she missed it when she was away. She was not a country
girl, however much one admired its beauty and tranquillity
and she didn't really think her mother was either. She
wondered how soon it would be before her mother got bored
once she was better. Alex resumed her stroll past the Inner
Temple to Waterloo Bridge before turning up into Fleet Street
and getting a bus home. Maybe there would be a message
from Hugo. But there was nothing and feeling desperately
tired again she had a snack and went to bed early.

It was one of those walk-in clinics that had sprung up in
London in the last few years. Alex was registered with a
London GP, but she preferred anonymity. She'd phoned for
an appointment and was told she would be seen the same
day. The charge for a consultation was sixty-five pounds.
The doctor was young, male, impersonal, businesslike, just
what she wanted. He confirmed what she had already thought
and tested with a home-made kit.

'You are about eight weeks pregnant, Miss Ashton.'

'No doubt?' Alex said.

'None at all. Am I right in assuming this is unplanned?'

'Unplanned and unwanted,' Alex confirmed. 'How long
would it take to get an abortion?'

'No time at all.' The doctor reached for the phone. 'I can
arrange it now, if you're sure. The sooner, the better.'

'I am sure,' Alex said.

The doctor lifted the phone and spoke for a few minutes
into it, then he scribbled a note, which he handed to her,
wished her good luck and asked her to pay on the way out.
It had taken about fifteen minutes. No earnest talk, no

counselling, no advice, no warnings. Just what she wanted. She was certainly old enough to know her own mind.

She walked slowly back down the Edgware Road, that big, impersonal cosmopolitan thoroughfare that seemed to encapsulate what London was all about. She got a taxi home and once there collapsed on the bed and gave vent, at last, to pent up tears, a combination of rage, regret and somehow remorse. She knew she would very much like to have had Hugo's baby.

It was a very silly, stupid thing to have got herself into. It had happened when she had run out of prescriptions for her pill and, well, she'd never thought about it; took a risk; she'd taken them before. It was horrible now to be alone in London and about to make an appointment for an abortion, which could happen tomorrow if she rang the number the doctor had given her. At this stage in her pregnancy it was a piece of cake he'd said. Nothing to it.

She felt vaguely sick. The slight queasiness she'd been feeling recently in the mornings was the only indication she'd had that she might be pregnant, that and the tiredness, tiredness like nothing she had ever experienced before; complete, total exhaustion. At first she'd tried to put it down to nerves. Well, she would have the abortion and would be again. She knew Hugo would never want a baby. He had two children already and was a lousy father. In all the time she'd known him he scarcely ever referred to his daughters and seldom visited them. It was as though they didn't exist. He would be a terrible father to her baby. She didn't want a baby either. She was thirty-one and there was still plenty of time for that sort of thing.

She got up from the bed and opened a bottle of wine, was pouring a glass to give herself courage before she went to the phone to arrange an appointment when her mobile rang. She seized it, as she always did, hoping it was Hugo.

'Hi, Alex,' Sara said. 'Good news. At least I hope it is. We had an editorial meeting and your idea to go to Iraq and write a piece on the women's angle is considered a good one. Are you still up for it?'

'Am I!' Alex said excitedly. 'I should say I am.'

'Are you sure? People are disappearing. There is nothing

we can do to guarantee your safety. All that is up to you. Also, all we'll pay is the normal rate for your piece. Think about it.'

Alex paused. It did seem a bit harsh, but it was work. 'Is anything open to negotiation?' she asked. 'Air fare, danger money?'

'I'm afraid not,' Sara replied. 'Really, I'm doing it for you as a favour. We have our correspondent there already, but he is mostly covering the military and political aspect. I pressed hard, but who knows what it might lead to?'

Death at the barricades, Alex thought, for no particular reason.

'I'm on,' she said. 'I just have one or two things to sort out and must go and see Mum, break the news, be sure she's OK. Next week, if I can make the arrangements, get a visa.'

'I'll send you a letter of confirmation, which should be enough accreditation for you and, by the way, I think you've got guts. But then I knew that already.'

Thirty-one. Slowly Alex put down her mobile. She didn't know why she suddenly thought about her age, still young enough to have a baby in a few years' time, but you could die at any time. Yes, she definitely wanted to go to Iraq, but how did one start with no Hugo to ask? She would ring the abortion clinic, but first, the Foreign Office.

Alex felt strangely reluctant to make either call. After all, she didn't really know what was involved. Maybe she should find that out before she contacted the FO, wait for Sara's commissioning letter? *Then* the abortion. That was the best idea. There was so much to do and she had to see her mum. She couldn't just leave without seeing her, tell her every-thing; get her advice. Suddenly, she felt she wanted to see her mother very much, wanted the warm reassuring comfort of Mummy. She was a little girl again and not thirty-one years of age at all.

It was the first time Eleanor had walked to the sea alone. She took it slowly, step by step, pausing frequently. She had taken her mobile phone with her in case she needed to summon help. She set about it with some trepidation, but soon gained confidence. It was such a lovely day, the lush, undulating countryside surrounding her at its best. On either side were the fields packed with sheep, and in the distance the hills rose steeply towards the sea. The path she was on inclined slightly and she slowed down, pausing frequently, and at the top she looked down on the view she never tired of: that great expanse of sea shimmering in the late morning sun. The vista widened as she walked down the hill, past an old converted watermill, windows wide open, its yard festooned with lobster pots and various nets and maritime paraphernalia.

She saw the village below her and the pub on its gentle slope facing the sea. A small stream of people headed towards the beach clutching the usual clobber of rugs, mats, fishing nets, picnic things, folding chairs and small tents with children and dogs scampering ahead. Overhead swooped seagulls with their shrill predatory cries dipping and rising from the sea, sometimes triumphantly with a catch and heading back inland to feed hungry offspring.

Eleanor sank onto a bench and surveyed the scene before her with profound satisfaction, deep gratitude that she had been spared to see and enjoy all the wonders of nature, the sight of flying birds and to feel the sun beating down on her.

After ten minutes or so she rose and walked into the village, taking another rest on the sea wall, then, feeling thirsty, she climbed the short path to the pub.

As a contrast to the bright sunshine outside it was gloomy inside and she blinked for a while before her eyes adjusted to the dark. There were a few people standing at the bar being served by Martin and his son George who gave her their customary affable greeting and pointed to a seat by the window. She removed her jacket and looked around, her eyes slowly adjusting to the gloom. In the dim light she saw a familiar figure sitting in the corner, his face half obscured by a newspaper, but unmistakable. At that moment he put aside his paper to take up his glass of beer and, looking over, saw her. Face wreathed in smiles he rose with his glass and came over to her.

'Mrs Ashton, how very nice to see you.'

'And you,' she replied. 'Please call me Eleanor, and I owe you a drink.'

'You don't owe me anything,' Henry Bankhurst said, sitting down next to her. 'How's the cat?'

'She's fine. She sulked for a bit but she seems to have got over that. Please, *do* let me buy you a drink.'

Henry looked at his half-empty glass. 'If you insist, I'll have a lemonade. I must be careful as I'm driving.'

At that moment, George came over and wiped the table in front of them.

'Very nice to see you, Mrs Ashton. Is your daughter not with you?'

'She's in London,' Eleanor said. 'In fact, this is the first time I have walked to the sea by myself since the accident. I feel very brave. I'd like a glass of white wine and Henry will have lemonade because he's driving. Are you sure?' She looked at him again.

'I'm sure.'

'You're very law-abiding if you've had only half a pint.'

'I am law-abiding,' Henry said with a smile. 'I also don't want to lose my licence.' They sat back while their drinks were served, then sipped them in an easy companionable silence.

Henry grew on her: a nice, generous, law-abiding man. He was not Adonis, but nor was she Venus and he would be eminently presentable in any company you cared to choose. She suddenly saw in him the possibility of a friend, a companion if nothing else, what the Americans called a walker. He was very different from Dick or Mike, but then she didn't want another Dick or Mike, did she? Her interest in him deepened. Henry looked at her as though in some way he could read her mind. 'How do you feel now after your walk?'

'I feel OK. A little tired but I am determined to become independent because my daughter won't be with me for long, and I always loved this walk before my accident.'

'I gather you weren't here very long.'

'Only six months.'

'That was very bad luck.'

'It was.'

'I don't suppose you know many people, either?'

'No.' She thought all this was leading very nicely to an

invitation, maybe to dinner or lunch. A small, welcome sense of anticipation stirred inside her.

'Do you live locally?' she asked. 'I don't really know much about you.'

'I live in a village between here and Lyme. I retired last year.'

'And what did you do?'

'I was a bank manager. I took early retirement because I was sick of banking; the bureaucracy and all the tedium. I am very keen on sailing and am thinking of buying a boat.'

'In theory,' Eleanor replied, 'I was keen on the idea of learning to sail, too, but I think I may have to postpone that adventure for the time being.'

'If I do get my boat, you must let me take you out. Have you ever sailed?'

'No. It was something I always wanted to do, but my husband wasn't keen and we always went abroad for our holidays.'

There was a silence while they finished their drinks and Eleanor imagined Henry wanted a bit more information without liking to ask.

'We divorced,' she explained. 'I was the editor of a woman's magazine and decided, like you, to take early retirement. Maybe an unfortunate decision in the circumstances.'

Henry nodded and drank deeply from his glass. 'Funny how life changes,' he said. 'It could have been me – your accident. I was just behind you and I saw this car swerve suddenly and bang right into you. I only just braked in time to prevent myself adding to the melee.'

Here was silence between them as if both their minds went back to that terrible day.

Henry looked at his watch. 'I should be going. I have to see a man later on about a boat. May I give you a lift?'

'Well . . .' Eleanor drained her glass. 'I did intend to walk back, but it is tempting.'

'Maybe just for the first day,' Henry said encouragingly. 'Break yourself in gently.'

'Then I'll accept,' she said smiling. He really was a very kind, thoughtful person, almost a soul mate. She felt this meeting was full of promise. How it would amuse Alex who had prophesied as much.

They said goodbye to Martin and George and went round to the car park where Henry showed her the spot where he had seen Melody.

'I think she'd have found her way home, eventually,' he said, 'but maybe it was lucky I'd heard about her from Alex.'

'I'm not sure at all.' Eleanor got into the car as he opened the door for her. 'I shall be forever grateful to you.'

She was about to invite him to supper one evening, take the initiative, but thought maybe it was a little premature. Didn't want to frighten him. A relationship like this between two mature people must develop slowly, if at all.

It was only a short distance to her house and as they stopped she said impulsively, 'I can't offer you very much, but would you like a sandwich, maybe in the garden as it's such a nice day?'

'I really would like that,' Henry glanced at his watch. 'But my wife is expecting me for lunch. Some other time maybe.'

He got out and helped her out of the car and she hoped he hadn't seen the expression on her face. It had never occurred to her that Henry might be married. He escorted her to her front door and she turned and thanked him just to see, behind him, another car draw up and Alex jump from it and, arms extended, run towards her mother.

'I *told* you he fancied you,' Alex said when, a short while later, they were sitting in the garden eating ham and egg sandwiches, a bottle of wine between them. 'Only I didn't think he was married, the bastard. He doesn't *look* married. Oh well.'

'I was actually just deciding he was rather nice,' Eleanor said wistfully. 'I could see him as a "walker" taking me sailing and for drives in the country. But honestly I never imagined him as a lover.' She reached out a hand for her daughter. 'Dream over. I shall now think of him as a boring little man instead, which he probably is, and put him completely out of my mind. Alex, this is really a lovely surprise. Tell me, what brings you down? Hugo coming back?'

'No.' Alex paused and took a mouthful of wine. 'Now,

Mum, I don't want you to be upset about what I'm going to tell you. Let me speak first. *Don't* interrupt.'

That horrible little feeling of apprehension, that little demon that was always lurking, waiting to spring emerged tugging yet again at Eleanor's heart.

'Go on,' she said trying to keep her voice steady.

'Well, you know for ages now I have been like a lost soul. I can't spend my life hanging about for Hugo. His attitude is odd, you know that. Besides it's not helped by the Niobe thing.

'That was all left suspended up in the air because when I got to London he'd gone again without telling me. Anyway I decided to take things into my own hands and started job hunting now that you are so much better and don't need me around. Well, Mum . . .' She paused and took a deep breath. 'I have got an assignment to do a piece on Iraq. It means I have to go there. You remember Sara Clements—'

She was interrupted by her mother's sharp exclamation. 'Alex, you can't *mean* . . .'

'Mum, I did ask you please not to interrupt. Listen to what I have to say.' Eleanor obediently clamped her mouth shut.

'It will only be for a short time and then I come back and write my piece and hopefully it will lead to more work. Sara is a very important contact and as good as promised me more. There, I've finished.' She sat back and downed the rest of the wine in her glass.

For a long time Eleanor remained silent. She knew her daughter well enough not to irritate her with negative comments.

'Well,' she said at last, 'if that's how you feel, and I'm sure you've thought about it, there is not much I can say. But you do realize darling, don't you, that Iraq is becoming an increasingly dangerous place? People are disappearing. Sectarian war is rife between the rival religious groups, to say nothing of their attitude to the people they regard as foreign occupiers.'

'I know that. I've been around, you know, Mum. I've read the papers and listened to the bulletins. I am a seasoned journalist. And as a woman particularly I know how careful I must be.'

'Have they offered you protection?'

Alex shook her head. 'No, but as soon as I get out there I'll try and get hold of Hugo. It will be much easier when I'm actually there.'

'You haven't spoken to Hugo about this yet?' Eleanor sounded incredulous.

'Can't,' Alex said defensively. 'I've tried. I simply can't contact him. I assume he's on some secret important job. Anyway, I want to give Hugo a bit of his own medicine. He didn't tell me he was going and I shan't tell him until I'm there.'

'I think, Alex, that is very foolish of you.' Eleanor began to lose patience.

'Mum, there is nothing I can do about it. You don't want me to be one of these awful clinging women do you?'

'No, I don't, but I thought you were a couple and couples share things, or should. You don't seem to share anything at the moment.'

Except the baby inside me, Alex thought, wondering how her mother would react to that. But as she had no intention of telling her it didn't really matter.

'When will you be going?' Eleanor enquired finally, a note of resignation in her voice.

'I don't know yet. I have to get a visa, various formalities, but I did want you to know, Mum, and don't worry. I promise you *nothing* will happen to me.'

Eleanor woke with a headache, a severe headache, the sort she used to have in hospital when she would yearn for the next dose of painkillers. There was always an hour between one wearing out and being able to get the next; an hour of excruciating pain. She hadn't had such a bad headache for a long time and, raising her head with difficulty, she reached out for the painkillers by the side of her bed, took them with a drop of water and sank back on her pillow waiting for the pain to subside.

Naturally, she associated it with Alex's news, which was the very worst she could have had.

Anywhere, anywhere but Iraq! Chaos in the streets, people disappearing all the time. If she couldn't get hold of Hugo how did she imagine her mother would be able to get hold of her? The whole thing was too awful to contemplate.

In her misery Eleanor imagined herself back in the hospital again, the darkness, just a light from the nurses' station at the end of the ward behind the glass partition. She would wait for the pain relief and sometimes it would be slow in coming due to some crisis in another part of the ward.

The awful pain and horror; the depression at her condition seemed to resurface again as though nothing had changed. Yet it had. It was nearly a year since her accident and she was a whole lot better. Her sight was better, her walking was more confident; hadn't she gone to the sea all by herself?

Her mood changed and she was able to think now with some amusement about Henry and the fact that he was married. What had she envisaged, for God's sake? What kind of relationship could she have had with an ex bank manager, a creature of habit, a careful, cautious man who spent a long time in the pub yet consumed only half a pint of beer for fear of losing his licence? One had to make compromises for companionship and security, but even if he hadn't been married she would soon have discovered that she and Henry had nothing in common to keep them together, not even sailing.

Gradually she felt her headache receding under the influence of strong painkillers and she was beginning to feel drowsy again when a curious sound jolted her wide awake and Melody, slumbering as usual by her side, sat up alerted too by what were clearly sounds of distress from the bathroom.

Alex was being sick, horribly sick by the sound of it. Just at the moment she couldn't get out of bed; her head still ached too much. Suddenly all the worry and anxiety about her daughter surged back. Alex had not seemed happy. Was the thought of going to Iraq making her ill; was it something she'd eaten? Yet, she hadn't eaten much and drank hardly anything at all. They had had grilled fish for supper and Alex had managed to leave most of it.

There was something very serious worrying Alex, maybe

the job, maybe Hugo, something very bad to cause such severe sickness.

Then there was silence. The light filtered through the curtained window. Five a.m. She often did wake up at five and didn't go to sleep again. She had begun to be able to get up and resume her morning inspection of the garden with Melody, feed her and then take her own milk upstairs to make her morning tea. It was the kind of ritual she liked, the sort of ritual that told her that she was better and life was almost back to normal again. By six a.m. her headache had lifted enough for her to get out of bed and she tiptoed past Alex's door, first listening outside for any sound. Silence. She continued down the stairs, made the customary tour of the garden with the cat, and leaving Melody downstairs went upstairs with her jug of milk and an extra cup in case Alex surfaced. But as she got to the top of the stairs her daughter emerged from the bathroom looking terrible, her face haggard, her eyes swollen and an all-pervasive smell of vomit surrounding her.

Eleanor nearly dropped her jug in alarm.

'Darling, what on *earth* is wrong?' She put her free arm round her and tried to draw her into her bedroom, but Alex impatiently brushed her away.

'Please, Mum, let me go back to bed. I feel so awful.'

'Have you got a bug or something?'

'I think I must have. Don't worry about it, Mum. I'll be OK, but I must lie down.'

She then went into her room and shut the door.

Eleanor made her tea and lay on her bed looking thoughtfully out of the window, worried to death about Alex. The best gloss that one could put on it was that it was a bug and not the manifestation of some deep psychological upset. As usual Eleanor worried and speculated too much; pointless, but habitual.

Alex came down at about eleven, still in her dressing gown. She looked ill and washed out and slumped in a chair running a hand wearily across her forehead.

'I must have picked up some sort of bug,' she said. 'I'm so sorry, Mum, being useless like this.'

'Darling, I am much more worried about you.' Eleanor

had been arranging flowers from the garden in a large vase on the sideboard. 'Can I get you a cup of tea? A piece of toast?'

'Tea might be nice. I couldn't eat a thing.'

'How long have you been feeling unwell?' Eleanor asked.

'It's been coming on,' Alex said. 'Maybe something I ate. Nothing serious.'

'Alex, if it's food poisoning you must see a doctor.'

'Oh, Mum, I don't *need* to see a doctor,' Alex replied irritably. 'It will pass.'

But pass it didn't and even before Eleanor had made tea she tottered up to bed and lay there wishing the earth would close over her.

Later Eleanor crept in with tea on a tray and put it gently on the table by the bed. She put her hand on Alex's brow. It was sticky, but not particularly hot.

'I don't think you have a temperature,' she said. 'Maybe just rest.'

She poured the tea and decided with so little response from her daughter that the best thing would be to leave her alone.

'Tea's there' she said quietly. 'I'll leave you to sleep and I'll pop up later to see how you are.'

'Mum, don't fuss,' Alex said crossly, and used to her daughter's outbursts from old her mother gently closed the door after her. Things were getting back to normal alright.

Alex spent the day in bed. She left the tea untouched and when Eleanor came up to collect the tray she was fast asleep. There was no more sickness and later Alex, still in her gown, made another attempt to come downstairs where she assured her mother that she was feeling much better, but said she didn't feel like supper. After watching a bit of television which was unfortunately, as far as Alex was concerned, full of bad news about Iraq she went upstairs again to bed assuring her mother she would be as right as rain by the next day.

However early the following morning Eleanor was woken again by the sound of retching in the bathroom. This time she got up and found Alex slumped by the bathroom door as though she was almost too weak to move. She took her by the arm and steered her gently back to bed.

'I am definitely calling the doctor;' she said.

'I forbid you to call the doctor, Mum. I hate doctors and I simply have some sort of bug. Besides I must make some phone calls or this trip to Iraq will never get off the ground.'

Eleanor desperately hoped that that would indeed be the case.

Still unable to concentrate on anything Eleanor occupied the morning as best she could, confiding in Cathy her anxiety about Alex's condition.

'It's so unlike her,' she said. 'I've seldom known my daughter ill. She must have picked up a very nasty bug indeed.'

'She looked all washed out to me,' Cathy, who had poked her head round the door of Alex's room, observed. 'She's doing too much if you ask me.'

And she doesn't even know about Iraq, Eleanor thought, wishing somehow that she could confide in her but not daring to. Relations between them remained strained. Eleanor was reminded about the old adage of not lending money if you wished to keep a friend, and how she wished she hadn't. What a lot of trouble they would all have been spared.

After Cathy had gone Eleanor was wondering what to do about lunch when there was a ring at the door and, to her surprise and as if in answer to some unspoken prayer, she found her doctor standing on the doorstep. She gazed at her with some astonishment, an expression the doctor misinterpreted.

'I just popped in to see how you were, Mrs Ashton, as you haven't been to see me for some time. I do hope I haven't disturbed you.'

'Of course you haven't.' Eleanor stepped aside. 'Please come in. I didn't know doctors made house calls these days.'

'Well some of us do,' the doctor said going into the hall, 'although I must confess I just happened to be passing.'

Eleanor didn't know her doctor very well, having had little need for one before her accident. She had just registered with the local GP as one does and was fortunate to have a rather nice, youngish woman doctor whose approach was informal and sympathetic rather than authoritarian.

She led her into the sitting room and offered her coffee.

The doctor refused and said she didn't really want to stay if everything was OK.

Eleanor sat opposite her. 'I am getting on very well,' she said, 'another eye op come September, and after that it's just a question of time, I guess.'

Dr Jennifer Beamish made a note on a pad she had produced.

'I could do with a prescription for some more painkillers,' Eleanor continued. 'I still get those headaches. I had a very bad one the other night.'

Dr Beamish got a pen and, looking at Eleanor's eyes invited her to follow her finger as she moved it from side to side.

'Mmm,' she murmured. 'Still not quite straight.'

'Mr Ferguson said that after the next one I should have quite good central vision.'

'Can you read?' Dr Beamish resumed her seat.

'I find talking books easier. I think I'm lazy.'

The doctor wrote out a prescription which she handed to Eleanor, rising as she prepared to go. Eleanor also got up.

'There is just something else, doctor. My daughter has come back from London and has not been at all well. She's upstairs in bed and I wonder if you'd take a look a her, just for reassurance.'

'What is the problem?'

'She's been terribly sick. Can't keep anything down. No energy. It's not a bit like her. She is a busy journalist, usually a hive of activity. She thinks she's picked up a bug.'

The doctor frowned. 'Has she been abroad?'

'No, but she is preparing to go to Iraq of all places. She has an assignment there. Needless to say I am desperately unhappy about it. I already suggested calling you but she refused.'

'Well it's lucky I popped in then, isn't it?' the doctor said with a smile. 'You are completely exonerated. Let me have a look at her.'

Eleanor gingerly opened the door of Alex's room and put her head round. Alex was awake but just lying staring at the ceiling. She raised her head as her mother entered and looked at the clock at her bedside. 'Sorry Mum, I was . . .' Her eyes opened wide in surprise when she saw there was a person standing behind her mother.

'Alex, don't be angry,' Eleanor said nervously. 'Dr Beamish popped in to see me and as she was here I asked her to take a look at you.'

Alex propped her arm on her elbow and stared angrily at her mother.

'I promise you I didn't call her,' Eleanor said.

'No, she didn't,' Dr Beamish said, neatly making her way past Eleanor. 'But I think it would put your mother's mind at rest if I just took a look at you. Would you mind?'

She said it so charmingly, so persuasively and unthreateningly that Alex slumped back on the bed with a sigh of resignation.

'I'll leave you to it,' Eleanor said and quietly shut the door.

The doctor seemed to be with Alex for an age which worried Eleanor more. She pottered about the house, not quite knowing what to do. She even went into the garden to pick some more flowers and the doctor still wasn't down when she came back. Finally she heard the upstairs door close and the sound of footsteps coming slowly down the stairs. She stood waiting in the sitting room and looked expectantly towards the doctor as she entered.

'Is she OK?' she asked at once.

'Everything is OK as far as I can tell,' the doctor said with a slight air of hesitation. 'Alex is pregnant, Mrs Ashton. I think this sickness is just normal, unfortunately, and it seems to have come on later than usual and to have affected her quite badly. Sometimes it does.'

Eleanor sat down quickly on the chair behind her. 'Pregnant?' she gasped. 'Alex is *pregnant?*'

The doctor looked at her sympathetically. 'You never guessed? Morning sickness? Tiredness?'

'Frankly it never crossed my mind. I thought she was on the pill or whatever. She is a very sensible young woman and has been with Hugo some time.'

'She found it very difficult to tell you. In fact she wasn't going to, but this has just brought it on. She asked me to tell you, easier than breaking the news herself. I've given her something to help with the sickness and another prescription.' She handed the paper to Eleanor. 'If you'd be kind enough to have this made up sometime? I've given her enough for today.' The doctor once again began to gather up her things. Eleanor rose too.

'But how did she expect to keep it from me? That's the part I don't understand.'

'I think you'll have to have a talk, Mrs Ashton,' Dr Beamish said as she went to the door. 'There are a lot of things you'll want to discuss. Let me know if I can be of any further help.'

Eleanor saw the doctor to the door murmuring her thanks and then walked slowly back into the sitting room where she stood looking for a long time out of the window, deep in thought, not knowing what to do next. She didn't know whether to go and see Alex or wait for her to come down. She decided to wait. Alex, like her, would realize that this was a watershed. Everything between them had been changed.

As the sun was shining she did what she invariably did at moments of agitation. She went into the garden and sat on the bench watching the birds in her bird feeders, the flowers growing in her borders, carefully cultivated before her accident and now some of them at their best.

There was a movement beside her and Alex sat down next to her, hands deep in the pockets of her dressing gown. Instinctively Eleanor put her arm round her and drew her close and, for an instant, Alex rested her head against her mother's arm. It was a profound moment for Eleanor whose heart seemed full of a kind of love, the intensity of which surprised her – a deep, heartfelt motherly love. She realized then that her relative estrangement from her daughter was partly, if not wholly, her fault. Alex had never been at ease with her, found it difficult to confide in her. She had been too involved with her work, her social life, her casual love affairs, her marriage, to pay enough attention to her children who she thought were self-sufficient like her. That was probably why James had gone to live in the USA, and Alex had wandered around the world forming relationships with unsuitable men like Hugo who led the same sort of shiftless, restless life as she did. She pressed her mouth against Alex's

forehead and Alex responded by putting her own arm around
her mother's so that for a brief moment they were entwined.
In the end it was Alex who spoke first, gently pulling away
from her mother's clasp.

'Nice woman,' she said, 'I mean I could talk to her. Thank
goodness it wasn't a man.'

'Does that mean,' Eleanor said after a while, 'that you felt
you couldn't talk to me?'

Alex brushed her hair away from her forehead. Her blonde
curls still clung damply to her forehead.

'I just didn't know what to say. I thought after Iraq it
would be such a shock.'

Eleanor turned to face her. 'But how could you possibly
consider going to Iraq if you were going to have a baby?'

'Because I'm not having it, Mum. It is out of the question.
How can I go to Iraq in this state? The doctor said I couldn't
possibly go. Anyway I don't want a baby. I'm not ready for
one and I'm sure Hugo isn't. He doesn't even know. I wish
I'd got rid of it before I came down here. I don't know why
I didn't. The clinic in London could have done it straight
away.' Alex shook her head as if the question still puzzled her.

'You've made up your mind?' Eleanor felt a chill clutch
at her heart.

'Oh yes. Completely. Don't you agree, Mum? You must
agree.'

Eleanor was silent. So silent and for so long that Alex
repeated her question.

'You *must* agree Mum, surely?'

Eleanor put her arm round Alex's waist again not wanting
to lose that precious moment of intimacy. 'I've never liked
abortion,' she said at last.

'No one *likes* abortion. But you can't want me to keep the
baby, surely?'

Eleanor let her arm drop and stood up. 'Yes, I think I do
want you to keep the baby. I would love it and I would
support you in every way I could. However, I know it is not
my decision but yours.' She looked at Alex who had sunk
back on the bench bent over, clutching her stomach and
looking so vulnerable and really quite ill. Eleanor had never
ever seen her like this before and wondered what battle was

going on inside her mind. Could it possibly be that she felt indecisive too?

'Did the doctor suggest anything?' Eleanor asked breaking the silence.

'No. She gave me some pills from her case and said she would leave a prescription with you. She said that after the thalidomide business years ago they had to be very careful, and the best thing with morning sickness is not to take anything, but I said I wasn't going to keep it and if it came away naturally that would be the best. She said nothing after that.' Alex ran her hand across her forehead.

'Mum, I think I'll go in again. I know it's feeble but I feel shattered.'

Eleanor took her arm as they went into the house. 'Would you like me to bring you up tea and toast?'

'Mum do *stop*,' Alex cried agitatedly, roughly brushing her arm away, 'you're treating me like a fucking invalid and frankly I'm sick of it. I wish to God I'd never come down to be mothered by you, that the whole thing was done and dusted, the baby down the pan and I was on my way to Baghdad.'

Ten

Niobe read the letter through and then read it again and again, scarcely believing her eyes. She looked at the London address then at the envelope, turning it over. It all looked very official; correctly addressed to her, typed, short, businesslike and to the point. If this was not a joke or a mistake but true, it was certainly the nicest, most moment-ous thing that had ever happened to her. The letter read:

Dear Ms Fletcher
Spring Exhibition
I saw your work at the spring exhibition in Battersea Park and have since been trying to contact you. I wondered if you would be interested in changing your gallery and would consider another representative? I have had many years experience in the art world and feel I could do a lot to promote your work, which I found startlingly original.

Please get in touch with me if this proposal interests you and if you would like to come and see me and discuss terms. Or maybe I might come and visit you?
Yours sincerely
Adam Winslow

'Yes, oh *yes,* Adam Winslow,' she said half aloud and ran to the telephone. She only got through to an answerphone. It was on answer: 'You have got through to the Adam Winslow gallery. Sorry there is no one to take your call at the moment, but please do leave a message and we will get back to you as soon as we can. Thank you.'

Niobe took a deep breath and quickly replaced the receiver, not daring to leave a message. It was a pleasant-sounding, slightly foreign woman's voice, but what would she say? What *could* she say? She would prefer to speak to a human being at the other end rather than an anonymous woman who might forget to give the message and possibly not return the call. In an instant Niobe's life was transformed from a general all-pervading feeling of discontent and depression, which had haunted her since the London exhibition, to be replaced by a sense of joyful expectation that seemed to offer a way out from a dreary and miserable lifestyle.

Niobe looked at the clock. Just past ten. She had a mound of washing to do, but instead she went to her studio and excitedly began looking at her canvases stacked against the wall. He had found her work 'startlingly original'. No one had ever said that before. She had found the attitude of most people indifferent or patronizing. Only she had really believed in herself and now here was someone else who believed in *her*. She began to sort through her canvases arranging the ones she thought he would like. She had not done any painting for ages. Owing to this feeling of hopelessness, the failure to make anything of the London exhibition, she had almost abandoned it. But now she could rapidly produce a few canvases and maybe take them up to London to show him. He suggested he would like to come down and see her. Here, with the kids screaming around and Francis hostile and sulking in the background? No, thank you, Mr Winslow. If they met it would be in London. She would buy some new clothes, have her hair done, maybe restyled, nothing fancy. She knew she was good looking enough without going to any additional trouble, but she did want to smarten herself up and not be too much the country girl from the back woods, which increasingly she felt she had been reduced to.

She decided to telephone again and went back into the house, made herself coffee and redialled Mr Winslow's number. This time there was a human, male, voice at the other end of the line.

After ascertaining that she was speaking to him she introduced herself, trying to keep her voice calm. 'Hello, Mr Winslow. My name is Niobe Fletcher. You wrote to me about my exhibition.'

There was a slight pause as though he were trying to place

her, then he said, 'Oh, yes, of course! I'm sorry we didn't meet at the exhibition. I left it rather late and when I returned you had packed up and gone. Well, how about it then?'

'I'd certainly like to meet,' she said with enviable detachment. 'I shall be up in London in a week or so and maybe we could talk?' She felt she was handling it very well. It wouldn't do to appear too keen.

'That is great, Ms Fletcher.'

'I could bring you some of my latest paintings.'

'Even better. Can we name a date?'

'Could I telephone you? I have to make some arrangements.'

'Certainly. Very nice to speak to you.'

'And to you. I'll be in touch.'

She replaced the phone, aware of how quickly her heart was racing. She swallowed her coffee. How had she sounded? Not too keen but, she hoped, not too indifferent. She looked at the clock and then she made a swift decision and ran out of the house and across the road.

Despite the medication Alex still felt lousy, not only in the morning but all day. Her mother had left her in the garden while Cathy took her to the shops. She had of course apologized for her rudeness and bad temper and, of course, her mother had said she understood. Wasn't that what mothers always did? They had to try and understand the behaviour, sometimes uncivilized and irrational, of their young and make allowances for it. She knew that if her mother seemed overprotective it was because she cared and at the moment was extremely concerned about her. Alex had felt too ill to have a deep and meaningful conversation on the subject. She didn't even really know how she felt herself.

Alex was stretched out in the garden luxuriating in the warm morning sunshine. She really was being dreadfully spoilt and should be grateful for it, not rude and cantankerous towards a woman who was only just recovering from a dreadful ordeal herself. But there had always been some conflict between them, two strong personalities invariably at times at loggerheads. She hardly had the strength to walk from her bedroom to the garden, let alone get to London for the abortion, which she now felt was becoming urgent if she were not to feel too guilty about killing a baby. As soon as she'd got rid of it she knew she would feel better. The dreadful sickness would be over and she would be able to get off to Iraq and fulfil her contract. She had already had a letter of confirmation from Sara. Maybe instead of trying to get to London she should try and have the abortion nearer here? She'd go and see nice Dr Beamish and discuss it all with her. Here the gentle tones of her mobile suddenly broke the peace and silence of the garden. She put it to her ear.

'Hugo!' she gasped.

'Alex? Alex can you hear me?'

'Yes, Hugo. Oh, darling, it is wonderful to hear you. Can you hear me?' She realized she was shouting.

'Just about. Alex, I can't be long but I wanted to tell you I am OK, though it's rough out here. The situation's deteriorating all the time.'

'Hugo,' she said, 'look, I've had a commission to do a piece on Iraq. I'm coming out as soon as I get a visa and complete the formalities.'

There was silence and for a moment she thought the connection had gone.

'Hugo? Did you hear me?'

'I heard you. Alex, I cannot emphasize too strongly how dangerous the situation is here. You must on *no account* think of coming out. In fact, as far as is in my power, I forbid you. I simply forbid you to come. Do you understand? It is no place for a woman and hardly a place for a man. Do you understand me, Alex? The place is chaotic and as soon as I can get out of here I'm coming home, too. I . . .' At that moment the line went dead and Alex realized that she was tightly clutching the phone with a hand that was shaking.

She was aware of her mother standing by her side looking down at her.

'That was Hugo,' Alex said tearfully.

'Is he all right?'

'He says he is, but the situation in Iraq shows no sign of improving. He doesn't want me to go. He says he *forbids* it. I wish now I had never mentioned it to him. Oh, Mum . . .'

'Look darling, Niobe is here and wants to talk to you. She came a few minutes ago but I told her you were on the phone and it seemed important. I suspected it was Hugo.'

'What does she want?'

'I've no idea. She says she just wants to talk to you alone. She seems sort of . . . agitated.'

'Oh, well.' Alex heaved herself up in her seat. 'I'd better go and see her.'

'Stay where you are,' Eleanor said. 'I have a few jobs to do so I'll bring her out here.'

'OK.' Alex slumped back in her seat again. Bugger Niobe.

Niobe came with unusual diffidence slowly across the lawn and stood by the side of Alex's chair.

'Sorry to trouble you, Alex. I hear you haven't been well.'

'It's nothing. Just a tummy bug.' Alex waved a hand towards the chair next to her. 'Take a pew.' Her manner was abrupt rather than friendly, which seemed to make Niobe even more nervous.

As she perched on the edge of the chair Niobe reached into her pocket and withdrew the crumpled note that she tried to smooth before handing it to Alex.

'Alex, the most fantastic thing has happened. Read this.'

Alex reached for the letter and quickly skimmed the contents. Then she raised her head. 'That's fantastic. Congratulations. You must tell Mum. The loan paid off. She'll be pleased.'

'Oh, it did!' Niobe was clearly brimming over with joy. 'Oh, it did and you lending me the flat and, Alex, I'd like to ask another great favour if I may?'

'And that is?'

'May I possibly borrow your flat again when I go to London? I'd like to spend a few days. Get some new clothes.' She slid her hands down her front. 'Make myself present-able. You know.'

'You look very presentable to me,' Alex said caustically. 'You always do. But I'm afraid I can't let you have the flat. I'll be going up myself in a few days and I'll need it.'

'Oh . . .' Niobe stared rather fixedly at Alex. 'I thought that being pregnant you might be staying with your mum.'

Involuntarily, Alex stiffened.

'Oh, did you? Where did you hear that?'

'Cathy told Francis.'

'Well, she told him wrong. I am not pregnant and I am not able to let you have the flat. I hope you can find somewhere else. I'm glad about this opportunity. Really, I'm very happy for you and Mum will be, too.'

After Niobe had gone Alex rounded furiously on her mother who came out into the garden.

'How on earth could you tell Cathy I was pregnant?'

Eleanor slumped into the chair recently vacated by Niobe.

'Of course I didn't tell Cathy you were pregnant,' she said indignantly. 'I never said a word other than that you had a tummy upset. You hurt me by even thinking such a thing.'

'Then how did she know?'

'She probably suspected it in a way that I didn't. Morning sickness. Country folk are very shrewd, you know. I certainly didn't say a thing.'

'Niobe has had a letter from a dealer who is interested in her paintings and she asked if she could borrow the flat again when she goes up to London. Bloody nerve! As if she hasn't caused enough trouble.'

'And what did you say?'

'Well, I had to say no. Besides, I need it myself. I'll be going up any day.'

'Alex,' her mother said firmly, 'you can't just yet. You know you're not fit.'

'Mum, I wish you would stop interfering. You know I simply have to have this abortion or it will be too late. I'm not happy about it and I don't want to feel I'm committing infanticide, which I shall if I leave it too long. I do want to try and get to Iraq because I need the work. I want the work. I need desperately to make some money.'

'What about what Hugo said?'

'I would expect him to say it. Of course there is danger. There is some danger everywhere. I thought I might ask Dr Beamish about the possibility of an abortion here.' She looked at her mother who had sat back, hands in her lap appearing to be gazing at some far distant place.

'I suppose you really *do* want an abortion, Alex?'

'Of course I do. Why would you think I didn't?'

'Your attitude puzzles me. Why didn't you have it before coming down to see me? It looked to me as though you were trying to delay it.'

'Don't be so Freudian, Mum.'

'I'm serious.' Eleanor paused again and resumed her inspection of that far off, invisible place. 'You know, I would love you to have a baby, Alex. It may seem very selfish of me, but I would. To have a grandchild here in England would give me so much pleasure. Also –' she glanced nervously at her daughter again – 'I don't want to sound corny, but life has always been precious to me and since my accident, doubly precious. I have never liked the idea of taking life away and somehow I feel you don't either. That's why you've hesitated for so long. I may be completely bonkers, but that's how I instinctively feel.'

Alex's reply was scarcely audible. 'Mum, you know what this would mean, don't you? Life would never be the same again and it would put an awfully big burden on you. I have no money. I have no idea how Hugo will react and . . .'

'Then it's yes?' Eleanor scarcely dared breathe.

'I'll think about it,' Alex replied, 'and I suppose I might as well let that ghastly woman borrow my flat. Who knows when we might need her again?'

Niobe opened the door to the Camden Town flat slowly and with care, almost as though she were afraid of disturbing someone. Why? Was she reminded of the time she came back and there was Hugo ensconced in front of the TV with a cigarette and glass in his hand, unaware at first of her presence. Did she hope the same thing would happen now? Was it ever likely, despite Alex's sudden and surprising change of mind? It was difficult to get him completely out of her head; something she almost couldn't admit, even to herself.

Niobe knew all this was a fantasy, yet how did one deal with it? She threw open the door half hoping, half expecting to see him sitting there, but the room was empty. Yet still she imagined she caught the strong whiff of foreign cigarettes as though Hugo had only recently been there. The truth was that she actually didn't want to deal with her fantasy.

Having a vision of Hugo as a possible lover represented
salvation, an escape from the stultifying embrace of her love-
less life with Francis.

Yet there was a strangeness about the room that at first
she couldn't pinpoint and then, as she put down her bag and
took off her jacket, she realized what it was. The large picture
she had left on the wall was no longer there. Instead there
was an empty space with just a dangling picture hook to
indicate that something tangible had once upon a time hung
there.

Niobe felt enraged that it had been removed. By Alex of
course. Hugo must have told her he'd bought it from her,
and that would explain Alex's attitude towards her; her reluctance to lend her the flat; an almost indefinable sense of
hostility directed towards her. He would have told her that
he had bought the painting for her and Alex would have
hated that and resented it suspecting perhaps an involvement.
In a sense she was justified. There may have been no phys-
ical contact, but Niobe knew that Hugo had been attracted
to her. This gesture was not just one of charity to help her
out of a tight spot. He'd gone to a lot of trouble to get to
the exhibition and no one did that kind of thing, went to so
much trouble without a reason.

Wearily, Niobe went into the bedroom with her bag and put
it on the floor, her jacket on the bed. She sat down and wondered
if she could be bothered to go out again to buy provisions, as
she once had. She felt like going straight to bed. Tomorrow
she had to have her hair done and buy some new clothes. It
was terribly important to look the part for the meeting arranged
for the day after, and not just like some impoverished country
bumpkin for whom success was a distant dream.

With sleep in mind she drew back the duvet and froze
immediately. The bottom sheet was rumpled and in disarray.
Of course it had not been changed and the last people to
sleep there were Hugo and Alex. She imagined them making
love, probably conceiving the baby Alex was carrying, In a
frenzy she drew the duvet up again and resolved that during
her stay here she would sleep on the futon in the sitting
room, and not come into the bedroom again.

*   *   *

Despite all her preparation, the expensive hairdo, the time taken looking for clothes and trying them all on in an incredibly short space of time, Niobe was extremely nervous as she was shown into a sitting room to wait for Adam Winslow. She was sure the sophisticated secretary who admitted her saw through her as a sham. Maybe her hair still smelt of hairdresser's lacquer, maybe it had been cut too short? Maybe she should have left it long, almost reaching to her shoulders instead of clinging as it was now like a close-fitting cap to her skull? Maybe her black, flared trouser suit was too formal, too obviously cheap, or her white lacy blouse too fussy? Maybe she should have worn a plain one or none at all? Maybe her heels were too high and made her look tarty? In short, maybe she looked too raw and provincial? Maybe she was.

Unaware of all these doubts the secretary – it was the woman with the foreign accent – offered her coffee. Politely, Niobe declined. Adam wouldn't be long, she was assured. All very informal. Adam, not Mr Winslow. Very London. She nodded and after the woman had left took a magazine from the table in front of the sofa, which she opened upside down and, unseeing, began to read until she discovered her mistake, thankful no one was looking.

It was quite absurd to be so nervous. Her life didn't depend on this. Well, in a way it did. This could be a start of the recognition, possibly the fame, that had eluded her so long and which she felt she deserved: an acknowledgement, finally, of the talents she knew she had. The detached, imposing, Georgian house was in a tree-lined street in Chalk Farm, an area of London she didn't know but which was quite near the flat, though she had taken a taxi. The room she was in was rather impersonal, functional, minimalist, with abstract pictures on the wall, obviously originals, stripped pine floors with a couple of expensive rugs, a long low sofa, two easy chairs, a polished table in the centre with glossy magazines mostly about art. Through the tall window with shutters on either side she could see into the garden of the house and the backs of the houses opposite.

It seemed that a long time passed before the door opened again and a rather short, stocky middle-aged man casually dressed in a blue denim jacket, jeans and an open-necked white shirt came bustling in, hand outstretched. His features were vaguely Eastern European. His black hair receded from a lofty brow and he wore horn-rimmed glasses with thick lenses. He looked powerful, someone used to money and authority; maybe even an intellectual, a professor, or he could have been a successful banker or businessman.

'Ms Fletcher, I am so sorry to have kept you.' His deep voice had no accent.

Niobe got awkwardly to her feet and found that she towered over Adam. 'That's perfectly all right,' she said indicating the magazine. 'I was reading.'

He took her by the arm. 'Come,' he said companionably, 'into my study and we can talk. When did you come to London?'

'Two days ago,' she said feeling some of the tension drain away. She decided she liked him, feared him a little.

'And do you have somewhere to stay?'

'I borrowed the flat of a friend in Camden Town.'

'How convenient.'

He led her into a large pleasant room overlooking the back of the house, which again had long windows through which she could see the garden and a small orchard against a high red brick wall.

Unlike the room in which she'd waited, his study was cluttered with heavy Victorian furniture, possibly Viennese, shelves of books lining the walls, and a huge old-fashioned desk facing the window and littered with books, files, an overflowing ashtray, small objects doubtless of sentimental value, a few heavy silver-framed photographs and a tray full of writing implements. In a corner, as though he wished to keep it out of sight, was a computer with a monitor and a printer. It certainly didn't fit in with the rest of the room, which resembled a well-loved and much used den. The walls that weren't covered with books were hung with heavy Victorian paintings of hunting scenes and elaborate land-scapes. From the side of the window a large Grecian statue of a nude woman seemed to be brooding thoughtfully over the whole scene. In front of the desk were two heavy, stuffed high-backed red velvet chairs with ornate curved armrests and Adam indicated one of them as he sat down at his desk and consulted a paper before turning to look at Niobe. He appeared to be studying her intensely for a few moments as though he were composing a portrait.

'You are exceedingly beautiful,' he said. 'How did you keep yourself hidden away for so long?'

Niobe was so startled she couldn't find the words to reply.

'I see I've embarrassed you,' Adam said. 'Maybe you don't get many compliments? If not, you should. Now . . .' He leaned back, hands splayed out on his desk. 'So we meet at last. I'm sorry I missed you at the exhibition. I saw you from a distance but when I managed to visit your booth you weren't there. I had so many other appointments I couldn't wait. I looked at your work, admired it, but when I returned you had packed up and gone. Imagine my disappointment! Let me explain my position in case it puzzles you,' he went on hurriedly. 'I have always loved art. My family were Viennese. My grandfather and father were art dealers and jewellers, but they came to England well before the Anschluss – there were a lot of Nazi sympathizers in Austria, and we were Jewish – managing to bring most of their money and some possessions as you see here.' His arms gestured expansively round the room. 'This is a relic of my family associations with my father's homeland, though I was born in England. My father died a few years ago – my mother predeceased him – and left me everything; this house and the fortune he had increased by his skill as a jeweller.

'As I never trained in the family business – my family spoilt me and I had no need to work – and loved art, I decided to build a small gallery and indulge my passion for modern art. I'll show you round later. I am interested in promoting new clients whose talents have not been fully exploited. Tell me, are you represented by the gallery whose name I saw –' he glanced down at the paper on his desk again – 'but with which I am not familiar?' He looked up at her curiously.

'It was something I made up,' Niobe said almost defiantly, deciding there was no point in lying to a man on whom her future might depend. 'You had to have a gallery in order to exhibit there.'

Adam smiled sympathetically. 'In fact you represented yourself?'

She nodded. Adam sat back and linked his hands across his stomach.

'Tell me about yourself, Niobe – if I may?' He raised an eyebrow.

'Of course you may,' she replied with a smile. 'Well, I live in the country, a village in Dorset, with my partner, Francis, and our two children. We have a smallholding – just sheep, a few pigs and some hens. Now that the children are older I decided that I wanted, needed, to do something with my life other than wash clothes, clean and look after a family.'

'Have you always painted?'

She nodded.

'And did you train anywhere?'

She knew this was not the time or the place or the occasion to tell tall stories about the Slade or St Martin's. He was too knowledgeable and too perceptive. As he obviously liked and admired her, honesty was the best, indeed the only, policy.

'I am virtually untrained. I took one or two courses at technical colleges.'

'Excellent,' Adam said with satisfaction. 'All the more commendable. As you have a gift, in my opinion, and you have developed it yourself, we will be able to do a good job in promoting you. In addition you are young and very beautiful. If you don't mind my saying so, that is no disadvantage. How does that sound?'

'I am speechless,' Niobe said sincerely. 'It all seems like a dream.'

'Did you sell many pictures in London?'

'No,' she confessed, 'only one or two. Lots of people, that is, both in my family and my partner's, have told me I'm not much good.'

'But you didn't believe them?'

'I've always had faith in myself.'

'And your husband . . . partner? He must believe in you, surely?'

'He has no faith in me at all and my art irritates him . . . *and* his mother,' she threw in for good measure.

'It must have been very hard?' Adam's expression was studiously sympathetic.

'It was. Very.' Niobe felt like bursting into tears.

As if sensing her distress, Adam stood up and, going over to her, took her arm and helped her to her feet.

'Come, let me show you round my gallery. It is very small but I think you'll like it and then we'll go and have some lunch. I hope you're free?'

They went downstairs, along a corridor and through a door at the end. The whole place exuded light and simplicity. Everything was white except for the paintings, carefully positioned, which adorned the walls, and the highly polished stripped pine floors. The gallery was a long room skilfully lit from the top by a series of skylights so that the walls were free for paintings. There were not very many and a whole wall at one end was bare.

'For you,' Adam said placing a hand lightly against the wall.

Niobe still felt she was in a dream. She would wake up any minute and find herself back home with a mountain of washing to do and the kids clamouring for their food.

'Do you like it?' Adam asked anxiously as if disturbed by her silence.

'I think it's marvellous,' Niobe managed to utter at last. 'It's all wonderful. I can't believe this is happening to me.'

Adam placed a well-manicured hand on her arm and gently squeezed it. 'I am so pleased,' he said in his soft cultured voice. 'Before you go we must discuss terms and . . .' He paused, looking expectantly towards the door that had opened and the woman who had let Niobe into the house came smiling towards them.

Adam extended his hand. 'There you are, my love. We are just going to have some lunch. I am pleased to say that Niobe is happy to have us represent her.' Then he addressed Niobe. 'You met my wife, Caroline, when she let you in. You see, we are a very small outfit and she is receptionist, secretary, art connoisseur and, above all, my beloved companion.' Drawing her to him in a possessive gesture he planted a light kiss on her cheek.

'I am so pleased,' Caroline purred bestowing an approving

glance at Niobe. She was possibly Scandinavian, Niobe thought and, like her, she towered above Adam. 'I've booked a table for us –' she glanced at her watch – 'in about fifteen minutes. That will give us time to powder our noses.'

Caroline took Niobe upstairs to a bathroom that had the same air of understated opulence as the rest of the house; sunk bath, tiled floor, white marble walls and fluffy white towels on the rails. Niobe guessed this was the guest bathroom as there were no personal items about; no toothbrushes, wash bags or little pots and jars of mysterious substances. She carefully redid her face, examining it closely. Adam thought she was 'exceedingly beautiful' – it was a long time since anyone had said that. She looked again at her hair, pulled down the back of her jacket and fastened all the front buttons in an attempt to disguise her lacy blouse. Yes, maybe it was a bit vulgar and the high heels *were* too high. Caroline wore an elegant, well-cut, royal blue trouser suit but with medium-heeled shoes that looked expensive. Everything about Caroline looked expensive. She wore no blouse or shirt under her suit, and Niobe realized without any doubt that she should not have worn one either. Useless to remove it today, it might give the wrong impression. Already Niobe was in awe of Caroline and a little afraid of Adam. They were powerful, controlling people.

Adam and Caroline, chatting intimately together, were waiting for her in the hall and looked up as she came down the stairs. Caroline had long blonde hair, artificially but skilfully coloured, a tanned, but not too tanned, face, so that one would not imagine she spent too much time on the sun bed, clear aquamarine-blue eyes and the sort of healthy complexion of one who took a lot of exercise and ate all the right kinds of food. She was about twenty years younger than her husband.

The restaurant to which they walked was only a short distance away and they were shown to a table on a shaded patio at the back, handed menus and asked what they wanted to drink. Niobe would have loved something strong and alcoholic but, in order to make a good impression, opted for water and Adam ordered a bottle. 'Sensible not to drink at lunch time,' he said opening the menu, 'we never do.'

Thankful that she'd done the right thing, Niobe began to relax again and ordered carefully. They all had salad Niçoise followed by fruit salad and when they'd finished and coffee was served Adam lit a cigarette and then leaned across the table.

'We take fifty per cent of all sales,' he said matter-of-factly. 'It might seem a lot, but it is not unusual and we are taking a risk with you, a completely unknown artist. We give you space in our gallery and put a lot of effort into promotion. That's where we score over other galleries.' He glanced at his wife. 'Caroline used to be in PR and is an expert. She knows everyone, all the gallery owners, the editors of art magazines, the arts people in all the main radio, magazine and TV channels. We think we'd make a very good story of you and how we discovered you and the little we know about you. Wouldn't we, Caro?'

Caroline had been watching Niobe carefully as her husband was speaking.

'Undoubtedly,' she said.

'Don't you think she is beautiful, Caro? Really beautiful?' Adam earnestly addressed his wife.

'She's lovely,' Caroline said warmly as though they were discussing an inanimate object, maybe a statue or a painting, something that could neither see nor hear. 'Really lovely.' She gave Niobe a look of quiet approval, a little nod of the head, a slight inflection of the eyebrow. Then, in her low, melodious voice, she added, 'Can you tell us a bit more about your life? How did you come to be in Dorset? A little about your partner. What does he do, for instance?'

'He's a thatcher by trade,' Niobe replied. 'We have a small-holding and we live a simple life. We have two children aged ten and eleven, Samantha and Freddie. I mostly do the house-keeping, cooking, cleaning and so on. I don't work but have little time for painting. In a rural area you spend a lot of time fetching and carrying the kids to and from school. We have a neighbour, a Londoner, who was the editor of a well-known magazine and was badly hurt in a car crash and I help look after her.'

'What's her name?' Caroline asked.

'Eleanor Ashton.'

'Eleanor Ashton!' Caroline gasped. 'I met her once or twice. She got divorced and decided to take early retirement two or three years ago and went to live in the country. I'm terribly sorry to hear about the crash. When did it happen?'

'Last September. She has made a very good recovery but still has problems, mainly with her eyes.'

Caroline grimaced. 'How awful. She has a daughter, Alex, who is also a journalist and has a very randy boyfriend who plays her up no end. I hear he has other women all over the place, but he never made a pass at me.' Caroline smiled tenderly at her husband. 'He wouldn't dare, would he, darling?'

'Not half,' Adam said contentedly, putting an arm around her waist.

'Hugo,' Niobe said quietly. 'Hugo did like my work. He bought one of my paintings.'

'Did he sleep with you, too?' Adam arched an enquiring brow.

'He certainly did *not*. There was nothing like that between us.'

'And what are they doing?' Caroline looked reprovingly at Adam. 'I haven't heard of them for some time.'

'Hugo is in Iraq,' Niobe said. 'Alex is having a baby. She says she isn't, but I know she is. She has constant sickness, looks washed out and stays all the time with her mother. It is her flat I'm using in London.'

'Isn't it a small world?' Caroline sounded amazed.

'It all seems very bucolic and ideal,' Adam said, 'and Niobe, darling, are you happy?'

'No,' Niobe was astonished to hear herself replying. 'No, not at all. I am not happy. I don't like the country life. I don't like farming and housework; I am not in love with my partner. I can't stand his mother and I would do everything I could to get away.'

Aware that her face must be deeply flushed, ashamed of her impromptu outburst, she stared at them, panting slightly, rather dreading their reaction to this sudden and unexpected loss of control.

Her two companions, carefully absorbing this torrent of information, seemed, from the expressions on their faces, transfixed by her and it was some time before either spoke. Eventually Caroline leaned forward, her hand closing tightly over Niobe's.

'It sounds like a plot for a novel,' she said softly. 'Don't worry, darling. We will look after you. I prophesy a great future for you.'

As soon as she opened the front door Alex knew there was something different about Niobe. For one thing, her appearance had changed quite dramatically. Her normally rather wild, shoulder-length hair had been cut so that it framed her face like a close-fitting cap, accentuating her oval chin and high cheekbones. She hardly ever wore make-up and now there was evidence of blusher, mascara and a pale pink lipstick subtly done, but nevertheless unmistakable. A different Niobe from the one who had left, had returned from London. She still wore her normal faded blue jeans and a loose-fitting top, sandals on bare, slightly grubby feet, but her manner was different, confident, challenging.

Alex had been in the kitchen doing a few chores while Cathy had taken Eleanor to Dorchester to shop.

'Come in,' she said, standing aside, 'Mum's gone out with Cathy.'

'I know.' Niobe stood looking at her. 'First of all, how are you?'

'I'm much better thank you.' Alex led her into the sitting room and indicated a chair while she remained standing.

'Can I get you coffee?'

'No, I'm OK.' Naomi sounded offhand. 'I shan't stay long.' She took the seat indicated and Alex sat down, too.

'How was London?'

'Great, really great. My visit was an enormous success. This gallery wants to take me on as a client and promote me.'

Alex made an effort to hide her astonishment. 'Really?'

'You seem surprised.'

'No, I think that is very good news. Congratulations.'

Instead of showing the pleasure Alex expected, Niobe's expression seemed to harden.

'Alex, what happened to my picture?'

'Picture?' For a moment Alex seemed bewildered.

'The one I gave you for the flat. It hung on the wall in the sitting room.'

Alex's eyes narrowed. She realized she had almost forgotten about it, and now all her old suspicion and jealousy came flooding back.

'You see, Adam, the gallery owner, would have liked to have seen it and it is no longer on the wall.'

'It's still in the flat,' Alex said offhandedly. 'I put it under the bed. I wonder you didn't find it when you used the bedroom.'

'I didn't sleep in your bedroom,' Niobe said icily. 'I used the futon. I didn't want to feel that I was trespassing on your privacy.'

While Alex was digesting this information Niobe continued, 'Didn't you like it?'

'It wasn't that,' Alex answered, 'it was more about the way it came to be there. It was not a gift, as you said. You lied to me about it. I understand that Hugo bought it from you.'

'As a gift for you,' Niobe said quickly.

'No, not as a gift for me. He bought it so that you could pay my mother back the large sum of money you borrowed from her. I wondered what you did to make him do something so generous.'

'*Did*?' Niobe exclaimed. 'What do you mean, *did*?'

Alex stood up and wandering across to the French windows stood gazing out into the garden, then she turned.

'What you forgot to mention when you thanked me for lending you the flat was that Hugo was there at the same time.'

'So?' Niobe's normally pale face took on an uncharacteristic blush.

'So, you were together for the night and he subsequently bought a painting that I understand he didn't particularly like, for a *thousand* pounds, which I guess was far more than it was worth.' Alex leaned towards her. 'Well, Niobe, what happened? What happened in that flat between you and Hugo, Niobe, can you answer me *that*?'

Niobe rose, too, and then the two women faced each other inches apart.

'Nothing happened. Absolutely nothing.' Niobe's voice shook with indignation. 'Hugo very kindly took me out to dinner as neither of us had eaten. It was a courtesy that I appreciated. We chatted, mostly about the situation in Iraq, which I knew very little about and he told me what he was doing and that was that. When we returned we slept in different rooms. I had previously offered to leave and go to a hotel, as Hugo was already in the flat when I arrived, but he wouldn't hear of it. I admit I was nervous about what you might say and think, but the next day he had left before I woke up. To my complete surprise he came to the art fair later in the day and said he wanted to buy the painting to help me pay your mother back. He chose the largest in the show and I nervously asked him for £300, but he insisted on paying me £1000. He'd written the cheque out before I saw the sum and I was overwhelmed. He realized that owing your mother such a large sum of money distressed me and I thought it was extremely kind of him.'

'And obviously it didn't distress you that he paid over the odds for, frankly, a rather ordinary painting?'

'I told him it was too much – naturally I don't consider it "ordinary". I was honest, but he insisted. He gave me a cheque, ran for his car and I didn't see or hear from him again. I swear.'

'But the whole thing had to be a secret from me?'

Niobe looked at Alex almost with pity.

'I think that was logical if you will forgive my saying so, Alex. I guessed you would be suspicious – I would have been in the circumstances – and jump to the wrong conclusion. Frankly, I'm rather surprised he told you.'

'He didn't. Somebody else did.'

Now it was Niobe's turn to look uncomfortable. 'Oh, who?'

'I'm afraid I'm not at liberty to say, but the whole thing has given a new meaning to the term "friendship", as far as I am concerned, and recently you have asked rather a lot of me and my mother. We were, and are, very grateful for what you have done for her since her accident and that certainly was in my mind and hers; but if indeed after accepting my hospitality you slept with my boyfriend, I do not think it was at all a friendly thing to do.'

'I did *not* sleep with your boyfriend.' Niobe's tone was shrill. 'I assure you, Alex, absolutely I did not sleep with him. I regarded him as a nice, generous person and if you want to believe something else that's your problem.'

And almost as though she could bear no more, looking quite distraught, Niobe turned to the door and went rapidly out of the room.

After Niobe had gone Alex sat for a long time in her mother's favourite chair by the window gazing at the garden, her mother's beloved garden, at the birds lining the fence queuing up for their turn at the feeders. It was a very beautiful tranquil scene and Alex realized why it was so important to her mother: the earth and nature being symbols of the eternal resurgence and renewal of life. Gazing at the life in her garden Eleanor had been reminded of how near she had come to death, and in a moment of intense illumination Alex realized then how very important her mother was to her, and how grateful they should be for each other.

What a contrast this peaceful scene was to the chaos of Iraq where suicide bombers were becoming a matter of routine and no one was safe no matter how innocent. What would happen to her mother if she did succeed in going to Iraq and became a victim too? Was it fair, after all she'd been through, to give Eleanor so much worry in the way that she herself constantly worried about Hugo? Alex's hand rested lightly on her stomach. Either she imagined it or could she already feel movement? Yes, it was imagination but might it not also be wishful thinking?

She knew that she was extraordinarily reluctant to get rid of the baby and that she always had been, not only because it was part of Hugo but it was life. By killing the baby she would be imitating all the senseless killing in Iraq as well as depriving the world of a sentient and maybe important human being.

Life was very precious. Her mother was right.

Having made her decision Alex felt uncharacteristically at peace, and started to doze off when she suddenly heard the sound of the front door opening, and soon after her mother appeared taking off her coat.

'Oh darling,' she exclaimed in surprise, 'were you asleep?'

'No, just thinking.' Alex frowned. 'Niobe was here.'

'I see.' Eleanor put her coat on the back of a chair and flopped down onto its seat. 'That must have given you something to think about.'

'It did. She is very cross with me for taking the picture off the wall of the flat and she insists she did not sleep with Hugo. Sometimes I could almost believe her. I don't know. Does it really matter?'

She turned her gaze once more to the garden and said slowly, 'Mum, there is one other thing. I am not going to go ahead with the abortion. I don't think I ever really wanted to and now, well, I have made up my mind.'

She then looked shyly across at her mother and the expression on Eleanor's face was all the reward she could ever have wanted.

Eleven

It would be a Christmas baby. Eleanor thought Hugo should be told, but there was no way to tell him. Since his brief call telling Alex not to come to Iraq there had been no further communication. Once or twice her mobile had rung, but when she put it to her ear all she heard was crackling and static as if someone were trying to get through from a long way away.

Alex's pregnancy was now public knowledge, but the really big news in the village was Niobe's success in finding an agent in London. Everyone was talking about it because she never stopped telling parents at the school picking up their children, people in the shops, though her partner was silent on the subject whenever it came up at work or in the pub. One should, of course, have been very pleased for Niobe, but few people seemed to be. She had never been popular, mainly because not only was she not one of 'them' but she had never tried to ingratiate herself with the villagers, most of whose families had lived there for generations. She had never joined or taken any interest in any of the local groups, the parish council, the mother's union, or participated in any of the activities that proliferated year round in a small rural community. She didn't even do anything for the school except take her children there in the morning and collect them later in the day. She attended church on special feast days only, like Christmas and Easter, and seldom went to the pub. Niobe had no close friends and kept herself apart. Not surprisingly people regarded her as stuck-up, and felt that this stranger from outside had ensnared a well-liked local man who should have married one of his own kind.

Cathy, who had never liked her son's partner, didn't help by putting the boot in whenever she could, stoking the flames of suspicion, distrust and ignorance and it must be said that Niobe did nothing to try and gain the affection of a woman who was essentially kind and caring.

Poor Francis, everyone thought. Poor Francis, indeed.

Eleanor was disturbed about the break-up of the relationship between Alex and Niobe who, after she abruptly left the house, avoided them. On the other hand it made Cathy closer and more inclined to confidence. So, whereas there was a break-up on the one hand there was reconciliation on the other.

Eleanor felt herself stuck in the middle, concerned for Niobe because in the past she had done a lot for her and she felt a certain sympathy for a woman who had striven all her life for success in a sphere that had so far eluded her. She saw a lot of good in Niobe, whereas others didn't see any.

It was this that made her decide to go and see her and one day while Alex was out she walked across the road and found Niobe in her studio, smock on, busy painting. She turned with some surprise as Eleanor knocked hesitantly at the door.

'Oh, hi,' she said coldly when she saw who it was.

'May I come in, Niobe? I won't stay long because I can see you're busy.'

Niobe was working on a large canvas full of broad, colourful strokes and stood aside to wipe her hands on a rag as if to indicate she was being interrupted and this had better be brief.

'Niobe, I wondered how you were? I haven't seen you for some time.'

'Well, I should have thought the reason for that was obvious,' Niobe said.

'But your quarrel, or whatever you call it, disagreement, I don't know, is with Alex not with me.'

'If you think I still owe you something because of the money . . .' Niobe began with a sulky expression on her face. 'I know I should have told you myself and thanked you, but . . .'

Eleanor held up her hand.

'Niobe, I don't think that at all.' Eleanor, still standing

and leaning heavily on her stick, began to feel tired. 'Might I sit down?' she said and Niobe grudgingly pushed over a chair.

Eleanor realized now why Niobe got so many people's backs up, because she could be so ungracious.

'I just came to see you to tell you how really delighted I am to hear that you have found an agent in London. I realize how important that is for you. I also wanted to see how you were because you have done so much for me and I am so grateful for it, and I have another favour to ask. I wondered if I could ask you to take me to the hospital for my eye op next week and bring me back as Alex won't be here? She has to go to London on business.'

'Mmm . . .' Niobe gazed distractedly at her canvas.

'I can see how busy you are,' Eleanor said, beginning to feel resentful at this complete lack of civility, 'but I would be grateful. Besides, you know I am very fond of you, Niobe. Believe me, I am really very glad you have this opportunity and no one deplores more than I the break-up of the relationship between you and Alex, which I am sure is based on a misunderstanding.'

With a gesture of impatience Niobe wiped her brush and placed it near her palette.

'I did *not* sleep with Hugo,' she said vehemently. 'If you can get your daughter to believe that then we may have achieved something. She seems convinced that I did and I did not. I liked him and I think he liked me. Maybe he was a bit sorry for me, I don't know, because I did tell him that I felt guilty that I had to borrow the money from you because of your accident and that, and I didn't know if you could really afford it. I felt awkward and embarrassed about it, I really did, and instead of *giving* or *lending* me the money he thought he could make it all right by buying the painting. Yes, he paid more for it than it was worth now, but if Adam really does for me all he says he is going to, in time I could be as famous as Tracey Emin or Damien Hurst and look what rubbish they produce!'

She smiled and Eleanor smiled, too.

'I don't think yours is rubbish,' she said, looking across at the new painting. 'I think it is interesting. Colourful. I'm sure you must have talent and now an important London dealer thinks so, too.'

'Alex doesn't. She put my painting under the bed. I think that is the worst insult an artist could have.' Niobe's voice rose as if to indicate the importance she placed on the snub.

'Whatever Alex thinks, it is her own opinion.' She beckoned to Niobe. '*Please* let us be friends again?'

But Niobe wanted to press home her point. 'Do *you* believe I didn't sleep with Hugo, Eleanor?'

Eleanor felt in a quandary. 'Niobe, forgive me, but I don't want to get involved in all this. I know nothing about it and it's not really my business. Alex is in a very emotional state, don't forget. Hugo has been gone now for some time and she doesn't know where he is or if he is OK. He is the baby's father. She wanted to join him in Iraq and was given an assignment. She decided to keep the baby for all sorts of reasons, and this has considerably complicated her life.'

Niobe was listening to her thoughtfully. Suddenly, to Eleanor's astonishment she went over and planted a kiss on her cheek.

'Thank you, Eleanor. I'm in an emotional state, too. Very emotional. I feel I am at an important crossroads in my life. A turning point. No one has ever believed in me and I have had to have faith in myself. Now, out of the blue, comes this man who has his own gallery and wants to give me an exhibition all to myself. Imagine that!' Niobe's pale face momentarily flushed with triumph. 'I want you to know that I do appreciate what you did for me, for the money. It made all the difference to my life and I have behaved badly towards you. I should have come to you straightaway to thank you. Instead, I was so angry with Alex and the way she treated my picture that I simply ignored you because I couldn't wait to have a go at her.' She sat down on a chair that she had placed next to her visitor and looked at her earnestly.

'You see, life has been very hard for me, too. You know I am not happy with Francis or my life here and I feel everyone is against me. They talk about me and criticize me. They always have because I don't fit into this boring little community. Francis has no sparkle. He is dull and boring, too, and that is about the long and short of it. Yet he is a good man and in many ways I am unworthy of him. Now, make what you can of that!'

'I make it a very sad story,' Eleanor said gently putting her hand on Niobe's. 'But what you're going to do about it, I don't know.'

'I want to leave him and start a new life.' Her eyes, as she looked at Eleanor, suddenly welled with tears. 'I really do. I want to go and live in London and enjoy my life before I am too old.'

The days were getting shorter, the nights longer. Alex looked mournfully out of the window of the London flat and noted that the cars already had their lights on although it was only five o'clock, but it had been a dull, late September day and the roads were wet and misty as she had driven up.

She didn't quite know why she had come. An excuse, perhaps, to get away, to see Sara and tell her the news about Iraq and, of course, the baby. At six months it was no longer possible to hide her pregnancy. She was still not sure she had done the right thing. She didn't long for a baby and she didn't feel ready for motherhood. She didn't really understand what had persuaded her: reluctance to destroy burgeoning life, the expression in her mother's eyes, her obvious sense of grief at the loss of a grandchild, or the fact that buried deep down she herself didn't know when or if she would ever become pregnant again.

As long as she was with Hugo there would be no question of a child, and she would be certain not to make any more mistakes about contraception.

She didn't know whether to stay on in London or go back to Dorset just to have the baby, or whether to let the flat and stay with her mother. Now it was a question of their needing each other instead of Eleanor being dependent on her. What Sara had to say, if she had anything to offer, would be important. They were meeting for lunch the following day.

Alex moved away from the window reflecting that she had never known such a difficult, indecisive time in her rather difficult and indecisive life.

The flat seemed a cold and unfriendly place. If Hugo were suddenly to return everything would change, including her plans and perhaps her current pessimistic mood. She went into the bedroom and looked around. In it was a bed, a wardrobe, a chest of drawers with a mirror and an armchair that had seen better days. The flat could do with a complete makeover. It was hardly a warm, friendly place into which to introduce a baby. It had a temporary feel, a refuge for birds of passage, which was essentially what she and Hugo had been, flitting from one continent to another, a life spent in hotels and boarding houses, sometimes tents, and on occasions without any shelter at all. In fact, come to think of it, she didn't know if it were a suitable place for a baby at all.

And what would Hugo have to say to all this? Hugo, who didn't even know he was an expectant father.

She drew back the duvet and saw how crumpled the bed was. She was quite shocked that Niobe had left it in such a bad state, and then she remembered their last conversation when Niobe had told her that she hadn't used the bedroom at all but had slept on the futon. So the dishevelled, crumpled bed was as it had been when she last slept there with Hugo. Suddenly she threw herself on the bed and pressed the sheet to her face, engulfed in tears of longing, regret and remorse.

Alex and Sara met in the same restaurant in Soho they had eaten in before. This time Sara was there before her, her face a picture when she saw Alex coming towards her and took in her bulge. Alex sat down with a smile.

'Surprised?' she said.

'Astonished,' Sara announced. 'You didn't tell me any of this when you talked about going to Iraq.' Her tone of voice was suddenly cool.

'I intended to have an abortion. It was fixed and then I changed my mind. I'm sorry. I should have written, but for a long time I was undecided and also quite sick.'

'Maybe you should,' Sara said, 'you certainly left it a bit late.' Her tone was still chilly as she agitatedly arranged and rearranged the cutlery in front of her. This was uncharacteristic, as she was a woman who seldom lost her cool.

'I guess you won't be drinking?' she asked as the waiter handed them their menus.

'Maybe a glass,' Alex said. 'And, listen, I'm paying. I feel I've annoyed you and I want to make it up.'

'Don't be ridiculous,' Sara said firmly. 'The company pays and unless you've come into a legacy you will need all the money you can get because you won't be going to Iraq.'

'True.' Alex stared at the woman sitting opposite her. She felt at that moment they were poles apart. One, the hard-bitten journalist, a ruthless go-getter, a career woman hell bent on getting to the top. That might once have described her, but it no longer fitted. She was now vulnerable, a quitter, a woman who had very little idea about her purpose in life or even its meaning.

'I know I've let you down, Sara, because you got me the commission.'

'Everyone was quite excited,' Sara said as she studied the menu. 'I'm just going to have something simple. Scallops and caesar salad,' she said addressing the waiter, 'and a bottle of Verdicchio.'

'I'll have the same,' Alex said and again addressed Sara as the waiter took the menus and moved away. 'Frankly, things have got so bad in Iraq I doubt I would have got a visa. Maybe you could tell that to your editor and forget about the baby. I promise not to put it in *The Times*. I will need work.'

'I'll see,' Sara said thoughtfully chewing on a breadstick. 'It's a valid point. We didn't bank on it, just admired your guts for trying. Tell me –' she nodded her head in the direction of Alex's bump again – 'what did Hugo say?'

'He doesn't know. I have not been able to contact him and, occasionally, if he manages to get through we are almost immediately cut off. Anyway, I don't think this is the sort of thing you announce on the phone. I'm not sure he would be too pleased. He has children already, you know, and is not exactly a good father.'

'So, why?' Sara's hostility seemed to be evaporating. 'Have you all this time been secretly longing for a baby?'

'No, not at all.　But frankly, I was never keen on the idea of an abortion. Also, there is the clock ticking and all that.'

'But, my dear, you're younger than I am. You're not yet thirty, are you?'

'Thirty-one, but I know I will never make a contraceptive mistake again, as I did this time and I am sure that if I stick with Hugo we'll resume our old nomadic lifestyle and a kid will just not suit.'

The lunch, having lost its purpose, was brief and the two women parted with routine kisses outside the restaurant. Alex had tried to bring up the subject of further work, but Sara wasn't interested and Alex knew for certain that that avenue of freelance work was now closed to her. Sara would never trust her again. There were plenty of other talented journalists waiting on the sideline.

Yet, feeling strangely and unexpectedly happy, free from constraint, once again Alex made her way to the river and wandered along the Embankment as she had that day which seemed such a long time ago now, but was only a couple of months past. She stood leaning over the wall by Cleopatra's Needle and stared into the muddy waters of the Thames, at the passing boats of river trippers and across at the South Bank complex and the Festival Hall. Autumn had set in and the ground was carpeted with leaves. A few idlers, like her, were mooching along. One or two people walked briskly as though they had a purpose. Alex couldn't explain just why she should feel so happy and at peace because here she was in a kind of limbo expecting a baby, unsure where its father was, pretty nearly penniless and dependent on her mother, and with no clear idea of what the future held. Not much really to be content about, yet she was.

She wandered back towards Tottenham Court Road, caught a bus for Camden Town and as she got to the outside door of the flat her mobile started to ring and she quickly groped in her bag for it before it stopped. This time his voice came loud and clear.

'Alex.'

'Hugo!'

'Darling, I think I'll shortly be on my way home.'

'Oh, Hugo. When?'

'I'm not sure. I'm in Baghdad again where phoning is easier. I've just come back from the Kurdish provinces and I have an awful lot to tell you, but . . .' The line went dead again.

Coming home. She practically ran up the stairs to the flat and frantically unlocked the door, almost as though she expected to see him on the other side.

Suddenly the flat took on a whole new aspect. Hugo would be coming home, here, and the place looked so neglected, deserted, and unwelcoming. It badly needed a fresh coat of paint and new furniture.

With their future ahead of them life took on a new meaning. Hugo would be with her. He would understand, and she realized then how very much she loved him and how much she missed him and how much she longed to see him again.

That feeling of joy and contentment and of inner peace that she'd had by the river seemed at last justified as though it had been an omen.

'What a clever boy I am.' Mr Ferguson had a smile of satisfaction as he looked closely at her eyes. The relief was immediate. She could look at him straight instead of turning her face sideways. He was a surgeon of the old school, a man who didn't give away much. There had never been any real personal contact between them, no chumminess, no chats about family and holidays. She didn't know if he was married or had children, or where he lived, but he did the business and that was all that mattered. She respected him enormously.

She was sitting in a chair looking towards the hospital window and he applied a local anaesthetic before beginning to stitch the muscle he had operated on. It was uncomfortable but not as bad as some of the previous procedures she had endured. Finally he stood back and surveyed his work once again and with a nod to the nurse left the room.

Eleanor was promptly sick in the bowl the nurse had been holding, just in case, and was wheeled back to her room.

All that day and the following one she was unable to eat or drink; even water made her nauseous. It was the effect of the anaesthetic she had been given for the main operation, and finally the anaesthetist was sent for and prescribed medication.

By the third day the sickness had subsided, she felt a lot better and was now resting on the top of the bed, dressed and waiting for Niobe to collect her. She gazed at the trees through the window, gently shedding their leaves with the advance of autumn. Autumn Eleanor thought of as a sad time, yet it was also one of hope, the earth shutting down for the winter in order to prepare for spring. She had a lot to prepare for: a grandchild. She still couldn't believe that it was going to happen and she was a little apprehensive because just before she went into hospital Alex had telephoned to say Hugo was coming home and she would stay up in London to prepare the flat for his arrival.

Who could say what would happen? All sorts of imponderables now that Hugo would learn, shortly, that he was to be a father.

The door opened quietly and Niobe put her head round.

'Ready for home?' she asked and Eleanor slowly swung her legs off the bed.

'Ready,' she replied.

She felt a little unsteady and clung on to her stick. Niobe took her case and holding on to her arm took her to the reception where Eleanor, after signing a few discharge papers, walked slowly towards the car parked outside. Feeling a bit dazed she sat in silence as Niobe manoeuvred the car out of the hospital drive.

'OK?' Niobe said, glancing anxiously at her.

'Yes, I'm OK.' Gingerly, she touched the patch over her eye. 'In a few days I should be able to remove this and have better vision. How are things with you?'

'Brilliant,' Niobe exclaimed. 'Couldn't be better. I am going up to London with my paintings for the exhibition. Francis has finally given in. He realizes he can't stop me and has agreed to drive me to London.'

'When is the exhibition?'

'They will hang some pictures straightaway. They have a lot of space. The proper opening, the gala launch for my work won't be until early next year.' She looked at Eleanor. 'I hope you'll come. You, and Alex, of course.'

'I will most certainly try and come. I don't know about Alex or what her plans will be or even where she will be. You see, Hugo is coming home. For all I know they may whisk off abroad again.'

'With the baby?'

'Who knows?' Eleanor gave a wry smile. 'Where are you staying in London?'

'With the Winslows. They've invited me. They have a lovely house in Chalk Farm. Oh, I can't tell you how excited I am, Eleanor, and all this is thanks to you.'

'There is no need at all to thank me. You hardly had the money for any time at all.'

'But you weren't to know that and it was very generous of you. You changed my life, turned it around. You took a risk and trusted me, which is why I was so anxious to pay you back. I want you to know how much I appreciate it and how much I regret what happened, you know, with Alex. And I assure you, I intend to pay Hugo back whatever he says.'

'But he bought the picture.'

'Yes, but at a greatly inflated price. Anyway, I want it back to hang in the gallery and I'll buy it back from them. They don't want it. They don't even like it. Alex lost no time in taking it down and putting it under the bed! That hurt, but now it doesn't matter. Nothing matters.'

Eleanor was silent as she reflected on the extraordinary turn of events that involved her and her family, just because she had lent someone a thousand pounds.

'No one believed in me. No one thought I could paint.' Niobe's tone was suddenly bitter.

'Often it is a matter of people liking your work, take Hockney, for example,' Eleanor replied. 'A lot of people even think Picasso is rubbish.'

'By the way,' Niobe said, 'Caroline Winslow told me she knew you.'

'Caroline Winslow . . .' Eleanor pondered the name. 'Yes, I do know her,' she continued after a moment, 'not well, but we've met a few times at exhibitions and things when I was on the magazine. Tall, striking blonde? I think she is Swedish.'

'That's her.'

'I didn't know her husband was an art dealer.'

'He's a little man, well, not little but Caroline and I tower over him. I think she is a lot younger than he is and maybe they haven't been married all that long. However he has a lot of charm and personality which makes up for his small stature. I like them both.'

'I do remember there was a buzz about her,' Eleanor said. 'She knew everyone. She'll certainly get you noticed.'

She lightly touched the arm that clutched the steering wheel. 'Good luck to you, my dear. You deserve it and I'm so glad Francis is coming round. I'm sure he is proud of you and maybe your relationship also will turn the corner. I hope so.'

The house was in such a pretty part of Hampstead, on one of those narrow lanes leading up to the Heath. You could have been in the heart of the country. It was a cottage, but had been cleverly extended with three bedrooms and a sizeable back garden. It stood back from the road in front and was surrounded by a high hedge making it very private. It was very expensive, but the owner who had inherited it from his mother was anxious to sell so the agent felt he would take an offer. However, it would have to be quick because a lot of people had shown interest.

'Can you pay cash?' the agent asked.

'Hardly,' Alex said with a smile, 'but I'm sure something could be arranged. My fiancé has to see it first.'

'Of course.'

Alex looked out of the window at the pretty back garden with a tall willow tree, a huge magnolia, a herbaceous border that needed a lot of attention. Like the rest of the house the garden bore a sad air of neglect. She had fallen in love with the house. Already she could see the pram on the lawn protected from the sun by the surrounding trees. Why, there might even be a dog scampering around and they would go for walks on the Heath, the three of them and the dog, just like a proper family. It would be a reminder of the family she had had so long ago when she was small, before Mum and Dad had got so busy and successful, which left them little time for family life.

They would take a few years off from travelling, may even have another baby, and she would learn to do domestic things in the kitchen and Hugo would be working in the study they would share. Maybe they would write books about the adventurous life they had led and the places they had visited. After the trauma of Iraq, she was sure even Hugo might want to rest and settle down at least for a time.

With three bedrooms, there was plenty of room. She had already decided which one would be the baby's room. She turned to the agent.

'I love it and I do want it,' she said, 'very much.'

They walked to the front door and Alex looked around once again. The old lady had been in her nineties when she died and quite a lot of work needed doing to it, but nothing structural. Once all the old furniture was out and they had theirs and the place had been repainted, well . . . dream on, she thought.

'When will your fiancé be home?' the agent asked as he locked the door behind him.

'Very soon. Please try and keep it for me.'

They shook hands. The agent offered her a lift but she said she wanted to walk and plan. After he had driven off Alex turned round again to look at the house.

Perfect.

She sauntered towards the Heath and stood looking at the pond and the children playing by the side of it, pushing their boats out, watched over by indulgent, happy parents.

It was chilly. Alex shivered suddenly and stuck her hands deep in the pockets of her coat. She was almost at a loss to account for this sense of euphoria that had somehow gripped her since she had heard Hugo was coming home. After all, the future was full of imponderables. It was a long time since they had been together, so much had happened. She had found she was pregnant. Against all her instincts she had decided to have the baby. Hugo had been in a war zone. They had been cut-off for months, unable to communicate. Sometimes she hadn't known whether he was alive or dead. And then there had been that last phone call, the warmth, the love and yearning in his voice, detectable even over so many hundreds of miles: 'Darling, I'm coming home.'

And from that moment everything had changed.

Mulling over her plans, her happy, optimistic plans for the future, Alex turned in the direction of Haverstock Hill towards home.

As she climbed up the stairs she could hear the sound of the television from within. Her pulse quickened as she laid her hand against the door and gently pushed it open. She was greeted by a strong, familiar smell of cigarette smoke and the sight of Hugo's back as he sat slumped in front of the TV, head sideways as if he were dozing, a glass tilted perilously in his other hand. She crept quietly across the room and gently removed the glass from one hand, the cigarette from the other, without his seeming to notice.

She stubbed out the cigarette and, putting the glass on the table, went behind his chair and put her arms around him.

'Wake up,' she said gently kissing the top of his head. 'You're home now. Safe.' She kissed him again and, stumbling to his feet, he turned and took her in his arms, his hand moving slowly down her body, lingering on her breasts, her hips, then to her stomach where it rested. Fully awake now his eyes opened wide as he stared at her.

'What's this?' he asked taking a step back. The expression of amorous delight and pleasure on his face changed immediately to one of dismay. 'You're not *pregnant*, are you?' His tone was one of outrage rather than pleasure.

Speechless, Alex nodded.

'Whose is it?' He stepped right away from her, searched desperately for his cigarettes and lit one.

'Oh, Hugo,' she walked over to him and attempted to put her arms round him again. 'Whose do you think?'

'It can't be mine.'

'Of course it's yours.'

'But when? We haven't fucked for ages.'

'When? When we last slept here in March, just before you went away. The baby is due about Christmas.' She tried to conceal the extent of her dismay at his reaction, her horror that he should even think it was someone else's. He had now taken up his drink again and put the glass to his mouth.

'I was somehow hoping you'd be pleased,' she said falteringly.

'Pleased!' he exclaimed. 'How can I possibly be pleased? You said nothing to me. I am amazed you should even think I wanted a baby and if you wanted one you should have told me and I'd have advised you to find another father. Anyway, I thought you were on the pill? What a nasty trick.'

He glared at her accusingly, his expression one of disgust, and she reeled at this sudden, abrupt change in mood from her wonderful sense of euphoria only such a short time ago. The dream was over, the thought of the pretty little Hampstead house with babies and dogs and walks on the Heath dissolved into thin air. How she had deceived herself.

'Of course I was on the pill.' She moved away from him and sat down in one of the upright chairs by the side of the table. 'But you arrived suddenly if you remember, un-expectedly, and I'd run out . . .'

'You could have told me, or did you do this deliberately?'

He went to the drinks table again and replenished his glass. Just in time she stopped herself remonstrating with him.

'Of course I didn't do it deliberately! It was not a nasty trick. I simply never thought. I was so excited to see you again. As for telling you, I didn't even realize I was preg-nant until the spring when I began to be horribly sick.'

'Then why didn't you get rid of it? That's what I can't understand.'

He slumped into a chair and rubbed his forehead in bewil-derment.

'I meant to, Hugo. I made an appointment at the clinic. I was coming out to Iraq, if you remember. It was all fixed up. Also, I wanted an end to this ghastly sickness.'

'Then why didn't you?'

'Well . . .' she hesitated. 'It's hard to explain but, among other things, Mummy wanted it so much.'

'Your mother wanted *what*?'

'She didn't want me to have an abortion.'

'But what in heaven's name did it have to do with your *mother*?'

He was now really almost out of control. She wondered how much he'd had to drink before she'd arrived. She had been house hunting all day. The Hampstead house was the last one she'd seen. She felt desperately tired and, again, nauseous.

'Mummy's been through such a lot,' Alex said quietly. 'She really wanted a grandchild.'

'And you were the milch cow who would give her one? God Almighty, Alex, I really don't understand you. Too late now, I suppose?'

'Don't be so horrible, Hugo.' She looked at him appealingly, but even as she did she realized the cause was a lost one. He'd always been low on empathy.

She put a hand on her stomach. 'Much too late. Besides, I rather want it, too, and, silly of me I realize now that I have seen your reaction but I was so hoping that you would want a baby from me.'

'Well, I don't.' Hugo stood up and replaced his by now empty glass. 'In short, I don't. I don't want a baby, Alex. I've got two and I've been a lousy father. I have no paternal instinct whatsoever. You've pulled a fast one on me.'

'I did *not* pull a fast one on you. How could I know I'd be so fertile? It was not intentional. It was not meant. But . . .' Her expression softened. 'Darling, it has made me so unbelievably happy. My sickness, which almost crippled me, stopped as soon as I came to the decision. I think somehow it was meant, if you can believe such a thing.

'It made me decide to take a rest from the wandering life, at least for a while. I hoped you might want to do the same after Iraq, and I wanted you to be happy and share it with me. Oh, and I saw a lovely house today in Hampstead, a little cottage with a garden. I could imagine the baby asleep in its cot and me pottering in the kitchen while you worked in the study. I thought we could write books.' Her voice quickened. 'And it wouldn't be forever. Mummy so wants the baby she can look after it when it is a bit older. I'm sure she'd enjoy being in London again, meeting all her old mates. It's not *forever*, Hugo. It's not a life sentence, just a chance for a different kind of lifestyle for a while.'

Wondering if he were even listening to her, he looked so distracted, she stopped and crossed to him again trying once more to put her arms round him, but he thrust her roughly aside and backed away, staggering slightly and putting a hand on the table to steady himself. She realized then that he was probably quite drunk and she should change her tactics.

'Hugo, you look terribly tired,' she said in a practical tone of voice. 'We'll talk about it tomorrow. We'll go through all the pros and cons and I'm sure you'll feel differently.'

'I am tired,' he said in the broken voice of a defeated man. 'I haven't slept for twenty-four hours. I couldn't wait to get back and see you. I was expecting a lovely relaxing time together. Instead, I find you're going to have a child. It is terribly unreasonable of you, Alex. It astonishes me. How on earth could you expect me to take that in without any warning?'

'Maybe tomorrow it will be better after you've had a good sleep,' she said soothingly, her hopes bolstered by his change of tone. It was a shock and she had not handled it well.

She looked across at the window and saw that outside it was now pitch dark.

'Would you like to go out for a meal or shall I fix us something?'

'I'm not a bit hungry,' Hugo said. 'I just want to sleep,' and he went into the bedroom and shut the door.

Later than night Alex crept in beside him, but there was no welcoming, forgiving arm encircling her, though she knew she had woken him. He turned his back on her and went back to sleep without a word.

She slept fitfully, but around dawn fell into a deep sleep and when she woke up the light of the mid-morning sun was streaming through the window. She put her hand out but found that the place beside her was not only empty, but cold and she knew then without any doubt that Hugo had gone.

Twelve

H e always had been unreasonable, Eleanor thought, disappearing and not saying where he was. In fact, despite his macho manner and appearance Hugo was a very immature, childish person and not for the first time she wished Alex had never got involved with such a man. But that was the attraction apparently and even now, despite the hurt he had caused her, she knew Alex missed him, wanted him and wished fervently that he would contact her again, maybe appear as he had before; just turn up.

It was early morning, always a favourite time when she had made her tea and lay with the cat resting beside her. They had made their tour of the garden, which looked increasingly bedraggled with the onset of autumn. As soon as she woke, that nagging, low-key feeling of depression surfaced again, more so today than usual because it was the anniversary of her accident. Her hand instinctively tightened on Melody's back as she recalled yet again that bright day, a day just like today, when she was undecided whether or not to walk to the sea and Jean had made a telephone call that changed her life.

Then there was Alex who had arrived home a few days before in a state, with the news about Hugo and his reaction to the baby. She had woken in the morning to find that he had just taken off and there had been no explanation or word since, not really that any were needed. That in itself was enough to make her feel depressed, never mind the anniversary. But as far as Eleanor was concerned it was typical of the man she wished her daughter had never met. Why did people get involved with unsuitable partners? It made one wonder again about this mysterious thing called *love*. She knew Alex would be better off without Hugo, but it might take her a very long time to realize this. She was glad the time for termination was past or maybe in her misery and distress Alex might have been tempted.

Her door opened and Alex put her head round. To Eleanor's surprise she was dressed and looked as though she were ready to go out. Eleanor glanced at the clock. 'Early for you, darling?'

'I couldn't sleep, Mum.' Alex perched on the bed. 'Too much to think about. I thought I'd walk to the sea.'

She gazed earnestly at her mother then, leaning towards her, unexpectedly kissed her cheek.

'I've been a pain, Mum, and I'm sorry and I know what day it is for you. I woke thinking of you.'

Eleanor smiled. 'Anniversaries are never very nice, at least not that kind.' She patted Alex's hand. 'Thank you for thinking of it. Off you go for your walk. It's a lovely day as it was a year ago.'

She listened to Alex going down the stairs and shortly after the front door closed. Something good had come out of that life-changing event of the year before: she and her daughter had become closer and had begun to understand each other in a way they never had before. But it had been at a cost. It was an irony that Alex had come to look after her and now their roles were reversed. Not that having a baby was an illness, but, in the circumstances, Alex would need her mother more than she needed her. Yet nothing was predictable, and she was sure that if Hugo did turn up he would be forgiven and their unsatisfactory peripatetic life would resume. The London flat was a very unsuitable place in which to bring up a baby, on the first floor with no garden and surrounded by streets full of traffic. On the other hand, the Hampstead house Alex had rhapsodized about was certainly also out of the question. She hoped with all her heart that for the time being at least Alex would stay with her, and she would have the incalculable pleasure of being near or with her daughter when her grandchild was born.

Alex sat for longer on the wall than she had intended. It was sunny but cold with the bay curving towards Portland in the east and Lyme Regis in the west. This was not a busy shipping route, but a couple of small boats could be seen almost as shadows on the horizon. There were one or two beachcombers looking for fossils, a solitary fisherman casting his line as the waves broke gently along the sea shore, continuous crests of soft white foam. The usual seagulls swooped hopefully over the water, occasionally diving and reappearing triumphantly with a catch and flying back towards the cliffs.

The sea had as usual a therapeutic effect. Despite her effort to appear calm that morning she was in a state of inner turmoil. A terrible bleakness, a sense of despair seemed to have completely taken possession of her. She had made an effort for her mother and also for herself, for her unborn baby. She knew Hugo wasn't worth all the heartache he'd caused, yet a part of her, maybe because she loved him, still made excuses for him. She could see why he was so upset and, to some extent, why he had left in the brutal way he had. It was a very great shock for a man who valued his independence and they had never discussed marriage in all the years they'd been together. But then she knew she always had been very adept at making excuses for Hugo, and failing to recognize his talent for opting out of difficult personal situations. In the field of his work he was a lion, completely unafraid, equal to any challenge; domestically he was a rabbit.

She felt she could have spent all day gazing out to sea, but she had begun to feel very cold and rather hungry so she got off the wall and turned towards home.

There was no activity at the pub as she passed. It was still very early and she walked up the road thinking about her mother and that awful day a year ago when she had had that phone call in India telling her about her mother's accident and that she might not live. Even then Hugo had been reluctant to let her go back, not taking in the gravity of the situation at all, because of course it didn't concern him. He had gone into a deep sulk and said he thought James should be the one to go, not her.

As she got near Niobe's house she was surprised to see the white van parked outside and Francis standing at the back busy loading it. He was not wearing his working clothes but a jacket and trousers and she hailed him as she approached.

'Hi,' she said.

'Oh, hi,' Francis looked awkward, even furtive, as if he had been caught out doing something he shouldn't.

'Going on holiday?' Alex knew it was a fatuous remark, even as she made it. No one went on holiday in late September.

'No,' he said, 'Niobe is going up to London with her pictures for this exhibition.'

'Oh, so soon?' Alex looked surprised and at that moment Niobe came round the house carrying a painting that was almost as tall as she was.

'Hullo,' she said, also looking slightly sheepish. 'Been for a stroll?'

'Just down to the beach. I find it hard to sleep.'

Niobe nodded and handed the painting over to Francis who took it carefully from her and re-entered the van. Alex could see that it was already half full.

'My, you have a lot,' she said. 'You must have been painting furiously.'

Niobe was smartly dressed in a black trouser suit with no shirt or blouse underneath, but a rather nice topaz necklace. Her new hairstyle framed her delicate features with a little kiss curl over her forehead. For make-up she'd used a light lipstick but a lot of mascara. She really had abandoned her country image, her casual informal way of dressing. She was halfway to being the complete cosmopolitan.

'Alex, might I have a word?' she said beckoning her inside. 'Won't take a minute.'

'Sure.' Alex and followed her into the house. Francis stayed out of sight inside the van.

As soon as they got inside Niobe came straight to the point.

'Alex, you may think this is a cheek, but I wondered if I could borrow the painting, you know, the one Hugo bought and which you put under your bed? It would be a focal point in the room for my exhibition. Eventually I would like to buy it off you for the price Hugo paid for it.'

'Oh, sure,' Alex said taken completely by surprise, but careful not to show it. 'In fact you can have it.'

'Oh, I couldn't . . .' Niobe's voice trailed off.

'Yes, you could. It doesn't have good memories for me.'

Niobe's expression immediately became defensive. 'I know you don't like it . . .' she began.

'It's not that.' Alex took a deep breath. 'You might as well know, if you don't already as nothing round here remains secret for very long, Hugo and I have split. I don't really want the picture any more.'

'But Alex, I assure you there was nothing between Hugo and me.'

'That has nothing to do with it and, frankly, I don't care much now. I just don't want the picture and you're welcome to it. Please don't feel offended. And by the way if you can find Hugo you're welcome to him.'

She paused at the door as she was about to leave. 'Tony in the cafe downstairs has a key. Good luck with the exhibition.'

'I was hoping you and your mum might come . . .' Niobe began, but Alex, having heard enough and thinking that perhaps she had said too much, went swiftly down the path waving to Francis who stood staring at her as she passed.

'What was all that about?' Francis asked as eventually Niobe joined him.

Niobe, her face flushed, stared with annoyance at Alex's back. 'Do you know, I can't stand the woman,' she muttered, 'no wonder her boyfriend dumped her. Now, let's go for God's sake or we'll be terribly late.'

The pair were very silent as they drove up to London, Francis doing the driving, his eyes fixed steadily on the road ahead. Niobe kept glancing at him, still scarcely able to believe they were on their way at last, pictures all packed up in the back of the van. They had had a terrific row the night before and, indeed, ever since she told Francis she was going up to London to stay for a while the atmosphere had been tense. The mood, the whole domestic situation affected both children who looked unhappy and insecure.

None of this deflected Niobe who had her eyes set on a single goal: to be acknowledged as a painter, to be exhibited by a prestigious gallery in London; in short, to be famous.

Francis, who seldom wore anything other than frayed jeans

and a shirt, had smartened himself up. He wore a pair of grey flannel trousers and a tweed jacket, a checked shirt open at the neck and a shiny pair of new brown shoes rather than boots on his feet. His hands were never particularly clean, nor were his nails, but both had had a good wash as had his hair. He looked, she thought, almost respectable, but she still wondered how she had ever fallen in love with him. Had she in fact ever been properly in love, or was it his Mellors' charm, as Lady Chatterley had discovered, his sexuality that at the time – and they were both quite young – had appeared irresistible? In her mind she was the Lady Chatterley figure, a city girl with a decent education, a good middle-class upbringing, a modicum of sophistication who, discontented at the time as she invariably was with her lot, had thrown herself at a rustic man of the soil. What a long time she'd had to regret it.

He glanced at her, maybe distracted by her gaze.

'Shall we pull in at the next stop and have a snack?' Both had skipped breakfast and the children had been at Cathy's for the night.

'Good idea,' Niobe said and shook herself out of her reverie.

Francis filled up with petrol at the next service station and they went into the cafe and ordered a late breakfast. Niobe was very hungry, having hardly slept and feeling almost desperately anxious to get out of the house in case something went wrong. The bitchy way Alex had shown contempt for her and her painting by offering it to her for nothing had made her feel diminished and insulted, and thus bad-tempered. More than ever she resolved to make something of her life, to make Alex jealous and envious of her.

For a while they ate, their silences now rather a matter of routine. She thought that Francis was more preoccupied than usual and he kept staring fixedly at her.

'Is there something wrong?' she asked at last. 'Have I got something on my face? A spot perhaps, a piece of food?'

'I just wondered when you planned to come back?' Francis said.

'Is that why you're staring at me?' she asked pointedly.

'No,' Francis put down his knife and fork. 'I was thinking

how beautiful you are, Niobe, and how afraid I am of losing you.'

His answer took Niobe completely unawares, surprising and even shocking her, the humble way he said it and the expression on his face. She also replaced her knife and fork, wiping her mouth on a napkin.

'What a funny thing to say.'

'It's true. You are beautiful and I love you, Niobe.'

'You have an odd way of showing it,' she said prosaically, resuming her meal. 'I don't think you have ever said anything like that to me before. It's a bit late now.'

'It's only because I'm awkward and bad at expressing myself. I know you've grown away from me, and I don't know what to do about it. I'm desperate about it at times.'

'Well –' Niobe calmly joined her hands on the table – 'I don't know what to say, Francis. If you cared so much about me you could have done something before.'

'I think I've made you unhappy and I haven't meant to. I'm an awkward man and I've made a mess of things, but I do love you and I don't want you to leave me.'

'Who said anything about leaving? I'm only going for a few days. I've got the children. Don't you think I love them?'

'Yes, I do.' He reached out a hand and put it over hers. 'Niobe, I'd like it very much if we got married.'

'Don't be silly, Francis,' she said crossly. 'What will that serve? Nothing.'

His grasp tightened. 'Promise me then you won't do anything rash?' His voice was tight with desperation.

'I promise,' she said, releasing her hand from his and partly rising from her chair. 'Time we got off. The Winslows will wonder where on earth we are.'

The lunch was simple, a selection of cold meats, salad and cheese with a delicious rosé to drink, all beautifully set out in their elegant dining room overlooking the front garden. The atmosphere of the house was one of restrained elegance, pervasive good taste, nothing over- or understated. Niobe felt so at ease here, as though she already belonged and the room to which Caroline had shown her was also perfection. It was at the top of the house and had a low sloping ceiling, walls a soft eggshell blue, stripped pine floor scattered with Swedish rugs, a white dressing table and chest, a double bed with a pale blue spread and an en suite with basin, shower and lavatory.

'Would you like your husband to stay the night?' Caroline had asked looking at the double bed. 'He is very welcome.'

'No, thank you,' Niobe had said hastily. 'He has to get back to feed the animals.'

'I forgot you had a farm. What a pity. Well, if you stay with us for some time – and you are welcome to stay as long as you like – maybe when he comes to collect you he could stay a night or two?'

Niobe said nothing and Caroline gazed at her searchingly for a minute. Her expression was warm and friendly, but curious, too. She had slipped her arm through Niobe's and squeezed it. 'I am *so* glad we found you, Niobe.'

Francis and Adam seemed to get on surprisingly well. While Caroline had shown her her room Adam had taken Francis round the gallery, where they had stacked Niobe's paintings, and then the rest of the house and garden. They'd met up in the hall and gone straight into lunch. Clearly the Winslows were busy people who didn't like wasting too much time on frivolities. There was a foreign housekeeper who wore a white coat and hovered discreetly in the background, leaving them after they had sat down and she was sure they had everything they wanted.

'Francis has been telling me all about thatching.' Adam seemed quite animated. 'It is absolutely fascinating, very skilled. He's promised to take me up and show me how it's done when I come and visit you.'

'Darling,' Caroline said with a pointedly sarcastic smile, 'I thought you were afraid of heights?'

'It's something I shall have to try and overcome.' Adam's way with her was very gentle, reasonable and almost protective.

Francis, who had been tucking into his food with gusto, paused for a moment, still chewing.

Niobe felt desperately ashamed of him, his gaucheness, his table manners, the way he held his knife and fork, fists clenched as though he were digging the garden. His hands were calloused and his nails blunt and grimy despite the obvious effort he'd made to spruce himself up. She could imagine the exquisitely turned out and elegant Caroline looking at them and thinking that these were the hands that embraced her when they made love, which, heaven knew was rare enough these days. Perhaps she would compare them to the soft, white, immaculately manicured hands of Adam, now correctly holding a knife and fork.

'It's not so bad once you're up,' Francis said, still munching away like a cow chewing its cud. 'Roofs that need thatching are seldom very high. Most cottages have only one upper floor. I'll gladly take you up, Adam.' He swallowed his food and looked animatedly over at Niobe. 'We'd like them to come and stay, wouldn't we, dear?'

Niobe gulped, thinking of the chaos the house was always in, piles of washing, kids' bicycles and gear stacked all over the place, to say nothing of the fact that it needed redecorating and a general makeover, which they were always too poor to afford to have done and too busy to do themselves.

'Well, we'll see,' she said nervously.

'I suggested that when you came up to take Niobe back you might like to stay on a day or two,' Caroline said sweetly, practically ogling him. There was something instinctively sexy and provocative about Caroline.

'We can't leave the animals,' Niobe said curtly.

'We could always arrange something . . .' Francis began and Niobe shot him a warning look.

'Anyway, we'll work something out,' Caroline said smoothly. 'Meanwhile, we have all the fun of hanging Niobe's paintings and preparing eventually for the great exhibition.'

As if taking a cue from Niobe's expression, Francis looked at his watch. 'I should be getting back,' he said. 'It takes a good three hours and as Niobe said there are the animals to feed.'

Caroline rang a bell and the maid sidled into the dining room as they all got up and walked to the door with Francis, who was obviously reluctant to leave, hanging back.

'You'll be OK, Niobe?' he enquired anxiously.

'Of course I'll be OK,' she said impatiently and, aware of Caroline's interested gaze, 'I'm in very good hands, don't worry.'

'Oh, don't worry we'll look after her,' Caroline said gaily putting an arm round Niobe's shoulders. 'And we won't let her out at night after dark!'

She and Adam thought it was a great joke and chortled. Niobe found it less amusing, but tried her best to smile and appear relaxed.

'Any idea when you'll be coming home?' Francis persisted.

'Oh, in a few days, I expect. I don't want to outstay my welcome.'

'No fear of that,' Adam said eagerly. 'We have to set up a lot of meetings for you.'

He put a reassuring hand on Francis's shoulder. 'Don't worry, old chap, but you take care you behave yourself, too.'

That again provoked more merriment between the Winslows, and Niobe began to feel as though they were treating them both like a pair of country bumpkins let loose in the big city for the first time. For the first time, too, she resented it.

They shook hands with Francis, Caroline artlessly kissing him hard on the cheek, which Francis was completely unprepared for and made him stumble backwards out of the door, nearly missing his footing, his face reddening as he did. Niobe watched him, thinking what a fool he made of himself, yet realizing that his clumsiness and naivety were made worse by the unconsciously patronizing manner of the Winslows.

They all walked down to the van and Niobe allowed him a quick peck on the cheek before he climbed into the cab and shut the door.

'Take care,' he said to Niobe, clearly feeling emotional. Putting the van into gear he listened politely for a few seconds as Adam gave him instructions as to which route to take in order to avoid central London before, with a wave, he drove off.

'What a charming man Francis is,' Caroline said as they turned back into the house. 'You will miss him.'

* * *

Alex pushed open the door of the pub having spent the past hour sitting on her favourite place on the sea wall and feeling now in need of a drink. Much as she loved her mother and appreciated the depth of their newly-discovered relationship there were times when she yearned to be alone. There was always the constant worry in Eleanor's eyes, the feeling that her mother was over-concerned about her, as any mother would be in this situation. Sometimes, however, her worry was too palpable and, to Alex, unnecessary. She was, after all, thirty-one years old, a woman of the world, an experienced journalist and traveller and had long ago left home. That's what she told herself anyway, but sometimes in her more vulnerable moments she did feel like a frightened young girl who still found it hard to believe that Hugo could abandon her in such a cruel and cowardly manner after all she'd thought they meant to each other.

The inside of the bar in this old sixteenth-century pub, with its beamed ceilings, was always dark and today it seemed more so than usual. The sea had been choppy with storm clouds rolling in from the west, and there was the sense that winter was not too far away. She went up to the bar and chatted to Martin who was polishing glasses, ordering a soft drink, which she took to her customary seat by the window.

'Hello, Alex,' a voice said and she looked up to see Francis, dressed in working clothes, a glass in one hand, plate in the other, standing in front of her. 'Mind if I join you?'

'Francis, I didn't see you,' Alex said shifting along the bench to make room for him.

'I was in the next bar and I heard you.' Francis sat down and put his glass and plate on the table. 'I'm glad of the company.'

He smiled at her and not for the first time she thought what an amiable bloke he was, and not bad looking either. Hard to see why he and Niobe didn't get on, unless it was Niobe's fault, which she rather suspected it was.

'Niobe still in London?' she asked.

'Yes, and the children are staying with Mum.'

'Unusual to see you here this time of day.'

'Unusual to be here,' Francis said brushing the froth from

his lips with the back of his hand. 'I've got work down here.'
He gestured vaguely towards the window.

'Any idea when Niobe will be back?'

Francis took a mouthful of bread and shook his head.
'None at all. It's a very nice place she's staying at. Very
classy set-up. Plenty of money.'

'Yes, I vaguely knew Caroline Winslow. I met her once
or twice, just at social functions.'

'They've taken to Niobe in a big way. They have a
specially-built gallery at the side of the house and a whole
wall for her paintings.'

'Do you happen to know if she got the painting from my
flat?'

Francis stared at her. 'Painting from your flat? I don't
know anything about that.'

'She just very kindly gave me a painting as a way of
saying thanks for letting her stay there. She wanted it back
for the exhibition.'

'She never told me that.' Francis finished his ploughman's
and sat back, arms folded. 'There's a lot I don't know about
Niobe,' he added thoughtfully and then he turned and looked
straight into her eyes. 'Alex, I hope you don't mind my
confiding in you, but sometimes I get quite desperate about
Niobe. I've failed her. I've never understood her properly
and I think she's tired of me and the fact that I have never
appreciated her work and, frankly, I haven't. I never took
it seriously. I just expected her to look after me and the
house and kids and I suppose I resented this other side of
her. Now I feel I am paying for it. I'd be glad of your advice,
to be honest.'

'But when you first got together and decided to live
together and have kids, wasn't she painting?'

'Not like now. She didn't have a studio. She didn't make
a career of it. It just came gradually. We were very passionate
about each other; really in love, then it just went downhill.
She never tried very hard to fit in with the village. At first
people invited her to do things and then stopped. I think they
thought she felt she was superior and perhaps she did.' Francis
drank deeply from his glass and gazed out of the window
as though, in his longing, he could imagine Niobe appearing

on the other side to make everything alright. 'Things do change, don't they, Alex?'

'They certainly do,' Alex said not really knowing what to say. Nor was she particularly anxious to be involved in the tortuous relationship between this curious, clearly ill-suited pair. She looked at the clock over the fireplace and began to make a move.

'I'm really not a good marriage guidance counsellor, Francis. I wish I could help, but I don't know what to say. My own life is a bit of a mess and no doubt someone thinks I should be straightened out, too.'

She looked at him sadly. She and Hugo had been really passionately in love, too, couldn't keep their hands off each other. And how badly that also had gone downhill, but she couldn't help Francis and he couldn't help her.

'I must get back to Mum,' she said getting up. 'She'll be waiting for lunch and will wonder what's happened to me.'

'I'll drive you.' Francis also rose. 'There are a few things I have to get from home to finish this job. It's starting to rain too.'

They went out into the car park and he helped her into the van.

'When is the baby due?' he asked looking at her.

'December. By the way, Hugo disappeared. I don't know if you know.'

'Mum said something,' Francis mumbled taking the seat beside her. 'I'm very sorry.'

'And you think *you've* got problems?'

'Maybe he'll come back?'

'Don't think so.' Alex stared hard out of the windscreen realizing the landscape was suddenly blurred, not by rain, but by her tears. Sometimes she couldn't bear it and felt overwhelmed with grief.

They drove the rest of the way in silence as if each were locked in their own special thoughts, their own special misery; Alex literally fighting back the tears. Francis stopped outside the door and for a moment they just sat in silence.

'It has helped talking to you,' he said earnestly. 'I hope I didn't bore you.'

'You didn't bore me at all. I just wish there was some-thing I could do.'

'You've got your own problems,' Francis said awkwardly. 'I was really sorry to hear about . . .' He stopped abruptly as if, having noticed her tear-stained face, he was afraid of making her misery worse.

Alex began to get out of the van just as the door of the house opened and her mother appeared looking anxiously around, then, seeing the van, smiled with relief.

'Cheers,' Alex said to Francis who raised his hand to Eleanor and, putting the van into gear, drove off.

Eleanor walked down the garden path and opened the gate.

'Worried again, Mum?' Alex asked sharply. 'I am quite grown up, you know.'

'I didn't expect to see you arrive with Francis.'

'Well, in case you think we had an assignation, we didn't.'

'I thought no such thing—' Eleanor began, sensing the beginning of a row.

Alex brusquely interrupted her. 'We bumped into each other in the pub. He'd done some work nearby and was having lunch. I was thirsty and popped in for a drink.' She tucked her arm through her mother's as they walked back into the house. 'I don't fancy him at all, but he's a really nice guy. Niobe doesn't deserve him. In fact, come to think of it, she and Hugo are well-suited, both selfish to the core.'

They entered the house and went straight into the kitchen where Eleanor had laid out a cold snack. Once again, as she slumped by the table and watched her mother move slowly around the kitchen bringing plates from the fridge, mixing dressing for the salad, Alex felt a pang of guilt that her mother was looking after her rather than the other way round.

She stared hard at herself in the kitchen mirror. She was beginning to look bulky and awkward and ugly. Then, hating what she saw, she turned abruptly away and realized that her mother was studying her, too, as she put plates down on the table and poured water for them both from the jug. Alex felt a surge of irritation with her mother for being so concerned, so over-possessive and it reminded her of being a child again with that hated childish dependence, that longing to get away. She found herself resenting those knowing eyes.

'You look very tired, Alex. Maybe you should go to bed for the afternoon?'

'Oh, Mum, do *stop*. What about you?' Alex asked beginning to boil over. 'You're the one recovering from an accident. I'm not even ill.' She gazed at her mother's bloodshot eye. The lid was half closed over it and it looked painful. She felt pity and anger at the same time because she was so helpless and her life so futile. Her mother, by making such an effort to be normal and uncomplaining, was irritating her in the extreme.

Suddenly, Alex felt like bursting into tears but Eleanor looked upset enough without adding to it, so she controlled herself by biting hard on her lips. She knew her emotions were all over the place; the price of getting herself pregnant by a man who neither wanted her nor the baby.

Eleanor sat down opposite Alex and for a while they both ate in silence as though Eleanor could sense that anything she might say would be out of place.

'Mum, what are you going to do when I leave?' Alex asked abruptly. 'I mean, have you thought about it?'

Eleanor looked up sharply.

'*Are* you thinking of leaving?'

'I have to leave sometime, Mum. I can't be a mother's girl again, ever. I don't know what you think about the future, or even if you do think about it.' She sat back, not hungry and nervously crumbled her bread on her plate.

Eleanor did the same, pushing her half full plate to one side.

'I do think about it, of course I do. I don't expect you to want to live with me permanently. I thought maybe a few months after the baby was born, in case I could be of help.'

'But a small baby screaming all the time will be very tiring for you.'

'I can cope. We can cope.'

Eleanor stood up and, taking their plates, scraped the contents into the kitchen bin and put the plates in the dishwasher, then she returned to the table.

'Alex, I am completely at your disposal. I want to do what I can to help you without getting in the way. You can stay or you can go whenever you want. I will help you in any way I can, financially or otherwise. However, I don't think the Camden Town flat is very suitable and maybe you should consider selling it if you want to stay in London.'

'Of course I want to stay in London,' Alex said sharply. 'I'm going to have to get work.'

Eleanor leaned across the table and looked her daughter in the eyes.

'Alex, you may not like what I'm going to say and maybe this is the wrong time to say it, but I'm wondering if you still hope that maybe Hugo will come back. Is that what's in your mind?'

'I don't know, Mum. I don't know,' Alex said and crashed her fist down on the table, glaring at her mother. 'I don't know, and I don't know what I want and that is the truth. One thing I do know, Mum – and I also hate saying this – is that but for you I would never have kept this bloody child and this would never have happened.' She stood up and gestured rudely at her mother. 'In that case Hugo and I would still be together.'

She then charged out of the room in a torrent of tears.

Eleanor, deeply shocked by what had happened, distressed by the violence of Alex's words, remained in her chair for what seemed a very long time. Indeed, she felt physically unable to move, even had she wanted to. She'd known Alex was in a state as soon as she'd got up that morning. She'd mooned abut the kitchen, largely silent and not wanting any breakfast and then saying she needed to go for a walk, clearly to get away from her.

All this she accepted. It was a very difficult time for Alex. Clearly, she had not got over Hugo's desertion, maybe was longing for the phone to ring as it had in the past. She was always inspecting her mobile for texts, had it close at hand, never switched it off or let it out of her sight. Yet living with Alex in this mood was very hard for her, too, and she was reminded of the difficult times they had had when Alex was an adolescent. and how relieved she and Dick had both been when their daughter finally made the break and left home.

Eleanor decided not to go to Alex's room to try and comfort her. She would not want it and it would only occasion another outpouring of her aggression, to which she might unwisely react. Alex, of course, had no intention of leaving at the moment. and her mother was only stirring up things by responding to her. Best say nothing and let the storm pass.

Instead she slowly made her way to her own room and, lying on her bed, wrapped her arms round Melody for the kind of comfort only a silent animal, who loved only you and never argued, could give.

Thirteen

The paintings did look splendid against the background of the white walls. Niobe's use of bright, primary colours made them stand out from all the others in the gallery solely devoted to abstract art. Some of them may have been more skilfully executed by trained artists, but Niobe's somehow stole the eye maybe because of her simple, untutored style. In the corner was the large one Hugo had bought and which she had retrieved from Alex's flat.

Niobe and Caroline walked round the gallery adjusting this one and that until they felt that everything was as they wanted it. In the background Tim, who looked after the gallery and did the hanging, stood silently watching them.

'Now for the next stage,' Caroline said and seized her hand and squeezed it tightly, drawing her close. 'We have to get you known, publicize you. It all helps –' she gazed at her for a moment and a finger reached out flicking a lock of her hair – 'especially with your looks. They will adore you, wonder where you have been all this time. Then we have the big launch sometime in the New Year.'

'I still can't believe it's happening to me,' Niobe said and, disconcerted by the intimacy, but more aware of the gratitude she owed this woman, the debt she had to repay, planted an impromptu kiss on Caroline's cheek to which the tactile Caroline responded.

'I think we've done all we can for the moment,' Caroline said prosaically. 'Adam will be waiting for us. Personally, I'm starving.'

'Me, too,' Niobe said. 'I'll just pop up to the loo.'

'See you in the dining room, darling,' Caroline said as they walked out of the gallery. She waved to Tim and gently pushed Niobe in the direction of the staircase.

Niobe scampered up the stairs to her room where, after completing her ablutions, she carefully applied fresh make-up and ran a comb through her hair, then she peered closely at herself for some time. They said she was very beautiful. Caroline couldn't seem to take her eyes off her. She peered closer. Was she that beautiful? Even Francis, that most prosaic of men, had called her beautiful, a word she couldn't recall him using in all the times they had been together. Had her recent experience changed her? She ran a finger from her forehead, around her eyes and down to the light cleft in her chin.

In this heady atmosphere Niobe felt as though she was a little in love with Caroline, almost like a schoolgirl crush, but there was nothing sexual in her feelings. Rather than desire Caroline she envied her, this superbly elegant, controlled woman with a degree of sophistication Niobe wished she could emulate. She may have been a little in love with Caroline, but she loved Adam too. The pair had completely changed her life, introducing her to a world of glamour and excitement such as she had never before experienced, indeed could scarcely have imagined.

Most evenings there were trips to the theatre or an exhibition, or a dinner at some fashionable restaurant in the West End or Hampstead. There were very late nights and yet in the mornings Adam and Caroline were up early while Niobe, who was used to little sleep, had no trouble keeping up with them, appearing at the breakfast table as fresh and as alert as they, ready for work, for consultation, hanging – oh and what a long, protracted process that was, deciding where each piece would go and instructing Tim who had endless patience. He needed it. A piece would go up and then come down and, after some discussion and repositioning, either go up again or be put somewhere else, and then the process sometimes repeated itself.

Yet though she had no difficulty keeping up, Niobe was weary, but the last place she wanted to go was home.

Adam and Caroline were already seated at the table, having helped themselves to food set out buffet-style on the sideboard by Marie the Thai maid who was also a brilliant cook. Lunch was always light and Adam, a diabetic, would

usually retire for half an hour afterwards to rest while Niobe
and Caroline read the paper or leafed through the magazines in the lounge until he appeared again at about three.
It was a very civilized existence and Niobe couldn't get
enough of it.

Adam looked up with a smile as she sat down, having
helped herself from the sideboard.

'I hear you had a successful morning?'

'Very.'

'Caroline thinks we're ready for the publicity. But your
husband phoned this morning and he seemed rather agitated.'

'Oh.' A sudden chill clutched at Niobe's heart.

'He said he is missing you, the children are missing you
and they wonder when you're coming home?' Adam coughed
apologetically. 'It has been a fortnight and he says you've
scarcely been in touch.'

'I've been so busy,' Niobe said with an offhand shrug of
her shoulders. 'I have rung quite a bit but he's never there.
His mobile is always turned off.'

This was a lie. Maybe she had tried a couple of times, but
what was true was that she had in fact been too busy to think
about anything other than her art and herself.

'Maybe you should go back for a while?' Caroline said
gently and took a sip from her glass of water, gazing at Niobe
over the rim. 'We can always send the journalists down and
a lot of the publicity here can be done without you. I'm sure
they would love to see you in your rural setting, the place
that inspired you and, who knows, it may even help?' She
looked at Adam as if seeking his agreement and obligingly
he nodded.

'We might come down, too,' he said. 'We'd love a glimpse
of the sea, wouldn't we, Caro?'

Caroline nodded. 'Of course we'd stay at a hotel,' she said.
'That'd be fun.'

Niobe sat back and stared at the table, pondering a reso-
lution that she had been gradually formulating in her mind,
one that had gathered momentum ever since she had come
to stay with the Winslows and had been seduced by their
lifestyle. She knew, without any doubt, that it was what she
wanted; not the rural, boring, stultifying life of a country

housewife. But she had not known when the moment to raise it was, or how it would come about: this was now the moment and seize it she must.

'You have been so kind,' she said, 'both of you. You have changed my life and I am so grateful to you, but it is not only that . . .' She paused dramatically and looked at them, her eyes going rapidly from one to the other. 'I don't quite know how to say this because I don't want you to mis-understand me.' She took a deep breath. 'The fact is that I don't want to go home. I have felt like that for some time, long before I came to London, and now I am ready to do it. I have reached a decision to leave Francis, and starting a new life here is the perfect opportunity. I've been looking for a way out for years and here it is.' She sat back, her expression solemn.

The ensuing silence seemed to echo and re-echo round the table. The faces of the Winslows registered neither shock nor disapproval. They just seemed impassive, carefully controlled, as though waiting politely for her to continue.

Niobe went on quickly: 'I have appreciated your hospi-tality and I don't want to abuse it. I think I could use the Camden Town flat after I've made a few arrangements. Alex, as far as I know, is staying on with her mother. If I could stay here for a wee while longer . . .?'

Of the two, Adam seemed the least comfortable about her announcement. He moved back from the table and lit a cigar-ette, blowing a long stream of smoke into the air as he stared at the ceiling as if seeking enlightenment. Finally, he looked at Niobe.

'My dear Niobe, I am very saddened by what you have to say. Personally, I liked Francis and I know Caroline did.' He glanced at his wife who nodded her agreement. 'We thought actually that you were well-suited; a handsome couple. Francis seemed particularly devoted to you. I noticed the way he kept on glancing at you at the lunch table. Clearly, he didn't want to leave you, so I am very sorry that you have come to this decision particularly while staying with us, as it might appear to the onlooker – and I am above all thinking of Francis – as though we were somehow conniving. However, you are our friend and we love you and enjoy having you with us. I'm sure I speak for Caroline when I say that having you here has been like a breath of fresh air. Of course we only know a little about the circumstances of your relationship with Francis, but obviously it has been bad enough for you to want to take such a drastic step, not done lightly, I'm sure. I think I am speaking for Caroline when I say that of course you must stay with us until you have found alternative accommodation.'

'Or changed your mind . . .' Caroline said, her voice scarcely audible. 'You may do that after you've had a complete rest and time to think it over.'

Niobe shook her head and was about to say something, but Caroline went on in the same low, even tone: 'Have you thought about the children?'

Niobe, who had expected more sympathy and under- standing from this sophisticated couple who, she was sure, must have been in and out of relationships all their lives, was rather taken aback by their reaction.

'Of course I have!' she said vehemently in an attempt to regain the ground that was sliding from under her. The last thing she wanted was to lose their respect by appearing an unloving and uncaring mother. 'I think about them all the time, but they will be well looked after by Francis and his mother until we can come to some arrangement about sharing. Of course I love my children and I want them with me. I think about Francis, too. I am not a monster and I want to try and do the best thing for us all. It has not been a happy home now for a long time. Francis and I have different interests and have grown very much apart. He has, as I told you, taken no interest in my painting and I find this hard. I am sure this is the way out for us all. The very best way out.'

'Are you suggesting you might stay in London?' Adam asked. 'Children and all?'

'I haven't made up my mind . . .' Once more Niobe hesi- tated. 'I suppose it depends on how well the exhibition does, how many paintings I can sell.'

Adam shifted uncomfortably and once again looked at his wife, whose eyes were downcast as though in deep contem- plation, or simply avoiding contact with Niobe.

'Niobe,' he said, 'though we have great hopes for you and your success, nothing is guaranteed. We are putting our faith in you, but please do not expect to make a fortune to begin with. After all, you told me you only sold two at the Battersea exhibition and one was to a friend. We intend to build you up gradually, but nothing can be guaranteed. Maybe we're taking a big risk. We're not sure, but it is our mission to encourage young talent.'

'And London is *very* expensive,' Caroline murmured in the same low, slightly reproving tone, seeming to indicate that she shared her husband's misgivings. Niobe could feel them almost palpably drawing away from her. The whole experience was proving an ordeal and she wished most fervently that she had kept her mouth firmly shut.

'Does Francis know how you feel? Has he any idea of this?' Adam went on.

'Oh, yes. For a long time,' Niobe said firmly.

'So it won't be a surprise to him?'

'Yes, it will,' she replied suddenly feeling an unwelcome sense of guilt and a kind of remorse remembering how she had promised him not to do anything rash. 'Yes, it will; a very big shock.' She looked appealingly at them. 'But it is something I have to do and if I don't do it now I know I never shall.'

Caroline rose and going round the table leaned over Niobe and put both arms round her shoulders, her soft warm cheek very close to hers. 'Don't worry, my dear, Adam and I will help you in any way we can, won't we, darling?' She looked across at her husband, who nodded.

'Any way we can,' he repeated. 'Any way at all.'

Shortly after this Adam got up from the table and said he was going for his rest. After blowing the women the usual extravagant kisses he left the room. To Niobe's surprise Caroline also announced that she, too, was going for a brief rest, thus breaking their normal routine and, with the customary quick hug, she also left the dining room leaving Niobe to suspect that she was going to join Adam to discuss the new situation that had just arisen. Despite the chill in the air, Niobe wandered out into the garden contemplating the undoubted fact that, somehow, everything had gone horribly wrong, and it seemed as if a pleasant idyll was, for the moment at least, at an end.

Alex read the letter and passed it to her mother who already knew the gist of the contents. Ten minutes before Francis had arrived at their door in a highly emotional state. Once they had brought him inside and made him sit down, he began to weep and thrust at them the already crumpled missive he had in his hand. Now he had stopped weeping, but sat slumped in his chair, head on his chest, a man in the grips of deepest despair.

The letter read:

Dear Francis
I am very sorry to tell you that I do not want to return home and that I am leaving you. There is no one else, but I think you know we have not been getting on and this has been affecting me and my work. I also think it affects the children, too.

I am taking advantage, unfairly maybe, of this new situation to make a clean break and for the time being I am staying with Adam and Caroline who have asked me to impress upon you the fact that they had nothing to do with this decision. In fact, I think I can say it has quite shocked them, but they are supportive.

Obviously we will have to meet soon to make arrangements about the children and I'll be in touch. I am sorry, Francis. I know I promised I wouldn't do anything rash, but you did sort of force that promise out of me and this has been on the cards for a very long time. I think you knew that. We just didn't face up to it. Now I have and you must, too.

Love
Niobe

Eleanor handed the letter back to Francis. 'Short and to the point,' she said. 'Is it really a horrible shock?'

'Like this it is,' Francis said his voice thick with emotion. 'It's the art business that got to her, the encouragement.' He looked at Eleanor and she was sure he was going to bring up again the matter of the loan yet again, but, whatever his feelings, he didn't.

'I know I have taken Niobe for granted, maybe not appreciated her enough. I should have accepted it and encouraged her instead of ignoring her. When she turned the barn into a studio I was annoyed instead of helping her, and she had to do it all by herself. I did love her and I do still, very much, but I suppose she thought I had an odd way of showing it. On the way to London I told her I wished again we could get married and told her how much I loved her.'

'And what did she say to that?' Alex had been leaning against the window sill, arms crossed.

'She said something like, "don't be silly". She was very preoccupied with seeing these people again and I don't wonder, seeing their posh house and the way they live. Niobe was clearly bewitched by them. I do think they have influenced her, despite what she says.'

Eleanor was trying to visualize Caroline Winslow, but it had been so long since she'd seen her it was difficult, except that she knew she was leggy, blonde, Scandinavian and charismatic. She could, however, imagine the set-up in a large house in Chalk Farm with its own picture gallery. She expected that to them Niobe was a sort of plaything, an amusement. No wonder they'd wanted to divorce themselves from any connection with her separation from their family. She guessed they might well be horrified. It would not fit in with their hedonistic lifestyle, their plan of things at all.

'We'll do all we can to help,' Eleanor said getting up. 'You have only to ask. I have my physio coming in a minute, Francis. I'll have to leave you now.' She looked across at her pregnant daughter and wondered, with her own preoccupations, just what help they would be able to give that was in any way practical. 'Have you told your mother?'

'No, I only just got the letter. My mother had no time for Niobe, as I think you know, and I had to talk to someone. I simply couldn't believe it.' He started to crumple the letter in his hand and once again seemed on the verge of tears. 'I don't know what I am going to say to the kids about their mum. I can tell you one thing, if Niobe thinks she's getting them she has another think coming. I will fight her every inch of the way. They're my children and they belong here.'

'I think you have every chance of keeping them,' Alex said. 'Judges are never very favourably disposed towards women who desert the home. The thing is, can you cope with them?'

'I can cope with them better than she could. Besides, where does she think she is going to live? I know for a fact she hasn't got any money and she can't stay with these people forever, can she?'

'Probably she hopes to sell a lot of paintings.' Eleanor shrugged. 'But, Francis, whether you like it or not you've got to arrange a meeting as soon as you can.'

'Let *her* do it.' Francis raised his chin aggressively. 'Let *her* make all the running. I have the house and the children. It's up to her, isn't it?' He looked at them each appealingly, but neither knew what to say, and as Eleanor went up to prepare for her treatment Alex led the way to the door and showed him out almost in silence.

She walked thoughtfully upstairs to her mother's room. Eleanor had slipped into a gown and was tying back her hair in front of the mirror. She had an hour's physio every week and then in the afternoon a massage. Looking after yourself was one of the best ways to recovery, everyone had told her and she thought everyone was right.

Alex slumped on her mother's bed cradling her head in her arms.

'It's very sad, isn't it? Francis is a real sweetie. The more I see him the more I can't understand Niobe. He is such a nice guy.'

'I hope you're not going to fall for him,' Eleanor said, half jokingly, regretting it immediately as this was bound to get a rise out of Alex, who couldn't take anything lightly at the moment.

'Don't be ridiculous, Mother, of course not. I can say someone is nice without falling in love with them, can't I?'

'Sorry,' Eleanor said contritely. 'I really meant it as a kind of joke.'

'Well, it wasn't funny.'

'No, I know. I'm sorry.'

It was so easy to upset Alex these days; one had to be so careful.

'He is such a contrast to Hugo, that's what I mean, Mum. Kind and thoughtful.'

'A bit dull, really.'

'Oh, I don't think he's dull at all,' Alex said indignantly. 'How can you say he's dull? But even if he is, he is a nice decent man and after a bounder like Hugo . . . Do you know what I wonder?' Alex said thoughtfully.

'What do you wonder?' Hands still pinning back her hair Eleanor looked up.

'I wonder if Niobe and Hugo have got something going in London after all?'

'Oh, darling that is a preposterous suggestion.' Eleanor turned back to the mirror.

'Why is it so preposterous? We never got to the bottom of that painting business.'

'I would put that idea right out of your mind. Don't torment yourself.'

Alex's next statement surprised her mother even more. 'In a way, I feel sorry for Niobe. You can bet she has been dazzled by the Winslows. I mean, why, really, have they done this? I am no art expert, but I know enough to say that by no stretch of the imagination is she good enough a painter to have her own exhibition, and you know that, too, Mum.'

'It's just that I don't understand the abstract,' Eleanor said, making a feeble attempt to be fair.

'No, but that is very ordinary stuff. I tell you, I think Adam Winslow fancied Niobe and maybe something funny is going on.'

'You and your imagination,' Eleanor said fondly as the doorbell rang. 'Would you go down, darling, and let Helen in, and then you have a rest yourself. You look all in.'

'Mum, please *stop* saying that! You know how much it irritates me.'

Yes, she did, Eleanor thought as Alex left the room. She kept on saying the wrong thing. Would she ever learn?

Eleanor had just finished her massage and was resting when her bedroom door slowly opened and she raised her head to see who it was as Alex had gone for a walk. To her surprise, Cathy put her head round.

'Sorry to disturb you at this time, Eleanor. I know it is your rest period, but could I have a word?'

'Why, of course,' Eleanor said sitting up and suspecting what it was about.

'I understand that Francis has been to see you.'

'Yes, he has. I'm really very sorry.'

'You know it's all your fault, don't you, Eleanor?' she said aggressively.

Eleanor felt a surge of indignation as Cathy came slowly into the room, clearly very upset.

'No, I don't,' she said as she pointed to the chair by the window. 'Do sit down and let's discuss this sensibly.'

But Cathy wanted her say and hurried on.

'If you hadn't given her that money,' she began breathlessly as she slumped on the chair, 'none of this would have happened. You know what I mean?' She stared hard at Eleanor.

'I think I do know what you mean.' Eleanor swung her legs over the side of the bed, feeling more able to cope in an upright position. She puffed up the pillow behind her and settled back. 'But if you think Niobe would not have left Francis you're mistaken. She was a very unhappy, restless woman, anyone could see that. She made no secret of her unhappiness, and that long preceded the London exhibition. It may have precipitated things and if it did, I am sorry, but I could not have known what it might lead to, no one could. You know that, Cathy.'

'She should not have gone to London. It unsettled her –' Cathy's eyes narrowed – 'and then Hugo bought that picture from her. That was all very funny. Luckily, I never told my son about it.'

'Oh, you didn't tell him? I did wonder.'

'Francis is a simple, straightforward man. I don't mean he's simple-minded, but he is uncomplicated. He would never have understood and I must say I didn't either, still don't. It would kill Francis to know that Niobe had slept with someone else.'

'We don't *know* that,' Eleanor objected.

'Don't we?' Cathy looked at her askance. 'I know what I think.'

'Cathy, where is this getting us?' Eleanor suddenly felt tired and dispirited. 'What is the point of raking over the past like this?'

'It's not the past, Eleanor. It is happening now. My son has been left in the lurch and he has a farm and a business and two children to look after. What I really came to tell you is that I can't come and look after you anymore. I have to move in with Francis, otherwise he can't cope. My house is too small to have the children permanently. I can't leave Francis alone. I don't know if Niobe is coming back or not. I hope she doesn't, because as you know I never liked her. I always thought she was trouble. From the beginning she had this air of being superior, not like us. But Francis was smitten. He loved her and says he still does, and it is my job to look after him and make things as easy for him and the children as I can. He is well rid of that woman and I hope eventually he does get someone who is worthy of him.'

She rose and stood at the bottom of Eleanor's bed and, looking at her, her expression suddenly seemed to soften.

'I know it isn't an easy time for you, Eleanor, and you did what you thought was best, but my advice for the future is don't interfere in the lives of people you scarcely know and certainly don't understand. You are not like us and you never will be and that goes for all the strangers who come and live in these parts. They buy a home so that the local people can't afford them and have to move away.

'There, I've said my piece, but I have become fond of you, Eleanor, and admire the way you coped. I *may* occasionally be able to pop over and give your place a bit of a clean, but when Alex has her baby, it will all be too much for me. I'm not getting any younger.'

'I understand, Cathy, and I shall miss you,' Eleanor said gently holding out her hand, 'and I do thank you very sincerely for everything you've done for me. I have appreciated your help and friendship and I hope it will continue.'

She stopped as, obviously embarrassed, Cathy abruptly turned and left the room, the door wide open. As she heard her running down the stairs Eleanor realized how upset the poor woman clearly was, and again wondered what degree of responsibility lay at her own door and what different decisions she perhaps could and should have made.

How easy it was to be wise after the event.

Niobe gazed out on to the garden which, now that winter had really set in, looked bare and desolate. The Winslows had used a lot of the space in the back garden for the studio extension, so it was quite small, but there were large trees, which afforded a certain amount of privacy from the house next door.

A journalist was expected to interview her and she felt nervous and unhappy. She had begun to feel without any doubt that she was outstaying her welcome. Ever since her announcement about leaving Francis the Winslows seemed to have distanced themselves from her. She saw less and less of them, which was easy in such a big house and for part of the day they were often out. The evening excursions had also practically ceased. The Winslows went out a lot on their own, and she would have a lonely meal served with a certain degree of insolence by the maid who clearly regarded her as an equal and once invited her to have it with her in the kitchen to save trouble. This was a suggestion Niobe bitterly resented as it seemed to emphasize her inferior status in the household, part of the servant class.

She felt a step behind her and turned to see Caroline, dressed elegantly as usual in a fake fur coat and high-heeled black boots, a silk scarf tied casually round her neck, pulling on long leather gloves.

'Are you sure you're going to be warm enough, Niobe darling? It's bitterly cold today. The heating is full on but . . .' Caroline rubbed her arms looking out of the window. 'The weather has got much colder.' She gazed with concern at Niobe. 'You look half starved and I'm sure you've lost weight. Are you all right? Are we looking after you properly?'

'I am really fine,' Niobe said with forced jocularity, 'and plenty warm enough. Maybe a little nervous about the interview.'

'Oh, there's no need for that, Tamsin Marlow is an awfully nice woman, quite knowledgeable, but I'm sure you'll hold your own. She'll be here soon. You'll like her. She'll do a good interview and, hopefully, it will appear soon to encourage the others.' She paused momentarily. 'Sadly, we can't be with you today to help out. We're just off for a private view in Hampstead. A rival gallery with a clientele we would die for.' Her expression became serious and she lowered her voice as if to impart grave news. 'By the way, Francis phoned again. Both Adam and I think you must talk to him. You can't hide your head forever. You must think about the children.' There was now a distinct coolness in her manner, an expression of reproof in her eyes and Niobe felt herself colour.

'I'll ring him,' she said, 'I promise.'

'Maybe you should go back, just for a while, until things get sorted out?' Caroline pulled a wry face. 'Unfortunately, we haven't been able to get all the publicity we wanted or expected; few have taken up on our press releases. There is a lot of competition about as you probably know; lots of talented artists out there. It was a scoop to get Tamsin. I pulled a lot of strings, but she will be more interested in you than your art. We told her you were a most fascinating, unusual person. She used to run a gossip column and is not really a critic; but do show her round the gallery. We're hoping it will all change after the exhibition, and that it will engender a lot of interest both in you and your work.' She paused again and gave a non-committal shrug. 'Maybe if you went home for a short while you could do a few more paintings?'

'But you know, Caroline, I am not going home. I have left home. I can't possibly go back. It will be like giving in.' She looked desperately at Caroline. 'Maybe I've outstayed my welcome?'

'Oh, not at all!' Caroline said placatingly. 'We *love* having you, you know that, but we did wonder, for your own sake how long that is going to be. You must feel terribly insecure and unsettled. Besides, don't you miss your children? I mean, I don't have any, but to stay away indefinitely . . .' Her voice trailed off.

'It is not indefinite,' Niobe said heatedly, 'and of course I do miss my children. I love them. But parents do stay away occasionally for a long time, and they have Francis and their grandmother; they love her. They probably won't even miss me they'll be so spoiled.'

In the intimate, slightly suggestive way she had Caroline moved across and gently ran her finger lightly down Niobe's cheek as though she were trying to recapture some of their former intimacy. 'Poor you. I know it is a stressful time for you, but I'm sure the exhibition will change everything. Oh, and we're invited for dinner tonight so shan't see you until tomorrow.' She leaned over and pecked Niobe fondly on the cheek accompanied by the usual impulsive squeeze of her arm. 'Marie will give you your dinner. I believe she's cooking something delicious.'

Probably a dead cat, Niobe thought sourly as Caroline hurried out of the door in answer to Adam who was calling her urgently from the hall.

Tamsin Marlow looked critically at the large painting that had hung in the sitting room in Alex's flat in Camden town.

'Don't say I go much for modern art,' she said to Niobe with a grimace. 'From the press release they sent out about you I thought it would be different.' She looked round at the other three walls. 'Are they all like this?'

'I'm afraid so,' Niobe replied haughtily. 'I'm sorry you came under false pretences.' She pointed to the press release Tamsin had in her hand, jabbing at it with her finger. '*There* is an illustration of one of my paintings. You might have known what to expect.'

'Country girl and all that,' Tamsin said ignoring the picture and studying the biography. Then she produced her tape recorder and pointed to one of the seats. 'Shall we do our interview? I don't have much time.'

'I don't either,' Niobe said, perching gingerly on the chair next to Tamsin to whom she had taken a dislike almost as soon as she entered the house. Whereas she had gone to some trouble to dress with style, elegantly but discreetly in her black trouser suit, the usual absence of shirt but the topaz necklace at her neck, Tamsin appeared to have taken no trouble at all. She was a tall, thin woman with untidy streaked blonde hair, which looked as though she had just got out of bed; no make-up and large tortoiseshell spectacles halfway down her nose. She wore a long beige coat almost down to her ankles, which she had merely unbuttoned to show a long shapeless shift of some kind, a monstrosity of dubious ethnicity that was also ankle length. A bag was slung over her shoulder and she kept on peering over her spectacles in a censorious manner as if from the beginning she had felt about Niobe the way Niobe felt about her. Above all, she gave the impression of someone who had very little time to spare, and that at the moment she felt she was wasting it.

Not at all a meeting of true minds, Niobe thought, as she waited for the first penetrating question.

'Tell me a bit about yourself,' Tamsin asked switching on the tape recorder and thrusting it towards Niobe. 'I mean, there is a lot in the biographical note about you, so we needn't go into all that but, for instance, where did you train?'

Niobe, who had been expecting this, went into a pre-rehearsed patter. 'No formal training, really. I went on one or two art courses. I am largely self-taught.'

'I *see*.' Tamsin glanced again at the large painting as if this explained everything, then turned to Niobe removing her glasses and started toying with them in the air.

'Adam Winslow is well known for taking unknown artists under his wing and making them, or trying to. Do you expect this to happen to you?'

'I hope so,' Niobe said.

'I hope so, too.' As if she had heard everything she wanted and was wasting her time Tamsin switched off the tape recorder and tucked it into her capacious bag. 'Now, if you don't mind, I really must fly. I'm late for my next appointment. I'll phone you if I have any questions.'

Almost speechless with anger Niobe showed her to the door, but just as they reached the threshold, Tamsin paused abruptly, turning suddenly and faced her.

'Look, darling, maybe I shouldn't say this, but I think you are a nice person, if a bit naive. As a friend I feel I must warn you that Adam Winslow is not highly regarded in the art world. He is notorious for taking up unknowns, especially good-looking ones . . .' She paused for a moment looking suggestively at Niobe. 'But if they don't catch on quickly, or fit in, he drops them like a hot brick. He is a

very wealthy man, you know, and does this for amusement
rather than business. Caroline, too, enjoys the fun, if you
know what I mean?'   Again there was that slight pause as
if to give her insinuation emphasis. 'Now I am getting into
the realm of sheer gossip, but that's what some people say.
Between them they play games with people, most of whom,
once their brief moment of glory is over, vanish from the art
scene, never to be heard of again. So if I were you, I wouldn't
give up the day job, you might well be better off sticking to
farming. Bye, darling,' she said and, swooping towards her,
gave her the usual de rigeur kiss on the cheek.

Niobe's chin was almost buried in her muffler, her coat wrapped
tightly around her as not long after Tamsin had left she walked
briskly along Haverstock Hill towards Camden Town. Her
pace was swift in order to keep herself warm. It was a bitterly
cold day and even the prospect of snow was forecast.

   After Tamsin had left she had sat for some time in her
room gazing out of the window at the almost bare trees, but
seeing nothing. The rage and humiliation she felt were almost
stifling her and she seemed to be looking not at the sky but
down at a great unfathomable chasm, a yawning pit that
contained the shattered sum of all her desires. A jumble of
words echoed and re-echoed in her brain.

   'Don't give up the day job.'
   *'Maybe you should go back, just for a while until we get
things sorted out.'*
   *'We want to build you up gradually, but nothing can be
guaranteed.'*
   'There is a lot of competition about.'
   Round and round they went, reverberating over and over.
   Publicity, Caroline had said, had been disappointing, but
Tamsin was influential. Oh, was she? Did Caroline know
what a malicious gossip she was, malicious, maybe, but true?
It had been a scoop to get her and the Winslows had told her
what an interesting person Niobe was. They didn't add that
Tamsin was one of the most revolting people in the world.

   She had allowed her every bit of fifteen minutes and had
managed to insult her by implying that her work wasn't
worth looking at, but she had also given her a warning

which, as well as being malicious, seemed at the same time sincere.

Adam was a rich man who took people up and then discarded them if they didn't catch on, or fit in. She thought that probably she had been too naive about their intentions, and she was beginning to understand other things. They liked to play games, maybe sexual games, and had found in Niobe a non-compliant playmate. Caroline's flamboyant, tactile manner had startled her, but Niobe had thought that was the way arty people behaved. She herself had never been a hugger and a kisser, not even with the children and certainly couldn't change for people she hardly knew. But they had got the message. They had wanted her to stay; now they were all too anxious for her to go. They were getting tired of her and anyway the publicity was not going too well, people were not interested in this untrained artist from the sticks. Tamsin had also given her an insight into something she had been beginning to suspect: that there was something bogus about the Winslows. Tamsin had not really told her something she hadn't already guessed, only confirmed it.

Slumped on her bed she had leaned over and put her head in her hands, her fingers tightening over the skin on her forehead as if trying to smooth out the winkles that she knew were there, and had surely increased in numbers in the short time she had been in London.

One thing she had realized, however, in those moments of intense soul searching: she no more fitted into this phoney arty London scene than she fitted into a completely different environment in rural Dorset many miles away from here. The stars had altogether fallen from her eyes and she felt she wanted out. Hence the purpose of her trip to Camden Town.

Time to move on – but where?

Deep in thought she hadn't realized how far she had come until she saw Camden Town tube station and crossing the road walked up towards her destination. For a while she stood outside the cafe gazing up at the flat. It looked deserted. The windows were very dirty. Then, hesitantly, she rang the door bell and stood for some time until she was sure there was no one in.

Had she half hoped that Hugo would come out? Perhaps she had. Hugo was the one person she had met in recent years who had, she felt, understood her. He was gentle and kind and had spontaneously given her a lot of money to help her out of a tight spot. Only his girlfriend had tried to turn it into something sordid and demeaning. Niobe turned into the cafe, glad that it was after lunch and the crowd had cleared. Tony stood behind the counter as usual drying cups and leaned across when he saw her, surprise in his greeting.

'Hello, I saw you outside the door but didn't realize who it was.'

Niobe took the muffler away from her freezing face and smiled bleakly.

'How are you?' Tony went on: 'Have you come to bring back the picture?'

'Not yet,' Niobe approached the counter. 'The exhibition isn't until after Christmas, maybe even February. January apparently isn't a good time.'

'How is it going?'

'Oh, fine.'

'You up in London for a while?'

She shook her head.

'I've left my husband. I'm staying here with my friends in Chalk Farm who own the gallery, only I wondered . . .' She looked round at though she expected to see Alex standing at her shoulder. 'Tony,' she continued hesitantly, 'I'm wondering if you could let me have the key to the flat? I'd like to stay there for a while. My friends are going away. Besides, I don't want to abuse their hospitality.'

Tony, his expression grave, put down the cloth and pulled a face. 'Well,' he said, 'I don't really know.'

'Alex won't mind, I'm sure,' Niobe went on breathlessly. 'She won't be using it. Is Hugo . . .' She paused. 'Is he likely to want it, do you know?'

'As far as I know,' Tony said, 'Hugo is in Iraq. He left a few weeks ago and will be there for quite a long time. He got a commission to do a major documentary. The opportunity of a lifetime, he said.' Tony resumed drying the cups. 'I hear they split up. Baby on the way, too, eh?'

Niobe nodded. 'Due in the next month or so. That's why she won't be using the flat.'

'Why don't you ask her? I can't just let you have the key, you know.'

'But you know I'm a friend.' Niobe's tone was pleading. 'There are reasons I don't want her to know. It's personal, but I'm sure she won't mind. I won't stay long. I'll look after it very carefully. I promise you I won't let you down. Let's just say I think I've outstayed my welcome with these people in Chalk Farm. They are making it a bit obvious and I also want a break. We haven't fallen out, nothing like that, but everyone wants their space and they didn't know I was leaving home. I didn't either until after I got here. It was a sudden decision, but the right one I know. I'll sort out something more permanent after the exhibition. *Please*, Tony, oh please say yes. I'll make it up to you.'

'In what way?' Tony asked with interest and Niobe, lowering her eyes, gave him a suggestive smile.

Fourteen

*D*ick *put his head round the door and said, 'The baby's crying.'*

'What baby?' Eleanor asked, preoccupied, busy at her desk, subbing an article she had brought home from work.

'Darling . . .' Dick said fondly coming into the room and putting his arms around her, 'our baby; our new baby.'

'Oh my God,' Eleanor sat back, appalled, and then she got up and hugged him. 'Fancy forgetting.' She leaned her head against his chest, grateful for his strong muscular body, the comfort that Dick always gave her when she needed it.

'You shouldn't bring work home, darling,' he said, gently pushing her away. 'You shouldn't have gone back to work.'

Suddenly she felt strangely fragile and weepy. She had returned to work within a fortnight of Alex's birth, only part time, a few hours a day and not every day at that, but it was what she wanted to do. She liked work and, frankly, she hadn't so far liked being a mother. Juggling work and motherhood was much harder than she'd expected, despite the number of articles she had read or even written herself on the subject. But in her case it was also with the help of a part-time nanny, a cleaner and Dick, never much good at changing nappies and the caring bit but a steady support. They had not really wanted children, being busy career people with a lifestyle they loved. Alex therefore was an accident but a delightful one as it turned out. They both loved her dearly and had no regrets but there would be no more. Dick promised to have the snip.

They both went into Alex's room and Dick lifted her from her cot and started to soothe her. She stopped crying at

*once and smiled at her father but when Eleanor took her
she started again.*

*And that's how it had always been with Alex . . . If only
they could get on.*

Eleanor woke with a start and sat up in bed, conscious of
a heavy weight on her chest like stone. She clutched wildly
at her heart, wondering if she were having a heart attack,
but then sank back on the bed knowing it was only a dream.
It was a long time since she'd dreamt about Dick or the
family. Dick had not had the snip and two years later there
had been James, not an accident but planned and loved
from the start. By then she was a more experienced mother,
more in control of herself and her job, and that was probably why she had always got on better with him because
he was prepared for, and wanted, and maybe because of
that she had always loved him best. And yet to repay her
James had gone to settle in America and now that he was
a family man himself she so seldom heard from him, especially since she had recovered so well from her accident.
It wasn't that he didn't care, he assured her in phone calls
and emails, he was just so busy. Eleanor scarcely knew his
wife or children, so it was no wonder she so longed for a
home-based grandchild.

It was not that Alex had been unwanted; it was simply
that as a new mother Eleanor had found it hard to cope. The
truth was that Alex always had got on better with her father,
even though she was both hurt by and resentful of the fact
that he had left the family home and her mother, though by
that time she was quite old and had left home herself.

She particularly resented the fact that he had married a
woman near her own age and had had another baby. Dick,
of course, had never had the snip. He would undoubtedly
have regarded that as a threat to his virility.

It was still very dark. She looked at her clock, only just
past one o'clock. A long time since she'd dreamt about
Dick. She never missed him now and seldom thought about
him, but he would be the new baby's grandfather and would
be sure to want to see it. She wouldn't mind. She could
look at Dick, contemplate his presence without any feel-

ings at all. Ruminating about the past she started to feel drowsy when she felt a movement by her side and Melody put a paw on her arm, which indicated that she knew her mother was awake and wanted a cuddle.

Eleanor drew her under the duvet and listened to the contented sound of her purring. She was just drifting off to sleep again when she was aware of sounds from the bathroom. In her state of advanced pregnancy Alex often used the loo several times at night. Eleanor pressed Melody close to her and shut her eyes, then opened them wide again as, hearing a sound in her bedroom, she put on the light and saw Alex leaning against the door.

'Mum, I think I've started. My waters have broken.' She clutched her stomach, her face creased with pain and was about to slump to the floor when Eleanor got out of bed with a speed she didn't know she was capable of, and was just in time to catch Alex and help her across to her bed to lie down.

'Oh Mum . . . the contractions are coming very fast.'

'I'll ring for an ambulance,' Eleanor said and seized the phone.

'Mum, I don't think there's time'

'I'll call Francis,' Eleanor said immediately and tapped in his number. She sat listening while the phone seemed to ring forever, and distractedly she began to wonder if she herself was capable of delivering a baby. Finally Cathy answered.

'Cathy, is Francis there? Alex has started and I don't think we have time to get an ambulance. I wonder if he would . . .?'

'I'll ask him,' Cathy said at once, without the objection that Eleanor had half expected and she could hear her banging at a door and the sound of voices.

'He's on his way,' Cathy said returning to the phone, but she was unable after all to resist a little dig. 'Lucky you've got me here,' she added grudgingly.

'Very lucky, Cathy, thank you,' Eleanor said and put the phone back on its base.

'Thank God for Francis,' she added half to herself.

* * *

As soon as they reached the hospital, which had been warned that Alex was on her way, she was taken immediately to the delivery room. Eleanor and Francis sat in the nearby waiting room listening to the sounds of other women groaning in various stages of labour, babies crying, the endless non-stop activity of a large hospital where babies are born as if on a conveyor belt.

'It's very good of you, Francis. I don't know what we'd have done without you. I was beginning to wonder if I would know how to deliver a baby,' Eleanor said at last.

'That's perfectly all right,' Francis mumbled, still looking rather dazed at being so abruptly woken from his sleep. 'Glad I had Mum there or I couldn't have left the kids.'

He looked towards the door leading to the delivery room. 'I just hope everything turns out all right.'

'Oh, it will. I'm sure it will.'

But still it did seem an age since they had arrived and their conversation was desultory. Finally Eleanor asked the question she had hesitated over.

'Any word from Niobe?'

'None at all,' Francis said. 'I phoned the place where she's staying a few times and then I gave up.'

His expression as he looked at Eleanor was bitter. 'I have the children, you know, the house and she has nothing. Good luck to her if that's how she wants it. I'll never have her back, even if she goes down on her knees to beg me.'

After that there seemed nothing more to say on the subject and they sat in silence until towards dawn the door opened and a nurse entered with a bright, reassuring smile on her face.

'I'm sorry it has been so long but we had a breech,' she said. 'However, all is well and –' she looked directly at Francis – 'congratulations Mr Ashton. You have a beautiful son.'

Being a waitress, albeit a temporary one, was not what Niobe had anticipated when she'd arrived in London a few weeks before with such great expectations, such high hopes. Tony had suggested it with a view to helping out with the finances. He was a waitress short and she needed the money, just really to get by on a daily basis.

The Winslows had accepted without question and with ill-concealed relief that she was staying at her friend's flat. However, she was careful to keep from them the fact that she was working in the cafe downstairs. She didn't want them to realize she was so hard up.

Nevertheless, it was an admirable arrangement that suited everyone and to some extent it took the heat off and improved her relationship with Caroline and Adam. Now that she was no longer around all day the tension had eased considerably. They dined or lunched together once or twice a week but personal chat, all sense of intimacy, was in the past. It had become strictly a business relationship, which is really what it always should have been. As far as Niobe was concerned it was another of those life-changing moments rather comparable to the time Eleanor had lent her the thousand pounds. If she had not stayed with them there is little doubt that she would have found it so simple to leave home, and she would probably still be there now eating her heart out.

In the new relationship there was no mention of Francis or the children and slowly but steadily the preparations for the exhibition had advanced, though they had been subtly scaled down. The Winslows had been unable to engender much interest in the art world – perhaps for reasons which Tamsin had hinted at – an unknown artist from the West Country, despite no mention of her age and a flattering picture of her on the cover of the exhibition programme. In addition, there was a handsome, embossed invitation embellished with one of her paintings. As Tamsin had indicated there would be plenty of acceptances because the food would be good. It would after all be in February when the Christmas season was well and truly over, and so were the ghastly sales that clogged London and kept people away.

Fortunately, in the circumstances, Tamsin had not delivered on her article. Guessing how unflattering it might have been Niobe was relieved and thought she had done her a favour. However, the Winslows were disappointed as she didn't return Caroline's calls. So they downgraded her in their estimation, changed their minds about her and said, Well really she wasn't much good and fickle too and, yes, she did dress dreadfully badly and looked a sight and most certainly they would not be asking her again. Niobe thought that if they had any idea how indiscreet she had been about them they would never have asked her in the first place. Despite all the setbacks Niobe still hoped to find fame and fortune as an artist, though occasionally that hope dwindled and seemed unrealistic.

The Winslows appeared to have the fortunate knack of adapting to each circumstance in which they found themselves, and remained resolutely optimistic and cheerful.

It was a busy cafe open from seven in the morning until ten at night and there was a lot to do. It was not a classy joint. In the old days it would have been called a workman's café, serving good plain food and lots of it on a plate, assisted by tomato ketchup, HP sauce, salt and pepper, tea and bread and butter. Tony usually came on at midday and stayed until closing time. He must have made a good living as the place was nearly always full though mealtimes were obviously busier than others.

To her surprise, Niobe quite enjoyed the work and found she was good at it which made her popular with Tony. At first he had been businesslike and silent, but now after a couple of weeks he was inclined to chat. She knew absolutely nothing about him and he never discussed his personal life. She didn't even know where he lived, or his surname, or if there was a Mrs Tony and little Tonys. She didn't know and she never asked. She wasn't really interested, immersed in her own thoughts and affairs. He was a good boss, popular with his staff and she liked him.

She guessed Tony was about forty to forty-four. He wouldn't have won any prizes for starry good looks being a long, thin gangling type of man with cropped greyish hair and the pale, lined face of the habitual smoker who seldom took exercise. He looked as though he'd been around, had lived a full life. He had an east London accent, but she didn't know where he came from, nor did she care. He didn't attract her and for his part he never made a pass at her or tried to take advantage of the blatantly flirtatious manner in which she had angled for the key to the flat. There was nothing at all personal in their relationship.

He paid her in cash and she had no working documents. She didn't pay tax or insurance or have a stamp so that every penny she earned, and sometimes with tips it was quite a lot, she kept. She was self-employed. Because she lived above the cafe she was down first thing in the morning to assist the breakfast chef who opened up. She usually left for her break when Tony came, and if she had no dinner date with the Winslows she returned in time for supper and worked until closing time.

It was eventually in the course of the evening shift that they began to know each other and in quiet periods to chat. Besides her there were two part-time waitresses, two chefs and three other staff in the kitchen. It was a good, well-run establishment, clean and hygienic.

Polishing the glasses one night shortly before Christmas, Tony watched as she cleaned the tables, put fresh cloths on for the morning and began to lay them up: knife and fork, spoon, plate, cup and saucer. She moved round the few people who were still there, occasionally pausing for a brief chat with one or two of the regulars, usually workmen coming off their shift. She was well-liked. The place was unlicensed so there was never any trouble, no rowdy behaviour of the type that got into the newspapers. She wore jeans and a shirt with an apron tied round her midriff, and while she was at work little or no make-up.

The last customers left, the kitchen was closed and the staff had gone. Niobe cleared the remaining tables and put the dirty dishes in the hatch, wiped the tables, put on the cloths and cutlery for the morning and began taking her apron off, putting it on its hook with a deep sigh as she pushed her hair away from her face. The work was tiring but she got a curious satisfaction from it, from its routine, its ordinariness. It was not unlike the kind of satisfaction she got from painting, only there she was able to shut the door and herself away from the outside world, whereas here she was right in it. Finally, with a routine glance in the mirror she went over to the counter as Tony came back from shutting and locking the main door after the last customers.

'I'll be off then,' she said shrugging on her coat. 'Night, Tony.'

'Good day?' Tony called after her. 'Everything all right?'

Niobe turned back and looked at him in surprise. She was tired, but obviously he felt like chatting.

'Fine,' she said as he leaned across the counter and offered her a cigarette.

'What are you doing for Christmas?' he asked casually, lighting her cigarette.

'I hadn't thought about it.' And she hadn't.

'It's soon.'

'Oh, is it really?'

'I suppose you'll be going to your artistic friends?'

'Oh, no, they're going away. Somewhere like Bermuda. In fact, they may already have gone.'

'Not thinking of going home?' Tony lowered his voice.

Niobe shook her head.

'Won't you miss the kids? They'll miss you.'

'I don't want to talk about it, Tony,' Niobe said firmly, stubbing out her unfinished cigarette.

'I wonder if you'd like to spend it with me?' he said. 'I'm not doing anything and I haven't got anyone either. I'll be closing the cafe for three full days. What do you say?'

Eleanor lay listening to the sound of birdsong. It literally filled the air as though hundreds of birds inhabited the large eucalyptus in the garden. It was a familiar song in the spring, a cacophony of glorious sound that seemed to herald the onset of a new day. As she grew more awake she realized that the space by her side was once again empty. Dick had not come home and it was time, she thought, that she realized that his relationship with his secretary was serious and that he might be considering leaving her as there was no longer any pretence. They never discussed it, but each knew what was in the mind of the other.

It was the one thing she was determined to avoid. They might go their separate ways, but she wanted them to be together at least for the sake of appearances. She didn't know that she could live on her own after all those years of marriage, over thirty. Their twenty-fifth anniversary had been an occasion with a large family party and it seemed to endorse all she felt about marriage; that whatever its drawbacks, its ups and downs and, contrary to current trends and the prevalence of divorce, it was for keeps.

Yes, she would tolerate Karen. Of course not in the house or acknowledge her directly, but that she was a fact of Dick's life. It had been some time since she had separated from Mike, but maybe it was time to cast her eyes round again; have a little fun before she was too old to enjoy it. Those furtive adventures at Marge's flat had been fun, kept the juices flowing, made her feel more alive. Trouble was, could she still attract a man? That was the rub. With men of her age it didn't matter; they could always get the birds as Dick had, a woman over twenty years his junior.

She got out of bed and going over to the window drew the curtains and looked down on the lawn and there, in the middle, she saw a very pretty small white and ginger cat. It seemed to look directly up into the window and gaze into her eyes.

And that was how it had happened. Love at first sight. She had not chosen Melody, Melody had chosen her.

And in the extraordinary way that coincidences happen that was also the day Dick came home and told her that Karen wanted a baby. And that was when she knew her life would change completely and forever.

Eleanor woke with a start listening for the birdsong. Of course there was none. It was Christmas Day; mid winter. Once more she had been dreaming about the past, life with Dick, many long years of marriage to a man she scarcely now ever thought about. It was extraordinary the changes that came into one's life and how it took a turn one could never ever have anticipated, like the day she met Mr Jones who had had a fatal heart attack as he came towards her on a busy road, swerved and nearly ended her life as well.

To survive that had been miraculous. Maybe some dreams served to review the past and make one grateful for the present, as she was now. As bad as the last year had been it had now been redeemed by the precious, unexpected gift of a grandchild. Then she realized what had woken her and she got out of bed as swiftly as she could and went into Alex's room to attend to the crying baby.

But Alex was already bending over his cot and he stopped as soon as Eleanor came in. Alex had him in her arms and was taking him back to bed.

Eleanor smoothed the duvet over Alex and her grandson and helped rearrange the pillow behind her back as Alex put him to her breast and began to feed him.

'Hungry little so and so,' she said. 'Did he wake you, Mum?'

'I think he did.' Eleanor perched on the side of the bed. 'I had a very odd dream. You remember that lovely eucalyptus tree in the garden that housed all those wonderful birds in the spring? Well, I dreamt about that and hearing them singing and when I woke, in the dream that is, I realized Dad hadn't come home and it began to dawn on me that his relationship with Karen was a serious one.'

'Do you ever miss Dad?' Alex glanced away from the baby to her mother.

'No, I hardly ever think about him, but he will eventually want to see Angus. I don't mind, but I don't particularly want to meet Karen again. Maybe when the time comes you might be able to arrange to see your father without me.' She got up and went over to the tea tray, putting on the kettle.

'I'll go down and get us some milk. Do you realize we have committed ourselves to cooking lunch for six people?'

Somewhat impulsively they had invited Francis and the children to Christmas lunch together with Cathy. As she began the preparations, stuffing the turkey, beginning the vegetables, Eleanor wondered if she had done the right thing. There was a lot to do and they had not done enough the night before. Alex took motherhood seriously, or used it as an excuse and had done practically nothing, but that didn't worry Eleanor. She welcomed Alex's absorption in a baby that at one time she was supposed not to have wanted. But she had no doubts now. The bond between mother and son was complete and it gave Eleanor the greatest happiness in the world.

Because they were up early, Eleanor's preparations were

quite advanced when the doorbell rang and there on the doorstep to her surprise stood Cathy.

'Happy Christmas, Eleanor,' she said.

'Happy Christmas, Cathy.' Eleanor stood aside. 'Do come in. I hope nothing is wrong?'

'Nothing is wrong at all,' Cathy said beginning to remove her coat. 'As you were kind enough to invite us all to lunch I thought the least I could do was come over and help.'

'That is very sweet of you, Cathy,' Eleanor said leading the way into the kitchen, 'but I was up early and have already done a lot. You could help lay the table if you like. Make it look all festive. I'm not much good at that kind of thing.'

'Gladly,' Cathy said and took a tin out of the bag she was carrying. 'I bought some mince pies and thought we could have one with our coffee.'

'Oh, Cathy, that's great.' Eleanor felt real pleasure at this change of attitude. Up to now, Cathy, although popping in from time to time to do some cleaning, remained aloof, still by implication blaming Eleanor for all the ills that had befallen her family. This was more like the old Cathy, the one she had missed for too long now.

'Let's have those now before we start work. I'll just pop them in the oven.'

'No need,' Cathy said. 'I heated them before I came.' And as though the old days had completely returned she went and filled the kettle and got the mugs from the cupboard and spooned coffee into them.

'How's the baby?'

'He's fine. Good as gold.'

'And Alex?'

'Alex is wonderful. I never imagined in my wildest dreams that she would take to motherhood so completely. She is utterly absorbed with the baby. He has taken over her life.'

'That's good,' Cathy sat at the table hugging her mug, her expression thoughtful.

Sitting opposite, Eleanor carefully studied her face, wondering what was going on in her mind.

Finally, Cathy looked up and their eyes met.

'Eleanor, I am sorry for the way I behaved,' she said. 'I have not behaved well.'

Eleanor stalled her. 'Look, don't let's even discuss it.'

'But I want to,' Cathy insisted. 'I was wrong to blame you for all that has happened. It was not your fault. It was the fault of that malicious, scheming woman and I feel now that Francis was well rid of her. I thought that some sort of sense of decency might make her want to come back and look after him and the kids, and for their sake and theirs alone Francis tried to persuade her to come back for Christmas. She flatly refused. She was spending Christmas with someone else and she hinted that there was a new man in her life. Can you believe it? She said she loved the children and was sending them presents, but so far nothing has arrived. Francis says he won't let her in the house again and if she tries to claim the children he'll fight her.'

Eleanor bowed her head. 'I see. I still think it is very sad. How are the children taking it?'

'They seem very unconcerned,' Cathy replied. 'You know what children are like and they are very used to spending a lot of time with me. In many ways Niobe was a distant mother, locked up in her studio, palming them off on to me or friends. Sometimes they'd come home and their tea wasn't ready. And when she was supposed to fetch them she was often late. Of course she was their mother and they loved her, but I don't think they'll really miss her in the long run. She is the loser. You may say I am prejudiced against Niobe because I never really liked her and maybe I am. How a woman can cut herself off from her children like that, I'll never know. Even Francis seems happier without her now that he's got used to it. He doesn't miss the rows and the scenes, that's for sure, and in the later days they never had a satisfactory personal life. I think she knew one day this would happen, which was why she refused to marry him. Even when he drove her to London that last time he suggested they got married and she told him not to be silly. What a thing to say! I think she was planning it then. Her studio was completely emptied, no paintings there at all and that's all that mattered to her, not Francis or the children. Even her wardrobe and drawers were almost empty. She was planning a getaway, the devious slut.'

Cathy's face was distorted with anger and Eleanor put out a placatory hand towards her.

'Don't upset yourself too much. I feel you're making the best of it and Francis and the children have come to terms . . .'

'And looking forward to their Christmas lunch,' Cathy said with a smile.

'Then let's give them a good one, the best we can. Let's *all* have the best Christmas we possibly can. It's been a difficult year for us all, but now we have a lot to celebrate, including a wonderful baby.' Eleanor got up from the table, crossed over to Cathy and gave her a warm hug.

'So glad it's all right between us again,' she whispered. 'I missed our friendship very much.'

It had in fact been a good and satisfying lunch, certainly the best they could have had in the circumstances Eleanor thought as, arms on the table, she looked round the room where Samantha was drooling over Angus asleep in his crib, perhaps hoping that he would soon wake up. Freddie, who was a studious lad, had his nose in the latest Harry Potter book he'd been given for Christmas, and Francis and Alex were sitting together at the far end of the table deep in conversation. Cathy had started to clear away and Eleanor, beginning to tire, was trying to force herself to get up and help her.

It looked just like a normal happy family. Eleanor experienced a glow of contentment, rare these days but getting more frequent, especially since the birth of Angus and the general improvement in her health. She didn't get quite so tired and her eyesight was much better.

She couldn't help noticing the attention Francis paid to Alex and whether or not it was reciprocated she could not tell. She thought not. She hoped not. It would be too much on the rebound, based on gratitude for all Francis did for them and went on doing, ferrying them to the hospital or baby clinic as though Angus really was his baby. She knew that Alex liked Francis as a friend, and it was actually impossible not to like Francis. He was a friendly, unaffected man, and that did not mean he was 'dull' as Eleanor had once unwisely suggested, and she recalled how swiftly Alex had reprimanded her. She thought it was not unnatural that the two would be drawn together, as each had been deserted by their partner. However, she also thought that Francis was just as unsuitable a partner for her daughter as Hugo had been. One was dynamic, the other not dynamic enough. It was easy to see why a dissatisfied, restless person like Niobe would tire of Francis and, like it or not, Alex and Niobe were restless, essentially dissatisfied people who had much in common.

She was about to get up and carry out some plates to the kitchen when the doorbell rang and, looking out of the window, she saw an unfamiliar car parked outside that she hadn't seen drive up.

She paused where she was as she heard Cathy go to the door and the subdued sound of voices. Almost immediately Cathy appeared at the dining-room door, a startled expression on her face. 'There is a man here who says he's your ex-husband, Eleanor,' she said as though she didn't believe it. 'He wants to wish you a happy Christmas.'

Alex stopped her absorbing conversation with Francis and looked up, startled, and Eleanor carefully put the plates down in order to try and conceal her shock.

'Dick? Did you say Dick?' she said as though she hadn't heard correctly.

'Dad?' Alex echoed and looked at her mother.

'He says he's your ex,' Cathy repeated, 'come to wish you a happy Christmas.'

The effect on those present was as though a pantomime fairy had cast a magic spell and frozen them all into blocks of ice. Everyone stopped what they were doing and looked up. Even Freddie took his nose out of the book and Samantha moved away from the crib, while Angus opened his eyes as if he too had been affected by this bombshell. It was left to Eleanor to break the spell as she quickly rose and hurried out of the room.

And yes, there on the doorstep stood Dick Ashton with a large bunch of flowers in one hand and a huge teddy bear in the other. There was a broad smile on his face as if he had no doubt about his welcome. He looked confident and relaxed for someone who had caused such a stir, and as Eleanor approached him he bent towards her as though he intended to plant a big kiss on her cheek.

'Happy Christmas, Eleanor,' he said as she stepped back quickly to avoid the gesture. 'I thought I'd give you a surprise.'

'You certainly did,' Eleanor replied in a tone not overly friendly. 'Whatever are you doing here, Dick?'

'I was anxious to see my grandson. I got Alex's note.'

'Well, you'd better come in and say hello,' she said ungraciously, stepping forward to shut the door. 'Hurry up, it's cold.'

Dick, however, remained where he was and gestured towards the car.

'I've got Karen in the car with the baby. I can't just leave them.'

Eleanor looked over to the car and saw Karen lean over from the passenger seat and give her a nervous, fluttery wave.

'Really, Dick,' Eleanor said angrily. 'What a thing to do without telling us.'

'I thought if I told you you'd tell me not to come.' Dick's smile vanished. 'We are spending Christmas in Bournemouth and it seemed such an opportunity. If you like, and as it appears we are not welcome, I'll go,' he said petulantly and he tried to thrust the flowers into her hands.

'Oh, don't be silly,' Eleanor said impatiently. 'Of course you must bring them in. Alex at least might be pleased to see you.'

Alex by this time had come to the door and as soon as she set eyes on her father she threw herself into his arms.

'Dad, Dad,' she cried clutching him. 'Oh, Dad, it's *lovely* to see you!'

'Glad someone thinks so,' Dick said in the same petulant tone of voice he had used before.

'Well, what do you expect?' Eleanor's face was flushed with irritation.

'Mum, it's *Christmas!*' Alex looked reprovingly at her mother.

'That's the trouble,' Eleanor said. 'One we shan't forget.'

Alex tucked her arm through her father's and went with him to the car where she also greeted her stepmother with a kiss and took the little boy into her arms. With conflicting emotions Eleanor watched this scene for a moment before taking the flowers into the kitchen where Cathy was loading the dishwasher.

'He's brought his bloody family,' Eleanor said. 'Honestly, I could weep with rage. We were having such a lovely day.'

'It will still be nice.' Cathy put a consoling hand on her shoulders. 'Maybe he won't stay long.'

'It's typical of Dick,' Eleanor said, unceremoniously sticking the flowers into a large vase without bothering to arrange them. 'He doesn't give a bugger about anyone, only himself. He probably got so bored with the family in a Bournemouth hotel he thought he would come and ruin our Christmas Day.'

'I thought you got on quite well?' Cathy looked puzzled. 'Didn't he come and see you in hospital?'

'He had no option. The police called him. He came and he didn't stay long; never came to see me again or sent any messages. I don't dislike Dick, I certainly don't hate him, but he is part of my past and it's over now. Funny, I have been dreaming about him recently. It must have been a warning of what was to come.'

Still angry, Eleanor took a quick look at herself in the mirror, made what adjustments she could to her face and hair (why she should bother for Dick she didn't know; must be pride) and went into the sitting room where Karen was being introduced to Francis and the children. She turned nervously towards her as Eleanor entered the room, hand outstretched.

'Karen, how nice to see you again.'

'And you, Eleanor,' she said shaking hands.

'It's been a long time.'

'It certainly has.'

In fact, the two women had not set eyes on each other since Karen had been Dick's secretary and as far as Eleanor had known, then, nothing more. She was at least twenty years younger than Dick. Eleanor was uncertain about her exact age, but she had worn well. She was a petite, good-looking brunette with clear skin, attractive brown eyes and Eleanor recalled that she'd always had good dress sense. It was no wonder her husband had swapped her for a younger model, though she'd doubted that he'd wanted more children. She also knew how bad he was at looking after them, no nappy changing or story reading for him. She imagined that Karen was a caring mother, in her late thirties and she had wanted a child.

'I heard all about your terrible accident, Eleanor,' Karen said. 'Dick was very concerned.'

'Was he?' Eleanor said with a slight inflection in her voice, but she was determined not to seem bitter and turned to look at Dick's new offspring. 'He's a dear little boy,' she said. 'What's his name?'

'Andrew. We try not to call him Andy, but nicknames do stick, don't they?' She looked despairingly at Eleanor who could imagine Karen spending the rest of her life vainly correcting everyone who used the diminutive name for her son. She was clearly nervous and very ill at ease.

'Sometimes they do,' Eleanor said wondering how long they could prolong this stilted conversation. 'Alex should be Alexandra, but I gave up on that years ago. Thankfully, no one ever tried to call James, Jim.'

'Pity, Alexandra is such a pretty name . . .' Karen began but, happily, at that moment Dick on the other side of the room was proving a diversion as he knelt on the floor to admire his grandson.

Alex picked him out of his crib and passed him across to Dick who hugged him and Angus obliged by greeting his grandfather with a big smile followed by a burp, which made Alex declare he was hungry. She took him from Dick at once, sat on a chair by the table and in the comfortable, unaffected way of modern mothers, bared her breast, pressed her engorged nipple into the baby's eager mouth where he began to suck furiously.

'How old is he now?' Dick asked gazing fondly at mother and child.

'Three weeks, just.'

'What have you called him?'

'Angus.'

'Angus?' Dick exclaimed. 'Why Angus? It has no family connection to ours that I recall. Is it something to do with Hugo?'

'It has nothing to do with Hugo,' Alex replied acidly.

'He's a great little fellow, isn't he, Karen?' Dick turned to his wife.

'Great,' Karen replied woodenly. Her own son was now occupying the interest of Samantha who clearly liked babies, while the bookish Freddie was once more preoccupied by the adventures of Harry Potter. Unnoticed by anyone Francis, briefly introduced to Dick, had disappeared probably into the kitchen with his mother. Eleanor, watching Karen, noticing her obvious discomfort, guessed she had been as reluctant to come as she was to have them. But she had little pity for this woman who, after all, had flagrantly gone after her husband and trapped him by saying she was pregnant. As usual, the only one who had got his way was Dick. He always had. He was the sort of tall, commanding kind of man who people, particularly women, instinctively took to and seemed to obey. He was undoubtedly good looking, even now, in a rather used kind of way with bushy fair hair, only slightly greying, a firm well-formed chin, rather narrow mouth and a pair of astonishing blue eyes that literally seemed to sparkle. It was very easy to see that he was Alex's father. He was a trifle overweight, but for a man in public relations who had spent a lifetime eating and drinking well that wasn't surprising. Looking at him now Eleanor could still see his fascination, remembered she had not wanted to lose him, and thought it was no wonder that the impressionable and much younger Karen had found him irresistible.

Even Alex remained devoted to him, the rather distant, always preoccupied father she had admired since she was tiny and whose defection had agonized her, even though she'd been quite grown up.

'How old is Andrew now?' Eleanor asked looking at the toddler who had returned to clutch the comforting hand of his mother, finger in his mouth.

'Coming up for fifteen months,' she said.

'He was born just about the time you had your accident,' Dick said beginning to unfasten his overcoat. 'Mind if I take this off? It is very warm in here.'

'You must all take off your coats,' Alex said expansively. 'Now that you're here you can't run away. You must stay for supper, mustn't they, Mum?'

Before Eleanor could reply, Dick bent to kiss the top of his daughter's head.

'You're a sweetie,' he said, 'but we must get back to the hotel for a children's party. Can't miss that.' He looked at his watch. 'In fact, we should be going soon.' He looked around. 'Is Hugo about? I'd like to say hello.'

'Hugo and I have parted, Dad. I told you in a letter.'

'Oh, I forgot,' Dick again looked around the room but saw no sign of Francis. 'Is the bloke you introduced us to, who was here a minute ago but has now disappeared, the new man in your life?'

'He certainly is not,' Alex replied robustly, heaving Angus over her shoulder to wind him. 'He is a very nice, helpful bloke who lives across the road. We are *not* an item. Just good friends.'

'I see.' Dick turned to Eleanor who was half-heartedly still trying to clear the table as Cathy had remained in the kitchen. 'You look awfully well, Eleanor. Considering what you looked like when I saw you in hospital I think your recovery is remarkable.'

'It is,' she said beginning to feel flustered as well as irritated by the way Dick had so obviously made himself at home. 'I have had a lot of help and I'm very lucky.' She stopped as Cathy entered the room and paused shyly by the door.

'I wondered,' Cathy said, 'if Mr and Mrs Ashton would like a cup of tea and a piece of Christmas cake.'

'Why not?' Dick looked at Karen who had already seemed on the verge of departure. She hadn't removed her coat and had begun to dress Andrew in his outdoor outfit.

'Well . . .' she began, clearly not pleased, but Dick didn't wait for her reply.

'An excellent idea, if it's not too much trouble.' He gave

Cathy a brilliant smile. 'Eleanor tells me how much you've done for her.'

Cathy blushed and looked at the ground and Eleanor could tell she was half in love with him already. Dick had, after all, been in PR all his life and knew all the tricks.

'I think we should all go into the sitting room,' Eleanor said briskly. 'Tea seems a good idea and it is very crowded in here. Where's Francis, Cathy? Will he join us?'

'He's gone back home. He says to say thank you for the lunch but he didn't want to disturb you and he has to feed the animals. I'll take the children with me when I go.'

'Seems an excellent woman,' Dick said when they were ensconced in the sitting room, him sitting in the best chair, legs outstretched before him, perfectly at home. 'Does she live with Francis and the children?'

'For the time being,' Alex said. 'His partner left him and his mum's helping out.'

'Talking of partners,' Dick said leaning forward, 'tell me about Hugo.'

'I'd rather not, Dad, not here, not now. It's a long story.'

'Pity, I liked Hugo,' Dick said. 'Does anyone mind if I smoke?'

'I mind,' Eleanor said, 'with the children about. I'm surprised at you, Dick. You really should give it up, with a young child.'

'Oh, stop preaching, Eleanor. You don't change, do you?'

'I agree with Eleanor,' Karen butted in and then, addressing Eleanor, 'I'm always telling him, but you can't tell Dick. He knows everything.'

'People don't change,' Eleanor said looking at her sympathetically, and for the first time feeling a bond developing with her successor.

Dick ignored them, but he didn't light a cigarette, instead he turned again to Alex.

'Darling, you must come and stay with us. Angus would be a nice little companion for Andy, in time. We'd love that wouldn't we, Karen?' He only paused long enough for Karen to nod before saying, 'Stay as long as you like. There is always a home with us, you know that. Your mother would be welcome, too. We'd look after her. There are no hard feelings about the past, are there, Eleanor?'

'I'd love that, Dad,' Alex replied, avoiding her mother's eyes. 'I'm not so sure about Mum.'

Not trusting herself to speak, Eleanor hurried back to the kitchen where Cathy was laying the best cups and saucers on a tray and cutting up pieces of cake.

'Nearly ready,' she said as Eleanor entered the room nearly bursting with rage.

'That man,' she said, 'suggesting Alex should come and stay with him and *me*, too! Trying to inveigle my daughter away from me.'

'Oh, surely not?' Cathy turned momentarily from her task. 'I thought he was ever so nice, very charming. Good looking, too.'

'I can see he's seduced you,' Eleanor said despairingly. 'That's just what you're meant to think. I just wish to God they'd go.'

It seemed like an eternity, but eventually they did go, surely too late, however, for a children's party. Alex saw them to the car with lots of hugs and kisses and promises to come soon, while Eleanor stood watching them from the door. It was getting dark and she knew they would have their work cut out to get to Bournemouth in time for Andrew's bedtime, never mind children's party. She suspected it was an excuse, but she didn't care. They couldn't leave soon enough for her and she was sure Karen felt the same. Her guess was that Dick had suggested the visit and his wife had had no option but to tag along. Alex returned with Angus in her arms and stood on the threshold waving until the car was out of sight. Then she turned with a pleased expression on her face.

'That was nice, wasn't it, Mum? I'm glad Dad came.'

'So I saw.'

'Don't be nasty, Mum. Don't be jealous.'

They both turned back into the house and Eleanor shut the door.

'I'm not nasty and I'm not jealous,' she said rounding on her daughter. 'I just think that your father might have phoned to say he was coming *with* his family. It would at the least have been polite on Christmas Day. I haven't seen him since my accident and I don't remember much about that, and I haven't seen Karen literally for years.'

'But, Mum, they're family.'

Alex sat on a kitchen chair and began to feed Angus again.

'They're not my family.'

'Then that *is* petty. He was anxious to include you in.'

'Alex, I find it impossible to talk to you rationally on this subject. You hardly ever mention your father. Did you often see him in London?'

'No.' Alex kept her eyes fixed on her baby's face. 'He's always so busy, and I'd been away such a lot. He and Hugo always got on. They were similar types; clever, dynamic, good looking.' Alex sighed deeply.

'Well, then. He didn't even know that Hugo had left you, did he? So it must be a long time since you had any contact with him.'

'I don't want to talk about it, Mum,' Alex said stubbornly.

'I simply want to know why all this affection, now?'

'Just because he is my dad, Angus's grandfather, and we are rather short of men in this family.'

As she looked up at her mother Alex's eyes were full of hostility, her mouth set in a thin line. Eleanor put a hand to her head.

'I have a splitting headache and I think I'm going to bed.'

'Maybe I *should* go and stay with Dad,' Alex said as her mother started towards the kitchen door.

'Maybe you should,' Eleanor retorted and stopped herself in time from adding, 'for good'. She tottered up the stairs and once inside her bedroom fell on her bed without undressing, her hand clasped to her head.

The day from which she had expected so much, maybe too much, had been a nightmare. She knew that although she had tried she had handled the situation badly. It was just that the sight of Dick turning on the charm had so provoked her. She had also hated hearing Karen being addressed as Mrs Ashton. Also the way Cathy had so obviously been seduced by Dick's charisma had seemed to bring back so much that had been good about her marriage. Everywhere he went Dick made such a good impression and, she thought, in the old days, so had she. They had been the golden couple, admired because they appeared to have looks, money, two clever, beautiful children and success. But now things were so different. Dick had kept his charm and looks and she hadn't. Her appearance had changed, and physically she thought she had shrunk. People felt sorry for her and she hated it. Above all she hated herself for being jealous of her ex-husband, for being so spiteful, bitchy and ultimately, by implication, so weak.

Above all, she hated the thought of losing her daughter and the grandson she adored and the possibility, now that they had started to fight as they used to often in the past, seemed a real one.

And all this on a day that was meant to be so perfect.

Eventually, Eleanor dragged herself off the bed and prepared herself for sleep taking painkillers to relieve her still aching head. She was surprised to see it was already past 11 o'clock and she lay down, Melody tucked in beside her, a hand resting on the back of the cat, whispering the usual endearments. Then she turned to put out her light, but sat up abruptly when she saw the handle turn on her door and it opened slowly to reveal Alex standing with a mug in her hand.

'I saw your light was on, Mum, and thought you might like a drink. Peace offering. Chocolate?'

'Chocolate is just what I feel like,' Eleanor said with a relieved smile and sank back on her pillow. 'How sweet of you to think of it, darling.'

Alex put down the mug carefully on the table beside her mother's bed and perched beside her.

'Mum, I am terribly sorry about today, about what I said.'

Eleanor instinctively put a hand on her arm, but Alex continued.

'I did go over the top a bit about Dad without under-standing your feelings. It is almost as though I did it to provoke you. I didn't . . .'

'Alex, don't distress yourself . . .'

'No, Mum,' Alex insisted. 'Let me have my say. Of course

it was wrong of Dad to come without warning, and I didn't realize how long it had been since you saw Karen and the effect that would have on you. I didn't take your feelings enough into consideration and that was selfish of me.'

'But I *was* bitchy and I *was* jealous, you were right.' Eleanor said, gently pressing her daughter's arm. 'I lacked, how shall I put it, magnanimity? Of course, your father wanted to see you and Angus, that's the sort of person he is, always has been: instinctive, and it has its good side and bad. I know him so well, you see.'

'Do you still love him, Mum?'

'If I'm honest and we are trying to be, yes, a bit. Today brought out the worst in me. It reminded me that I was lonely and disfigured and basically on my own. I can still see Dick's attraction, even Cathy fell for him.

'I was very upset when he told me he wanted to leave me for Karen. I felt sure we would stay together all our lives, whatever our transgressions. I thought they were small and insignificant compared to the strength of our marriage. It was the last thing I expected, although of course I knew about her. I thought I'd get over it in trying to make a new life for myself, but my accident has thrown me in on myself and the new life I envisaged didn't quite materialize. Well, perhaps it did, but in a different way. Still, it has its positive side. I don't suppose you and I would have become as close as we have, and I can't tell you how much I have appreciated it. But you must go and stay with him whenever you like. I shan't, naturally, that would be ridiculous. But I would like you to have a relationship with someone you adored as a child and it will be important for Angus too.'

'You're very generous, Mum.' Alex leaned over and embraced her and, for a moment, they hugged each other in silent, mutual harmony, Eleanor's responsive arms fastening tightly round her daughter.

'You look very tired,' Alex said at last breaking away and gently stroking her mother's brow as if she were trying to banish all the wrinkles that had accumulated in the past year. 'All forgiven?'

'Of course all is forgiven,' Eleanor said, her heart very full, 'and forgotten.'

'And you are not alone, you will always have me. Whatever happens, I'll always be there for you.'

Eleanor nodded, incapable of speech, but already she could feel her eyes, heavy with sleep, closing as Alex crept to the door, leaving the untouched chocolate growing cold on the bedside table.

Fifteen

Niobe lay in bed gazing out of the window of the bedroom in Tony's flat. She could just see the tops of some of the trees in Regent's Park and there was a delicious smell wafting in from the kitchen where Tony was cooking breakfast. She hadn't been so spoilt for a long time. Francis hadn't spoilt her for years; the Winslows had spoilt her, certainly, but not as much as this.

It had only been for a very few days and were the relationship to continue it would certainly pass, but for the time being it was very pleasant. She snuggled beneath the duvet and closed her eyes thinking of sausage, bacon and egg, hot tea and warm toast.

She felt movement as Tony plonked himself on the bed beside her and she opened her eyes.

'Ready,' he said, 'when you are. Do you want to eat in the kitchen or shall I bring it to you?'

'I'll get up,' she said throwing back the duvet and he gazed lasciviously at her for a moment in open admiration of her body, as though for two pins he would forget about breakfast and climb in beside her.

'I'm starving,' she said giving him a teasing, playful look and, putting on her gown, glanced in the mirror, pulled a face and ran a comb through her hair. They had had plenty of sex and now she wanted food.

'Ready,' she said with a smile and Tony followed her into the kitchen. She sat at the table while he dished out the food, finished the toast and poured water into the teapot, seeming to do it all at once with a dexterity born of years of experience.

'You are spoiling me,' she said. 'I was just thinking I hadn't been spoiled this way for years.'

Tony put the plates on the table, brought over the teapot and began pouring tea.

'Didn't Francis spoil you?'

'Not after the first few months of being "in love", before the children were born,' Niobe said spreading butter on her toast. 'After that he didn't know the meaning of the word.'

'Did you spoil him?'

Niobe appeared to think. 'Not after the honeymoon period, no. We were very practical, busy people and by the time I left we had been out of love for a long time. And the babies came soon, one after the other.' She indicated her plate with her knife as if she were anxious to change the conversation. 'You make wonderful bacon and eggs, Tony. Anyone would think you kept a restaurant.'

Tony grinned and they fell into a thoughtful silence while they ate their food.

Afterwards Niobe went to the shower leaving Tony to clear up. She spent a long time over her toilet because in the past few days his compliments had made her very conscious of her appearance and her body, and she wanted to please him. She had known he was a nice, kindly man, but had never previously fancied him or remotely imagined him as a sexual partner. However, once in his home the intimacy had been immediate. Getting into bed with him had seemed a natural progression of their relationship. He had obviously had it on his mind for a long time, had prepared for it, planned it and lost no time in demonstrating his feelings for her.

He was a good lover and knew how to give a woman pleasure rather than keeping it for himself. She thought that that was what made them such successful bed mates, because she liked to keep a man happy too. Moreover, she was grateful to him for rescuing her from a melancholy Christmas on her own and she felt she owed it to him.

She knew it was lust not love, but she didn't mind. She had been deprived of raw, violent passion for such a long time that she enjoyed it, felt carried along and swept away by it and they had spent a good deal of the three days over the holiday in bed. In between sessions they had enjoyed huge meals and had plenty to drink. He did all the cooking; turkey on Christmas Day with a bottle of vintage Bordeaux because he liked good wine. She felt it was the best holiday she had had for years, and the thought of it ending was sobering.

Tony lived in a luxurious modern block in Primrose Hill and had an almost new foreign car in the garage underneath. He was much more affluent than she expected, having only ever seen him behind the counter in the cafe polishing glasses or drying mugs, taking money or helping out in the kitchen or dining room when staff were late or away. Though there was no reason why he shouldn't be. He worked hard. The cafe was always open seven days a week from seven in the morning until ten at night and was nearly always full at peak times, though people would come in for meals at all hours of the day. He had few staff who he also worked hard thus saving on wages, even though he paid them above the average rate, gave them good holidays and kept their loyalty. He was a good boss; she had never doubted he was a nice man. It seemed now that he had no family. Or if he had, that part he hadn't told her about and she was reluctant to ask in case he had a wife and children somewhere tucked away out of sight. She just wanted to enjoy the here and now. He had in fact told her very little about himself, but he was interested in her and asked her endless questions.

Ruminating about the past few days Niobe was almost ready, just finishing her make-up as Tony came into the room and gazed appreciatively at her over her shoulder and into the mirror. He, too, had showered, shaved and dressed in jeans and a sweatshirt.

'You look lovely,' he said leaning across and kissing her cheek. 'Fancy a walk in the park?'

'I thought you were going to suggest we went to bed again,' she said coquettishly turning to look at him.

'Well I wouldn't mind.' He made a mock gesture of unfastening his trousers, but Niobe jumped up, put her arms around him and kissed him. He smelt of a very subtle, undoubtedly expensive aftershave. She really was beginning to fancy him quite strongly. She liked his strength and his positive attitude. Away from work he had hidden attributes which she had never considered before, such as where he lived, his lifestyle and, most important, what he was like in bed.

'I wouldn't mind either,' she said breaking away and, taking darting glances in the mirror, fussed again with her hair. 'But all the time I have lived here I have never really seen the park and it is such a nice day.'

It was mild for midwinter, a clear but cold sunny day and hand in hand they crossed the bridge and walked into the park, past the children's playground and round by the pond. There were people walking dogs, children playing with balls and flying kites, families with prams, youths messing about, solitary people, quite a few of those who perhaps had nowhere to go for Christmas and no one to see, and some amorous couples like themselves strolling arm in arm or hand in hand.

They took a circuitous route to the inner bridge and stood leaning over the iron railings gazing into the water alive with birds of all descriptions, some of whom came hopefully to the bridge to see if they had anything to eat.

Niobe leaned over staring into the water and wished so much she could see into the future. Tony had his arm round her waist and pressed her close.

'Penny for them?'

'I was thinking what a lovely time we've had and that tomorrow it all comes to an end.' She gazed up at him. 'Like Cinderella leaving the ball.'

'It needn't,' he said. 'You can stay on with the prince if you like. Give it a shot. I can't promise happiness ever after, but you never know.'

She remained where she was, staring into the depths, but her heart had done a somersault and then she stood upright and turned to him.

'Are you absolutely sure that you mean this? You're not having me on?'

'Sure I'm sure,' he said with a smile. 'I fancied you from the day I set eyes on you nearly a year ago.'

'No!' she exclaimed, looking at him incredulously.

'Yes, but I thought you were sleeping with Hugo. You fancied him, didn't you?'

'Yes, I did at the time, but I never slept with Hugo. I'm not saying I didn't want to and would have if he'd asked me, but although we spent the night in the same place we slept in separate rooms and the opportunity never presented itself then or again. Alex thought we had an affair, but she was wrong. However, it did change both our lives, hers and mine, and it made me determined at some stage to leave home and start a new life in the city –' she waved her arms around – 'a place like this where I belong.'

'I fancied you rotten and thought I'd never get you. Now that I have I'm not going to give you up so easily.'

'You haven't got a wife and family tucked away somewhere?' she asked facing at last the question that had haunted her.

'I have never been married, I swear,' he said. 'I didn't find the right woman, but you never know, one day that might change.'

They went to bed early that night because both had to be up at dawn to open the cafe. They had discussed plans over supper, each excited like young people newly in love, though they never mentioned the word.

'I'm not going to let you go on working, you know, after I've found a replacement.' Tony finished setting the alarm and turned to her.

'But I don't want to be a kept woman.'

'Why not? You can do your art and when you become rich and successful you can keep me.'

'It's a deal,' she said. 'But I can't paint here.'

'I thought I'd find you a nice little shed or something and you can use it as a studio. In fact I have a place in mind.'

'You sound as though you had it all worked out. I can't believe this is happening to me.'

She lay on her back and looked into the dark where now she was able to imagine a glorious future free from debt, doubt, insecurity and struggle.

'I did have it worked out, but I didn't know how to put my plan into operation. I didn't know if you were going to go back to Francis or if you really wanted to stay in the flat in the hope Hugo would return.'

'I never thought about that, well not much. I was mainly worried about Alex finding out.'

'Then that will be one worry off your mind.' He paused and she could sense he was trying to gauge the expression on her face. 'Unless, that is, maybe you still want Hugo to come back?'

'Don't be silly,' she murmured. 'I'd never swap you for Hugo, not now that you've promised me so much.'

'Little gold-digger,' he said, chuckling.

'I'm not,' she whispered. 'I'm Cinderella who just found her prince.'

'Well now, that frees you from that worry. And you can have the kids here whenever you like. There is plenty of room.'

It was a dream come true and, lying wrapped in Tony's arms, Niobe fell into a dreamless sleep.

Francis sat in the hospital waiting room leafing through a magazine, but paid little attention to it and kept raising his head and looking towards the door. Angus had had a temperature in the night, had appeared listless in the morning and Alex had telephoned him and asked if he could possibly take them to hospital as she was afraid it might be meningitis.

He seemed to be there for a worryingly long time before Alex finally appeared without the baby and still with a worried look on her face.

Francis threw down his magazine and got up immediately expecting, from her expression, to hear the worst.

'It's OK,' she said putting a hand lightly on his arm. 'They don't think it's meningitis, but they want to do a few more tests. We may be here all day. Look Francis, I can get a taxi back. You've been terribly good waiting as long as this.'

'It's quite OK,' Francis replied. 'I'll stay.'

'But what about your work?'

He pointed to the window where outside the rain was beating down.

'No work today. Too wet. I was doing things in the house. Can you get away for a coffee or snack?' He consulted his watch. 'It's nearly lunch time.'

Alex nodded. 'I've got a few minutes. I could do with a coffee. We can go to the cafe here.'

'Fine by me.'

They walked along to the hospital cafe where Alex ordered a coffee and Francis fish and chips.

While Francis waited for his meal Alex took her coffee to a table near the window and sat gazing out at the wet, desolate scene. She had been terribly worried about Angus, but her mother had been, as usual, practical and consoling and it was she who had suggested calling Francis as Alex didn't want to drive all the way to Dorchester with a sick baby in the car.

Francis joined her with his full plate to which he had added several slices of bread and butter and a cup of tea.

He sat opposite her, knife and fork poised. 'So that is good news?'

'So far, yes. They are pretty sure it is an infection, but they are doing a battery of tests. If they're still not sure he will stay in and of course I'll stay with him. It is terribly good of you, Francis. I do feel we're putting you out and using you.'

'I'm sure you would do the same for me,' Francis said gruffly. 'In fact, I may be calling on you a bit more because Mum is restless to get back to her own home. It is understandable. It is a lot to ask Mum, but it puts a strain on me.'

'I'll help in any way I can,' Alex said. 'Mum will always keep an eye on Angus, though I think she is getting a bit sick of me, too.'

'Maybe you should come and live with me?' Francis said unexpectedly, and he didn't appear to be joking.

'That's a bit drastic,' Alex said jerkily.

'Why is it drastic?' Francis who was a fast eater cleared his plate and took a sip of his tea. 'I think it's a good idea.'

'I'll have to think about it,' Alex said rising. 'I must get back to the ward.'

'I'll be here, waiting.' Francis winked at her broadly.

Did he mean it? Could he possibly be serious? It was hard to know, she thought as she walked swiftly along the corridor. Had she ever thought about it? Well, yes, she had, fleetingly. They had seen a lot of each other in recent weeks. He seemed to enjoy her company and for her it was nice to get out of the house. They had the odd meal at the pub, and her mother seemed to encourage it. He had almost become part of the family.

She thought in a way they were both wounded people who needed each other.

But moving in together? Was that a step, perhaps, too far?

'Francis has invited me to go and live with him,' Alex dropped the bombshell that evening as she fed Angus before his bedtime, just as Eleanor had got his cot ready and begun sorting through his clothes.

'He what?' Eleanor asked without turning round, then she straightened up and stood staring at the wall.

'He said his mother wanted to go home.'

'Oh, and he wants you as a housekeeper?'

'Something else, too, I think.'

Eleanor turned in the act of folding baby clothes. 'And how do you feel about that?'

'I'm not sure.' Alex wrinkled her nose and began to wind the baby over her shoulder. 'Part of me finds it quite exciting. I do like Francis. I'm even vaguely attracted to him I've decided.'

'And I think he is more than vaguely attracted to you. The first time I noticed it was at Christmas a year ago, the Christmas that caused all the trouble or it seemed, in retrospect, to be the beginning of it.'

'Oh, yes, I remember. Hugo thought Francis and I were flirting and I thought he and Niobe were doing the same. It did cause a row.'

'It was the same this Christmas, and you do seem to be seeing a lot of each other.'

'Well, not a lot, but we do like each other. We get on well, sort of.'

'It's hardly a basis for cohabiting.'

'But it is something. Sex is not the last frontier, Mum, you know. I would like a man again. It's something I need; something I miss. You can have a sexual relationship without being in love. I'm a bit in the wilderness, Mum. I don't know whether to go back to London or stay here. I don't know how much longer we should stay together, you and I. We've started our old fights. We bicker, get on each other's nerves. I'd only be across the road, near but not too near. If I didn't move in with Francis I might seriously consider going back to London and trying to resume my career.'

Eleanor sat on the bed and wrapped her housecoat closely around her. There was something quite attractive at the idea of having the house to herself again but her daughter nearby. The idea of her going back to London was unthinkable. It was true that they had resumed their old state of semi-hostility, lots of silly little arguments and disagreements, quickly regretted but irksome all the same, more so since Cathy had only come in part-time, and Alex contributed so little to household chores. It reminded her of how pleased she had been when, long ago, Alex had decided to leave home. They found it hard to live together. She had the same sort of feeling now.

'If it didn't work out it would be a disaster.'

'No, it wouldn't. I'd just move back here again.'

'Like a shuttlecock?'

'Sort of.'

Eleanor got up, went across and kissed first her head and then the baby's.

'We'll have to talk about it. There's no hurry, is there? It is a big decision and a big new life. Don't rush into anything. You would also have his children, think of that.'

'I have thought about it and I like them a lot. I've seen quite a bit of them and Sam adores the baby. That's no problem. They badly need a mother and I might be quite a good one.'

'I think you would be, without doubt.'

'I have an idea you are quite in favour, Mum,' Alex said slyly. 'Want to get rid of me?'

'Not at all, I just want the best for you and at the moment I'm not sure what that is.'

'Francis and I are a bit like two orphans in a storm, aren't we?' Alex said. 'The truth is we have both been ditched by our partners and have only each other to turn to.'

It certainly didn't sound an ideal situation for a relationship.

Alex walked round the back of the house and saw that the doors of the barn that used to be Niobe's studio were wide open. Outside was a collection of flotsam and jetsam as if someone were having a good clear-out. For a horrible moment she wondered if Niobe had unexpectedly returned after all, in which case all her doubts would be settled right away. She popped her head round the door, saw the room was empty and Francis, in a pair of white overalls, was painting the walls with a long-handled brush, a cigarette dangling from the corner of his mouth.

'Having a clear-out?' she called.

He turned and greeted her with a smile. At that moment she felt she did fancy him, a lot.

'You bet, a new broom . . .' He put down his brush, wiped his forehead with the back of a stained hand and walked towards her. He threw down his cigarette and ground it out on the stone floor. 'How's the baby?'

'He's fine. No temperature and the district nurse is popping in later on.'

'That's good.' He looked at her and as he came towards her she thought he was going to kiss her.

'Do you want a coffee?'

'I can't stay, really. Mum is holding the fort with Angus. I just wanted to say thanks for yesterday.'

'No problem,' Francis said. 'Just a *small* coffee, maybe?'

'Well, alright then.'

She could tell the atmosphere between them had completely changed since the day before.

Changed altogether. They walked purposefully towards the house in step, in harmony with each other. She had a sense of excited anticipation such as she had not felt for a long time.

Inside the kitchen Alex stood by the table while Francis got mugs down from a shelf and spooned coffee into them.

Then he took the kettle from the hob and poured hot water on the grains.

'Milk?' he enquired. She nodded and he added milk and pushed her mug across the table towards her.

'Your mum not here?' she asked.

'She's gone to, what she calls, make her house habitable again. That's partly why I'm doing up the barn. I may have to put it all on the market.' He paused to light a cigarette, his hand shaking slightly.

'Oh,' Alex studied the floor. 'Isn't that very drastic?'

'Not unless you move in with me.'

'Did you mean it? Really?' She raised her head and their eyes met.

'Really,' he said moving closer so that he stood directly in front of her, nearly touching. She could feel the heat of his breath. The atmosphere was almost unbearably charged with sexual tension.

'You'll have to stop smoking if we are to live together,' she said.

Eleanor stood at the door of the exhibition hall, almost shaking with nerves. She had had her hair done, nails and a facial and taken a lot of time selecting what to wear: a knitted woollen suit in her favourite blue with mid-calf skirt and dark blue, medium-heeled court shoes. She had worn a coat, which was taken at the door by a maid in a white coat and then she'd walked by herself to the exhibition room after being courteously directed towards it. But the noise would have shown her the direction to take. She looked now on a sea of bodies and unfamiliar faces and wished Alex had come, but wild horses would not have dragged her there, besides the fact that she was busy with her new life, she and Francis, doing up his house and making all sorts of changes.

In the old days she would have had no difficulty entering a room full of strangers, but no longer. She was not the woman she had been and this was the first visit to London since her accident.

Suddenly, a familiar face swooped down on her. 'Eleanor Ashton!' Candy's voice boomed above the crowd. 'My God, darling, is it *really* you?' She peered closely into Eleanor's startled face. 'How you've changed.'

Reluctantly Eleanor proffered a cheek to be kissed. 'I had a very bad accident.'

'Darling, I *know*. God, I know. It was awful. And I did mean to come and see you. I mean you've made a wonderful, wonderful recovery. I'm sure you'll soon get back to your normal self.'

Her expression, however, was doubtful as she lifted a finger and practically poked it into Eleanor's eye. 'Is there something wrong with your eyes still, darling?'

'A little,' Eleanor said curtly, 'but it is improving. It will never be completely OK.'

Candy slapped a hand to her mouth; eyes wide open in mock horror. 'My God, how awful.'

'You get used to it.' Eleanor was trying hard to keep her composure. 'You can really get used to anything if you try hard enough, Candy.'

'I'm sure . . . *and* you've got a stick!' Candy squeaked, stepping back, as if she were forever discovering fresh disasters. 'Did you break your leg?'

'My injuries affected my balance. That will be permanent, too.'

'Oh, I could never have imagined you with a *stick.*'

Eleanor was finding this close inspection very tedious and also unnerving. She felt she had shrunk in comparison to Candy who was scarcely able to keep her own balance on very high heels. She could see herself now through Candy's eyes: an object of pity, and compare it with the woman she used to be. Apart from Candy's behaviour, the way she was peering at her made Eleanor call her sight into question and she felt like asking her if she were sure she'd got her contacts in. However, that would have been too rude and as Candy seized her arm and started to propel her through the crowd, anxious now to get rid of such damaged goods, Eleanor tried hard to remind herself that this was a woman she had trained from being an office junior and who was now trying to intimidate her.

'What an enormous number of people there are here,' she said trying to make herself heard through the din.

'They are mostly pals of the Winslows or pals of pals,' Candy confided. 'Hardly any art critics. Their new discovery Niobe Fletcher's stuff actually isn't very good. We all only come here for the food, which is always fabulous.' She waved a hand towards the paintings adorning the walls. 'Have you had the chance to see much of it? I don't think you'll be impressed.'

Eleanor nodded. 'I'm actually a friend of Niobe's,' she said. 'She's a neighbour of mine in Dorset.'

Up went the hand to the mouth again. 'Oh my goodness, have I put my foot in it?'

Eleanor was rather pleased that she had scored with Candy, when she saw Niobe coming towards her and she stared at her in open admiration.

Niobe looked beautiful, stunning in fact. She also appeared years younger, and Eleanor realized how she'd been kept back by country life. She wore a gown of shimmering turquoise Thai silk with long sleeves and a low neckline. She was quite heavily, but skilfully, made up and her hair, now cut very short, closely embraced her head like a snug-fitting black cap. It was very attractive. There was a little jewel, skilfully placed on one side.

She kissed Eleanor with what seemed like genuine warmth.

'Eleanor, I am so thrilled you were able to come.' She glanced behind her. 'Did you manage to persuade Alex to come, too?'

'She couldn't leave the baby,' Eleanor said, half truthfully.

'A lovely little boy, I hear.'

'Angus,' Eleanor said with a nod. 'Gorgeous. Such a joy. Seriously, you look fabulous, Niobe.'

'Thanks,' Niobe said, and, keeping a hand tightly on Eleanor's arm, 'don't think I'm not grateful to you for making this change happen.'

Eleanor was rather appalled to be thanked for being responsible for breaking up a home, but thought it inappropriate to comment.

'We must have a little talk, Eleanor, after you've said hello to Caroline,' Niobe went on.

By this time, Candy had somehow disappeared to Eleanor's intense relief, probably to bitch about the artist to someone else and tell them about the terrible change in her. Holding Eleanor's hand, Niobe fought her way through the throng, who were mostly consuming the delicious canapés and drinking the best champagne rather than admiring the pictures on show. Caroline was standing at the end of the room with a group of young, prosperous looking men gathered round her, lecturing about one of the paintings.

She turned to greet Eleanor with that mystified expression that indicated she thought she knew her but couldn't quite place her, as Niobe interrupted her.

'Caroline, this is Eleanor Ashton to whom I owe so much.'

'*Eleanor!*' Caroline said warmly detaching herself from the circle of admirers. 'I have heard so much about you and your terrible accident. We knew each other years ago, didn't we?'

'We did,' Eleanor replied. 'It seems a very long time ago now.'

'I don't think I'd have recognized you, but you have made an excellent recovery, Niobe says.' Then, as if aware of her initial gaffe, she hurried on: 'Doesn't she look beautiful?'

'Beautiful,' Eleanor echoed with sincerity.

'She has changed enormously since she's been down here. Mind you, I don't think that's entirely due to *us* –' she gave a suggestive smile – 'but aren't her paintings wonderful?'

'Wonderful,' Eleanor agreed, 'and you do them justice. They are also beautifully hung.'

'Thank you, Eleanor.' Caroline's unnaturally smooth brow showed a tiny crease. 'Unfortunately, we don't have *quite* the number of serious art critics we hoped for today. Our intense publicity has failed to draw them in, which is disappointing, but there is so much competition. There are a number of very good artists out there fighting to be noticed, but I think if Niobe perseveres, and persevere I know she will, one day she will break through. Now, if you don't mind I must attend to my other guests. Niobe, when you have had a word with Eleanor do come and meet Nigel el Farouk. He is a rich and discerning buyer who has come especially today to see your work. I'm going to ply him with Roederer,' she said with a wink and, with a flutter of her hands and a little wave to Eleanor, moved away.

'Let's go into the room next door,' Niobe said. 'I can't hear myself think here. First, there is someone I want you to meet.'

She took Eleanor to another part of the gallery where a tall, thin, rather ungainly looking man stood alone, his back to the room pointedly studying the large painting that once upon a time had hung in the Camden Town sitting room. Niobe caught his arm and as he turned towards her he instinctively put an arm round her waist in an intimate gesture.

'Eleanor, this is Tony.'

Concealing her surprise, Eleanor took Tony's hand and shook it. 'How do you do, Tony?'

'How do you do, Mrs Ashton? I've heard such a lot about you, and I know Alex.'

'Oh, do you?' This was another surprise.

'Tony runs the cafe underneath the flat in Camden Town.'

'I see.'

Tony was smartly dressed in a black pinstriped suit with white shirt and maroon tie. He looked very ill-at-ease and the palm of his hand was sweaty. But his handshake was firm and there was something masculine, powerful and appealing about him that made Eleanor see why he might attract Niobe, despite his obvious lack of conventional good looks.

'He is going to find somewhere for me to paint.' Niobe tugged impatiently at her arm. 'We must have a brief chat, Eleanor, and then I'll go and see the rich, important man Caroline has lined up for me. I don't think any paintings have been sold at all yet, but it doesn't really matter.'

She rather ostentatiously kissed Tony lightly on the lips and, scarcely giving Eleanor time to say goodbye to him, led her into the room next door, which was pleasantly furnished and had French windows that opened onto the back garden.

'Lovely place, isn't it?' Niobe pointed to a chair and then sat down next to her.

'It is very pleasant,' Eleanor agreed resting her stick against the side of her chair, relieved to be off her feet again. She looked across at Niobe. 'I'm glad things have gone so well for you. And Tony . . . ?' Her eyebrows formed a question mark.

'He's my new man.' Niobe's voice faltered just a little. 'It was very sudden. He gave me a job working in his cafe. I was very short of money by this time and felt I'd sponged enough off the Winslows. By this time, too, I knew I would never go home. One day he invited me to his place and I just stayed, you know how it is? One thing sometimes leads to another, doesn't it, Eleanor?

'I suppose it does,' she said with a smile. 'He seems very nice,' she added politely.

'He is very nice. He's not much to look at, but he is a good man and he also has quite a lot of money, which is a help as frankly I don't think I am going to get all that much out of the Winslows.'

'Oh, dear, why is that? I thought they were promoting you . . . all this caviar, champagne and the very best, Roederer Cristal.'

'That's what they do. I've learned quite a lot of things about them that I didn't know. I won't go into too much detail, but I think they were more interested in me than my art. I'm sure you understand what I mean. I didn't. I guess I am very naive. They collect people, especially women. I'm not into that kind of thing, so I moved out. When they realized I wouldn't play they lost interest. It helped that they were also very put out about my leaving home, as it left them with the sort of responsibility they didn't like. I think they imagined Francis might sue them or something ridiculous, as if you can imagine poor old Francis doing such a thing. I think all this is just an excuse for a party. I haven't seen too much of them lately and most of the interviews they promised did not materialize. So thank goodness for Tony, or I'd have been on the streets.'

'I'm very sorry to hear that, Niobe. I thought you'd landed on your feet.'

'I have,' Niobe said brightly, 'not perhaps as I expected, but by meeting Tony. He appreciates me in a way Francis never did. Francis took me for granted. I don't think Tony ever will. He will let me get on with my art. He even has a studio lined up for me and I don't have to worry about money. He has a very nice flat in St John's Wood. He is very happy for me to have the children to stay. I don't know much about his personal life because he never told me and I didn't ask, but I think he has been a lonely man. He assures me he's not married and never has been. He's built up a good business in his cafe and I admire him for it. I don't admire the Winslows at all, frankly. I think they're artificial and insincere. I don't even like them very much.

'Look, Eleanor, I haven't told Francis. You can tell him if you like. I know that I should have contacted him, but I didn't want to turn back the clock. I'm hoping the kids will forgive me one day, understand what I did and why and come and stay with me. I do love them and when the time is right I'll try and explain what happened. It may be for their own good. Some mothers do that, don't they? I'm not saying it's right, but it's happened. It's a fact. I know Francis loves me very much and will be desperately unhappy, but he'll get over it and he has his mother who never liked me anyway, never even tried. Besides, the whole thing is so much less complicated as Francis and I never married and, in time,' she added as an afterthought, 'I'm sure he will find a new life, too.'

Eleanor didn't want to tell her that this had happened sooner than she might have expected. Niobe was so riveted on herself, on her new life, that she didn't think it was the time or the place to introduce what might be a shattering revelation, might even undermine her self-esteem, namely that the man she'd rejected, who was supposed to love her so much, had lost no time in acquiring a new partner, too.

Sitting in the train on the way home Eleanor reflected on her London visit and all that she had learned, both about other people and about herself. She didn't think it was her place to tell Francis about Niobe's new life any more than it was to tell Niobe about Francis, and she wouldn't and hadn't. Some things were best left unsaid. Let them find out about each other, as they would in due course. She and Niobe had parted friends, which was as it should be.

As for herself, it was like revisiting her past and then deciding to put it right behind her. There were certain things about it that she no longer wanted. She'd stayed in a small, smart hotel near Harrods, so that she could pop in and remind herself what it used to be like when she had money and position and was living in London. But even that pleasure had palled. She had drifted through, had coffee and an expensive cake in the cafe and bought a few items of make-up. Once upon a time she had had an account there and regularly spent a small fortune on designer clothes and vintage wines.

That Eleanor was no more.

She was not sorry to say goodbye to her past. This was a new, different Eleanor, grateful to be alive, to be close to her daughter and grandson, to have a new extended family, possibly in time to develop fresh interests and make new friends.

The past was behind her, the future yet to come.

The train drew in at the station and the guard helped her out with her suitcase. She peered along the platform and there stood her small family anxiously scanning the carriages; Alex with Angus in her arms, Francis beside her with Freddie and Sam. As they saw her they started towards her, Sam breaking away and excitedly running ahead. A big smile on her face, Eleanor threw open her arms wide to embrace them all.

Her family.

It was so very good to be home.